QUENTIN BRENT

THE REASON

A THRILLER

IT'S ABOUT MORE THAN JUST THE MONEY

BEAVER'S
POND
PRESS

ISBN 13: 978-1-59298-871-6

Library of Congress Catalog Number: 2015906069

Printed in the United States of America
First Printing: 2015
19   18   17   16   15   5   4   3   2   1

Cover and interior design by James Monroe Design, LLC.

Beaver's Pond Press, Inc.
7108 Ohms Lane
Edina, MN 55439–2129
(952) 829-8818
www.BeaversPondPress.com

*To Shannon, the love of my life and the reason
this book is in your hands right now.*

If I'd have known better, I'd have done better.

—Maya Angelou

The dollar, under the Fed, has achieved something no God, no prophet, no messiah has been able to do.

—ADAM DAVIDSON,
NEW YORK TIMES MAGAZINE, MARCH 1, 2015

1

Pain was Ray's constant companion. It was his normal. He couldn't remember a day without it.

He needed to share the pain he felt at that particular moment. That thought drove him up the stairs, dragging his broken leg behind him and screaming the asshole's name.

Ray threw open the door at the top of the basement stairway and stepped into a large formal room. His hand was throbbing where it had been sliced open and was now dripping blood on the thick, beige Berber carpet. The room was sparse, but what there was seemed expensive. Ray didn't know how he knew that since he'd never shopped for home furnishings in his life, but he knew. He was seeing the opposite of destitution, which had been his close companion for the last several years.

Ray could smell him. Somewhere on this level. It was the stink of pride. He'd remove that smell. Slowly, and with a lot of blood. Replace it with the smell of death.

Ray wanted him to beg. If not for his life, then for a quick end.

Ray knew he wouldn't grant either.

He found the asshole in the kitchen. Leaning against the counter, sipping a beer, harmonious with the fierce events that had just taken place in his basement.

1

The kitchen was all white from the floor to the ceiling. The cleaning lady earned her keep.

He looked relaxed. Maybe because he was standing next to a large butcher knife. It had a well-worn wooden handle and looked recently sharpened. Its gleaming blade reflected back the sterile environment. Ray decided he'd use the knife to cut out the asshole's tongue first.

"You are a tough son of a bitch," the asshole said.

"You'll need more than that knife."

"It's for you," the asshole replied as he grabbed the knife by the handle and tossed it to Ray.

"Have it your way," Ray said as he caught the knife in midair and held it by his side.

Ray moved toward him, but the asshole didn't back up, with distress seeming a distant emotion.

"Are you going to do it? Or do you want me to talk first?" he asked. He didn't look scared or concerned.

Against his better judgment, Ray stopped. "Why would I want to hear anything you have to say?"

"I'm not going to beg for my life, if that's what you want."

"Too bad. But that doesn't matter. I'm just wondering if you're going to fit down the garbage disposal when I'm done."

"Good question. Before we consider the answer, you need to follow me," the asshole said as he turned around and walked toward the back of the house.

The white tile floor in the kitchen would have been easier to clean, but Ray was hoping blood came out of hardwood floors almost as easily.

Ray was right behind the asshole with the knife poised to strike. It brought back memories of a different day and a different weapon—but the results would be the same. A lot of blood and a lot of satisfaction. Ray was happy.

A fat, orange cat was curled up in a sunny windowsill across the kitchen. It raised its head, looked at Ray, licked its lips, and went back to sleep. Ray wondered what would happen to the fat cat after the asshole was dead.

The asshole walked down a wide hallway with dark walls and stopped in front of the last door. The door looked heavy. He turned back and smiled at Ray while opening the door. Then he stepped aside so Ray could look in.

Ray froze.

The knife slipped out of his hands and stuck in the floor. It wasn't possible.

"Go in, Ray. Just know you won't come out the same person."

2

U sually the drive home was therapeutic. Not today. Zane was exhausted and didn't want to go home and act like the person he knew he'd never become. The traffic was heavy, but it parted like the Red Sea every time he was about to slow down. Where the hell was gridlock when you needed it?

Zane and Tina Donovan lived in Deephaven, an affluent suburb of Minneapolis, Minnesota. It was a bedroom community that bordered Lake Minnetonka, a prime recreational location for the well-to-do of the Twin Cities. Zane loved living in Deephaven and was always proud when he gave out his address. They'd lived there for the last three years but had moved twice, both times into bigger, better homes. It was impossible to imagine a more ideal spot for his desired haven.

The final few miles of his commute wound around the deep blue lake, and as he navigated, Zane gazed at the sailboats and the yachts bouncing from wave to wave. It was the perfect picture of serenity and prosperity. The gorgeous lake homes populating the shoreline were straight out of a Norman Rockwell painting—husband, wife, two children, and a dog in every one of them. The perfect life in a picture-perfect place.

Zane didn't fit in. Not anymore. Or perhaps the picture didn't fit him now. He'd worked his entire life for this, and now the scene mocked him. Everything he'd wanted was so close, but it would never be his if his past foretold his future.

No question, they were doing well, at least financially. They were debt-free, except for the mortgage, and both children went to exclusive private schools. He couldn't help but feel proud of what he'd accomplished, especially considering the path he'd traveled to get there.

Pink Floyd's song "Money" startled him out of his reverie. It was his cell phone. He looked at the screen: work. Zane pressed the Ignore button. He was determined to keep his two lives separate. And never the twain shall meet.

To hell with it. He wasn't going home. At least not yet. He hung a tight U-turn a mile from his house and headed back around the lake. He needed to think. And he needed a drink. Drinking helped his thinking.

As he pulled into the parking lot of Lord Fletcher's, the local watering hole, "Money" began to play again. This time, it was his best friend, Tec.

Zane pulled into a parking spot, shifted the car into park, and shut off the engine. He didn't want any distractions while talking to the one person who really understood him.

He watched as two young women in sexy summer attire waved at him as they walked by his car into the beach area of the bar.

"What's going on? I thought you had class tonight," Zane asked after he hit the Answer button.

Tec owned a local mixed martial arts school, the Warrior's Den. Zane trained there on a regular basis.

"I'm not Tec."

"Who is this?" Zane asked.

"Somebody who cares."

"Who is this? And why are you using Tec's phone?"

"You need to go home. Now."

Zane's heart began to pound, and his palms started to sweat

as he began to finger the key on the chain around his neck.

"What makes you think I'm not home? You must have the wrong number," Zane said.

"We have the right number."

"Just tell me who you are."

"It doesn't matter who I am. All that matters is that we know what you did. And that means your problems just got a lot worse."

3

MINNEAPOLIS, ELEVEN YEARS EARLIER.

When they recruited him, they had assured him it was the right thing to do.

Tec should have known better. But they made it sound good, and not just good for him. It was immediately after 9/11, and patriotic fever was running hot. Justification was easy to come by, but that didn't make it right. He'd listened, and once he'd let them explain and hadn't objected, they knew they had him. The longer he'd stayed and heard them out, the harder it had been to leave. They'd made it sound inevitable. And maybe it was.

They met in an office on the forty-sixth floor of the tallest building in downtown Minneapolis. That certainly lent an air of credibility to the whole thing. The luxury of the surroundings stood in stark contrast to his simple home at the time.

They were nice—professional in a way that didn't allow you to question their motives or their way of conducting business. There were three of them. They all appeared to have bought their suits at the same store, and that store wasn't cheap. He felt out of place in his old army surplus fatigues and T-shirt with a rising sun emblazoned across the chest. They took him out to lunch without asking him where he wanted to eat.

They asked a lot of questions, focusing in particular on his past and his skills. Tec explained how his experiences and beliefs had made him want this job. He wasn't sure they believed him. It was as if they were reading from a script that he didn't have, but he was still reading his part word for word. That should've bothered him, but it didn't. That's the funny thing about hindsight. We see clearly things that we couldn't discern in the moment, maybe because we don't want to. Our egos bind us to only one course of action.

Tec realized that they'd done some research into his background. More than some, actually. But he had nothing to hide. He'd have told them, anyway. So what difference did it make if they knew already?

As it turned out, it made a big difference.

When the time came for them to lay out his task, he was ready. They had him where they needed him to be. They'd done this before. Still, the words were shocking to him. They would be to anybody.

Tec asked how he would know the bad guys from the good guys. They told him not to worry. It would be a target-rich environment.

He still should have worried.

They told him the mission was for the greater good. And not just their greater good—but to benefit a lot of parties, almost everybody. They asked him if he could do it.

As it turned out, he could do anything.

After the interview, Tec took the long way home.

4

The chairman of the Federal Reserve sighed as he was going over the introduction he'd been asked to write for the Federal Reserve's new website.

The Federal Reserve System is the central banking system of the United States. A series of financial panics, the worst occurring in 1907, convinced Congress that it couldn't fulfill its constitutionally mandated authority to maintain a stable and sound currency. So, on December 23, 1913, Congress created the Federal Reserve Bank, a federally chartered, but private, bank.

The Federal Reserve Bank was created with three clear mandates: maximum employment, stable prices, and moderate long-term interest rates. Over the years, its role has grown to include conducting the nation's monetary policy, regulating banking institutions, and maintaining the stability of the national financial system.

After being appointed by the president and confirmed by the US Senate, the chairman and board of governors—along with twelve regional Federal Reserve Bank presidents—set the Fed's institutional policy.

This structure is unique among the world's central banks. The Federal Reserve's monetary policy and all of its decisions do not have to be approved by the president or any-one else in the executive or legislative branches of govern-ment. It does not receive its funding from Congress; instead, it is self-funded through its member banks and other profit-making endeavors. It is truly independent.

The US Department of the Treasury creates the currency the Federal Reserve regulates. This is also unique among the world's governments. It creates a system of checks and bal-ances against the Federal Reserve manipulating the nation's money supply, in good times or in bad.

At least that's the way it is supposed to work, the chairman thought as he stopped typing.

But quantitative easing had changed that. The Federal Reserve was mandated to regulate the money supply, not create it. Purchas-ing bonds issued by the federal government had never been part of the Federal Reserve's roles as they'd been designed by Congress. Quantitative easing was creating money. Off budget. It was the gov-ernment borrowing from the government. In fact, several mem-bers of Congress were irate and calling for his head. Some of those Tea Party do-gooders who seemed to like nothing except arguing. Fuck them and their conservative bullshit. The near depression of 2008 had changed the fiscal equation. In his role as chairman, he had to make sure the house of cards didn't collapse—which was a challenge, because there was too much debt caused by too much deficit spending. The elected officials didn't think creating $85 billion a month of virtual money could be described as little, but compared to the deficit, it was very small. Why even tell Congress? All they could agree on was more disagreement.

An insolvent nation required desperate measures. And if those measures required putting a little money into the system, well, that's what he would do. With the perfunctory board of governors' approval, of course. Each of their districts needed this money just as badly as the other.

The chairman got up from his palatial desk and stepped onto the veranda outside his home office. He looked out at the expanse of earth that was also known as his yard. The sun was beginning to set, and the view of the bucolic back of beyond was breathtaking. It was easy to understand the rebel Civil War fidelity to Old Virginia. He continued out onto his lawn, sat down in the grass, and then spread out on his back like he had when he was a kid of five. He didn't care if the grass stained his $2,500 suit. He stared up at the sky. A few puffy white clouds were floating by, apparently without a care in the world.

He never wanted to be like them.

5

As he turned into their long, winding driveway, Zane knew something wasn't right, but he couldn't put his finger on it until he neared the house. The garage door was open, as were all the doors to his wife's car. Tina was meticulous about keeping the interior of her precious diamond-white Mercedes spotless. She would never leave her car doors sitting open. Guilt kicked in; he should've come home sooner.

Zane pulled his Range Rover in front of the garage and jumped out almost before it stopped rolling. Prepared to defend himself and his family, he fought his fear as he ran into the garage.

Looking into the front of his wife's car, he saw that the keys were still in the ignition, and her purse was on the floor mat. The backseat was empty, but something was scrawled on the back of the front seat. In yellow crayon. On his wife's precious black napa leather.

Daddy, WWHDT

He couldn't make sense of the scribble made by his five-year-old son, James. Zane's mind spun in circles. He turned around quickly, half expecting to find James sneaking up on him as part of one of his childish pranks. He ran back out of the garage and surveyed the driveway and their spacious front yard. Everything appeared normal. He could smell the fresh-cut grass and realized that the lawn must have just been mowed by their landscape service. The brick pavers in the driveway looked as immaculate as they day they had been laid. Their dry cleaning was even hanging outside next to the front door, exactly where the delivery boy always left it.

Zane ran back into the garage and could feel the bile in his throat as his heart raced. Nothing else in the garage was out of place; even the kids' toys were in their assigned spots—the result of his wife's organizational habits. He rushed to the side door, which led from the garage into the house, and ripped it open.

"Tina!" he yelled. "Anybody home?" No answer. He stepped through the door, afraid of what he would find. But more afraid of what he wouldn't.

6

A search of the house confirmed his worst fear. They were gone. Zane had long dreaded that Tina would take the kids and leave him. But this didn't feel like that. Her car was still in the garage, and the doors were wide open. Could she be playing a game with him? That would explain the call from Tec's phone. It would be just like him to participate in some prank. But it didn't sound like something Tina would do. She was a lot of things, but she wasn't a practical joker.

Zane sat down at the breakfast counter and placed his palms flat against the black granite countertop. As the coolness of the stone seeped into his hands, he took a deep breath and tried to think. He looked at the calendar on the wall in front of him. Under today's date, it said: *Zane: Pick up James from soccer practice.* Damn, he'd forgotten again. Instead, he'd been contemplating the lies he was going to tell this evening. Picking James up might have prevented whatever had happened to Tina and the kids.

He took his phone out of his suit pocket and brought up his contacts. He quickly searched through the list until he found his mother-in-law, Betty Lawson. Despite all of the timeworn clichés about difficult mother-in-laws, he had a wonderful relationship with Betty, though they couldn't be called close. She was a bit quirky and right wing with her conservative Christian beliefs, but he trusted her to always tell him the truth. She was blunt and had a bullshit barometer that was equal to none. He would need to be careful. She answered on the first ring.

"This is rare," Betty answered.

"Tina and the kids are gone."

"I guess you'll be eating leftovers tonight."

"Her car is in the garage with all of the doors open. Do you know where they are? Did she call you?"

"No, I don't—and, yes, she did. Tina called me this morning to tell me about your argument, or whatever it was, and some other things, but she didn't mention that she was planning to go anywhere. She certainly didn't seem upset enough to walk out on you, if that's what you're thinking."

"I'm—I mean, no . . . I'm not sure."

"She might leave you, Zane, but she'd never leave her precious car behind, I'm sure about that." Betty laughed. "Did you check in the backyard or with the neighbors?"

Zane didn't answer.

"Zane?" As if she finally registered his fear, Betty's voice had taken on a new urgency. "If her car is there and she's not, something's wrong." She waited for him to respond, perhaps to hear that everything was fine, but there was nothing but silence. "I'll be over in a minute; I'm leaving right now."

"No, I got this. I'll keep you posted," Zane implored. He didn't want Betty to come over. He feared his illegal business dealings had something to do with whatever was going on. The mysterious phone call from Tec's phone had hinted at that very thing. He needed to deal with this alone.

"Remember, she's my daughter, so do the right thing," Betty said.

"Of course. I'll talk to you later."

Zane stood up and walked over to the refrigerator and pulled out a bottle of Budweiser to wash down some of the dread stuck in his throat. As he closed the door, he noticed a picture of James holding a medal he received for his hitting prowess at T-ball this summer. Maybe it was last summer. He couldn't remember.

He set his beer down, unopened.

Betty was right; he needed to do the right thing. If only he knew what that was.

Zane was the vice president of Strategic Acquisition Services, also known as SAS, a national merger and acquisition firm. Their specialty was acquiring businesses nobody else wanted, businesses that were circling the drain financially. The plug had been pulled, and their options were limited. Bankruptcy was one choice; SAS was the other. Zane was their lifeline. He gave them hope, even when there was none to give.

When people are facing what seems like a Mount Everest of a problem, they want to believe that there's a way out. Any option that might preserve their dignity, protect some money, and most importantly, safeguard their legacy. If you tell them they can save those things, they listen—but not closely. They hear the big picture but can't absorb the details. They're focused on getting out with their lives intact but not on the ways and means required to accomplish that.

Zane's job was to investigate. He listened to them describe their problems and pretended to be paying attention. When he had all the data and understood the reasons for their imminent demise, he sat them down and relayed the diagnosis. The disease was always terminal—except for a miracle treatment only Zane could provide. He'd explain it succinctly, always summarizing with the same words. "Good news: it'll work. Bad news: it'll be costly." As in, someone-has-to-die costly.

Right now, he was the one who needed help, and he could only think of one person who might provide it. Tec.

He hoped Tec would answer and not the people who'd apparently borrowed his phone earlier.

He was afraid to imagine who they might be.

7

Tec was in between classes when Zane's call came in. Tec's school was located in one of Minneapolis's historic districts. His building blended perfectly into the neighborhood of old buildings and crowded tenements. Tec liked it that way. His old-style art worked best when crowded. Tec believed in keeping things simple, low key, and efficient. That was best when time was critical and lives were in danger. Leisure was often a commodity in short supply. His call with Zane indicated that this might be that kind of situation.

Tec pulled up to Zane's house on his Harley, the *blat-blat* of the pipes jarring Zane out of his deep thoughts.

Tec uncoiled himself from the bike and hooked his helmet on the handlebar. Not as tall as Zane, Tec was solidly built with long, black hair and a nose that had been broken more often than he would admit. Tec had some Native American ancestry that was revealed in his high cheekbones and forehead. Tec was short for Tecumseh. His mom had named him after the famous warrior. Nobody could recall Tec's last name, if in fact he'd ever tendered that piece of his identity. Some women considered him attractive, although most would have to admit it was more a factor of his calm, confident demeanor than his actual looks.

He walked to the garage in that easy swagger of men who are sure of themselves. Nevertheless, Tec had a dark side that wasn't only mysterious but also unnerving.

"Tec, did somebody use your phone within the last hour?" Zane asked.

"Hello to you too," Tec responded while entering the garage. "The only person using my phone was me when I answered your call."

"Well, somebody used your phone earlier to make a very disturbing call to me. Then I came home to this," Zane said while pointing to the open car doors.

Tec seemed surprised, but it was hard to tell, as his dark features clouded his true emotions.

"People can fake the caller ID. What's going on?" Tec responded while walking up to the car and looking inside.

"Tina and the kids are gone, but her car and purse are still here," Zane explained. "I called Tina's mother. She has no idea where they might be, particularly without a car or money and credit cards. I have a feeling something bad happened."

Zane watched as Tec circled the car slowly.

"My life is spinning out of control, and it doesn't seem like you give two shits," Zane continued as he plopped down on a bench in the garage.

"I'm here, aren't I?" Tec turned around to look at his friend. "Relax. Freaking out doesn't help anybody."

"Easy for you to say; it's not your family!" Zane stood up, walked to the workbench, and grabbed a hammer off the meticulously organized tool board.

"Let's go over to the neighbors. Maybe they heard or saw something," Tec suggested calmly.

"That wouldn't do any good."

"Why?"

"Tina told me the neighbors on both sides are on vacation."

"Both?"

"Isn't that what I just said?"

"How about the kids' friends? Tina's friends?"

"I don't know their friends."

"That close, huh?"

"Listen to me! I need your help, not your useless ideas, and certainly not your sarcasm!" Zane yelled as he swung the hammer and drove it through the Sheetrock on the garage wall.

Tec walked up to Zane, put a hand on his shoulder, and spun him around to look in his eyes. "What's really going on here? Just tell me. Fucking BFFs, right?""

"I can't. A real friend wouldn't ask a bunch of stupid questions. He'd just help me find them. He'd trust me."

"I can accept that. For now. Have you tried calling her?"

"Goes right to voice mail."

"Did you check the house?"

"Of course I did. They're not here." Zane's arms hung by his sides limply, signaling his despondent mood.

"I get that. Did you find any clues?"

"Clues?"

"Yeah, clues. You know, things that might suggest where they might be. Like did they take their swim suits to go hop in the lake?"

"No, I didn't."

"Let's check together," Tec suggested and took the lead as they walked through every room of the house.

The house was huge, with several wings and high ceilings. The hardwood for the floors had been imported from the Philippines. The furniture had been custom made and would never be duplicated. The kids' rooms looked like kids' rooms, with toys strewn about in James's room and dolls and boy-band posters on the walls of Zanese's room. Otherwise, Tina kept the house clean and orderly, straight from a spread in *Architectural Digest*. Tec couldn't remember if they had a housekeeper, but he sure hoped it wasn't Tina who spent her days keeping this house so immaculate. *What a waste of time that would be,* Tec thought, *for a smart, beautiful woman who surely could use her talents better elsewhere.*

They walked through every room. There was no sign of a struggle, which would've left obvious signs in this immaculate home. In fact, there was no sign of anything. Except for the kids' rooms, you couldn't tell if anybody really lived there. Maybe that was the clue.

Tec stepped out on the back deck that overlooked his friend's backyard, which gently sloped down to Lake Minnetonka. He walked down to the lakefront and then out on the dock. Zane and Tina seemed to have the perfect life. Just like this backyard, everything was well groomed, and all the accessories fit proportionately. But looks can be deceiving. Tec had done some landscaping in a previous life, and he knew all too well that appearances don't tell the whole story. Sometimes you had to pull out the flower with the weed, because you couldn't tell which was which by sight alone.

8

COLOMBIA, FOUR YEARS EARLIER.

Tec hadn't wanted to go on this mission. Had he stayed home, nothing would've changed. He wouldn't be a different man today. But he went—and he changed. Now he was capable of doing things to and for people that he'd never have done before. Was it fate, part of God's design? Or was it just dumb luck? He'd never know, because he didn't want to. Ignorance is bliss.

He'd learned his mother was sick the day before he left for Colombia. She knew it could be a long trip, so she wanted him to know. But she told him not to worry about her. She had her hobbies, and the dog, and her writing. Always her writing. She wrote poetry, and it was good, but it made him sad. It expressed her life's regrets and reminisced about people she wished were still around. He hoped that when he was her age, he wouldn't feel that way. He wanted to live life with no regrets. He'd read that somewhere, and it seemed like a good motto. When he left, he didn't know that he'd never fall back on that motto again. His mother was still alive when he returned, but she'd changed. Not for the better.

Tec was going to Medellín, Colombia. Into the heart of Drug Lord Inc. He was part of a paramilitary, black-ops unit that specialized in locating and neutralizing the bad guys. Wherever they were in the world and regardless of extradition treaties. They were in the K-and-K business—killing or kidnapping. Never any other option. He didn't like to think about what happened to the ones they kidnapped. It helped him to believe that whatever it was, they deserved it. The three suits would tell him what had happened sometimes, but only when it was in their interest to tell him. He'd stopped listening after the first time. The more he listened to their justifications, the more confused he became. Confusion didn't fly when a split second meant the difference between life and death.

That time, the bad guys were Aguilas Negras. They were all that was left of the former terrorist organization known as Auto-defensas Unidas de Colombia, the AUC. Aguilas Negras stood for Black Eagles. They were a dark organization consisting of former death squad members of AUC, which was the military arm of the drug cartels. Over 70 percent of the Black Eagles' income came from cocaine trafficking. The US government had sent Tec and his black-ops team to stop cocaine at its source. They were there to send a lethal message.

Tec never asked permission from any local authorities for what he did. If you had to ask permission, then you weren't doing it right. That's what the suits said, anyway. That had never made sense to Tec, but he didn't care. He let them worry about political repercussions. He was always told he'd be protected. Deep down, he knew that couldn't be true. And it wasn't.

Tec was one of six members of a killer team. His closest friend on the team was a large man with a shaved head named Nito who didn't care about much other than action. He lived for the action. Nito had no fear and loved a fight, especially a good firefight. Tec learned a lot from Nito. Maybe too much. Nito taught him that killing was good as long as it was sanctioned. Nito had saved his life more than once. Tec always felt better when he saw Nito's bulbous ebony biceps cradling his rifle beside him.

They landed in Medellín early on a Saturday morning. He felt depressed the minute they stepped off the plane. Part of it was the oppressive heat, but the abject poverty they saw everywhere played a part too. As they drove out from the city center into the poorer neighborhoods, packs of small, naked children roved through the streets begging for money and crumbs of food. Their desperate pleading stood in stark contrast to the armed groups that populated every corner, gangs and police alike. He felt as if he'd dropped out of their cool, comfortable, and swanky jet directly into the pit of hell. This place didn't seem worth fighting for. Certainly not worth dying for.

Tec and his team were billeted with an army general in a better part of the city, beyond Medellín's poor neighborhoods. The house was Spanish in architecture but American in decoration. The back wall of the largest room on the main level opened completely to a small but lush backyard that had a stunning view of a rich Colombian valley. The coolness of the home belied the fact that the hot sun was bearing down on the red clay roof without forgiveness.

The general had a beautiful wife and three children. His children weren't naked, and they weren't begging. They benefited from their dad's power and prestige, which came from the end of a gun. But his power also brought danger and fear to their lives.

Their mission was America's token effort to stem the flow of cocaine flooding the country from this impoverished nation. It seemed like the proverbial thumb in the dike. Nobody in Colombia seemed to care. Even the general made money fighting on the side of good in this drug war, profiting from its ongoing battles. Nobody wanted it to stop. The drug war made money—and illegal or legal, from the end of a rifle or the stroke of a pen, it all spent the same.

Tec and his fellow warriors went out during the night in two-man, hunter-killer teams to hunt drug gangs in the jungles. They received information and leads from the general, and two members of Tec's team always stayed behind to protect the general's family.

Tec's team had gone out for ten straight nights without making contact. It was hot, and the work was boring and backbreaking. The unforgiving rain forest seemed to sense their frustration, but it wouldn't yield. They didn't come across any Black Eagles, and they began to wonder if they even existed.

The wondering ceased on the eleventh night.

9

While Tec was checking out the backyard, Zane stood in the picture window of his dream home and noticed a car pulling up the long driveway. He knew it was for him. It was a plain maroon Buick, and the two men sitting in the front seat didn't worry him. But when the car stopped and a third man emerged from the backseat, Zane became concerned. He could handle two, but probably not three.

All three men were dressed well and exuded power. They were hard, the type confident women found alluring and some men feared. Though Zane didn't fear them, he feared the reason for their visit. The consequences of his actions might finally catch up with him in the form of these three men.

Zane walked out his front door to meet them. Zane was six four, and though he was lean, he was well muscled. His dark hair was cut short to keep grooming to a minimum. He worked out at the gym daily and took mixed martial arts twice a week. He was ready. Had to be.

The first two men approached him on his front lawn, and the third man hung back.

"Can I help you guys?" Zane asked.

"You know why we're here," Number Three answered.

"Perhaps, but why don't you tell me, anyway? And if you don't have a good reason, get back in your car, drive away, stop at the beach, and have a nice cool swim in the lake before you go home. Or wherever scary guys like you go," Zane retorted.

"We have your wife and kids," Number Two answered.

Zane's heart stopped beating for a second. He'd feared the worst, but now that it was confirmed, he wasn't sure he could handle it.

Zane looked past the three men at a weeping willow tree he'd planted two years ago. James and his friends had used its drooping branches for their fort as they fought off imaginary intruders. Their cries of fake pain and courage echoed in his ears as he tried to focus on the present.

"You'll get them back unharmed if you do some things for us. If you're smart, you'll keep this quiet. If you're not, we'll gladly show you we mean business. But it'll hurt," Number One chimed in.

What had he done? Zane wondered. His family didn't have anything to do with his work. They didn't even know what exactly he did, so why did they have to suffer? He should have known his business partners would go to any extreme to keep him in line. He'd been stupid. What kind of man did this to his family?

He knew he couldn't take time now to ponder that question. Zane had to send them a message and send it fast.

Zane knew these men weren't intimidated by him. They'd seen danger, and while they might not have won every fight, they looked like the kind who persevered. But Zane had surprise on his side. He didn't enjoy violence, but many times in his life, it had served a purpose. It was a tool, no different from the pen he used at SAS—and just as dangerous.

Number One was on his right, about a foot away. He'd made the mistake of getting close to his quarry before assessing his abilities and intentions. Zane quickly raised his right foot and brought it down hard on top of Number One's right foot. He heard something crunch. Number Two turned to face him. Immediately, Zane spun to his left with the same leg and brought his knee up to Number Two's groin. He heard the satisfying crunch of his knee against another man's vital manhood as Number Two went down.

Number One was still in the fight, though, and Number Three hadn't even been heard from yet. Number Three stepped into Zane and, using a palm strike, hit him hard in the solar plexus. Zane felt like his world stopped as he struggled to catch his breath. Before he could recover, Number One kicked him hard in his right kidney—hard enough for Zane to see stars and swear his body had been broken in half as he fell. Zane was sprawled on his finely manicured front lawn writhing in pain as he fought back the bile that seemed to rise involuntarily from some part of his body that was intertwined with his soul.

Zane knew he needed help. "Tec!" he yelled as loud as he could.

Number Three picked up Zane by both ears and pulled Zane's face close to his. "You got yourself into this, and now you get yourself out. If you're half the man you think you are, you need to realize that you really screwed up. You brought this whole shit storm down on your precious wife and kids. You should've thought about how your choices would affect them. You're the only one to blame if something happens. You know what to do, so do it. Don't make us send you another message."

Tec came running around the corner of the house just as they were getting in the car. Tec yelled after them to stop—as if that would do any good. Tec didn't know if they'd seen him. Not that it would have made a difference to them. It did to Tec, though.

"What the hell is going on? Zane, are you all right?" Tec asked as he reached Zane. "What did you do to bring these men here?"

Zane was still coughing and sputtering, some of it blood. "They have my family. You are right; they took them because of something I did."

Tec helped Zane to his feet and over to a small decorative

bench on the front lawn. It was now serving a more practical purpose as Zane sat down. Zane felt like a knife was sticking out of his back, and each breath felt like a new sensation, as if he were learning how to breathe again. But worse than the physical pain was the stabbing guilt.

"Zane, you really need to tell me what's going on. I can't help you unless you tell me. I'm your friend. I don't care what you did or didn't do. All that matters is getting your family back. Understand?"

"I know, Tec. You're my closest friend, but if I tell you anything, you're in danger too, and I can't risk that. I can't involve you in this. Get the hell out of here. I'll figure it out somehow."

"Don't be an idiot. You probably can figure this out, but two heads are always better than one. I've been in difficult situations before; I know how to fight my way out."

"Let me think. Can you please get me some water and leave me alone for a moment? I need to make a call. Please don't tell anyone about this. I have to keep this quiet. You have to trust me."

Tec turned to go into the house for water. At least Zane hadn't shut him out completely, as he needed answers to help both of them.

Zane sat on the bench wondering what his family might be going through. Was James crying, hoping his daddy would come rescue him? Was Tina trying to console Zanese? Zanese was old beyond her eight years, but she was sheltered in so many ways nonetheless. And Tina, was she wondering why this was happening to them?

Zane stood and walked two steps but then fell to his knees. He looked up to the sky and began to cry. What had he done? He fell back onto the lawn and yanked up handfuls of the precious turf—over and over again, crawling in circles, ripping up as much of his finely manicured lawn as he could reach.

Taking his family had been a huge mistake. As he wiped the

tears from his face, he felt something growing deep inside him. It was cold and hard, and he'd felt it before.

10

COLOMBIA, FOUR YEARS EARLIER.

On the eleventh night, the Black Eagles came for the general. There were ten of them. The night was moonless and as black as the conscience of the country they lived in.

The general had been branded a traitor for asking greedy foreigners to protect his precious wife and children. Inviting American greedmongers to his home had brought danger and bloodshed directly to his doorstep.

Tec and his fellow team members returned to the general's home from that night's hunting expedition as the sun rose to form a bloodred dawn sky. Tec knew something was wrong as soon as he stepped from the SUV. The family's two pit bulls had always met them at the gate, but that day, they were nowhere to be found. The wrought iron gate was swinging open, as if inviting him toward the incredible sight that would brand his mind forever.

As they walked through the front door, Tec recognized the sickly, coppery smell that meant the gates to hell had been opened. There was blood on the beautiful tile floor in the entryway—and more blood the farther they moved into the picturesque home. Blood didn't bother him; in fact, at times he reveled in it. But this wasn't a lot of blood; it was a *lake* of blood. He'd never seen this much blood in his life. Not even when he helped clean the kill floor of his uncle's meat locker.

Their weapons drawn, they proceeded to clear the house the way they'd been taught. They secured the front of the home first and then the upstairs. All the beds were unmade and looked as if they'd just been slept in. There was no sign of a struggle, which meant the general must have known his attackers.

The dining room was last. It was the room with the most blood. Once they looked at the magnificent dining room table, they knew why. For the rest of his life, Tec would dream about the dining room table and its macabre setting.

He closed his eyes and remembered the two girls playing in the courtyard the day before, trying to keep a soccer ball away from their little brother. The boy had told them repeatedly to stop teasing him, but his giggles gave away how much he enjoyed his big sisters' attention. And then in the evening, all three had been laughing hysterically at Nito's stupid card tricks. They never worked but also never failed to make his young audiences happy. The innocence of children is common to all cultures.

Tec slowly opened his eyes. The table was set with five white linen place mats. On top of each sat a severed head: the general, his wife, and their three children. Tec had seen many a mutilated body, but never children. Now their ashen faces were burned into his memory as blood dripped from the table onto the teakwood floor. As Tec looked closer, he discovered the tracks running down their faces where their tears had mixed with their blood. Their mother's face was frozen into an anguished scream. He imagined they'd made her watch the savage beheadings of her daughters and son. He carefully picked up her head and held it to his chest while stroking her long hair. Her blood dripped on his boots.

Tec's mind burned with a fever that made him want to kill and maim and put out the flame. He'd never felt like this before. He needed to kill. He had to kill. He had to do it now or he'd lose his grip on reality forever. He pleaded with God to give him the strength for vengeance so he could show these savages that this massacre had been their biggest, and last, mistake. Tec gently placed her head back on the table with her blood still soaking into his shirt and pants.

On the wall behind the table was a message scrawled with the precious blood of this innocent family:

WE ONLY FINISHED WHAT THE GENERAL STARTED.
LEAVE NOW AND NOBODY ELSE GETS HURT.
YOUR TWO MEN WILL SOON WISH THEIR HEADS WERE
ON THAT TABLE TOO.

Tec's unit had left behind two team members to protect the family. The savages had them. Tec wished he were one of them. Torture would be preferable to what he was going through now. He couldn't live knowing what the children and mother had gone through as they watched each other die. All that mattered now was revenge.

Nito grabbed him by his shoulder.

"Standing around in this slaughterhouse does no one any good. Get out to the yard. Now!"

Tec slipped in the blood and fell to his hands and knees, but he stood up quickly and followed Nito to the front yard. He wiped his bloody hands on his shirtsleeves. His breath came in quick, shallow bursts, and he couldn't stop shaking. The pain in his chest threatened to spread throughout his organs with the pressure of a thousand boa constrictors. It felt as if he were dying. Or maybe that was wishful thinking.

"Tec! You have got to get a fucking grip!" Nito shouted in his face as he shook him hard. "The sons of bitches who did this are just men. They don't deserve to draw another breath. We can't be scared of them. They need to fear us. They're lucky we weren't here. I don't care if it's just me against them. I'll kill every last one of them." Nito made that dark promise to no one in particular. "They made a big motherfucking mistake. I'll find them and make them pay."

"I'm not afraid, Nito. I want a piece of them. I'll do anything."

"Damn right you will. First you have to stop shaking and calm the fuck down. We can only do this in the right frame of mind. They're bad motherfuckers, but we're worse. You hear me? You have to get mean—real fucking mean. We're the righteous hand of God, carrying out His glorious retribution. These sorry sons of bitches are going to wish they'd never pissed in our pool. We won't fail, and we won't stop until they're all sucking dirt six feet under."

Tec stared at him, concentrating on his breathing.

"Do you understand?" Nito asked.

Tec nodded, still trying to control his breathing. He focused his thoughts on his last R&R in South Beach, where the hot sun had been baking him as he cooled himself in the teal-blue ocean. He was trained to control his thoughts and his fear so he could survive and thrive when others couldn't. He was trained to think clearly and patiently. He just had to concentrate, and then he'd be fine for battle. This situation was no different. He could find opportunity in even the worst situation. He'd find a way to carry out his revenge. He was good to go.

His radio buzzed as he was checking his weapons. He keyed the receiver and listened as their intelligence team gave him the intel that would help complete his revenge.

11

Still lying on his front lawn amid the evidence of his grass-pulling tantrum, Zane realized he had to make the phone call. It was a hard call to make, because he'd screwed up. He'd done what he'd been told he must never do.

Zane would have to make him understand.

Zane sat up with his legs spread-eagled and pulled his phone from his pocket.

He had the number memorized.

"Is he there?" Zane asked the receptionist.

"Yes. May I tell him who's calling?"

"Tell him it's the one guy who can burn his ass forever."

"Uh, okay. I think it might be better if you give him that message yourself. Just give me a name."

"Zane."

The receptionist placed him on hold, and he listened to Stevie Wonder sing the question "Isn't she lovely?" *Yup*, he thought, *Tina is lovely, if she's still breathing.* After mere seconds, someone bellowed in his ear.

"This had better be important. You know better than to call me, especially now."

"It is important. My family has been taken."

"Why?"

Zane thought he seemed too calm.

34

"Because you're an asshole. You lied to me."

"I have never lied to you. If they were taken, they were taken because you betrayed SAS's trust. You had to know there would be consequences."

"People work their whole lives building their companies, their future. Then I steal it with the stroke of a pen. I can't do that anymore. Especially with what I know. You need to rescue my family without me going back in to find what you need."

"I can't do that. You're responsible for your own family. It's up to you to get them out, not me. Own up and do what they want."

"Get me out—now. Take what you can, and end my involvement. In the name of all that's decent and right, back off. My God, you're allowing innocent people to get hurt. My family doesn't even know what I'm doing. Why should they pay?" Zane asked.

"You agreed to see this to the end. You took an oath to see this to the end. The only way for your family to be saved is to do just that."

"That's insane. I promised to do my job, but you changed the rules. We can do it another way without me screwing people. Just listen—"

"I have listened to you. Long enough." The man hung up.

Zane's heart sank. There had to be some other way. Yes, he was going to save his family. But did that responsibility include going back and acquiring more companies illegally?

Zane stood up and turned toward the house. He dreaded talking to Tec. Tec couldn't learn the truth. Not ever. There was no way he could tell him what he'd done. He couldn't bear the thought of losing his respect. But maybe he could tell Tec a different story—something, anything—and enlist his help. Was that fair? No. Tec was too good a friend to lie to, especially when helping him could be dangerous. He hoped part of the truth would be enough.

Zane trudged up to the house. He would've loved to just keep going past the house and jump in the lake. He could swim to the other side and disappear. He could head north, move to Canada, and never come back. He had the money to do that. But then he thought about James and Zanese and Tina. As tempting as escape sounded, he couldn't do that to them. Especially on top of what he'd already done. There were still some lines even he wouldn't cross.

Tec was sitting at the breakfast counter when Zane walked into the kitchen. He was staring at the calendar for today. He looked at Zane sadly and handed him his water.

"Did you make your call?"

"Yeah, but it did no good. I have to take action myself. I need to find a way to save my family," Zane replied while sitting down next to Tec.

Tec stood up and leaned against the counter and crossed his arms. "Why not start finding that way by telling me what the hell is going on? Maybe I can help. No matter what the problem is, just lay it on me, brother. I've seen some shit in my life. Shit always stinks, but I can shovel it with the best of them."

Zane put his head down on the cool granite. "I'm sure you can. I don't know where to start. But I'm sure you'll never look at me the same again."

"I've heard a lot of bad things and done some bad things myself, so I'm sure this won't shock me. Surprise me, maybe," Tec said, nodding as if deep in thought, "but it won't shock me."

"You heard about the Taliban in Afghanistan putting their women and children at sites of great military and strategic value? That way they can claim the Americans are slaughtering women and children if they bombed those sites. What do you think of that strategy?" Zane asked as he brought his head up and looked at Tec.

"I think they're cowards and need to receive whatever bad shit comes their way."

"What I did is worse. Much worse," Zane flatly stated as he

stood up and walked to the kitchen window and stared out at the lake.

He ran his hands through his short hair, turned around to look at Tec, and proceeded to tell him his story.

He was right; it did change how Tec looked at Zane. And he hadn't even told him the whole story.

B en Guardian hated clearance sales. He hated convincing people they were getting a superior product by lowering the price. He'd rather sell less at a higher price. Value meant more to him than volume. However, having fifty-seven branches in five midwestern states meant he had to sell a lot of product at any price.

Ben was the sole owner of Guardian Jewelry, a high-end jewelry retailer headquartered in the Twin Cities. He'd started with one small store and then slowly expanded to become the largest retail jewelry chain in the upper Midwest. Expansion had come with a price. He couldn't remember his last restful night; he ate just to fuel his body, not to enjoy the food, and his marriage was approaching its demise. And on top of all of that, his business was failing. In fact, this sale was his last-ditch effort to salvage his golden empire. Guardian Jewelry was a privately held corporation, owned solely by him, and now that it was in trouble, he couldn't go public even if he wanted to. Investors weren't interested in failing jewelry stores.

New customers came in regularly, but visits didn't translate into sales. Customers often found what they wanted but were unwilling to pay his price. Most of them didn't understand or care about diamond quality. Guardian Jewelry was fast becoming an

38

unintentional showroom for Amazon and other online sellers. And prices at Walmart were significantly lower. They didn't sell quality, but the average diamond buyer didn't seem to care anymore. Ben's personal designs didn't hold much sway, either. Everybody was a jewelry designer these days, and he had to admit there was some really cool stuff out there.

He still maintained a few wholesale customers. They bought his diamonds at a low markup in large lots, cut and uncut, and resold them who knows where. While the net profit wasn't as high, the volume made up for it. Ben relied on the wholesale portion of his business. Right now, one of his wholesale clients was way behind in his payments. As a result, Ben was behind in his payments to his suppliers. It was a vicious circle that had long ago turned into a box. A coffin-sized box. Ben needed to do something to make this guy pay up. He didn't want to alienate him, though, because he was a large source of Guardian Jewelry's profit. When he paid.

Ben thought he might have to start drinking again.

Guardian's corporate offices were in a high-rent section of Edina, a wealthy suburb of Minneapolis. If you were a jeweler, you had to look and play the part. There was no cube farm for his corporate workers; everybody had a dedicated office. All the artwork on the walls was original. Even the silverware in the break room lived up to its name. No expense had been spared.

Ben was standing on the plush carpet in his office mulling over his options. He'd considered closing and filing for bankruptcy. Even if he could get over the stigma of that, he knew that wouldn't satisfy his suppliers. Many of them were international organizations that didn't recognize US laws, including bankruptcy statutes. Diamonds had to be paid for. Somehow. After all, they were a woman's best friend.

Growing up, Ben had been taught that every problem had a

solution. If you couldn't find one, you weren't looking hard enough. *Can't* wasn't part of Ben's vocabulary. He walked to the window, gazing out at the pond in his corporate backyard. He wanted to go outside and walk around the pond until his problems disappeared. Unfortunately, the last time that had worked for him, he'd been ten.

He heard the main office door open. It was early afternoon, and most of his employees had gone out to a birthday lunch for one of the administrative staffers, so he wasn't sure who to expect. He hadn't felt in the birthday mood, especially for someone he didn't know. It had been a long time since he'd personally known all the people who worked for him.

As he counted the ducks on the pond, he felt a presence behind him.

"Hey, Dad. I have some good news for you."

It was his son, Tim. He was a good son, concerned about his dad.

Ben turned around slowly. "Great. I need some really good news. As long as it doesn't involve you finding your dream sailboat."

Tim was the Guardian Jewelry's CFO, but the title was just window dressing. Tim's most developed business skill involved going to lunch.

"I just went to lunch with a guy named Zane, and I think our problems are solved."

13

COLOMBIA, FOUR YEARS EARLIER.

Intelligence satellites are beautiful things. Unless they're watching you. You can give up trying to hide, even behind walls. The government doesn't need a reason, because most of the time, nobody knows about it. On a clear day, these satellites can watch anything a person does—or doesn't do. On a cloudy day, drones work just as well.

The morning after the slaughter at the general's house was humid, clear, and hot. The call from the intelligence contact had given Tec the information he'd wanted to hear. The satellite had a clear view of the house, and the analysts could track the attackers as long as they hadn't returned to the rain forest. They tracked them to a house in a rural zone of Medellín and provided an 80 percent probability that at least some of them were still there. Tec had a hard time maintaining his heart rate. He could taste revenge.

Tec and the three others in his group spent the next thirty minutes getting ready. They cleaned their weapons and secured their gear. Tec was tired, but the adrenaline surge was overriding his exhaustion. He liked this feeling. He was on the knife's edge, and that made him more dangerous.

Nito knew he didn't have to motivate Tec. If anything, he needed to rein him in. But Nito didn't care. Fuck it. That was his

41

motto. Two very simple words.

They spent the next forty-five minutes on the road toward their target, driving a crap car so they could blend in. Advertising their presence meant more scrutiny, and that was the last thing they needed. Tec hated this terrible place and hated the people. Why couldn't they just rise up and throw the Black fucking Eagles out? Why did he have to help? He liked the work, but not the collateral damage.

Tec understood that he'd broken the cardinal rule: don't get close to the natives or the people they were protecting. The indelible image of the severed heads of the general and his family served as motivation to bring severe, swift, and merciless retribution. Patience wasn't a virtue that day.

Tec and the three other team members arrived as the humidity of the day started to weigh in. Recon was their first priority. They spent the next several sweltering hours working concentric circles back to the subject house from a one-mile diameter. Once confident they weren't walking into a setup and that they could strike without interference, they were ready to go by noon. It was a white-hot and intensely bright afternoon. They wouldn't have the cover of darkness, but they didn't care.

The house was a wooden structure not too different from those found in lower-middle-class neighborhoods of American cities. It was one story with large, modern windows and was painted a tawny color. It looked to have a footprint of about fifteen hundred square feet. It didn't look as if locating and seizing its occupants would be difficult.

The heat signatures in the house suggested three people were present. One was an adult. It appeared they'd stumbled upon one Black Eagle's family. But the satellite had tracked all of the attackers to this house. They could've left since the last check of the satellite data—or the whole gang could be hiding in a basement. There was only one way to find out.

The other two team members waited at the rear of the home while Tec and Nito waited just outside the front door. The sweat formed by the hot day was mixing with the blood on Tec's camouflage khakis, creating a stench that matched the violence that created it.

As soon as he heard the ready sign from the back-door team, Nito and Tec kicked in the front door with several angry blows that did little to quell their appetite for more. The four Americans cleared the house within two minutes and determined their initial assessment had been correct. The only people present were a mom and her two children.

They came up with a plan.

After a team member who spoke Spanish interrogated the mother, they learned this was the house and family of the gang leader. They couldn't believe their luck. They had his family. They wouldn't do as the Colombians had done, though. At least that's what Tec told Nito. They'd use the woman and her children to bait the Colombian lieutenant and his men back to the house. His wife radioed them and feigned an emergency.

The Colombians took two hours to get back to the house. The Americans waited until all ten were in the house and sprung their trap. Surprise, speed, and violence of action provided the Americans with the edge. The Colombians never knew what hit them. Tec took out half of the Colombian team himself. His disregard for his own safety was evidence of the haze of hatred filling his mind. It didn't take long to brutally kill all of them—but they spared the leader. He repeatedly cried out for his family, who were sequestered in the basement. The plan was working. In fact, it all seemed a little too easy.

Had they overlooked something?

14

Tina was scared and confused. Scared about what would happen to her and the kids and confused about what her husband could've done to invite this. That's what her abductors had told her—Zane had done something to cause this, and he needed to do something else to get them back alive. She had no idea what they were talking about, but she was certain her husband of eleven years would never intentionally hurt her or the children.

These men reeked of violence and death. How could Zane possibly be mixed up with them?

They'd been blindfolded as they'd traveled for less than an hour to the house where they were now being held. It was a tiny, single-level rambler with wood floors and old, threadbare furniture. It reminded Tina of her aunt Tillie's cabin on the lake, except they weren't in the woods enjoying the view of a picturesque lake. They were locked in a back bedroom with one twin bed and no available bathroom. The windows were blacked out, and they had no way to communicate with the outside world.

One of their abductors was a large, muscular black man, and the other was a short, wiry white guy. They wouldn't answer her questions. When she kept asking, they told her to keep her mouth shut, or they'd do it for her. She didn't want to find out what that meant, so she kept quiet.

James was taking the whole experience fairly well. He seemed to look at it as an adventure—as was almost everything that happened to a five-year-old. Zanese, however, wasn't dealing with it as well as her brother. She'd begun crying as soon as the bedroom door was locked shut. Tina was trying to console her and get her to calm down, but it wasn't working. Zanese was heaving up big, tearful sobs and was having trouble catching her breath. James was lying facedown on the bed playing with a small metal truck that someone must have left behind. *The previous abductees, perhaps*, Tina thought with uncharacteristic sarcasm.

Tina went to the bedroom door and began to pound. "We need to use the bathroom. My daughter's going to be sick. Please help. I know you can hear me."

She could hear footsteps coming her way down the hall, and then the door was thrown open, pushing Tina onto the floor. She scooted backward up against the wall.

"You need to shut up. You'll get three bathroom breaks a day, no more," the skinny guy told her as he began to leave.

"That's not enough. I'm a woman, for God's sake. And they're kids. That's just not going to work."

He stepped back into the room and walked over to where Tina was lying on the floor. He picked her up by the front of her tank top and brought her face close to his. "You're very lucky to be alive after the shit your husband pulled."

Tina mustered up her best brave face. "My husband won't stand for this. He'll rescue us, and you'll be sorry."

He began to laugh as he grabbed her by both shoulders and threw her against the wall. Her head hit hard as it left a dent in the Sheetrock. He was on her quickly and picked her up again, this time by the hair.

She screamed.

He slapped her in the mouth and drove his boot into her stomach, letting go of her hair and driving her into the wall again.

45

Zanese was screaming, and then she suddenly stopped and began to vomit. James rushed to his mom's side without looking at the man. Tina was bleeding from a cut lip and was holding her stomach, obviously in pain. The sour stench of fresh vomit filled the room as Zanese tried to wipe her mouth on her shirt while continuing to retch.

A large black presence filled the doorway. "Spaz, dead hostages don't do us any good. At least not yet."

Spaz moved and stood over Tina, smiling and licking his lips. "She's mine, Rocker. I get all of her, including that nice, tight ass. I haven't had that for a while."

"Just remember, dead ass is no ass, and we have a job to do first," Rocker replied as he waited for Spaz to leave.

He turned to Tina. "Just stay quiet. This will all be over soon."

That's what she was most afraid of.

15

COLOMBIA, FOUR YEARS EARLIER.

Something was wrong. Even after they'd killed nine of the ten men from the kill squad that had brutally murdered the general and his family, Tec's bloodlust wasn't satisfied. The revenge had been so quick that he didn't get to savor it, like eating a favorite candy bar and then looking at the empty wrapper and having no memory of how it tasted.

Tec wasn't in control of his mind or his body. He was controlled by his need for more death and suffering. He grabbed Nito and took him to the main room of the house.

"We need to find out what the leader knows about our two missing guys. I want him alone for five minutes. Take the other two outside and post them as sentries. Do it now."

Nito nodded and looked him straight in the eyes. "Don't do anything you'll regret later. This place isn't worth it. Remember, you'll have to live with what you do today forever."

"You were the one who said we needed to show these dudes how bad we are. You said we needed to make them pay. I'm that payback."

"We have made them pay. If this druggie knows where our teammates are, then by all means, find out. But do it in a way that doesn't destroy you. Don't lose yourself. You can't become one of them."

"Give me five minutes. I'll get the information. Don't worry about how. None of us will be able to live with leaving two team members behind."

Nito called the other team members outside to give them new orders to stand guard. One went to the back, and the other stood with Nito in the front yard. The sun was as unyielding as the thought of how terribly this day had gone. Nito looked up and down the barren street, hoping for any kind of interruption.

Tec went to the kitchen and faced the Colombian leader, who was gagged and tied in a chair. The furnishings here and in the rest of the house were simple but well cared for. The mechanically cooled air didn't remove the heat from the suspense from what was about to happen. Tec took out his combat knife and placed the blade on top of the leader's right ear. He removed the gag and asked the man if he understood English.

"My English is better than your Spanish will ever be," he spat.

"Then you'll understand when I tell you that for every question you answer with helpful information, you get to keep an appendage. If you withhold information, you lose an appendage, starting with your right ear. Do you understand?" Tec asked.

"Do *you*? There's a lot going on here that's beyond understanding. You are just a stupid, ignorant tool of the trade. *Comprende*?" the Colombian retorted as he spat on Tec's bloody boots.

Tec couldn't control himself. He was all bloodlust. He was the tip of the spear of retribution. He pictured the severed heads of the general and his family and the lake of blood that flooded their dining room. Tec calmly and cleanly sliced off the Colombian's right ear. He felt nothing.

The Colombian gargled a primal scream as blood bubbled out in a red fountain from where his ear used to be. "Take more!" he taunted. "Come on. Show me you're a man!"

Tec calmly placed the knife above his other ear.

"Maybe you should cut off your own ears, since you are not listening to me. Your guys did this, not mine," the Colombian spat out as he thrashed from side to side with blood spraying onto Tec and around the room.

Tec stopped. What was he talking about? That made no sense. His vision swam in red, and he grabbed the Colombian's hair and held his head while he cut off the left ear.

The Colombian screamed louder.

"I'm telling you the truth. We got a tip about your team being at the general's house. The tip came from an American. An American, you hear? I don't know what's going on, but neither do you. Fuck me, kill me, do whatever you want—just get me out of this house. My family is listening!" he cried.

Tec's mind was racing, and he couldn't concentrate. An American tipped them off? Why? He knew he needed to stop, to find out more, but he couldn't. The only thing he could focus on was the memory of the children's heads. He looked down at the mother's blood on his shirt. He tried to wipe it off with his left hand, but all he did was add the Columbian's blood. He looked at the man before him, and all he could see was blood. But it wasn't enough. He raised the knife to strike again.

At that moment, Nito buzzed his lapel mike. It took all of his willpower to answer.

"Yeah?" he asked.

"We can hear what's going on. You need to stop," Nito commanded.

"I haven't heard what I need to know yet. I don't have answers. Just more questions. Stay out of this."

"You need to get out here. Now. This is not a request."

Tec screamed and kicked the kitchen table over and watched it hit the wall. He looked up at the ceiling and began to shake. He continued to scream and then turned around quickly and walked up to the Colombian. He wiped his blade clean on the Colombian's jeans and stuck it into the chair between his legs, an inch from his balls. He walked to the front door, opened it, looked outside, and froze.

There stood the two missing team members.

They were clean and unhurt. With a broad smile on his face, one of them asked if he was ready to go home.

16

WWHDT? What did that mean? Zane's son, James, was advanced beyond his years. He had the body of a five-year-old but the mind of a twelve-year-old. If he knew he was in trouble, James would try to leave him a clue. Any clue. Many evenings when Zane arrived home from work, James showed him a picture he'd drawn, representing something the boy had done that day. Then he'd wait impatiently for Zane to decipher the picture. Zane was sure those words were a puzzle for him too. He needed to concentrate. Those letters had to mean something.

Zane slowly walked upstairs and stood at the foot of the California king bed in the master bedroom. Tina had found the $5,000 snow-white comforter on a recent trip to New York. He stood there and imagined Tina making their bed that morning, unaware of what chaos the day would bring.

Zane approached her walk-in closet and stepped inside. Many a person wished their bedroom was this large. Her clothes were hung with all the hangers pointing the same way and every pair of shoes carefully aligned and organized by style. He supposed he should be able to figure out what she was wearing by the process of elimination. But he had no idea. There were too many clothes. Most of them he couldn't remember ever seeing her wear.

He walked into Zanese's room and stood by her desk. She'd been writing a thank-you note to Betty for taking them up to the family cabin and teaching her how to swim. She ended the note by apologizing for Dad and his absence at this year's annual retreat. She was sure Dad was busy and would be there next year.

Zane couldn't read more.

He was exhausted.

He'd spent the whole night going through their home, going through memories. They'd built the home together with love and lies. Now as he watched the sun rise over Lake Minnetonka, he was beginning to fear that maybe his love was also a lie.

He needed Tec's help, but his confession yesterday had left out some critical details. He couldn't cop to his own deceitful role in SAS. Then Tec would know he was working for them. He told himself that he was keeping secrets to protect Tec, but somewhere inside, he knew he was protecting himself. He couldn't let Tec know what he'd done, how he'd crumbled under pressure.

Zane was a whistleblower. He was passing on information he'd sworn to keep secret. Was he doing it because of his moral compass? No, it was much more complicated than that.

Two months ago, he'd gone to the Treasury Department. He'd considered going to the FBI but decided against it because he knew Treasury offered whistleblower protection.

They offered him a way to make it right. They knew he'd want to make it right. It would be Zane's way out.

Except it wasn't.

He was to go undercover and obtain evidence. Zane would use his position within SAS and give the Treasury Department enough evidence to prosecute. He would keep deceiving his clients and provide evidence of all illegal transactions. They told Zane it was risky. SAS might find out he was a snitch. He didn't care; this was his way of keeping some part of his life intact. He was ready and willing to be the government's stooge if it meant he could get out and keep his family safe. He worked late nights, alone, copying and stealing incriminating data.

It was never enough, though. The government always wanted more. The days turned into weeks, and the weeks into two months, and he still hadn't gathered enough evidence.

Then the unthinkable happened. One of his clients caught him downloading the details of the transaction that effectively purchased the client's company. As if that wasn't bad enough, the client was able to track him e-mailing details of the transaction to the government. He was busted. His only option was to tell his client the truth—that he was cooperating with Treasury in an investigation of SAS. The client freaked out. After all, he'd liked the SAS plan that would've let him sell his insolvent company and reap a big profit. He couldn't care less that it was illegal or what part of his soul he had to sell. The client wanted a solution and would do anything to get it. So the client went to Zane's boss.

The Feds weren't doing anything with the evidence he'd provided. And worse, now his boss knew he was a mole.

That had been two days ago. And now his family was gone.

Zane was sure SAS was behind his family's abduction. But he wasn't entirely sure why. If SAS wanted to shut him up, why not just kill him? Because they wanted him to keep making their dirty deals. But now they knew they couldn't trust him to keep their secrets, so why force him back?

The answers to these questions would help him figure out how to get his family back. Zane wouldn't put anything past his employer. The stakes were high: money (lots of it) and life and death.

Tec had left abruptly after hearing Zane's story. But Zane knew he'd be back. There was something about Tec that made him help people in need. He'd seen Tec reach out to his students and involve himself in their lives as a mentor. Tec believed the world was bigger than just us and ours. That core belief fueled him and gave him purpose.

Zane showered and dressed quickly. He put on an old pair of jeans, a worn T-shirt, and a pair of work boots. He had to do something they wouldn't expect, although he wasn't sure yet what that would be. He had some ideas, but he wasn't at all sure he had the balls to go through with them. He needed more encouragement before he'd dare to take bold action.

He took his laptop, which held all the evidence he'd collected. He backed his SUV out of the garage and drove down the long driveway. He loved this house and the land it occupied. It was private and secluded. So private that you could kidnap a family without anyone knowing. You could do a lot of things without anyone knowing.

He stopped at the end of the driveway, looked for traffic, and turned onto the road.

He felt the rumble before he saw it. As he turned to look back at the house, his mind couldn't register what his eyes were seeing. His Range Rover slid sideways across the road as his dream house exploded in a cacophonous eruption of flame, smoke, and debris.

Encouragement.

17

Zane's explanation didn't wash with what Tec had been told by the suits. But it was beginning to look like they hadn't told him enough. He went back for a visit. This time there was only one of them.

Tec hated the sterile office. It reminded him of his high school principal's office, where he'd spent a considerable amount of time during his teen years. There was an empty desk and three chairs, one behind the desk and two in front. The room was just one of the man's tools, and it was cold and impersonal. Tec knew he had a more luxurious office, but he wouldn't use it. At least not today.

The man was polite but aloof. He always used as few words as possible. There was no wasted motion. He only smiled when he knew he'd won. He claimed that he wanted Tec to understand—but Tec knew he was becoming a problem, because they didn't share the same definition of understanding.

Tec asked if he could see the subjects. As if they weren't real people.

"No," the man flatly stated.

"I need more than that. I did what you asked. I'm not sure anybody else could have pulled this off. I deserve to see them, and I need answers to my questions," Tec demanded.

"You got your money. Ignorance is your protection."

"I'm touched by your concern. But I need a favor."

"This favor will cost more than you're willing to pay."

"You know what I'm capable of. Let me see them. Just once."

"This is not Colombia. These aren't the same circumstances."

"You sent me to Colombia, said it was necessary for our country. Then innocent people got killed. Because of what you did. I won't let that happen again."

"War doesn't discriminate between the innocent and the guilty."

"I didn't know who the subjects were when I took this assignment. Had I known, I never would've done it."

"You could've pulled out when you discovered who we were asking you to take."

"It was too late to back out."

"It's never too late for that."

"It is when you told me that the security of our country is at stake and that this job is for the greater good," Tec explained while looking up at the ceiling.

"So even though I screwed you in Colombia, you believed me in this instance?" the man asked sarcastically. "Why the sudden faith?"

Tec looked at him with a mournful expression that seemed to come from another time. "I trust the war, just not you."

"And now I'm supposed to believe you're worried about them?"

"Believe what you want. I just need to know."

"If your friend does what we ask, nothing will happen to his family," the man replied, pushing his chair back and crossing his legs.

"What does he have to do?"

"Keep doing his job. And keep it to himself. Very simple."

"You know I have no qualms about hurting people who lie to me."

"You did a job. We paid you. That's it."

"You may think you know me, but you don't. I'm not afraid of you, because I don't care what happens to me. You'll never understand, but know that it's true. And fear it."

"Fear isn't the best emotion to motivate people. I learned that a long time ago. I actually think love works better."

"I don't love you, and I don't love them. I did what I thought had to be done, and now I just want to make sure."

"But you do love."

Tec stood up and put both hands flat on the desk. "Don't."

"You already did. You made a mistake, and that mistake can still cost you. All three."

Tec quickly backed up and stumbled over the chairs, almost falling down in the process. "Please. Don't do that."

"Then be a team player."

Tec stared at the man for a moment with pleading in his eyes and his hands balled up into fists. He couldn't reason anymore. He turned to leave but stopped at the door and looked back one last time.

"Have a nice day," the man said, grinning from ear to ear.

18

Zane pulled the Range Rover to the side of the road as soon as he could. He was shaking so much he could barely drive. His house was gone. It was a house built on the broken backs of those he'd deceived, but it was still his. All of his hard work gone up in smoke. He wanted to go back and find out if anything was left, but he knew there wasn't. Except perhaps an evil presence.

History is full of ordinary people who do extraordinary things when faced with extreme circumstances. People who weren't perfect, who'd had their share of failures, but when pushed, they'd answered the call. They didn't place their lives over the lives of others. The pressure of impossible situations created an opportunity to do what they could never have done otherwise. Zane found himself in a similar situation. This was bigger than himself, even bigger than his family and friends.

Zane decided his next step was to find Tec. He wouldn't tell him more than he already had. The explosion of his house should provide any additional incentive that might be required. Tec would be as pissed as he was. He loved Zane's family.

After years of friendship, Zane knew Tec's schedule. Right now, he'd be at the Lifetime Fitness gym, about four miles from Tec's dojo. He'd be lifting this morning. Tec was a fitness fanatic. Like everything else in his life, Tec was very disciplined with his workouts.

Zane strategized the best course of action. All he needed was the courage to carry it out. Take the fight to them before they had any way of reacting. It might endanger his wife and kids even more, but he had no guarantee of their safety, anyway.

Zane could do his enemies at SAS a lot of harm. Just not in the way they feared.

19

Tina couldn't sleep as she lay in the dirty little bed with Zanese and James by her side. She couldn't stop thinking about their abduction the day before. She kept analyzing and reanalyzing the scene. There had to be a clue that could help her somehow. She had picked up James from soccer practice, because Zane had forgotten yet again. As they drove home, she and James were discussing how maybe they could help relieve Dad's busy schedule. She noticed that a plain van followed her into their driveway. Three men with masks emerged, and before she could dial 911, she'd been shot with something electric. It paralyzed her, so she couldn't resist and couldn't scream. It was the most terrifying moment of her life.

Her thoughts drifted to earlier that day. She and Zane had argued that morning over the same old subject. Zane seemed removed lately, into two different parts. Like he had their family and something else. Something that she could never touch. It would never become part of her and the children. Replaying the argument in her head made her angry all over again. Would that be her last memory of Zane?

Zane had stormed out of the house without saying good-bye. She called him several times during the day, but he didn't pick up and didn't return any of her texts. That was unusual. No matter how mad he was with her, he'd always returned her calls and messages. She'd only ever been with one man—Zane.

Growing up, Tina had lived a sheltered life. She was the only child of the pastor of a large congregation in the Twin Cities. She'd attended a small Christian school with limited exposure to the real world. Other than two mission trips to Central America she took in high school, she hadn't left the Twin Cities until their marriage. Her life had been orderly and neat and safe. At the moment, though, she felt like Alice in Wonderland. She wondered how deep this rabbit hole was.

While Tina was young, her mom, Betty, had played the role of a dutiful, subservient wife. As Tina got older, she discovered there was far more to her mother than that. Her dad had never taken advantage of her mother's subservience. Until he did. With one of the young female church members. He left, and now her mom was the pastor. The church growth tripled. Everybody enjoyed and benefited from her no-nonsense, biblical approach to life. Tina wished she were here now.

While her mom got along well with Zane, they weren't close. Her mom thought that Zane was torn between two elements. She agreed that he seem separated, as she put it, to another God. And this other God was driving him away from the light toward something fueled by his passion, and it would not be erased until he either allowed the real God to abolish it forever or until Zane faced it with all the brutality and fury that would bring it to a close.

Tina never bought into that scenario, as her mom was always a bit over the top.

But now, maybe she was right.

20

Lifetime Fitness was a monument to exercise. It was more of a suburban-soccer-mom gym than a sweat-and-pain gym, but Zane loved it. Working out made him feel good. He liked belonging to the chosen few who were truly in shape. Not today, though.

He held open the door to the gym as two elderly women dressed in red velour tracksuits walked in ahead of him. He was too distraught to register their thank-you. He went to the front desk to swipe his onyx membership card, the kind only held by premier members.

As he started down the crowded hallway to the weightlifting area, he noticed a large bearded man heading his way. He raised his eyebrows at Zane and smiled.

"Hey, I know you. It's been a while, but I know we've met." He stood in front of Zane, not allowing him past.

"Wrong person," Zane responded as he gently tried to move past him.

"No, I'm sure you remember me. Jeff Riley. It's been a long time since we've last seen each other. New Orleans, right? And all that Katrina made us become."

"You have me confused with somebody else. Excuse me," Zane said as he looked around furtively. People were looking at them, registering their unusual exchange. He needed to get rid of this guy and find Tec. This wasn't the time to have a revealing discussion about his past.

"We're all in a hurry. Anyway, here's my card. Give me a call sometime. We can bullshit over a couple of beers. I'd really like to find out what happened with you."

Zane took the card and shook his hand. "I'm not your guy."

"Of course not," Jeff said as he patted Zane on the back while moving on.

Zane resented the idea that after so many years and so much distance between New Orleans and here, he was still expected to act like he knew this man—if he ever had. But there wasn't time to think about that now.

The gym was packed with its usual morning fitness fanatics, more focused on their next repetition than on Zane walking through in street clothes. He found Tec at the squat rack. He wasn't lifting heavy. Tec thought bulky muscles slowed you down. He did high reps, which gave him a leaner look. Zane had learned his fitness regimen from Tec. It dovetailed well with mixed martial arts.

Zane couldn't hang back and wait for Tec to finish. "How much of your workout is left?" he asked as he walked up.

"As much as needs be. Working out gets my struggles out of mind for a bit," Tec answered as he racked the bar. "But it isn't working today."

"My family is missing. Things have changed and not for the better. I need your advice and your help. I can't wait."

"Relax. Let me grab my stuff," Tec answered while looking around for eavesdroppers.

Zane turned, left the weight area, and went to wait for Tec by the main door. A few minutes later, they walked out to Tec's aging two-door Monte Carlo.

"They blew up my house," Zane flatly stated as soon as they sat in Tec's car.

"What? They blew up your house? What do you mean? Who?"

Tec asked, not looking at Zane.

Zane didn't respond right away. He stared at a mother and daughter leaving the gym. The mother took her little girl by the hand, both holding a drink in the other hand and struggling to also carry their matching pink gym bags. As they tried to cross the street, the little girl dropped her drink and began to cry. The mom set her bag down and gave the little girl her drink while consoling her.

"My house is gone," Zane explained as he leaned back in the seat. "There was a huge explosion a second after I left my driveway this morning. I'm sure it was no accident."

"That's some radical shit. I'm not sure what's going on or who *they* are, but they seem like some mean hombres. What do you want to do?" Tec asked, leaning back in his seat and staring at the roof of the car, becoming even more concerned about the increasingly complicated situation.

Zane rubbed his eyes, leaned forward, and briefly detailed his plan to Tec.

"Well, that's one way to go. You might get some answers. But are you the kind of guy who can do this?" Tec asked him.

"I have to be," Zane replied, now looking out his side window as the mom and little girl walked by the car. The little girl was laughing and sipping her mom's drink. Crisis averted.

"Okay, what's the first step?" Tec asked, somewhat taken aback by Zane's cool demeanor.

"I need to call my office."

"Do it."

His boss's personal secretary answered on the second ring. "Hey, Delores, is Holmes in?" Zane asked, wondering for the millionth time if Holmes was his real name.

"No, he's not, Zane. But what on earth did you do?" she asked, her voice dropping. "Are you all right? I told them that I didn't think you did it, but I'm not sure they—"

Delores was rambling.

"Yes, I'm all right," he interrupted. "What are you talking about?"

"Mr. Holmes left as soon as he heard. He almost ran out of here."

"Heard what?"

"Geez, Zane, I'm surprised you're not dead. Your house blew up. The news said they found three bodies in the wreckage. A woman and two children. Doesn't take a genius to figure out that's your family. I mean, my God, your family! The police called here looking for you. They say you're a person of interest. I told them you'd never hurt your family, but I've got to ask. Did you kill them?" Mixed with her concern was the sensationalist desire to hear any scandalous news straight from the horse's mouth.

"I don't think I should talk to you anymore." Zane ended the call and threw his phone on the dash.

Tec grabbed the phone, opened it, removed the battery, and asked, "What's up?"

Zane opened the car door and stepped out, too preoccupied to wonder why Tec had removed the battery from his phone, not knowing or caring that nobody could use his phone to find him if the battery was removed. He walked out on the lawn in front of the gym. He was going to be sick. His legs were weak, and his head felt as if it was being split open like a coconut. His family was dead? There were no bodies in the house when he left this morning. Had they been planted there after the explosion?

They really weren't giving him any room.

He turned to one of the large trees and grabbed a branch for support. He pulled it so hard it broke off. He took a few deep breaths and then walked toward his own car, unaware that the branch was still in his hand. When he noticed, he dropped it on the asphalt, opened his SUV, leaned in to grab his laptop, and relocked the doors.

Then he rushed back to Tec's car. He knew he couldn't drive right now; he was far too off balance. He was a person of interest in the death of his family, which probably meant the police were searching for his Range Rover. How could he have let it come this far?

"Drive. Go to Monique's. She'll help me." Zane clenched his teeth. Against his better judgment, he needed to involve another person.

21

Ray didn't have a happy childhood. From the outside looking in, it probably appeared happy. He had everything a normal boy his age had. Toys, a few friends, and a nice house to live in, albeit a small one. And he had a family. At least a type of family.

But Ray was afraid to sleep. The darkness scared him. The noises in the dark scared him. It wasn't bad when they just argued, but too often, the arguing would lead to sounds of flesh hitting flesh and screams of pain. He couldn't remember when the nights didn't hold horrors for him.

He often thought of running away. They wouldn't care. His dad was more interested in getting drunk and raising hell than in caring for him. The older he got, the more tempted he was to run, but worry about what would happen to his older sister, Joan, stopped him. He often wondered why their parents put them through this never-ending cycle of violence and terror. Didn't they care that they were just kids? That they only wanted to feel safe?

Sometimes his parents would go out. He relished the time he and Joan were alone, away from them—but then he was even more scared when they came home. Those nights were the worst. The outside world was more than his parents could handle. When they came home, they'd both be drunk and ready to fight. Ray wondered why people drank if it changed them so much, so badly. Didn't they like who they were without drinking? And if they didn't like themselves, why didn't they change? When his dad was drunk, he became someone his mom hated. Ray hated him then too. He wished and prayed that his dad would just realize that and stop. But his dad had no control over the alcohol. It was a demon inside him, and that made Ray think his dad was weak. Just not weak enough.

Ray worked hard to please his dad, but it was an impossible task. Didn't he understand he was trying to do his best? Ray was a curious boy. He needed to know how things worked, and he asked questions. But according to his dad, kids were supposed to be seen and not heard, so pain was the answer to many of his questions. Ray couldn't sit or lie down many nights while trying to absorb that difficult lesson.

Life wasn't always terrible for Ray as a boy. His parents took him and his sister places sometimes. Usually those family trips were fun. One wasn't. It was the time his family went to the county fair just outside their little town of New Ulm in central Minnesota. It was held every year in August at the Brown County Fairgrounds. The hot summer nights held great intrigue for a ten-year-old boy who imagined any and every type of life different from the one he had. Ray loved the rides on the midway and the carnival games. It was fun to try to win stuff. He'd always wanted a big stuffed animal, and that night, he was trying hard. Joan laughed at him. But he was so close. He tried game after game without success. His sister had found friends and was riding the Tilt-A-Whirl again and again. Then suddenly his sister came running up to him and said they had to leave.

"Why so early?" Ray asked as he struggled to keep up with her.

"Mom's sick! She is puking in the bathroom, and she says we need to go!" Joan yelled back toward Ray. "She says to meet her at the car and wait for Dad."

"Where's Dad?" Ray said as he stopped.

"In the beer garden," his sister replied as she kept on running.

"I'll get him," Ray said as he turned around and ran back into the fairgrounds.

"No, no, please don't. You know better than that," Joan pleaded, stopping and running after him for a few yards.

Ray went, anyway. He found his dad drinking away the humidity with several other guys. They must have been there awhile, because they'd reached their destination: drunk. Ray was scared, but his dread about his mom being sick was stronger than his fear.

Ray ran up to his dad and told him they needed to go. His dad said no, he had to finish his beer first. Ray pleaded with him, and then out of desperation, he took his dad's beer and dumped it on the ground. Time stopped. Everybody looked at Ray, waiting for what would happen next. One look at his dad and Ray knew he had to run. He'd barely made it out of the beer garden when the first punch caught him on the back of the head. It stunned him and drove him to the ground, which was slimy with the putrid mud of spilled beer. His dad kicked him, hard. Very hard. In the back. Ray tried to curl up to protect himself, but the pain was overwhelming. His body wasn't working right. He started to cough up blood. Then, some brave, brawny soul intervened and tried to stop his dad. That only gave his dad a new target. Ray felt sorry for his would-be rescuer. The last Ray remembered, his savior was on the ground with his dad on top and teeth flying from the Good Samaritan's mouth in between his dad's vicious blows.

This had to stop.

Someday, Ray vowed to himself, he would make it stop.

22

Monique Mantel lived in Uptown, a trendy Minneapolis neighborhood where the cool people lived. Cool was a relative term—relative to how many birthdays you'd experienced. Located on the shores of several lakes, Uptown was picturesque and usually busy. That's why Monique lived there. She loved running around the lakes in the mornings and later visiting all the trendy shops. Especially the bookstores. At times, though, she tired of all the passersby, mainly the men dressed in their skinny jeans, wearing big, dark-rimmed glasses and carrying a skinny-half-caff-mocha latte. What had happened to real men?

She needed some danger in her life, some excitement. She fulfilled that need by practicing mixed martial arts at Tec's school. She trained with the men, and on most nights, she could hold her own. Monique was a well-respected fighter. But that wasn't why Zane needed her.

Sometimes after training, Zane and a few others went out for beers, and Monique joined them occasionally. In time, they'd become friends. She was attractive in a subtle kind of way, with a dark complexion. She told him that her mom was Jamaican and her dad was Israeli. Whatever her past, she always seemed to know things that nobody else knew. He liked that about her.

Tec obtained her address from the Warrior's Den records. That was one benefit of being the owner. They drove to her place directly. Zane was lying down in the backseat. After all, he was a wanted man. In more ways than one.

Monique paid her bills with freelance computer programming through her company, WSYN Consulting. She would write code for anyone who wanted a program to make life easier, among other unorthodox assignments. One night at the bar, she'd confided in Zane and admitted that in a past life she'd done her share of hacking. She was good at it. She'd even told him some of the systems she'd hacked. Zane was shocked—and impressed. That was why he needed her now.

She lived in an old brown fourplex crammed between two others of similar size and style. The hallways were narrow and creaked out their protest as Tec and Zane walked to her apartment, which was upstairs and in the back. A faint smell lingered from her neighbor's dinner last night. It could have been spaghetti or some other Italian dish.

She answered the door in cut-off sweats and a T-shirt. The T-shirt wasn't pink.

"Come on in, boys. A little early in the day for beers, or are you here to test my skills? If so, then at least let me warn the neighbors. I don't want them calling the po-po as I drag your sorry asses out to the garbage," she teased.

"Have you seen the news?" Zane asked.

"Well, judging by the long faces and short sentences, I guess this isn't a social call. No, I haven't watched the news. I like to start my day on a positive note. Come on in and sit down," Monique answered. "Fill me in over a cup of coffee."

They followed her in and sat on barstools at her kitchen counter and then watched her pour two cups of coffee. While old, her place was bright and cheery and decorated abundantly with an eclectic taste. Zane set his laptop on the counter and began to rub his temples with his fingertips while Tec stared at him and sighed.

They told her some of the story. The more she heard, the quieter she became. Zane was relieved to note that fear never entered her face. He sensed that she'd faced tough situations before. When they were done, she leaned back and picked up her cup. She swirled the contents around a bit and looked up at them.

"Wild stuff. Have you thought about just turning yourself in? No, scratch that. You could die of old age before the authorities figure out what's actually going on." Monique laughed.

"Yeah, this is a fucked-up deal," Tec said, taking a drink and setting his cup down. "This is on a level that none of us understand. Are you in, Monique?" Tec asked her, looking at her inquisitively.

"That depends. I don't really know you, Zane." She paused, waiting for Zane to protest. When he didn't, she continued. "I know you're not giving me the whole story. That's fine. I'm used to not getting the whole story from my clients. Just answer this: did you have anything to do with your family's disappearance, or did you harm them in any other way?"

"No, I didn't," Zane responded, his eyes meeting her straight on. "I don't know if you believe me, but that's something I could never do. I have no idea what happened to them."

Tec stood up and walked to the kitchen window, trying to get rid of some nervous energy. He looked down into the small courtyard where two kids were kicking a ball around. Unable to watch their innocent play, Tec turned around quickly and walked back to the kitchen counter. "It's obvious his family isn't dead. The kidnappers would lose their leverage over Zane," he said, trying to calm himself as much as the others. "They're still alive."

"Just so you know, I could never help a person who would hurt his family. Never."

Monique's words hung in the air, prompting Tec to cringe and Zane to wonder if—even though he'd never physically hurt them— he'd hurt them in a more insidious way. Exposing them to danger and not telling them was tantamount to hurting them himself. He shuddered but put the thought aside as Monique finally continued.

"What do you need from me?"

"So you trust me?" Zane asked.

"Trust but verify."

Zane looked at Tec, who shrugged his shoulders. Zane didn't have many friends left, so he proceeded to ask for her help. "I need you to find somebody. His address isn't listed."

"I'm going to need more than that."

"The guy who's behind the abduction of my family."

"And what will you do when you find him?" Monique asked, already knowing the answer.

"Ask him where they are," Tec interjected.

"*Ask* may be too nice a word," Zane said grimly.

Monique looked at both of them and smiled. "I've been up this mountain before."

After absorbing the details, she powered up her laptop and assured them that this wouldn't take long.

23

MINNEAPOLIS, TWO WEEKS EARLIER.

Tim and Ben Guardian had been talking for over an hour, and Ben still didn't understand what Tim had in mind. In fact, Ben was convinced Tim didn't know what Tim had in mind. Sometimes Ben rued the day he brought Tim into the business. He began to rub his temples with the heels of his hands.

Ben stood up and walked to the window in his office and then turned to face Tim. "You have to slow down. You aren't making a damn bit of sense. We need money, not management expertise. It doesn't take much expertise to figure out that the only way we can get money is by increasing sales. But how do we do that? Online competition is eating us alive," Ben said.

"Zane's going to increase our sales by helping us manage better. Slow sales are just a symptom. Management deficiencies are the real issue. How much plainer can I be?" Tim replied, moving uncomfortably in his chair.

"Don't be a smart-ass. I guess it's better than being a dumb ass—but just try not to be an ass at all. I'm the only one managing anything in this company. Are you saying I'm doing a bad job, and finding someone else will save us? I'll step aside in a minute if I can get out with some money, buy a lake home for my retirement, and sleep for a year."

"The problem's not you. It's how we're all managing things. Maybe we have to sell and turn it over to someone who can manage better. Perhaps we can get out with our money. Don't you think that would be best?"

"I'll keep an open mind, but this sounds too good to be true," Ben answered, wondering what Tim meant by "our" money. The last time he checked, the little money he had didn't have Tim's name on it.

"It isn't. Zane will be here in a few minutes."

"How did you find this Mr. Zane?"

"Zane Donovan. He called me out of the blue. Said he heard we might be having financial issues and wanted to take me to lunch."

"How did he know we were having financial problems?"

"He said he'd heard about our issues through a mutual acquaintance. He couldn't divulge which one. What difference does it make?"

A lot, Ben thought. *It could make all the difference in the world.*

Just then, Rita, the receptionist, knocked on Ben's door to announce Zane's arrival. Tim went out to show him in.

Here we go, thought Ben. *More bullshit.* He didn't have time for this crap; he had a business to save.

Tim introduced Zane to his dad as they shook hands.

"Hello, the mysterious Mr. Donovan," Ben said.

"Hello, Mr. Guardian. Pleased to meet you. But there's nothing mysterious about me," Zane replied with a self-assured smile.

"Well, I quizzed my son for over an hour, and he couldn't really tell me what you and your associates do. I'll have to admit that bothers me. I'm open to almost anything, but if you can't even explain it, something must be wrong," Ben said, sitting down behind his desk while Zane stood.

Ben thought he noticed Zane wince.

"Nothing is wrong," Zane replied quickly. "It's difficult to explain what Strategic Acquisition Services does and how we do it. But I'd love to try."

"Have a seat, then. Sorry if I jumped all over you."

"I get that a lot. We're not going to come up with the answer in today's meeting. I just want to ask some questions. Based on your answers, I'll need to look at some business practices and financials, and then we can talk about survival. I have a signed nondisclosure form to assure you about the privacy of your information," Zane replied as he took a seat and set the form on the desk.

"Fire away. I have very little pride or time left," Ben replied as he perused the form.

"My first question is, what's your goal?"

"First and foremost to save Guardian Jewelry. But if that's not attainable, I'd be willing to sell or liquidate as long as the deal will get me out whole. I didn't work hard my whole life for nothing."

"I understand. The answer to my next question helps me determine which direction to go with this. How far are you willing to go to save your dream and financial future?"

"What the hell does that mean?"

"Relax. All I need to know is whether you'll at least listen when I propose a way out. Our methods involve some out-of-the-box thinking, but I promise that whatever I propose will involve no risk to you."

Ben swallowed hard. He opened his top drawer, took out a nearly empty bottle of TUMS, and put two in his mouth. He wasn't sure what Zane meant. There were certain things Ben wasn't willing to do, but he'd admit that the list was growing smaller every day.

"I'm open to almost anything. If you show me a way out of this mess or out of the business, I'm all ears. Seriously."

"Let's get to work, then. From what Tim told me, there's a good chance we can reach your goal. Trust me."

"I hope I can."

24

Monique was quick. She could find out anything about anybody. She'd designed hundreds of firewalls and knew how to find all the hidden back doors. She'd stopped looking up information about her friends and associates long ago. The more she knew about people, the fewer friends she had and the more associates. She wanted just the opposite. Ignorance was highly underrated.

They'd barely finished a second cup of coffee when she had Robert Holmes's address, along with his credit score, bank balances, and golf handicap. The sources of her ill-gotten data would stay secret. She'd help them, but she wasn't stupid. She could get in trouble, and consequently, she trusted no one with details of her methods.

Zane and Tec took several more sips of coffee and were soon on their way, leaving Zane's laptop behind with Monique for safekeeping.

Monique wished them luck and offered future help. She secretly hoped they'd be back. She found Zane attractive and loved his dark aura. Part of Zane was remote and inaccessible. Monique was sure she could find that hidden part but not so sure she wanted to. She liked him without a past.

Zane and Tec walked to the car in silence. They both knew the plan but were reluctant to discuss it. Zane feared that talking about it might expose its flaws and weaken his resolve. Tec had serious reservations, yet couldn't come up with an alternate idea. He had to help his friend now, and the best defense was a good offense. Surprise can sometimes shake things up enough to force the enemy into making mistakes. While he wasn't sure Zane could or would take advantage of his enemy's mistakes, Tec knew he had to go along to preserve his own interests. And to hide his motives.

"I want to talk to you," Tec said as they got in the car. "You need to listen to me. Closely."

They were parked in Monique's parking lot, which faced the lake. It was hard to believe that anything bad could ever happen when looking out at the beautiful scene. People were jogging by in their designer shorts and sports bras, oblivious to what was going on in Tec's car. Everybody had challenges, but it was hard to believe that anybody could be facing as ominous an obstacle as Zane's. He was close to despair but would fight on.

"Zane, you need to make sure this is what you want to do. Trust me, you'll live forever with what you do today. Have you thought about that?"

"I have, Tec. I've thought about it a lot. If my wife and children are still alive—and I have to believe they are—I need to get them back. I'll do anything, anything at all. I'm nothing without them. And if they're not . . ."

"Trust me, they're alive. They need them alive to control you. Otherwise, they would've killed them at the garage. I know. But I understand your fear."

"No, you don't," Zane stated calmly. "I brought this on them, and I have to make it right. I need to act, not react."

"Okay, I'm here for you, man," Tec promised with more vehemence than Zane expected. "I just need to know that you're mentally prepared for what happens next."

"Come on, Tec. My wife and children were taken, my house was blown up, three charred bodies were found in the smoking remains, and I'm wanted for questioning. I don't have a choice."

Tec looked at Zane for a long time and finally looked away. "There's always a choice," he said heavily as he started the car. He headed for Highway 100 south. Robert Holmes lived in an exclusive golf club community in Eden Prairie, a southwestern suburb of Minneapolis that was about a twenty-minute drive away. More time to think, Zane figured, but he realized there was nothing to think about. He was ready.

When they arrived, they discovered Holmes's house was in a gated golf community. The high stone walls kept the undesirables out and the golf balls in. They hadn't come up with a plan for getting past the gatekeeper.

"Keep driving," Zane said as they passed by the main wrought iron gate, which was manned by an armed security guard. "I noticed a service entrance on the side. Let's check that out."

As they drove up, a landscaping truck was being let through. Tec pulled his car right behind it and simply followed it inside. Nobody noticed but the landscaping crew, and they didn't care. No skin off their ass. Zane and Tec were in.

Holmes's house was easy to find. It also was stone and the largest in the development. It had more windows than walls, and it faced the eighteenth hole. Tec cautioned Zane that the house would likely have some level of security.

They parked the Jeep behind a maintenance building next to the cart path. It took them all of three minutes to find an excellent lookout underneath some hedges within twenty-five yards of Holmes's front door. Zane's heart was beating so hard he thought Tec could hear it.

"Make yourself comfortable; we may be here for a while. We need to observe the place so we know who's inside. We can't just rush in," Tec reminded him.

Zane nodded, and they both lay prone under the hedges and

waited for what was next. He said a silent prayer for his wife and kids. Then he said a private prayer for Robert Holmes.

God rest his soul.

25

Evening was approaching. Zane's biggest fear as they were lying under the hedge was that an errant slice would land near them and some Tiger Woods wannabe would come looking for his ball and find them instead.

He couldn't take this much longer. His legs were sore, his shoulders ached, and his shirt smelled like he felt. Foul and ready for a new day.

In contrast to his desperate and restless discomfort, Tec was the epitome of cool. Zane marveled at Tec's ease with surveillance. He wasn't sweating, and he didn't move. He was a rock. Normally, Zane could have mirrored Tec's composure, but not today. Not with his family in danger. Or dead. Either way, his skin was only a paper-thin barrier for the emotions that were threatening to erupt at any moment. Zane took a deep breath and tried to stay silent, lest he pierce Tec's Zen state.

They didn't notice a single person at Holmes's residence. Nobody came, and nobody left. They didn't know if anybody was home. Zane felt that the time to act had arrived. Fuck Zen.

"Tec, I'm going in. I can't wait any longer. This is bullshit," Zane whispered.

"Going in isn't our best move. But we do need a closer look. We'll try to look in the windows without touching anything. Do you understand?" Tec whispered back.

"Yeah. Let's go." *Finally.*

Zane stood up, stretched, and boldly walked to the house as if he belonged there. He was walking with a purpose. They started this, and he would end it.

Tec trailed Zane and kept a close watch on the rest of the neighborhood. Zane's picture was all over the news, and they needed to be observant. Foolishness wasn't the same as fear. Tec wasn't afraid, but he also wasn't a fool.

They were approaching the back of the house where a large window faced the golf course. It offered a great view on the multitude of golfers trying to shave a stroke or two off their handicaps.

"Remember, Zane, keep cool. We're just going to walk around the house. Then we'll casually cop a look. Act like we're at a friend's house, trying to figure out if he's home. We don't want the police or golf-course security here. Be careful," Tec restated.

"Yup," Zane said as he picked up a large landscaping boulder, about two feet in diameter, strode up closer to the house, and threw it through the large window. Immediately, a loud, obnoxious siren began to blast.

"Or throw a damn boulder through the window," Tec muttered under his breath as he looked for observers to Zane's rock-throwing party. Given Zane's mood, this move didn't surprise him. Maybe he wouldn't have patience, either, if it were his family in trouble. He tried to push that thought out of his mind as pangs of guilt washed over him.

Zane followed the boulder through the window. He didn't have much time. He wished he had a floor plan. He wished Tina and the kids would be inside. But that would be too easy.

Tec stayed outside keeping watch. He was getting more nervous by the second. He wasn't sure of the police response time, but figured they had five minutes at most. And course security could be here even sooner.

Zane was one of his top students. But there was more to it. Zane fought with a passion and energy best described as controlled abandon. Zane seemed to relish injuries. It was payback for his past, he said.

Tec knew the feeling. They were kindred spirits. Tec wouldn't leave without Zane. He couldn't manage what he couldn't control, and Zane was dangerously close to being out of control.

Tec turned back to the house just as Zane appeared in the broken window.

Over his shoulder, he was carrying a man who looked a lot like Holmes.

26

At first, Tec feared Holmes was dead. On closer inspection, his chest was moving. At least Zane was innocent of murder. Kidnapping wasn't as unforgivable as murder. At least that's what Tec told himself. He trailed Zane as he utilized the fireman's carry to transport Holmes back to Tec's car.

"Open the damn trunk!" Zane grunted as he shifted Holmes into position to dump him.

"Trunk? Wow. You're serious," Tec replied as he popped open the trunk.

Zane noticed that Tec had some duct tape in his trunk. *The man was well prepared,* Zane thought as he threw Holmes on top of the spare tire and other assorted implements commonly relegated to obscurity for the rest of their trunk-bound life. He didn't struggle. Fear had paralyzed him. But just to be sure, they bound his ankles and wrists and taped his mouth. Duct tape is truly multipurpose.

Tec slammed the trunk shut. They were in the car within seconds and then out the service entrance with nobody the wiser.

"The plan was to question his ass. We don't need any more abductions. Now we have a body."

"We're abducting the bad guy. They abducted an innocent woman and her children," Zane said.

"Bad to some is good to others."

"Morality is subjective?"

"Isn't it?"

"Holmes must know something. Otherwise, why would he have run home?"

"Maybe he was scared."

"Of what?"

"If I had to guess—you," Tec said pointedly.

"Or the people he's working with."

"Maybe he thought you killed your family and were coming for him to clean up all the loose trash."

"Or SAS and the people running it have my family, and he knew I'd be coming for him. We both know I didn't kill my family, so let's go with my theory."

"Rather than guessing, let's find out. We both need the truth," Tec said, keeping a close watch on the rearview mirror. "How did you get him?"

"I snuck up behind him and used the sleeper hold you taught me," Zane replied.

Tec gazed at Zane out of the corner of his eye and wondered where this would end. Zane knew more than he was telling him. But, then, that went both ways.

"We have to figure out where we're going to take him," Tec continued. "I don't want him in my house, and you don't have a house. We need somewhere else. Remote."

"Let me think."

"We have something else to solve first. There's a cop behind us. He's been following us for the last few blocks. Here, put on these old sunglasses and this cap and turn away. It'll have to do for now," Tec said.

Sure enough, as they rounded the next corner, the cop turned on his lights and sounded his siren. Tec hoped the cop would get close enough for him to take him out without hurting him. He took several deep breaths as they pulled over.

The officer walked up to Tec's car, looking it over carefully.

"I need you to turn off the engine and get out of the car," the cop said as Tec rolled down his window. He was standing at the back of the car, and Tec couldn't see his face in the rearview mirror.

Oh shit, Tec thought. *Maybe I should run for it.*

He slowly got out of the car. The cop had his back turned toward him, looking at the trunk.

"I'm going to need you to open the trunk. Something weird is going on here."

"Why was I pulled over? Don't I have some rights? You can't just search my vehicle without cause."

"You don't have shit for rights, you punk-ass MMA wannabe. You do what I tell you—when I tell you, and how I tell you. If I say I want you to bend over and grab your ankles and spread 'em, then that's what you do. You got that, boy?" the cop barked at Tec.

Tec glanced toward the front seat and could see Zane going through his glove compartment, where Tec kept his Glock 19 pistol. Tec needed to end this now, before Zane found the gun and did something he couldn't take back.

"Did you hear me, son?" the cop bellowed as he turned around slowly.

As he did, Tec recognized him, and the cop had a grin from ear to ear. It was Rick, one of his students.

"That's payback for all the shit you put me through!" Rick exclaimed as he was doubling over in hysterical laughter.

"The beatdown is coming. You have been warned," Tec retorted as he began to playfully punch Rick in the chest.

They exchanged several punches and some more play cop-suspect banter, laughing as if this was the funniest joke on earth. As they parted, they promised to take it out on the mat.

As Tec got back in the car, he could sense the relief wash over

Zane as he removed his hand from the glove compartment and closed it.

"That took years off my life. I don't need this today. Or ever."

"That was a bit stressful, I'll admit, but it's all good. Now have you thought about where we're going to conduct our little illicit interrogation?" Tec asked, hoping Zane hadn't found the gun.

"One of my clients has an old office in downtown Saint Paul, on the twentieth floor of a decrepit building. It's scheduled for demolition in a few months. Let me look up the address," Zane said, pulling out his phone and reinserting the battery.

Tec got on I-494 and headed east to downtown Saint Paul. They parked in the empty underground garage of the building. Holmes was awake and staring at them when Tec opened the trunk. Zane grabbed his shoulders, and Tec took his feet as they carried him to the freight elevator. Between the two of them, it was an easy carry. The elevator clanked and yawed its way up to the twentieth floor. Zane couldn't help feeling its resistance was a sign the aging machine was conspiring with Holmes.

It truly was a deserted building. The air-conditioning had left along with the former tenants. Zane and Tec were soaking wet with exertion by the time they deposited Holmes in the abandoned office. Luckily, it hadn't taken them long to break in. The office door had seen better days.

There was no furniture. There was no ventilation whatsoever, and it stank like an old man's armpit.

Perfect conditions for what Zane had in mind.

With or without Tec's Glock.

27

Holmes wasn't doing well. The duct tape had been removed from his mouth, but he was silent. He didn't appear to be afraid as he sat calmly in the leftover chair. He was confused, his eyes darting between Tec and Zane and back again. Zane wondered if it was all an act. He needed to find out. And he would.

"We need to step outside for a moment," Tec said as he pulled Zane out into the hallway.

"What's the matter?" Zane asked as he reluctantly followed him.

"We need to seriously think about what we're doing here, or rather, what you're doing here," Tec said.

"This shithead knows something, and I plan to find out what that is. If you want to stay out here, that's fine," Zane said, turning to go back in.

Tec grabbed Zane's shoulder and looked him in the eye. "It doesn't work that way. Whatever you do, I do." Tec knew he had to stay in control of this interview in order to protect all parties. "In fact, I'll handle the questions. I'll start slow. Just watch. Okay?"

"Fine. If your methods aren't working, I'll take over," Zane said as he shrugged Tec's hand off his shoulder. "It's my family they have, just remember that."

There was no chance Tec would forget.

Zane stood in the corner as Tec grabbed an old chair, turned it around, and sat down facing Holmes.

"Okay, Mr. Robert Holmes, is it all right if I just call you Holmes?"

"I'm not the guy."

"You didn't answer my question. We'll call you Holmes," Tec said.

"I know what you want. But I'm not the one who can give it to you," Holmes answered.

"It doesn't work like that," Tec said with a worried smile. "Rule number one: speak only when spoken to. Rule number two: answer the questions honestly. Stick to those rules, and things won't get messy. *Capisce?*"

"Yes," Holmes answered.

"Good. You're learning. Now, Holmes, what do you know about Zane's family?"

"I know what the news reported. Their bodies were found in the wreckage of Zane's home." He looked at Zane and yelled, "I know what you did, Zane!"

"Don't listen to this shithead!" Zane yelled as he leaped toward Holmes. "I'll get the truth."

Tec turned to Zane and put his hands on his chest to restrain him. "Chill."

Zane glared at Holmes but stepped back.

"I really want to believe you. It makes it easier on all of us. But I need something to help me believe." Tec smiled.

"Let me loose and I'll talk. Just you. Alone."

"Come on, Holmes!" Zane screamed at him but kept his distance, not understanding why Holmes wanted to talk to Tec alone.

"I told you, I got this," Tec said, privately wishing Zane would wait in the hall so he could talk to Holmes openly. "You give us something, Holmes, and we'll give you something. So far, I haven't heard shit."

"We're using ill-gotten proceeds to purchase financially troubled businesses. Hasn't Zane told you?"

Zane smashed his fist through the Sheetrock on the cheap office wall.

"Holmes, you're really not getting this," Tec said, shooting a glance at Zane. "I ask you a question, and you give me an answer, not another question. I know that SAS takes over businesses by illegal means. I know that Zane went to the Feds. You probably took his family to shut him up, but it was too late, and now—"

"You know damn well that I don't have his family!" Holmes interrupted, shrieking at the top of his lungs and close to losing whatever composure he still had. "What kind of game are you playing?"

Tec slapped him in the face.

"Don't you dare interrupt me again, Holmes," Tec said, the threat in his voice belying the smile on his face. "Now I suggest that you give me straight answers to my straight questions, or I'll turn this interview over to Zane. Look at him," he said, pointing at Zane, who was pacing the room. "He looks like a hungry lion waiting to be let out of its cage."

"You should be asking Zane, not me," Holmes said. "I know no more than you do." Tec winced, but luckily, Zane was too upset to pick up on the deeper meaning of Holmes's response.

"Bullshit. You're just covering up," Zane said as he walked up to Holmes, grabbed him by the shoulders, and shook him. "We can see right through you."

"I don't know where your family is! I had nothing to do with taking them! You're asking the wrong person!" Holmes yelled back in his face, his eyes on Tec as much as on Zane.

Zane grabbed Holmes by the front of his shirt and punched him in the forehead hard.

"You have to know something. SAS is your fucking company,"

Tec said as he pulled Zane away.

Holmes looked like he was about to cry. He was sniffling furiously.

"Why did you run when you heard about Zane's family? Were you afraid Zane was coming after you?"

"Yes. I thought he'd come after me, but it isn't me he wants. He should be worried about the money people. We all need to be afraid of them," Holmes said, staring at the tops of his shoes and then looking up at both of them. "Zane, I think you know who's really behind this, don't you?"

28

Zane was confused. Holmes wasn't behind the kidnapping of his family or the explosion of his house. He'd worked for Holmes several years and knew when he was lying. Holmes was scared—of what he had done, of what Zane had done, and of what the people who'd kidnapped Tina and the kids had done and would do. That fear prevented him from lying, at least for the time being.

Holmes said it was the money. That was the one part Zane had never been able to figure out. The money trail greasing SAS and its illicit moves had always been kept hidden. Is that why his handlers at Treasury were waiting to prosecute?

Whoever had his family had to have a motive. If he thought about it long enough, he could probably figure out what that motive was, and that in turn would tell him who it was. But he didn't have time to think.

He had to get out of this decrepit, condemned building for a bit and talk to the Treasury agents. He should've gone to them as soon as he knew his family was taken. It was a risky move, because not even they knew the full extent of Zane's involvement in this whole mess. Only one other person knew how deeply he was involved, and Zane had already talked to him and received no help.

Zane walked back out to the hallway. Tec followed.

"I have to go somewhere, Tec. Can you stay here? I'll be back soon."

"Famous last words. So I get to stay here in this dump and watch Holmes?"

Zane nodded.

"Okay, but get back soon. I'll call Monique and see if she can teach my night class."

"I have to get some information. I think Holmes might be telling the truth," Zane said.

"I'm not sure. I still think Holmes knows more than he's letting on. What does he mean when he says you know who has them?" Tec asked anxiously.

"I'm not sure, but I'll find out," Zane said to him. "I'll bring food when I come back. Hang tight."

Tec tossed him the keys to his car.

Zane walked to the elevator, his head hung low and his eyes glued to the floor, thinking about how to approach the Treasury agents. He didn't find any revelations in the used condoms and drug needles littering the floor. He wished he could turn back time, drive to his beautiful home, and hug Tina and the kids. Paradise lost.

His phone rang as he neared his car. He almost pressed the Ignore button until he noticed it was Betty. She deserved better.

"Hey," he mumbled as he leaned against his car.

"'Hey' isn't going to cut it, Zane," she said in a quiet yet firm voice. "I heard about the explosion and the bodies. You need to pick me up and drive me the fuck over there. Now."

Her use of the F word drove his distress and strain even higher. She'd never used that word around him before. "It's not what you think it is."

"Doesn't matter what I think. What matters is—are they still alive? And did you do this?"

"I'm still gathering information, but they're still alive," he said, hoping he hadn't just told her a lie. "But, yes, some of this is my fault."

"You're wanted for questioning," she stated matter-of-factly.

"Yes, I did something bad. But I'll get them out of this."

"I can help. Come get me."

"How can you help?"

"I've dealt with bad people before."

"Not like this."

"We all have a past, Zane. How soon will you be here?"

"Give me two hours. I need to do something first."

"Okay," she answered reluctantly. "But Zane?"

"Yes."

"Don't make the mistake of underestimating me. I can take care of myself and you too, if you know what I mean."

"See you in a bit," he answered as he clicked off, worried that he knew exactly what she meant.

Zane's usually acute observation skills were dulled by his preoccupation with his circumstances. He didn't see the police car behind him as he approached the ramp to I-35E southbound, his route to the Treasury office in Bloomington. The next thing he knew, flashing lights were in his rearview.

Zane silently cursed his earlier decision to turn his cell phone back on.

It was unlikely that this officer was another friend of Tec's. If he could get into the heavy traffic on 35E, he could lose the patrol car. It was worth a try. Zane needed some answers and feared he wouldn't get them if he were detained for questioning.

The closest car was about a quarter mile ahead of him. Zane pushed the gas pedal to the floor in an attempt to catch up. Tec's Monte Carlo was old, but it was fast. He was up and around the car in no time. The police car stayed right on Zane's tail as he began to weave in and out of the heavy traffic. The traffic was running at a steady fifty miles per hour, and he was doing about sixty-five, so he was able to get in and around most cars easily. The cop hung on Zane like his life depended on it. More cops would be coming soon.

Zane decided to take the next exit east on Highway 110. His plan to lose the cop on the freeway hadn't worked. If anything, he was even tighter on his tail. The lights were flashing, and the siren was wailing. He fingered his fat money clip through his jeans pocket. The feel of it gave him comfort.

The 110 was now taking him across the river, turning into Crosstown Highway. Maybe he should just go home. Except he didn't have a home. He rested his head back on the headrest and took a breath.

The sirens jarred him from his trance. They seemed louder. As he looked back, he noticed another cruiser had joined the parade. Not good. The speedometer read ninety-five. The sirens parted the traffic for him, which only made him press the gas pedal harder. Zane didn't have a plan. He remembered the traffic parting for him coming home from work the night before. That seemed like a century ago. So much had happened in the last twenty-four hours.

All of a sudden, he heard a helicopter above. They were tracking him by air. He had nowhere to hide. He wished there was time to pull up his map from his phone. No GPS in a '98 Monte Carlo.

Then off to the right, on an entrance ramp from the Minneapolis–Saint Paul International Airport, he saw two more police cars pulling ahead of him. They had him boxed in. Front, back, and above. The memory of watching O. J. Simpson fleeing alleged murder charges in his infamous white Bronco brought a quick nervous laugh.

The cop cars in front of him were slowing down, and he had no way of getting around them. Noticing an exit coming up, Zane quickly veered into the exit lane. One of the cop cars in front of him turned and hit his brakes hard. Zane was going to hit him, so he swung the wheel hard to the left and went down the grass embankment leading back to the freeway.

There was a wire guardrail between him and the freeway. He knew Tec loved this car, but he could always fix it up for him or even buy him a new one. Money could fix most problems.

He was going about thirty now and hoped that would be enough to get him through the guardrail. It wasn't. The car hit the wire and two posts hard, and they bent over, performing just as it was designed. The Monte Carlo was ensnared in its web, and Zane was stuck. He quickly looked around him for an escape route. He could run away on foot, but he knew that was useless.

The police car that had first been trailing him pulled over on the shoulder and stopped. The cop exited the car with his weapon drawn, yelling at Zane to get out of the car, put his hands on his head, and drop to his knees. Zane opened the driver's door. The helicopter hovered above, announcing to the world that the fugitive had been caught. Zane looked at the glove box, thinking of the hidden gun.

The cop yelled at him to get out of the car.

"Let me get some identification from the glove box!" Zane yelled.

"Negative! Keep your hands laced behind your head where we can see them, and get out of the vehicle!" the cop yelled back.

Zane looked around and counted five more policemen walking toward his car with guns drawn. Zane wasn't interested in suicide by cop. He slowly got out of the car and stood next to the car with his hands laced behind his head.

"Yeah, it's Donovan. What do you want us to do with him?" After a pause, the cop continued, "That's crazy."

What the hell was that supposed to mean? How did they know his name?

Zane sensed someone coming up behind him. His hands were roughly yanked behind his back and cuffed.

A bag was slipped over his head.

Zane wasn't read his rights.

29

Tina figured their chances of survival were slim to none. They could identify Spaz and Rocker, and that knowledge would mean their deaths. The third kidnapper had left his ski mask on, and she hadn't seen him since the abduction. She thought she knew why.

Tina was sitting cross-legged on the small bed with her back against the wall. She was cradling her daughter's head in her lap and stroking her hair as Zanese dozed fitfully. The room still smelled like sour vomit. So did Zanese. The smell was distracting her. James was sleeping, curled up on the hard floor. He didn't realize that they were in real danger.

Tina gently laid Zanese beside her on the bed and stood up. She stretched and walked around the room to get some blood flowing and to build up her resolve. She had to use the little knowledge she had and try to get them all out of here.

She walked up to the locked bedroom door and began to pound on it while yelling that she needed to talk to somebody. Zanese woke up, climbed off the bed, and sat in a corner with her knees pulled up to her face. She began to cry.

The door was suddenly thrust open, and Tina was face-to-face with Rocker. He didn't look happy.

"You woke me up. There had better be a good reason."

"I need to talk to you and Spaz."

"You don't get it," Rocker said as he grabbed her behind her neck, pulled her into the little hallway, and shutting the bedroom door again. "Spaz will fuck you, and then he'll kill you. In front of your children. I'm not too sure he won't fuck the little girl too. There's something seriously wrong with him. Shut up, and go back to bed. You're lucky Spaz didn't wake up."

"Oh, but I did wake up, and the time for fun has come," Spaz said as he stumbled down the hallway toward them.

30

Zane became disoriented very quickly. He'd always imagined that he could approximate where he was heading even when blindfolded. At least the general direction. Now he found out that wasn't true. As the car made turns and stops, he lost all sense of direction. Not that it mattered. He expected the worst.

They drove for what he thought was a half hour. After a series of sharp turns, the car suddenly stopped, the back door opened, and he was pulled out. They entered a building and walked down a tile hallway until they stopped and pushed a button. A minute later, they got on an elevator. The elevator went up several floors and stopped when a recorded voice announced they'd reached the forty-sixth floor. The doors opened into a carpeted area. They then proceeded down a series of corridors that must have been narrow because Zane kept bumping into the walls. It made him think of the corn maze they'd visited with the kids last fall. Except there was no corn, and nobody was stationed at the corners to help in case he got lost. James and Zanese hadn't needed any help. He'd been proud of them.

Finally, they opened what sounded like a heavy metal door. Chairs were scraped back against the tile floor, and Zane was dumped into one of them like a sack of garbage. His hands were uncuffed and then cuffed again through the back of the chair. Then his captors left, and he sat in utter silence for what seemed like an eternity. If this was meant to make him crack, it was working. The more he thought about his predicament, the guiltier he began to feel. The guiltier he felt, the more depressed and frustrated he became. He'd caused this mess, and now he had to get out of here. He had to get out to help Tina and the kids.

Finally, the door opened, and two people entered the room. One person sat down, and the other stood behind Zane and pulled the bag from his head. Zane blinked rapidly against the fluorescent light assaulting his eyes. It was an interrogation room. One window, white walls, white floor, gray ceiling, gray steel table, and gray steel chairs. If he weren't in so much trouble, Zane would have laughed at the absurdity of it all. It reminded him of *The Matrix*. It was a cliché of a cliché. He looked at the two men in the room. He'd met them in the altercation at his now blown-up home. Number Two was behind him, and Number Three was seated in front of him.

"Where's your other associate? Did he need to see a podiatrist? Foot injuries can be a bitch," Zane stated.

"Please don't underestimate your situation," Number Three responded.

Zane had surprised himself with his smart-ass remark. He didn't want to antagonize his captors. He might need them.

"You guys need to give me more information so I can properly evaluate my situation."

"You fucked up."

"You with the Treasury Department?" Zane's head was hurting, and they hadn't even hit him yet.

"No."

"Who are you, then?"

"Doesn't matter."

"Matters to me. How am I supposed to help you when I don't know who you are or what you want?"

"All you have to do is go back to SAS and do your job," Number Three said. "And I believe you will."

Number Two didn't utter a word. Obviously, he was the muscle. Zane wished he'd crippled him when they fought earlier. He hated their smugness, he hated their air of superiority, but most of all, he hated that they weren't answering any of his damn questions. He brought his head down on the table and banged his forehead against it several times. The pain was a relief.

Suddenly, he broke out in a clammy sweat, and his throat clenched. "Why are you so sure I'll go back?" Zane quietly asked.

"Tina, Zanese, and James," Number Two flatly stated behind him.

Zane stood up with the chair still bound to him and slammed back as hard as he could. Number Two had seen it coming and quickly sidestepped him. Zane slammed back against the wall and fell to the floor. Number Two calmly kicked him in the nuts. Zane rolled to his side, retching. Number Two picked him up in the chair and slammed it back against the table.

"I'll give you this, you don't quit. In another place, at another time, that would be useful. Today, you just need to shut up, stay calm, and listen. Lives depend upon it," Number Three said.

Zane was coughing and trying to catch his breath. Holmes was right. His employer didn't have his family. These guys did. Whoever they were.

"I'll go back. But what do I tell the Treasury agents?" Zane coughed out.

"Don't tell them anything. Cut off all communication."

"They won't like it. And after a while, they'll come after me. They'll prosecute me, or Holmes, or both."

"That's your problem. Just don't tell them about us."

"I don't even know who you are, so what could I possibly tell them?"

"Good," Number Three said as he leaned across the table staring into Zane's eyes. "And try not to be so sad."

"What?"

"Just because they're all dead doesn't mean they can't enjoy life."

31

Spaz raised his arms over his head and began to stretch. He was smiling as he came up behind Rocker and propped his chin on the other man's shoulder to look at Tina.

"You and me, baby. In a moment, that's all that's going to matter," Spaz said as he opened his eyes wide and began to moan.

Rocker turned to face Spaz. "Business before pleasure."

"Fuck that shit. My business is pleasure," Spaz said as he reached around Rocker and grabbed for Tina's breasts.

Tina screamed.

Rocker put both of his hands on Spaz's chest to restrain him, but Spaz was expecting that and quickly spun out of his grasp, grabbed Tina by her hair, and dragged her down the hallway to the living room.

Tina was screaming all the way. Rocker followed. "Take it easy! You know they don't want damaged goods!" he yelled.

Spaz threw Tina on the ratty couch and punched her hard in the jaw. He began to move his hips in a rhythmic motion. "I don't give a shit what they want. It's time for what Spaz wants."

Tina struggled to sit up. Spaz leaned down and grabbed her by her ears as she screamed again.

He brought her face next to his. "I heard you praying earlier. Your God isn't here. Your man isn't here. It's just you and me. So shut the fuck up and show me what you got," Spaz said as he brought out a knife from his pocket that he flipped open while he put a knee on her chest, put his free hand on her throat, and pointed the knife at her crotch. "I promise it'll be good for both of us."

Tina resisted, desperately trying to hold her head back as she mumbled, "I know the third kidnapper. It was Tec. He wouldn't want you to do this."

Rocker grabbed Spaz by his shoulder and spun him around. "You know the lady is right."

32

Tec's stomach growled as the protein shake he'd had for breakfast became a distant memory. He knew Zane wouldn't be back. The call he'd made after Zane's departure would ensure that.

"Zane will be back soon," Holmes said. "Or he won't."

"Thanks for that wonderful piece of wisdom. Now be quiet."

"You've only seen the tip of the iceberg."

"Maybe you're right; I don't know what Zane is messed up with. But he's my friend."

"You sure have a strange way of showing that." Holmes smirked.

Tec turned around, anger burning in his eyes.

"Relax. I don't know what game you're playing, but your secret is safe with me," Holmes continued. "Besides, I'm not sure you'd want to be his friend if you knew who Zane really worked for."

Didn't Zane work for Holmes? That's what Zane had told him. And that's why Tec had assumed Holmes was involved in the kidnapping, because after all, the whole point had been to keep Zane in line at SAS. And somehow that was for the greater good.

However, Tec knew Zane didn't tell him the whole story. They were both holding back. But the possibility of Zane concealing his true employer hadn't even occurred to him.

"Okay, Holmes, you got me. Who does he work for?"

"The government. The Treasury Department. I don't have all

the answers, but I do know Zane isn't all he's cracked up to be," Holmes said.

"I know he took evidence of SAS's corruption to the Treasury. Is that what you mean by working for them?"

"No. Yes. I don't know. I just think he's involved in much more than we know or think we know."

"I suspect neither of us has Zane's full story. But I have a hard time believing anything a lying bastard like you tells me."

"I admit I'm selfish. But Zane is a snitch. And I'm sure there's more to it. Follow the money, as they say in the movies, right?" Holmes said with a nervous cackle.

"Are you telling me *you* don't know the moneymen behind SAS, either?"

"That's exactly what I'm telling you. I'm nothing but a cog in a big, faceless machine that keeps turning and turning. I do it for the money, just like you."

Tec took a few threatening steps toward Holmes, his fists balled, but Holmes continued unfazed. "And just like you, I don't know or care who's paying."

For a moment, Tec contemplated using his considerable skills to force more information out of Holmes or to punish him for knowing too much about Tec and too little about SAS. But he decided against it. Holmes was telling the truth. He wasn't one to withstand even the thought of torture. And no matter what pain he'd inflict, Holmes's suffering wouldn't ease Tec's guilt. He was sure of that much.

He had to get out of here. There was someone he needed to talk to.

33

When Tina mentioned Tec's name, Spaz jumped off her immediately. He got quiet and looked scared.

Within minutes, he and Rocker quickly put Tina and the kids in the van.

Tina had no idea where they were going. At least they were out of that depressing house. She couldn't dwell on bad outcomes, so she decided to consider their change of venue a good thing. She was a mom; she had to be strong.

As Rocker pulled into a parking garage, Tina could see a large building through the windshield. Rocker parked in a spot that seemed to materialize out of nowhere. Tina's door automatically opened, and she stepped out.

Spaz was waiting. He grabbed her by the throat and slammed her against the van. Tina gasped but glared directly into his eyes.

"Don't try anything. You and your sniveling little kids are still our captives, and we can do whatever we want, whenever we want."

"Do what you want to me, but leave the kids out of this. My God, they're children," Tina begged.

Spaz slammed her into the van again. Hard enough to leave a dent.

He reared his fist back to hit her when two black hands grabbed him around his neck, and he began to choke.

"Keep your hands off her. No one touches her. Got it, fuck

stick?" Rocker quietly said into his ear.

Spaz dropped her and spun out of the choke to face Rocker.

"You have a weakness for pussy too. You're just like me. You just won't admit it. That will come back to haunt you," Spaz spat out at him.

Rocker quietly and smoothly swept Spaz's legs out from under him and dropped him hard to the cement floor with his knee placed firmly on his sternum. He had Spaz's right arm in a joint lock and was controlling the left arm with his other knee.

"I'll never trust you," Rocker whispered in Spaz's ear. "You know the shit we've pulled and where the bodies are buried. When this is over, I'm going to make damn sure nobody else ever finds out."

Rocker carefully got up, and Spaz followed, glaring at Rocker. Spaz turned away and slowly walked to the elevator.

"Thank you," Tina said as she followed Rocker to the elevator with the kids in tow.

"Shut up. Don't assume I'm on your side. You have no idea who I am."

They stepped in the elevator. Rocker pushed the button for the forty-sixth floor. Not a word was spoken on their short trip until a recorded voice announced they had reached their destination. Spaz led them down a series of corridors to a bland gray door. He swiped his card and opened it. It was a steel room with four chairs and a gray table. There was one window, but it didn't have a view. The white tile floor was polished to a sheen that reflected Tina's fear.

"We'll be back," Rocker said as he and Spaz left the room. The door closed with a sound that tried to suck dry the last bit of hope Tina had left.

Suddenly, she heard a loud slam against the wall in front of her. She jumped up, and the kids jumped back.

She needed Zane. Now.

34

Zane was alone in the interrogation room. He tried to keep his mind blank, but it was impossible, even after he concluded there was no way out. He had to go back to SAS, continue to mess with people's businesses and lives and implicate himself and Holmes. Or else his family would die. Some stubborn part of his mind couldn't accept that there was no other way to stop the madness.

Obviously these guys were the money—or worked for the money—and the money was more important than SAS, Zane, and Holmes combined. They could find another SAS if Zane and Holmes ended up as scapegoats and were left to rot in prison. Zane had to track the source of the money. The money was the key. Always is.

Would he ever see his family again? He only had one option, and that was to do what they wanted. That would give him time to unravel this mystery.

Ten minutes later, Number Three opened the door. He stood there for a second just smiling at Zane. The smile seemed to say, *I'm glad I'm not you.* Zane stood up and smiled back. He refused to give them the satisfaction of seeing him fret. He shuddered to think what he would do if he had a gun right now.

Number Three came closer, holding the keys to Zane's cuffs in his hand.

"Come with me. We'll give you a place to stay. Personally, I couldn't give a shit where you stay. But the boss cares. I'm not sure why. Maybe it's because he really likes that pretty wife of yours, and he just wants you happy and whole for her."

"I'd love to have a minute with you alone. In fact, come in and shut the door. Let's see what you got. It is easy for you to talk like that when my hands are cuffed behind this chair," Zane said.

Number Three laughed. "You sucker punched us the other day, but I guarantee that'll never happen again. My life won't be complete until *I* get a minute with *you*. But that'll have to wait. Unfortunately."

"Aw, come on, just sixty seconds. Let's see who's better," Zane implored.

"Now, now, play nice."

Number Three then said into his cuff mike, "Hey, come on in. Apparently, we can't trust Mr. Zane Donovan. Bring your gun."

Number Two arrived within a minute and was pointing a gun at Zane while they uncuffed him. Zane stood up, stretched, and flexed. It was some small satisfaction that it took two of them to escort him from the room. Maybe he could use that to his advantage sometime.

As they stepped into the corridor, Zane got a whiff of something familiar. Euphoria, Tina's favorite perfume.

$ $ $

Tina was worried about Zanese, who was becoming more despondent by the second. She was sitting on the floor doing nothing. Tina crouched down next to her and put an arm around her.

"This will be over soon. I need you to hang in for a bit longer."

Zanese didn't respond.

"God is here for us. Even in this place. He won't abandon us," Tina encouraged.

"Dad will save us. I know. He would never let these men hurt us," James said as he cuddled up on the other side of Zanese.

"You're right. Your dad is our hero. I promise, soon we'll all be together again," Tina said.

Zanese began to cry, and James crawled under the table. "Just in case Dad doesn't come, it's always better to be under heavy furniture. At least that's what the National Weather Service says."

Tina smiled at James and his brave joke. Then she stood up and began to pace. She'd been sitting most of the day and needed to move. As she walked back and forth in the small room, the thought of Zane gave her comfort. She knew all men had the capacity for evil, but not Zane. At least not as much evil as it would take to hurt your own family.

Suddenly the door opened, and Rocker entered.

"Can you leave the kids here and come with me?" Rocker asked.

"Absolutely not. I'm not leaving the kids in this place. I don't even know where we are."

"Okay, okay. I need to have you talk to somebody, and it would be better without the kids, but bring 'em along; we'll figure something out."

"Who?" Tina asked.

"You'll find out in just a minute," Rocker said as he held the door open for them.

35

Tec had lent his car to Zane, so he had to find alternate wheels. He decided on a taxi. The bus was too slow.

It took five minutes for him to get a taxi and another twenty to get to the building. It was late, and everything was locked up tight. He called the man. Although his last meeting with him had not provided additional information about why they had taken Zane's family, another attempt was worth a stab.

"We need to talk."

"We don't have anything to talk about. You delivered Zane. That's all that matters."

"I'm downstairs."

"What the hell. Come on up, then. I could actually use you right now. I'll send someone down."

Tec knew enough to be suspicious when things were that easy. He wasn't sure he wanted to know what was really going on, and his feet felt glued to the ground. Suddenly, the door opened. Tec had met this man before.

"Come on up; we may have another job for you."

His escort turned to go back into the building. He was walking with a limp, obviously in pain.

Tec followed him in. He'd been here before and knew his way around. But the circumstances were different today. Drastically different.

For one thing, the building was deserted. And for another, Tec had become one of them. Sort of. He didn't like to think of himself that way, but it was true.

Although they went up forty-six floors, the ride in the elevator was mercifully quick. The less time Tec spent with this escort, the better. He didn't like him, and he was sure the feeling was mutual.

He followed him out of the elevator to the office. It was deserted too, except for one person sitting at a large desk. The office was spacious and well appointed but also utilitarian with businesslike furniture. It seemed to suit the man perfectly.

"I thought we had an understanding," the man said as soon as Tec's escort had left the room.

"Grabbing his wife and kids may have been a mistake," Tec challenged him, standing at the edge of the desk while crossing his arms.

"Really?" the man asked as he stood and walked around the desk to sit on the front edge, facing Tec.

"You've unleashed a monster. I know him. He'll do anything to get his family back."

"Well, that's what we were hoping for," the man answered while motioning for Tec to sit in one of the chairs facing his desk.

"He may do things you don't expect. Or want," Tec said while uncrossing his arms and also sitting on the front edge of the desk facing the man. Tec refused to give him any height advantage in this conversation.

"We'll just have to see to it that he doesn't. Thanks to you, we have him in the first place. Which makes you the perfect person for that job," the man said, smiling and staring intently at Tec.

"Not unless you tell me what's going on." Tec stared back.

"I told you enough."

"How is grabbing his family helping other people? At least give me that."

"I told you, it keeps him in line. Motivates him to cooperate. At least we think it does. Actually, we need to make sure. Or more precisely, we need *you* to make sure." The man smiled as he looked at Tec expectantly.

"I'm not sure I can do that."

"Of course you can. You do have people that you love."

Tec stood up and began to shake slightly. He clenched his hands into fists and willed them to stay at his side. "Not unless you answer my damn question. How did this, or will this, serve the greater good? What kind of shit is that?" he asked through clenched teeth.

"We'll need you to expose yourself a bit," the man said, standing up and moving to sit in one of the chairs. He crossed his legs and casually picked a piece of lint off his jet-black trousers.

"Expose myself?" Tec asked, walking over to the wall and looking at himself in a frameless yet graceful mirror that was more suited for decoration than reflection.

"Yes, confess to him what you've done. Sort of. Eventually, that will allow you to gain his trust."

Tec suddenly brought his palm up and struck the mirror hard in the center, causing it to crack like a spiderweb. Tec spun around with his fists clenched. "How would admitting what I did to his family help me gain his trust back?"

"Mirrors are replaceable; friends are not," the man said, folding his hands in his lap.

"*True* friends aren't replaceable," Tec corrected him.

"When people are desperate, they grasp at straws. You know that. He's alone. He has nowhere to turn. You're his best friend." The man leaned back and laughed. "In fact, you're his only friend, true or not. Make that clear to him, and stick with him to monitor his cooperation. Then you'll learn the answer to your question. I promise," the man answered, getting up and standing face-to-face with Tec.

"Your promises don't mean shit," Tec replied, glowering at him.

The man put his hands on Tec's shoulders. "Fine. What will it take to secure your cooperation?"

36

Shuffling along slowly to buy some time to think, Zane followed Number Three through the corridor. The smell of Tina's perfume had thrown him. It couldn't be a coincidence. These people had abducted her and the kids and were holding them here. She was here somewhere. The thought of it was floating in his mind like a puffy cloud on a sunny day. It was beautiful and peaceful, but if he couldn't touch it or taste it, was it real?

Zane briefly considered jumping Number Three. Number Two had left them after they exited the room, and this would be a perfect opportunity to see who the better man was.

"Don't even think about it. I would put you down before you could say Tina," Number Three said.

They'd made a couple of turns and now walked through a long corridor that passed by what Zane assumed to be office suites. They stopped in front of a steel-gray door marked with the number 4604 underneath the empty slot for a nameplate. Apparently, gray was their favorite color. It probably matched the mood of most abductees they brought here.

"How do I know you really have Tina and the kids—and that they're still alive?" Zane asked before they entered. "If you want me to do anything, I need to know they're still breathing. And I need to know now," Zane demanded. "I need proof of life."

"Proof of life? Why should we prove anything to you? If you

don't want to do what we're asking, then don't." Number Three sneered. "However, unless you want proof of death, you *will* do what we are asking. Anything else would be a dangerous gamble."

"I like gambling if the odds are right. I'm risking a lot by going back, and at this point, I'm not sure why. At least give me a reason, prove to me that they're alive and well."

"You know what? You caught us on a good day. I think the man likes you. We'll give you proof of life. Living, breathing proof of life. But remember that it can easily become proof of death."

Number Three grabbed Zane by the arm and led him past the front desk to another steel door. This one just had one number on it: seven. Lucky seven.

Number Three opened the door. Grays dominated there, as well. The carpet was gray, the walls were gray, and the wood desk dominating the room was gray. Even the uncomfortable-looking chair in front of it was gray. There was a curtain midway up one of the walls.

The curtain was blue.

"Here, sit for a minute. Remain calm. If you don't, your family could get hurt. What happens to them depends on you. Do you understand?"

Zane nodded.

He stared at the curtain. He knew it wasn't for decorative purposes.

$ $ $

Tina held Zanese's limp hand as they followed Rocker. Zanese seemed to have given up caring about anything, and Tina feared she was losing her. Depression was a dangerous opponent anytime, and particularly in this situation. She had to find a way to raise her daughter's spirits. She was lucky that James seemed to take care of himself. He was walking ahead of them as if he were anxious to reach their destination.

The hallway was narrow and dark, and Tina quickly became disoriented. Rocker opened a steel-gray door that led to an office suite. Tina caught a glimpse of an empty slot for a nameplate on the door and wondered if the building was deserted. Once they entered, they passed what seemed like a front desk and then walked past other doors on both sides of the hallway. Tina considered taking the kids and running, but she knew they wouldn't get far. She had a sinking feeling.

James counted down the office doors, "Six, seven, eight."

Rocker opened the door, and they entered. It was a sparsely furnished office without any decoration. Grays dominated. As she took in her new surroundings, her confidence sank further. That was probably what they wanted.

She would give almost anything to see Zane.

There was a table and one chair, both gray. The kids immediately fell down on the gray carpet. Zanese curled up into a ball, and James sat cross-legged, waiting for the adventure to unfold. As far as she was concerned, there had already been too many adventures today.

"Stay here for a minute," Rocker said and turned to leave.

"I don't really have another choice, do I?" Tina yelled after him as he locked the door.

One of the walls seemed to have a window covered by a blue curtain. Knowing she was so deep inside a building that the window couldn't offer a view, Tina assumed it was a two-way mirror. She had seen enough interrogation scenes in movies to know that.

Rocker returned quickly. He placed a small video recorder on the desk very quietly.

"I want you to see this. It's your husband. Listen to what he says. Calmly. Quietly. Some of what you see and hear may be hard to take, but I don't want you to panic."

"What did you do to him?" Tina asked. "If you're about to show me how you tortured him, please spare my children."

"Don't panic. We haven't done anything to him. He's done it all by himself." Rocker looked at her with a genuine smile. "He's not the man you think he is. Never was. You deserve better."

Rocker pressed the Play button, and a husband Tina never knew and a father the kids wouldn't recognize began to take shape before Tina's eyes.

$ $ $

Zane knew the curtain would open into another room. He was uneasy about what he would see. They held his wife and children, he was sure of that. And he was sure these people had great potential to maim and murder. The charred bodies in his burned home were proof of that. He knew these people had no scruples. They'd do whatever it took to ensure his cooperation. Would they go so far as to hurt his wife and children in front of him? Zane wiped his face with his sleeve. He didn't want Number Three to see him sweat.

"You don't have to show me this. I'll cooperate," Zane said.

"We believe you will. In fact, we know you'll cooperate, if you ever want to see your family again. You asked for a proof of life. Well, here it is, with a little twist."

Number Three began to draw back the curtain. Zane had trouble breathing. A flame had started burning in his head and was spreading throughout his body, rage mixed with fear. Fear of what was on the other side. He closed his eyes.

Number Three grabbed him by the shoulder and shoved him closer to the window. Zane stumbled and almost fell into the glass.

"Open your eyes. Time for truth and consequence."

Zane's heart raced. It took all his willpower to open his eyes.

What he saw made his fear and rage burn hotter, but what he heard made his whole being wither.

He was looking at a table in a room similar to his. Tina was sitting at a table in the center, Zanese and James sat on the floor next to her. A tall, muscular black man was standing watch. His presence threatened Zane's family more than a ticking bomb.

They were watching a small, handheld video recorder sitting on the table. Zane couldn't see what they were watching, but he could hear it. It was his voice. He was talking to the Treasury agents. Tina was stone-faced. Zanese and James transfixed their eyes to the little screen.

Zane banged on the window with both fists and screamed at the top of his lungs. He had to make this stop. But Tina couldn't hear him through the soundproof window.

Number Three grabbed his arms.

"Calm down," he said almost gently.

Now she'd know what a terrible person he was. She'd hear about the laws he'd broken and the many lives he'd ruined. She'd find out he'd been playing both sides—that he'd lied to his employer, his colleagues, his clients, and to her. And that was just the beginning of his sordid tale. Would she ever be able to forgive him? Would she still love him?

All the energy left his body. He plopped down on the lone chair in the room. He had to talk to her, but he wasn't sure she'd want to talk to him.

"Just tell me why. I told you I'd go back," Zane said.

"We want you to do a bit more than just go back. This little scene today is just to show you how badly we can fuck with you. Your wife will look at you differently from now on. Her trust in you has been violated. That will be hard to earn back. This is just one small example. You have no idea. We can make your life a hell on earth. So do what you're told, and we'll all work our way through this together."

Zane spun quickly to his right, with his fist in a spear aiming for Number Three's throat. He wanted to end the smug man's miserable existence. Then he could throw a chair through the window, get to his family, and beg them to forgive him.

Zane didn't see the stun gun in Number Three's right hand. He brought it up in a smooth arc, and Zane went down. Hard. He lay on the floor convulsing and trying not to spew the little that remained in his stomach onto the bland, gray carpet.

He refused to stay down, though. He struggled back up. Rasping and retching, he turned to Number Three.

"How about you and me, mano a mano? Come on. Put that woman's weapon down. Badass."

Just as Number Three was beginning his retort, they both heard Tina begin to speak. Her words would change Zane's life forever.

$ $ $

The kidnappers had told Tina that Zane was involved in illegal business dealings, and that's why she and the kids had been abducted. While she couldn't deny they were in the hands of some vile criminals, her ardent hope had been that it was a misunderstanding. But when she heard Zane confessing crime after crime to the Treasury agents, she knew she'd been the one who'd misunderstood.

She didn't understand what Zane and his employer were doing, but it was clear that it was wrong and that they'd been taking advantage of a lot of hardworking people. People had lost their livelihoods, others had disappeared, families had been left in ruin, and somehow, SAS had been involved—had even benefited. Zane's voice seemed to be in a foreign language. She could hear it but couldn't comprehend it.

But she knew one thing. He was her husband, and nothing he did would ever change that. She could never leave or forsake him. Her beliefs and salvation only gave her one option.

When the tape stopped playing, she began to speak.

"I don't understand what Zane did. I don't need to understand it to know that he ruined a lot of people, that some people are missing, and that he made money for himself and his company by hurting these people. No doubt what he did was wrong, despicable even, and I apologize for him. I also know that Zane wouldn't have done this just for the money. Zane would never have done this unless he felt he had no other option. I'm sure he had a good reason. So I'm not interested in what he's done; I'm only interested in why he did it. I love Zane, and I trust him. He's my husband, my partner, the love of my life—and that will never change. Nothing you can show me and nothing you can tell me will ever change that."

$ $ $

"Please follow me," his escort said, pointing out into the corridor.

Tec knew he had no other option. He had to see where this was going, although he had no idea what he was going to say to Zane. Tec had done what he thought was right, but in hindsight, he wasn't so sure anymore. With the luxury of time, decisions made for reasons that seemed clear in the moment were brought into even sharper, often different focus. But time was a luxury that Tec usually couldn't afford.

They passed the front desk and several offices before they entered a door marked with the number eight. The man slowly took out his card key.

"Are you ready?" he asked.

"Open the damn door."

The man began to turn the knob.

$ $ $

Zane wasn't sure what grace was. Except he was pretty sure he'd just seen it. Grace didn't need a definition. It just was.

Tina's unconditional love for him inspired his own unconditional love for her. He knew he didn't deserve her, but love wasn't about merit. It was about acceptance. Tina accepted him no matter what he'd done. And that filled him with gratitude. He would never be the same. Now he could and would do anything for her.

Number Three turned off the sound to Tina's room.

At that moment, the door opened.

37

Tina knew a split second before her eyes told her. Tec was standing in the doorway. Was he here to hurt her?

She couldn't comprehend friends who hurt friends. Yet, all people had been given free will.

"Tec. I knew it was you! You have the nerve to show your face?" Tears rolled down her cheeks, betraying the profound sadness that threatened to overtake her justified anger. "Why did you do it?"

Tec took a few tentative steps into the room when James realized who had stepped in and jumped up and ran toward him.

"Tec! You came back! Is Daddy here too? I knew Daddy would come to help us," James said as he rushed toward him. "This was all just a game? But it's over now, right?"

Tec couldn't help himself; he knelt down and embraced the little boy.

"This isn't what it looks like," Tec said as he looked up at Tina, who had risen from her chair. "Trust me."

"Trust you?" Tina cried out as she watched the scene, which to everyone who couldn't hear what was being said must have looked like the happy reunion of long-lost friends. "Yes, I trusted you. The kids trusted you. What am I saying? They still trust you! They don't know better, but I do." She struggled to stop crying as she approached James, gently touched his shoulder, and pulled him away from Tec. "Do you know what we've been through? Do you even care?"

She was beginning to calm down. She stood tall in front of her children as if to protect them from the evil Tec had brought into this room. "How could you do this to us? How could you do this to Zane? He's your friend. Or was this all just an act? Do you even know what friendship is?"

Her words were penetrating Tec's soul, cutting like a razor.

"All is not as it seems. Please, Tina, there's a bigger picture. People got hurt, and someone needed to put it right. Sometimes pain is gain. I'm so sorry you and the kids had to go through this, but the ends may justify the means. I'm working for the greater good," Tec said.

"The ends don't always justify the means. Sometimes we have to do what's right and know that God will work it out in the end," Tina said as she backed away from him, keeping her children close to her.

"I know you believe that, Tina, but sometimes we have to do what God can't do. We're in control of our own destiny. I took control when Zane lost control."

"God is always in control. He is always there. Zane is my protection and always will be, no matter what he's done. You can't take his family hostage and then claim you did something evil in the name of the greater good. I don't even know what that means."

"I can't tell you, Tina. Please, just trust me," Tec implored.

"We are well beyond that," Tina said quietly.

Tec had no response. Seconds ticked by as Tec and Tina stared at each other.

The room grew quiet. Rocker looked at Tina with a respect he'd never felt for any woman before.

$ $ $

"*Tec?*" Zane exclaimed when he saw his friend entering the room, approaching Tina.

What was Tec doing here? Talking to Tina. Who was watching Holmes? How had he found them? A lot more questions than answers. Tec must have followed him. But how did he get into the building? And why wasn't anybody trying to restrain him? This wasn't right.

"Tec is one of us," Number Three said as he pointed at Zane, making a gun with his thumb and finger and shooting it.

"Bullshit! Tec's my best friend. He was helping me."

"Your hand has been dealt, buddy. There are no cards up your sleeve. Face facts—Tec works for us. Your wife knows you're a crook, and no matter what she just said, she'll never look at you the same way again. You're screwed, so grow up and act like a big boy."

Number Three switched on the sound button.

"I took control when Zane lost control," he heard Tec say.

And that's when it hit him hard. WWHDT. *Why would he do this?* That's what James's scribbles had meant. James knew one of the kidnappers. A five-year-old's perception is not clouded by preconceived ideas.

Suddenly, he knew what he had to do.

Zane turned his back to the window and put his head in his hands in a look of despair. He then turned to Number Three.

Zane slowly put his hands on the top of Number Three's shoulders and began to cry.

"Maintain control. You have a lot of shit to do for us."

Suddenly, Zane brought his hands up and clapped hard on both of Number Three's ears. It had the desired effect. Burst eardrums. The pain was immense. Number Three began to scream and put his own hands over his ears in a futile attempt to stop the pain.

Zane took the opportunity to grab the weapon from Number Three's belt. But he didn't go for the stun gun. He went for the Glock in the small of his back. He had seen the bulge earlier, and he was rewarded when his hand closed around it as he swiftly withdrew it from his holster.

Gun in hand, Zane then put his right leg behind Number Three and grabbed his right arm and swept him to the floor in one smooth move. Once he was on the floor, Zane put his knee hard on Number Three's sternum and slammed the barrel of the Glock in his mouth as he switched the safety off.

"Okay, fuckhead, give me one good reason to let you live."

Pieces of broken teeth and blood oozed from Number Three's mouth. Zane realized that he couldn't hear him through busted ears. He'd never hear anything again.

"It was a rhetorical question," Zane said.

Zane's finger tightened on the trigger. He trembled. Every fiber of his being wanted to kill Number Three. This was a time to be violent.

Number Three didn't deserve to live, but he, Zane, didn't deserve Tina and her grace, either. He pulled the gun from Number Three's bloody mouth.

He stood up. Number Three's head was rolling from side to side, trying to ease the pain. His eyes were wide with panic. Zane saw the pain and the panic, but his hatred outranked them. He stared down at Number Three. With a hard black thing where his heart should have been, he pointed the gun and pulled the trigger.

And again.

And again.

38

Zane ran into the hallway. He had to find Tina quickly. He had to know that the vision of her acceptance and grace wasn't some ghostly apparition.

Tec and Tina were in the hallway running toward him. Maybe she needed him too. He ignored Tec and rushed to Tina.

They fell into each other's arms. He hugged her ferociously. They were united again. And his relief was overwhelming.

"Daddy!" Zanese and James screamed, joining the hugging melee. Zane thought his heart would explode. He couldn't believe it was over. He had Tina back; he had his kids back. Yet, his joy was not full.

"I'm so sorry, Tina. I love you, I love you, I love you," Zane whispered in her ear.

"I love you too. I knew you'd come for us. I knew you'd save us. I forgive you. I just want our old life back. Thank you, God, for this wonderful restoration. My prayers have been answered," Tina whispered into his ear, ignoring the gun she had felt in the small of Zane's back as they joyously hugged.

"I know you've forgiven me. I heard you. Your words changed things. They changed me. More than I can ever show. But I can try. I'll explain everything. We need to get out of here and go somewhere. Anywhere," Zane said.

"I'm not sure that's going to be so easy," Rocker chimed in.

"I don't think so, either. We need to review options," Tec said.

Zane turned and glowered at Tec. He wanted to pull the gun and end this now. Yet deep down, he couldn't extinguish all his faith in Tec. He knew there had to be more to his story.

"Let's go talk, but I wouldn't plan on just reuniting as one big happy family," Rocker said.

"With God, all things are possible. Nothing is too hard for Him," Tina said as she stared at Tec. "But there are consequences to the decisions we make. You need to remember that, Tec."

"I realize that," Tec said looking at no one. "However, in this place, at this time, Zane may be learning that lesson more than me."

"Shit rolls downhill, and Zane here is at the bottom of a mountain," Rocker replied.

Zane knew that was true. How could he even begin to believe this would somehow work out?

"Let's go. Whoever is in charge has to be able to listen to reason," Zane said.

Tina smiled. She took Zane's hand and squeezed it as they began walking down the hallway. Zane squeezed back.

"Keep your guard up," Tec whispered in Zane's ear.

"Of course," Zane replied. "Trust has to be earned."

Tec opened his mouth as if to say something but then thought better of it. He walked behind Zane and Tina, staring at their intertwined hands.

Rocker led the way as the small group trudged deeper into the darkened hallways, looking for redemption and closure. They passed doors numbered nine and ten. James jumped into Zane's arms suddenly, telling his dad all about their wild adventures over the last two days. Zanese was holding her mom's other hand and wasn't going willingly. She was scared of what another confrontation would bring.

They arrived at a locked double door. This door wasn't plain gray, but black and well appointed. Whoever resided here needed to project power. Rocker's knock was loud. Moments later, the door opened. Spaz stood in the doorway, grinning from ear to ear. Number One and Number Two stood behind him. Spaz motioned them all in. The door closed with a tomb-like finality.

Behind the large desk sat the man himself.

39

The Man, as he was sarcastically referred to, wasn't an imposing figure. He was five foot ten, with a slight build and a full head of white hair. His large, hawkish nose lent a predatory quality to his features. This was compounded by steely eyes that bored holes through anyone he looked at. He made people feel guilty just by being in the same room. That was the coveted effect.

Whatever needed to be done, wherever it needed to be done, he was the Man.

Zane, Tina, and the kids were ushered to a simple black leather couch and were seated with the formality shown to the biggest client of a prestigious law firm. James looked excited for the next twist in this adventure, while Zanese looked like she might get sick again. Rocker and Tec sat in adjoining modest chairs as did the Man. Spaz and Numbers One and Two stood.

"Let's start with my name. People call me Mr. Moore or Tom Moore. You can call me either and safely assume that whatever you call me is not real." He smiled for a brief second before his features turned serious. "Let's get right down to it. Do you have your laptop?"

"Not with me," Zane told him. "And even if I did, I wouldn't give it to you."

"We'll get it. For now, let's keep it simple," Moore said.

"Yes, it is simple. I'm not sure who you guys represent, but haven't I done enough? Just leave me and my family out of it. We'll go on our way, and you go on yours. You don't need me anymore," Zane flatly stated.

"We need you. But what's just as important, you need us. Trust me. Without our protection and involvement in your life, I'm not sure any of you will make it through the day. We need to work together."

"We'll take our chances. I have to put an end to this. If I'm facing prison, so be it. We'll get through this," Zane replied.

Moore sighed and laid his head back on the chair. He stared at the ceiling for a moment. "Tec, what do you think? Is Zane's plan a good one? You're his friend. Give him your honest opinion."

Tec looked down for a minute. He seemed to be deep in thought. Or perhaps he didn't want to answer the question. Maybe both.

"You're asking Zane to make a life-changing decision without all the facts," Tec responded.

Moore was trying to at least appear as if he was concerned with Zane's well-being. "Facts? As if the truth will set you free. Sometimes the truth is what keeps us bound. You need to look beyond the truth, and don't think having that laptop is going to protect you—or your family," Moore said.

Tina cleared her throat. "No. With all due respect, you're wrong, Mr. Moore. The truth *will* set you free. Just lay it all out for us, and let God have His way. It's the best way. It's the only way."

"Let God have His way. Doesn't your God always have His way? Isn't your God always in control? He knows what we're going to say before we say it, what we're going to do before we do it. So what difference does it make?" he challenged.

"I do believe that. But God also gave man freedom to choose. He knows what we're going to choose, but we still have the freedom to choose it. You need to choose life, Mr. Moore. Not more lying and death," Tina replied, sure of her words and her beliefs.

"I've already chosen. Do what we ask, and everybody will be fine. Tell him, Tec," Moore prompted.

"Not before we know where the money trail leads. Tell us who's behind SAS and its machinations. We know it's not Holmes. And I assume it's not you," Tec said, wanting to appear on Zane's side.

"It's not who, but what. Money is a commodity that can be used for good or bad. Of course, there's a money trail leading to and away from SAS. But that's not your concern. You just need to go back and do what you were doing, and everything will fall into place," Moore asserted as he stared intently at Zane.

"I think what Mr. Moore is trying to say is that sometimes a step backward is needed to go forward. He may not have your best interests at heart, but if he says you're safer going back to SAS, I'd believe him," Rocker piped in.

"Don't listen to them, Zane. Let's go. Just walk out. Believe it, Zane," Tina implored.

Zane wanted to go, but he couldn't. Perhaps it was what Tec said, or perhaps it was Rocker's words. He didn't believe they'd let him just walk. Either way, he couldn't make his feet move toward the door. He knew he was letting Tina down.

"Okay, Mr. Moore, answer this. Would you let us just get up and walk out that door?" Zane asked. He wasn't sure what he wanted the answer to be.

"Even if I would, you'd want to come back. With the laptop," Moore said as he stood up and leaned against his desk. "You may think that if you go back and continue to provide evidence of the crimes you and SAS are committing, then you won't be prosecuted because you have whistleblower protection. It's not that simple."

"Make it that simple," Zane said.

"A man after my own heart," Moore replied as he stood up, walked over to the counter, and grabbed a bottle of water. "If you don't go back and do what you were doing before, then those who are at the end of the money trail will step in. Just like Tec said. They'll kill you because of what you know already and because of what you could still find out. They want you to be a team player. Taking your family was to get your attention and to keep it. Is that simple enough?"

"Fuck all of this talk. Let's just grab the wife and kids to make sure Zane has the proper incentive," Spaz broke in as he lifted his Beretta M9 to the side of Zane's head.

It became very quiet in the room.

Zane moved to the edge of his seat as Rocker stood up and held up a hand to stop him from going any further. Zane wondered how quickly he could pull the gun in the small of his back.

Tec stood up and moved ever so slightly toward Spaz.

"Well, another world heard from," Moore murmured. "You can put the gun down, Spaz. Let's give Zane the freedom of choice that Tina's God died for," he finished with only a hint of sarcasm.

"You may pay me, but I take orders from someone else," Spaz snarled. "I've got the authority, and all of you can go straight to hell if you want. I'd be happy to send you there, as a matter of fact. Except for Zane, Tina, and those ratty ankle biters. So get up, Tina, grab the kids, and follow me. Now."

Zanese began to cry, covering her face with her arms. James cowered down into the couch cushions, looking for any available protection.

"No. Look at me, Spaz, and remember, just remember what I can do," Tec said, moving slightly closer to Spaz.

Spaz slowly turned to Tec with a perplexed, disgusted look on his face. "You seem to forget that I have the gun. Come on, Tec, you're not that fast."

"Do you want to find out? Colombia won't happen again. I'll make sure of it," Tec firmly stated.

"Come on, boys. Remember that you all work for me. Do you really want to go over my head?" Moore quietly asked.

The room was dead silent again, except for Zanese's quiet sobbing. Everybody was waiting for someone—anyone—to do whatever needed to be done. Good or bad. It would soon be over.

Tec slowly turned to face Spaz. Spaz backed up one step, but the gun was now pointed directly at Tec. Tec showed no fear as he began to move toward Spaz. Spaz stood his ground. He looked determined as he turned the gun back toward Zane. Tec stopped.

"Okay. Bring it, Tec. Maybe you are fast; maybe you are better than me. But you aren't faster or better than my trigger finger," Spaz stated. "The next move you make, toward me or anybody, I pull the trigger. The man in the room we can least afford to lose will be dead. Your friend."

Tec cringed at the word *friend* and stole a glance at Zane.

Seconds from now, this moment would be history.

Tina was praying and seeking God's wisdom and strength. She recalled happy times in her life. Her wedding, the birth of her children, moving into their new home. Zane had provided a good life. He was a good husband. Once Zane explained his reasons for his actions, she knew she'd be able to forgive him and move on. Regardless of what might happen today.

Time slowed to a crawl. Stress and pressure compress time in ways the human mind will never comprehend.

Tec moved toward Spaz, which caused Spaz to slightly move the gun away from Zane. Tina saw her opportunity, uttered a quick prayer, and jumped in front of Zane and toward Spaz.

Zane was sitting back and didn't have time to react and go for his gun. At least that's what he'd tell himself for the rest of his life.

Spaz caught Tina's movement in the corner of his eye, turned back toward Zane, and pulled the trigger.

"Violence is rarely the answer, but when it is, it's the only answer."

—TIM LARKIN

40

Caleb Rider was having a long, fun night. He loved training and fighting. It came naturally to him. He'd lost more fights in his life than he'd won, but that didn't matter. It wasn't about the victory; it was about the lesson.

The Warrior's Den was a long, low building that hadn't been well maintained. The red stucco with brown trim on the outside was faded, and the old, bent awning angled over a cracked window. The dark wood paneling inside was beginning to show its true worth as it warped and split beyond repair. Nonetheless, the dojo felt like a second home to Caleb, even though he'd only started training there a month earlier. The art of fighting was taught and hammered home well, regardless of the condition of the physical structure. The memory of many a true fighter lived in these worn walls, along with their distinct combined aroma. But that smell of sweat, blood, and exertion excited him. He knew most of the fighters and loved how tough they were. Iron sharpens iron.

Tec hadn't been around much lately. He hadn't sparred with any of the students for a long time. Tec loved sparring, so Caleb figured he was busy.

Other longtime students taught most of the classes. His favorite among them was Monique. She was definitely easy on the eyes

137

but was his favorite for other, more practical reasons. She was tough, gave no quarter to man or woman, and always maintained the same even calm, whether beat or beaten. He really respected that in a fighter, since a single loss taught more than ten victories.

Tonight's instructor taught a new move at the beginning of the class, and then they spent the first hour practicing it. Practice was at something less than full speed. The second hour was open gym, which meant sparring. It could be Brazilian jujitsu—grappling on the ground trying to get your opponent to tap or submit. Or it could be standing and striking, which Caleb preferred because he loved to punch with elbows, hands, knees, or feet. MMA was a combination of both, and that's what he loved most. Use all the tools God gave you to see who was the better warrior.

Open gym was winding down, and Caleb was considering leaving when Monique walked up with a new student. Dan was wiry and tall, with sinewy arms. The scowl on his face matched his sullen, but brash, walk.

Monique had spent the open gym teaching Dan a few basic moves, and now he wanted to try them. Caleb possessed excellent control and would work with Dan without hurting him.

"Hey, Caleb. I know it's been a long night, but do you have a little bit left?" Monique asked.

"Sure. Anything for you. Just tell him to take it easy on me," Caleb replied.

"Dan, this is just for you to try your moves on a live person. Caleb is one of our better fighters, so you can learn a lot."

"Hi, Dan." Caleb stuck his hand out.

Dan held his hands to his side as he replied, "I'm in the army. Just honing up my skills. I've been trained as a killer, but don't worry. I won't try my lethal moves on you. I haven't been in a combat zone yet, but don't let that fool you."

Monique raised her eyebrows at Dan's reply and worked to

suppress a grin.

"Yeah, I guess a handshake could be a killer move. So let's get started," Caleb said. "I have the utmost respect for anybody brave enough to be in the military."

"All righty, then," Monique said. "I want Dan to parry a jab from you and respond with a palm strike to your chest. After we try a few of those, I want you to put him in a standing headlock for him to escape. Simple enough."

They both assumed fighting stances as Caleb threw his first jab. Dan parried effectively with his left, stepped outside the jab, and threw a palm strike to Caleb's chest, hard. Caleb turned his body sideways at the last moment to divert the majority of the blow. He looked at Monique with mild curiosity, and Monique shrugged her shoulders.

"Again, but lower the speed, Dan."

They repeated the move several times, with Dan throwing the palm strike harder with each repetition. Caleb didn't mind, because he figured it helped him perfect his response time.

"Okay, enough of that. Let's try the standing headlock and escape."

Caleb put Dan in the standing headlock, and Dan perfectly used his left arm for the block against Caleb's neck while grabbing Caleb's right arm with his right hand and twisting out of the headlock, while putting Caleb in a standing arm bar, behind Caleb's back. He brought the arm up hard while applying extreme pressure with his left against Caleb's neck. He let Caleb out of it after a couple of seconds. Caleb grinned at Monique while trying to act concerned for the validity of the move.

Dan performed the move three more times, applying more pressure with each successive application.

"You know, I could try resisting," Caleb told Dan.

"You could, but then I might have to hurt you. Seriously hurt you," Dan replied.

Caleb looked at Monique with a wry look of amusement. Monique's wink back was all Caleb needed.

They performed the move again, but this time as Dan brought Caleb's arm up very hard behind Caleb's back, Caleb grabbed Dan's left, brought it across his own chest, and used a hip lock to throw Dan over his shoulder and land him hard on the mat, controlling his right arm.

All fighters stopped and turned to look at this exhibit. Everybody loved to see a new asshole taught his place in the gym. Or for that matter, any asshole.

Dan attempted to spin out of the arm hold and throw a left hard at Caleb's face. Caleb expected that move and quickly got Dan's back, putting him in a rear naked choke. Dan was unconscious within several seconds.

Caleb stood up, shrugged his shoulders, and walked to the edge of the mat.

Monique shook Dan's shoulders hard to wake him up. He wasn't happy.

"You motherfucking loser. I'll get your ass. Count on it. If I wasn't taking it easy on you, I would've killed you. Watch your back. I'm one badass fucking killer," Dan spat out as he stood up.

"If you say so," Caleb responded while walking away to put his gear in his bag. "Take it easy. Everybody can learn."

All of the fighters slowly turned back to their sparring. They had witnessed this scene before. Nothing new.

"Chalk this up as a learning experience, take a cold shower, and try again in a couple of nights. No harm done. But a word of advice: don't mess with Caleb," Monique said.

Dan glared hard at Caleb as he walked to the showers.

Caleb expected this wasn't the last he would see of him.

Sure enough, Dan was waiting for him outside the Warriors

Den with two of his buddies. Two large, muscular buddies. Caleb suspected they were army. If their high and tight haircuts didn't give them away, their studied I-am-a-badass expressions did.

Caleb sighed. He just wanted to go home.

He walked up to the three of them slowly but confidently. "Okay, guys. Dan is a badass. I shouldn't have dumped him. You guys don't need to teach me a lesson. I get it."

"That's not the way this is going to work. We don't need to teach you a lesson, but we want to. You're going to be practice for us. Too bad, so sad, but we're going to mess you up. Big time," Dan claimed.

As he finished, the biggest one walked up to Caleb, faked a left jab and threw a right hook. Caleb ignored the jab, since the attacker never sold him on the fake, and then stepped inside the hook and kneed the big guy hard in the balls. He went down, clutching his manhood, with a baboonish growl coming out of his mouth.

Instantly, another big guy on the right came in low on Caleb with both arms outstretched, attempting to tackle him. Caleb easily sidestepped that, grabbed an ankle as it went flying by, flipped his would-be assailant over, put him in an Achilles lock, and repeated his testicle kick. This big guy rolled around moaning.

"You really need to learn that kick-in-the-balls move. It works quite well. Especially against the parking-lot assailant. In fact, it's probably best against parking-lot assailants. Case in point," Caleb said as he pointed to the two big guys on the ground.

Dan just stood there with his mouth open as Monique exited the dojo and locked the front door.

She briskly walked by them, staring straight ahead. "I told you not to fuck with Caleb." Then she turned to Caleb. "Hey, are you hungry? Let's go get something to eat."

"Sounds good. We can talk about you putting me on the payroll, since I seem to be giving more lessons than you," Caleb replied.

They were both laughing as they got in her car.

Dan stared after them, wondering who had given Caleb lessons.

४१

He ran in the morning so he could be alone in the dark. His feet were pounding the wet pavement as he knocked back the miles. His back hurt, his knees hurt, and he was short of breath. Rain, shine, cold, or heat—he ran. He'd run ten miles so far and wanted to run two more. The pain was intense, but physical pain took his mind off his mental anguish. It also helped him sleep. For a couple of hours. After that, sleep was as elusive as clearing his mind of the regret that controlled his every moment.

He ran back to his small apartment in Saint Louis Park before the clock hit 6:00 a.m. Saint Louis Park was an inner suburb of Minneapolis—nice, but not nearly as opulent as his former sur- roundings in Deephaven. Zane felt he didn't deserve to live there anymore. His dream house had blown up, along with his dream life.

He now had a one-bedroom apartment with a small com- bined kitchen and dining room that opened up into an equally small living room. The place had come furnished and could best be described as a showroom example of the Early Shit style. The car- pet was a threadbare brown, which was probably best so as to hide the stains of the former tenants. The walls were yellow, though Zane couldn't tell if that was the color of the paint or the result of years of nicotine floating around in a deadly fog. He grabbed a bottle of water out of the fridge since the kitchen sink moaned like a dying frog whenever he turned on the faucet, which spat out something brown that bore no resemblance to drinking water.

He showered but didn't shave. This was his new life. He didn't have to be at work until eight, so he had some time. He poured himself some cereal, added milk, and thought about his former life. Life before sadness and regret consumed everything he did and didn't do. He recalled how Tina always made fun of him for eating cereal as a meal any time of day. She would laugh at him and set out a bowl of cereal for him when he came home from work and sarcastically inform him that she had been toiling in the kitchen for hours making his supper and he'd better appreciate it. If only the clock could be turned back. He fought back the tears as he began to slowly eat his breakfast.

Tina had been laid to rest on a bright, sunny day. The weather was in stark contrast to the inside of Zane's heart and soul. He didn't cry. He had to be strong for the kids. The whole day had been a blur. Many of the people who attended expressed their sorrow that she had to die so young. Zane didn't want their sorrow. He had enough of his own. Tina's mom, Betty, was sad, but her faith seemed to give her some buoyancy and hope beyond the grave. She presided over the funeral, though she called it a celebration of Tina's life. Betty hugged Zane, told him she was praying for him, and that this day would soon pass into the recesses of his memory. Tina was with God, she assured him, and someday Zane would be with both of them. Zane knew better. As she ended her hug, Betty told Zane that someday he'd be ready to tell her the whole story, and until that day, he had her love but not her trust. And if he didn't want to be with Tina real soon, the story had better be the truth.

As he had so many times in the last several weeks, he relived the key moments of that fateful day. Was there something—anything—he could have done differently? After being reunited with Tina, he'd been so sure things were going to end on a happy note.

Nothing in his life ever seemed to turn out that way.

The bullet from Spaz's gun had entered the right side of her neck. Zane caught her before she hit the floor.

Tec had moved between Zane and the kids as Rocker grabbed them and buried their heads in his legs.

Zane put a couch pillow under Tina's head and stroked her hair while using one hand to put pressure on the wound. Tina was still conscious, and her mouth was slowly moving.

Zane told her to be quiet and that help was coming, that it would all be fine. And that he loved her.

She put her finger on Zane's lips, and he'd leaned down so he could hear his wife's last words. "I love you. You are an amazing and strong man. Do what you need to do. Go in the Lord's strength. Show our children a blessed life. You can do it."

She would never tell him she loved him again. Never do Zanese's hair again. Never laugh at James's silly questions again. Never snuggle with him as he whispered his love for her just before they'd fall asleep.

Tina looked into Zane's eyes as she took her last breath and went to meet her God. Part of Zane's heart had gone with her.

He didn't understand why God didn't answer his prayer.

Maybe he'd ruined his karma by shooting Number Three. Three times. Once in each knee and once in his right hand. He had needed to send his family's captors a message. He had left Number Three alive, he was sure of that. Reasonably sure, anyway.

Tina wouldn't have approved. Live by the gun, die by the gun. An eye for an eye. When Zane thought of the love of God, he wasn't sure he had that kind of love in him. He'd read about it in the Bible that Tina had bought him, but how did he know if he had it? He must not have it, as evidenced by crippling Three, possibly for life. Since he didn't exhibit that kind of love, maybe God wasn't showing that kind of love to him, either. You reap what you sow.

Wasn't that in the Bible too?

Zanese and James didn't deserve any of it. The brutal murder of their mother would be seared into their memories forever. He couldn't even imagine their nightmares, their daydreams, or their prayers before they lay down to sleep every night. He had brought this on them. At least Tina was at peace and with God. He had to go on with the pain of loss every single day.

Zanese and James were living with Betty, who was a bit eccentric with her militant Christian beliefs, but he needed them out of his life for the time being. Seeing them every day hurt too much. And he wouldn't be any good as a father right now. At least that's what he told himself whenever he wondered if his refusal to be with them meant that his children had lost both their parents in one day.

After the shooting, Tec had deftly disarmed Spaz and rendered him unconscious with a blow to his chin. As Tec was holding the gun on Moore and Rocker, Moore had told them all to leave. He would clean it up. Zane couldn't leave. He couldn't leave his gorgeous dead wife with that evil group. Tec helped him collect himself, and Rocker helped him pick up Tina's body and retreat to another room. He held Tina in his arms, caressing her lips, not ever wanting to part with her.

Zane lost track of time—and everything else, for that matter. His eyes had been dry, mostly for the children's sake, but his heart had hurt so badly that he was having trouble breathing. Each breath was labored, and he began to hope that it would be his last. Then he would look at Zanese and James, sitting there in a stunned stupor, and he knew he had to go on, for them.

Moore found them fifteen minutes later and told them that the situation had been cleaned. Zane wasn't sure what that meant but figured *clean* had to be a good thing.

Moore proceeded to explain to all of them how it was going to go down. Zane didn't really care. His grief was washing over him like a tidal wave, taking all common sense with it.

The explosion at Zane's house would be explained as a random gas line leak that ignited. Tina's body would be one of those found in the debris. They would control any cause of death and subsequent inquiry. The other two bodies found would be explained as the children of friends she was babysitting that day while their own children supposedly were with Zane. Zane assumed he'd never know whose bodies really were found in the rubble of his house, and he didn't care. Moore must have incredible pull with the authorities and the press to be able to sell that story.

Zane was free to leave with Zanese and James, along with the implied threat that if he didn't go back and carry on as before, his kids would pay the price. Although Monique still had his laptop, he knew he couldn't use it. He had to go back to Holmes and SAS and continue his work. Whatever organization Moore represented, and whatever end they were seeking, their reach was infinite. That much had become clear to him on that eventful day. Tina's tombstone was dead proof. Zane couldn't take a chance with his kids.

Zane didn't tell Holmes anything. When he cut him loose from his imprisonment in the abandoned building, they didn't exchange a word. Holmes's silence acknowledged the fact that this was beyond him. He didn't want to know what was going on. He just wanted out.

Moore told Zane to act like nothing had changed with the Treasury Department. Zane would continue to feed them information, but only after it had been approved. Moore would decide what information the Treasury would get. Zane assumed it would only be information that implicated Zane and Holmes as the masterminds of this criminal enterprise.

He went back to his Treasury contacts the next day and told them Holmes was playing hardball with him and that was why

Tina had died. However, he'd go back and work at getting evidence of the murder. He spent hours with the Treasury agents; they were more interested than ever. They expressed their regret at Tina's death, but it seemed to Zane as if they were secretly pleased. Murder had a bigger penalty than fraud, and most times, it was easier to prove.

Nothing much had changed since this ordeal began, except his wife was dead, more people were going to be hurt, and Zane had lost something deep inside of him. He wasn't sure what it was, but he was sure he'd never get it back.

He finished his cereal, dressed for work, and stumbled out to his shitty little car.

As he turned the ignition, he silently prayed, please let this be the day for something—anything—to happen to reignite his hope.

Without hope, he was doomed.

42

Along with handling many economic, currency, and policy issues, the chairman of the Federal Reserve was supposed to keep the three branches of government happy, or at least marginally informed. After all, he was up for reappointment and Senate confirmation in three years. While the politicians had no authority over the Federal Reserve, the chairman knew he needed friends on Capitol Hill. A few key, influential friends would ensure his legacy of prosperity. Or at least the illusion of it.

A perfect opportunity presented itself that Friday in the form of a fund-raising dinner for the wounded veterans of the last two wars. The chairman's wife was the chief organizer and had managed to invite and confirm the attendance of many political elites from both houses of Congress. Even the president had promised to come. Drinks and dinner that evening would be the perfect opportunity to pitch quantitative easing and push for more aggressive use of it. Inebriated partygoers always cozied up to easy money.

The chairman got out of bed and walked into his personal bathroom to perform his morning ablution. Now that he had money, he wouldn't share a bathroom with his wife. Why put up with hair all over the place and tons of beauty and feminine hygiene products when you didn't have to?

He slipped on his robe and slippers and went downstairs to the kitchen. His wife was up making breakfast. She was wearing yoga pants and a sports bra with her back turned toward him while frying bacon and eggs.

"What a beautiful sight to wake up to," he observed while sitting down at a kitchen barstool. "My wife has done her workout, shaping that nice ass of hers for me, and is now slaving over a hot stove to make me breakfast. A man couldn't ask for more."

"You're damn right," she said without looking around. "A lot of men would kill to have this."

"And I'm one of them," he said while putting on his reading glasses and perusing the headlines of the morning paper. "Luckily, I didn't have to."

His wife poured a cup of coffee, turned around, and put it in front of him. "The story isn't over yet."

He took a sip and uttered a sigh of satisfaction. "Ah, the nectar of life." He turned the front page. "What I did to earn your hand was help people. I didn't hurt them."

"We shall see," his wife said while putting the eggs and bacon on a plate and setting it in front of him, as well. "Speaking of earning my hand, what about him? Have you talked to him lately?"

"You can mention his name, you know," he answered, putting the coffee down, sliding the plate in front of him, and picking up a piece of bacon. "I talked to Ray a few days ago. He's having a few minor problems, but overall, he's doing well."

"What? You talked to him?" she exclaimed while grabbing the paper in the middle and pulling it down to the counter. "Why didn't you tell me?"

He slowly took off his glasses. "It involved business and not you," he said, staring at her.

"Anything to do with Ray involves me, business or not," she said, putting both of her hands on the counter and leaning over it toward him.

"Not really, but again, he is well."

"What are his few minor problems?"

"I won't go into that. He is looking at the problem and not the answer. The problem lies within him. The answer does too."

She took her hands off the counter and walked around to the other side. She sat on the stool next to him and put her hand on his knee. "I'm concerned. You know why. Don't tell me any specifics, but you need to tell me when you talk to him. That's all I ask."

The chairman shoveled the last egg into his mouth and began to chew. "I understand you need that. I'll try to accommodate you, but you have to understand that you need to keep your eye on the final goal. Don't worry about the path we travel to get there."

"I don't worry. I love him, and I need to know he's alive. That's all."

"So what we did still bothers you?"

"Of course it does. Doesn't it bother you?"

"I don't let it. He was lost. He needed direction. We gave him a purpose and meaning. We showed him how to find his soul."

"Yes, but this has become something none of us expected," she said as she took her hand off his knee and looked beyond him to the serene morning view out the kitchen window.

"Ten dollars or ten billion, it's still the same."

"If you asked him that, I don't think he'd agree."

The chairman grabbed a napkin and wiped the crumbs off of his commanding chin. "He needed me. We both shudder to think what Ray would be today without my help. Now he has a chance to bring it all home and become the hero."

"No matter the cost?"

"There's nothing in life that doesn't cost something," he said, putting his glasses back on while taking another sip of coffee and picking up his paper. "And sometimes the cost can be our life."

43

They went to dinner at Chipotle. Caleb figured one place was as good as the next, and he loved Mexican food. And he didn't have a car. So since she was driving, it really was up to Monique. He was secure enough in his manhood to sit on the passenger side and eat her choice of food. He thought all women should be liberated.

He paid, though. He had to draw the line somewhere.

He had a large burrito and water. Caleb loved water. He didn't understand why anybody drank anything else.

He began eating immediately. Kicking the shit out of people made him hungry. He loved the feeling after an adrenaline high and a good workout. Food only enhanced the rush.

"Wow, you are hungry. Slow down, big boy. We can always get more," Monique said.

"Sleep when you can, drink when you can, and eat when you can. You might not always be able to," Caleb responded with a mouthful of burrito.

"We aren't in a war zone right now. Although I guess you were a bit earlier," Monique said.

"Not a worthy enough opponent to be considered war."

"You smoked through those dudes like a hot knife through butter. Where'd you learn to fight like that?"

"The circus," he mumbled with a mouthful of food.

"Right. And I'm the reincarnation of Princess Di. Tell me. I've seen you fight with the best fighters we have night after night, some of them black belts, and you've never even come close to losing. You could go pro and clean up."

"Pro fighting's not real fighting. Close, but too many rules," Caleb said as he finished swigging a huge drink of water.

"I agree, but you still aren't answering my question. Don't tell me you learned to fight in the three-ring circus."

"Okay, I won't."

"Come on, dude. I looked at your application form for the Den, and you said no pro fighting and a lot of real-world experience. Whatever that means."

"It means I learned to fight in the circus."

"As a performer?"

"No."

"I think pulling teeth would be easier."

"I don't like to talk about it."

"Not even to a beautiful woman?"

"Especially to a beautiful woman."

"At least you're here now. I'm happy about that."

"I'm not who you think I am."

"I hate guys who are what I think they are. Surprise me."

"I'll surprise you with dessert."

"Dessert? I had something else in mind."

44

The moon was hiding, making the night as black as the wrath in a hateful soul. It was one of those warm and humid Minnesota nights that made a person forget winter even existed. They were driving the last mile with no headlights so as to avoid detection by law enforcement.

Caleb didn't care. He was getting to fight—in the closest thing there was to a real fight. He loved training at the Warrior's Den. He'd learned a lot of Brazilian jujitsu, which was helping his ground skills, and the Muay Thai was making him a more effective striker. Many sparring sessions felt dangerously close to the real thing. But sparring wasn't real fighting. Fighters learned control the hard way or didn't stay around long.

Tonight was different. It was a local fight club. Held in a barn somewhere west of the Twin Cities on what looked to be an abandoned farm site. Everybody paid a hundred-dollar fee to fight or to watch. Some of the money went to small purses; the rest went to the owner of the site. There were no real rules. Caleb had seen his share of unconscious, messed-up fighters being carried off the premises. He knew they'd been hurt in such a way as to leave permanent evidence to fuel many a fight story for a lifetime. He loved watching.

This night, Caleb was fighting.

"I always wondered why you never entered any of the local

MMA tournaments. I guess that pales in comparison to this," Monique said as they both got out of her car. She was looking at some of the fighters warming up outside by the barn. Their warm-ups looked more dangerous than some of the MMA fights she'd seen.

"It is fun," Caleb replied.

He brought Monique against his better judgment. Caleb couldn't think of it as a date. They were just enjoying a mutual pastime. Blood didn't seem to faze her; he'd seen her deal with plenty of blood at the dojo. However, this could get a lot more crazy and the crowd a bit unruly. Sometimes there were more and better fights in the parking lot than in the ring.

Their dinner at Chipotle had ended in dessert at her house—homemade apple pie with homemade cinnamon ice cream. Delicious. Monique had invited him to stay, but he wasn't ready. Caleb thought sex too early could mess up a good thing. He really liked Monique. He had left awkwardly and walked home. It wasn't far.

Now he'd invited her here. What a guy.

"How do you know when you fight? And who you fight?" Monique asked as they walked into the slightly dilapidated barn.

"You register, pay, and then wait. It's the luck of the draw."

"Weight classes?"

"No. It doesn't matter what you weigh here. The size of the fight in the man and the number of fights in the man."

"How long are the fights?"

"Until one guy wins by knockout or submission or until the other guy just pussies out. I've seen some long fights here."

"I take it you don't want to pussy out."

"Not if you want to be able to walk out under your own power."

The barn sat on an old farm site that had seen better days. Pre-Great Depression days. Someone had made an attempt to clean it up, but sweeping the sand off the beach may have been easier. The floor was dirt, combined with grease and oil from untold years of exhausted farm implements. Looking down, it was hard to tell where the outside ended and the inside began. The smell wasn't bad, but not pleasant, either—a mix of staleness and dirty, unwashed hair. It was hard to imagine that people were tearing down these sheds to reclaim the wood for furniture with the weathered look. There was a market for everything.

The animal stalls had been removed to make space for folding metal chairs, and a crude, raised, chain-link cage had been set up in the middle. The bottom of the cage was lined with a worn canvas floor marked with old blood and sweat stains. There were no advertising logos on the floor, only a bold hand-lettered sign that claimed "Pain is your friend."

A wide variety of people seemed to be in attendance. Some of them were dressed nicely as if out on the town for cocktails and dinner. Some of them looked like bikers just released from county lockup. A crude plywood bar had been set up across the side of the shed serving setups and ice. Fight fans could be seen carrying their own coolers full of beer and brown bags with various other libations. Most of the fans appeared to be well on their way to feeling no pain.

Caleb paid the fee for himself and Monique and led her over to the bar. They hadn't brought any refreshments.

"Would you like a pop or something stronger? I'm sure I can find some Southern Comfort or something here for you," Caleb asked.

"No, pop is fine. I think I want to be sober tonight."

Caleb let out a short laugh and grinned back at her.

"Sobriety is a good choice," he said as he bought her a Coke for five dollars and handed it to her. He then led her over to a seat in the third row.

A couple of people acknowledged Caleb as they walked to the

seat. They continued to point at him and talk hurriedly among themselves.

"Do a lot of these people know you?"

"Yeah, some of them have seen me fight. I don't do this very often, just once in a while to freshen things up."

"Freshen things up? I would never associate fresh with fighting, but what do I know?"

"I'll go find out when I fight and then sit with you. I don't need a lot of warm-up time."

"That doesn't surprise me. You seem like a zero-to-sixty guy."

Caleb left her and was back in ten minutes. He had a piece of paper with him.

"I'm the third fight of the night. It's a round-robin, single elimination. So if I keep winning, I'll have three fights. It shouldn't take long," Caleb stated matter-of-factly.

"I guess I should return that book I bought you on self-confidence."

"It is what it is."

"Well, don't make it too quick. You promised me a good time."

"I'll try, but I usually like to end it fast. It's more merciful that way."

"Mercy. What will be next?"

"By the way, after my last fight, we should get out of here, as in right away. I'll come get you, and we'll skedaddle."

"Understood, but this girl can watch out for herself."

Caleb nodded, but his attention quickly went elsewhere, as the first fight was being announced. The barn had filled up fast, and now was there was standing room only. The cheering grew loud as both fighters were announced. Blood, sweat, and tears were on the card for this evening.

The first two fights were quick. The losers were seriously overmatched. Both were knocked unconscious within two minutes each. Blood did flow, though. Tomorrow, they'd have the marks to prove their manhood to their friends and enemies alike.

Caleb stood up as the second fight ended.

He pulled his T-shirt over his head and pulled off his boots and socks. He was tall, with a medium build. He didn't possess six-pack abs, but he was muscular. He had tattoos on his chest and back portraying trapeze artists in various flying positions. *The circus, after all*, Monique thought. Caleb had short brown hair that framed his bony face. He was attractive in a rough-cut way.

He turned to Monique and handed her his clothing and boots. "Here, hold these for me. And please promise me one thing."

"Yes, I will still love you in the morning."

Caleb smiled and shook his head. "Don't judge this dish by your first bite."

Caleb turned and walked calmly toward the cage as the barn filled with hard rock music and bloodlust from the crowd.

Monique screamed over the crowd, "What the fuck does that mean?"

45

Zane knew he was a sinner. His past afflicted him with memories that proved it. It never bothered him until he met Tina. She was the promise of a better life. A future allowing him to move beyond his sins. That dream had died with Tina, and now he was back doing what he did best.

Guardian Jewelry had set up his own office for him. He spent the bulk of his time poring over past financial statements and accounting records. He reviewed their general ledger and receivables and payables. He had to make it look good even though most of it was just for show. More than anything, he wanted to get an idea of what the company was really worth and who their wholesale customers were. He spent a great deal of time interviewing the management staff, including Ben and his son. He went to lunch with them and for drinks after work. The better he knew them, the better his chances of them accepting his plan. Usually, it took him a couple of weeks to prepare and convince them his review was thorough and complete. Guardian would be a hard nut to crack, but Zane was confident. Confidence was the key.

A knock at his office door announced Ben's arrival. The door opened, and he stood there with his hands by his side looking like an adolescent home late with Dad's car.

"This party is just about over," Ben said as he sat in the chair across from Zane.

"Not yet. I've actually reached a conclusion," Zane said as he stood up and walked over to shut the door. As he walked back to his desk, he briefly pondered what it would be like not to shut the door but instead to keep walking and never look back. But Zanese and James kept him coming back.

"Tell me, Ben, what keeps you coming to work every day? Even with all your problems, you're here every day like clockwork. What drives you?"

"Family. By family, I mean my actual family and my employees. I have a responsibility to all of them. I've worked hard to build this business, and I just need to take something from it. My wife and children deserve that. I deserve that. I can't ride off into the sunset with nothing."

"I get it. Sometimes, at first blush, an option doesn't sound workable, either from a family, personal, or economic standpoint. I urge you to keep an open mind."

"I will. Just what kind of options are you talking about?" Ben said as he wrung his hands and moved in his chair, trying to find that elusive comfortable position.

"All options. Keep the end goal in mind. We'll take care of everything else. Relax."

"Okay. Just what are we talking about?"

"Well, looking at your finances, it's obvious your condition is dire. Your biggest issue is your debt to your supplier. This debt wouldn't be eliminated in bankruptcy. The agreements you signed with him would allow him to take over your whole business. We must deal with him first. Second, there are some serious deficiencies in your management staff. Tim, your CFO, is the biggest issue. Without having a sharp, knowledgeable CFO, no business can survive. Last, your business model is antiquated. Online sellers are eating you alive; your product is dated. You would need capital to create a viable web presence and design some new product. Capital you don't have."

Zane paused to let his analysis sink in. He leaned back and watched Ben squirm in his seat. These were well-rehearsed moves meant to maximize the impact of his words. The tension was rising. The key was waiting until the client couldn't stand the suspense.

"If you need my firstborn, who is also my CFO, not a problem. Take him. As you so succinctly stated, he's a horse's ass. No argument there," Ben replied.

"You get to keep him—as a son, not a CFO."

"Whatever."

"It appears you have very little life insurance. I could only find one policy."

"Yes, that's accurate. It is a $1 million policy. That doesn't seem little to me."

"When you have a business that was once worth over $20 million, it's insufficient. You should have enough life insurance to cover your business worth."

"Well, that problem is solved. I'd love to sell Guardian for a million. I should have sold when the business was worth twenty."

"Hindsight is always perfect."

"So true. Why bring up the life insurance?"

"I think you need more."

"Why?"

"Life insurance policies are assets. Marketable assets. They can bring you money."

"I'm not sure what you mean."

"Life insurance policies can be as good as cash."

"Yeah, over time."

"No, right now."

"Enlighten me," Ben said warily. He was now sitting upright in his chair. "How much money are you talking about?"

"Enough."

"Enough for what?"

"Your goals. Enough to meet all your goals and then some."

Ben got up and began to pace around the room. He stopped in the far corner and turned to face Zane.

"Who's going to write that much life insurance for me? I know that life insurance normally can't exceed the net worth of the insured."

Zane smiled at him and put his hands flat on the table. He looked directly in Ben's eyes.

"SAS can make that happen."

"Are you also a life insurance company?"

"No, we are a licensed agency, though. I can write and sell you a policy," Zane replied.

"So the life insurance is the real money?" Ben asked, staring intently at Zane.

Zane didn't reply. He seemed to be elsewhere, staring into space, deep in thought.

"Hello, Zane," Ben prompted. "The life insurance is the money behind the purchase?"

"Yes, yes," Zane replied haltingly. "They must be."

46

Caleb loved the walk to the cage. It put life in its proper perspective. Focusing on a dangerous task always obliterated every thought except one. *Why am I doing this?* There was great potential for bodily injury, possibly even permanent damage. Legal entanglements were another distinct possibility.

Caleb chose not to focus on the danger but instead on his one reason for doing this. He loved the challenge. Win or lose, he always came out a better man. He loved the adrenaline rush and the strategy of a good fight. It was like a chess match, except with blood. It made him feel alive.

He stepped into the cage and waited.

Then he heard it.

The door was locked.

No gloves, only bare hands.

His first opponent was a big, heavyset, strong-looking bar brawler. He had long hair that was tied back in a ponytail. His pupils were dilated, and he had a thousand-yard stare. Caleb wasn't concerned. Ponytail didn't need to feel pain; he just needed to be unconscious.

They were both announced like in a real UFC fight and told to come out fighting. There were no referees at this fight since there weren't any rules to enforce.

Ponytail thought the best defense was a good offense. Not

tonight. They traded jabs, swung in the air a bit, and tested each other for a minute or so. Ponytail was the aggressor and kept backing Caleb up. It was just like chess: think a couple of moves ahead, and lure your opponent into making the moves you wanted him to.

As Caleb was quickly backpedaling, he feigned slipping and losing his balance while leaning back and leaving his lower body exposed. Ponytail bought it like a Kmart special. He dived and went for Caleb's legs, looking for a double-leg takedown. Caleb simply regained his balance and brought up his knee, hard, right into the diving Ponytail's chin. There was a large crack as his chin split, and he was unconscious before he hit the mat. Blood was gushing from the split as new stains were added to the well-worn canvas. Caleb turned silently and calmly and walked to the cage door, waiting for it to be opened.

"Not yet," the announcer told him. "You pay, you play."

Since he had fought last and won, he would keep fighting until he lost or won two more matches. Caleb shrugged his shoulders and turned around to face his next opponent.

The next opponent was a slightly built guy. Caleb was always wary of his type. Usually they were deceptively fast and fought hard—the small-guy syndrome.

This guy was yelling about Caleb's mother and what he'd done to her last night. Caleb just smiled and kept his mouth shut. That usually pissed them off. It made them wonder what was wrong with Caleb. Caleb loved that edge. He lived by the adage that it's better to keep your mouth shut and be thought a fool than to open it and remove all doubt.

They stood face-to-face in the middle of the cage while they were announced. Caleb wished this guy knew how to keep his mouth shut. It smelled like he had eaten a shit cake for dessert before he entered the cage.

"If we're going to be this close during the fight, I need to introduce you to a breath mint. For real," Caleb said as they stared into each other's eyes.

He continued to spout obscenities about Caleb, his mom, and all his relatives as they went back to their corners. Caleb just continued to smile, which made Bad Breath call him a goofy idiot. Let him think that.

Bad Breath rushed him at the sound of the bell and then stopped right as he got to Caleb. At first, Caleb thought he might just be dumb enough to continue rushing him. That would have made this an incredibly short night for Bad Breath. Well, shorter, anyway.

As Bad Breath caught up to him in the middle of the cage, Caleb went into a defensive posture with his hands and forearms covering his face, and he crouched down. Bad Breath knew that was a bad position for Caleb and threw a side kick at his head. Caleb absorbed the kick on his forearms and fell on his back with his legs still in the air. Bad Breath took that opportunity to rear back his front leg and go for a kick to the manhood. That put Bad Breath on one leg for a brief second as Caleb snaked his right leg up and around that leg and expertly took him down, right into a knee bar. Bad Breath yelled, but that wouldn't do him any good. Caleb sunk it in hard. Caleb was looking for the tap. He waited a few more seconds. Bad Breath was doing a lot of screaming but wasn't tapping. *Shit.* Caleb looked over at the announcer, who just looked back and shrugged.

Caleb had nothing against orthopedic surgeons. He was sure they were good people and needed to make a living. They had families to feed, kids to send to college, and big houses to pay for. Why deny them a living?

He leaned back quickly and heard the tendons pop. Maybe just the ACL, but probably the MCL and possibly the LCL too. It would be an expensive surgery and a long rehab. Should have tapped.

Bad Breath lay there screaming with his knee bent at an impossible angle as Caleb walked away.

Caleb smiled over at Monique. She was clapping and whistling with two of her fingers in her mouth. You gotta love a girl who loves to see an ass kicking. Caleb smiled back and held up one finger. Two down and one to go.

His third opponent was of medium build and medium height. As he made his way to the cage, he grinned at Caleb. There wasn't an ounce of fear or concern on his face. Only eagerness. He had the look of a fighter and the scars to prove it.

The announcer whispered into Caleb's ear, "This dude knocked out his first two opponents within two minutes. Watch his hands. He was the unofficial bare-knuckle fighting champ of Ireland."

The luck of the shamrock. Good strikers and boxers can cause problems. Especially if they're quick.

The announcer brought them to the center of the cage and announced them. Knuckle just grinned at Caleb, who grinned back. It was contagious. Everybody was just one big happy family. Until the bell sounded.

Knuckle walked right in and started punching. Fast. It was all Caleb could do to keep his head and body away from his punches. Caleb bobbed and weaved and barely eluded the strikes. Knuckle kept coming and didn't seem to tire. Caleb tried to counterpunch, but he had to pick his spots so as not to leave himself exposed.

After one of Knuckle's jab-cross combinations, Caleb had his spot and threw a palm strike to his solar plexus, hoping to take his breath. Knuckle had seen it coming, turned slightly sideways to slip and parry Caleb's strike, and threw an elbow into Caleb's ribs. It lit Caleb up. He would feel that tomorrow. As he took the elbow, he maintained enough composure to throw a left hook to Knuckle's temple. It connected hard, and he staggered. They both moved beyond each other and regained their stance. Both were hurt. And grinning at each other.

This was going to be fun.

Caleb went after him, this time aggressively, trying to stay ahead of Knuckle's punches. He needed to work off the counter, but he was having problems breathing. He had to buy some time. He feinted to the head and caught Knuckle coming in with a hard side kick. Knuckle's body folded around the kick, but he maintained presence of mind to throw an uppercut that connected hard to Caleb's chin. The whole nighttime sky passed before his eyes as he laid out flat and landed hard on the canvas. The jolt from the canvas jarred him awake, and he kipped up to his feet. You could only stay down a few seconds or they called the fight. He'd been knocked out so many times he'd stopped counting, but not tonight.

They both took a few seconds to recover and get their poop in a group, and they went right back at it.

The crowd was going wild. Caleb caught a glimpse of Monique. She was chewing her nails, and she seemed worried. Not a particularly inspiring sight.

This wasn't going to be quick.

They were circling each other warily, probing with feints and halfhearted strikes. Then they would engage, hurt each other, and recover. This pattern continued. Strike, counterstrike, and counter the counter. The chess match went on without either side making a fatal mistake. They kept their kings and queens covered up well. At various times, they would get into a clinch, but they were so slippery with sweat and blood it was impossible to hurt each other. It did allow them to catch their breath. At the fifteen-minute mark, it was hard to tell who was the better fighter and who had the advantage. Fifteen minutes felt like sixty in a fight like this. Caleb was glad he'd eaten a light supper.

Knuckle was a worthy opponent, and Caleb respected that. Each time they would hurt each other, they would flash those silly grins, telling their opponent that all is good, I'm still standing. Come on and bring your best. They loved it. This was almost as much fun as another favorite activity of his that started with an *F*.

Caleb didn't want to, but he had to end it. He couldn't go on much longer. He was drenched with sweat and blood, and not all of it was his. His breathing was labored. He was running on pure adrenaline. He had to take the fight to the ground. Knuckle was a striker, and Caleb was confident his ground skills were minimal, at best. The problem was to get him to the ground. Caleb had tried several takedowns, but Knuckle had stuffed them all. He might not be a good ground fighter, but his takedown defense was world class. Caleb would have to set it up.

Caleb went in for a clinch and got it, but he took a hard hook to the temple in the process. It stunned him good, but he had his clinch. Caleb backed up his legs enough to allow some room between their lower bodies. It wasn't much room, but enough for Knuckle to get his right foot up on Caleb's waist. He then leaned back, put his other foot on Caleb's waist too, and fell down on his back, holding Caleb up in the air. The next move for Knuckle was to drop Caleb, catch an arm in the process, and get an arm bar. Fight over. Apparently, Knuckle did know some ground fighting. Hopefully just a little. Caleb used the momentum of Knuckle going to the ground and just kept going over Knuckle's head. Knuckle knew that move too, and he just backward somersaulted into a mount position on Caleb. Mount was a superior position. However, the momentum was still going, and Caleb used it to rise up from bottom mount, flip Knuckle off him, and end up in guard, which was between Knuckle's legs. Before Knuckle could catch his breath, Caleb passed guard to side control, grabbed an arm into an arm bar, and sunk it in hard. Knuckle didn't want to, but he wasn't stupid, so he tapped. Fight over. Checkmate.

After a few seconds, they both stood up, bruised and blood-ied. The crowd was going apeshit. Caleb lived for this. Knuckle looked at him out of his swollen, bloodied eyes and mumbled, "Good fight," from between his swollen, bloodied lips.

"Likewise," Caleb mumbled back.

They stood for a second, and the cage was unlocked. The announcer came in and announced Caleb the night's overall winner, taking the overall purse of $1,200. Not a lot, but enough. Enough for all the wannabe champions to keep coming back.

Caleb took his cash and walked out the victor, grabbing a dirty towel along the way. He found Monique standing at the edge of the crowd. Everybody was yelling at Caleb and slapping him on the back. This crowd knew they'd been part of a special evening. Fights don't get much more entertaining than that.

"We'd better make like seagulls and get the flock out of here," Caleb said.

"Why is that? Are you afraid of some retribution from some of your vanquished foes?" Monique responded.

"No, I just want to leave. The fun is over. Time to vacate the premises," Caleb said as he tried to towel off some of the blood and sweat. He pulled on his T-shirt and boots and turned to leave.

"Okay, but I think someone wants to talk to you," Monique said as she was pointing to two men walking up to Caleb. They were both wearing khakis and polo shirts that looked more yuppie than fight club.

"Hey, Caleb, are you back?" the first man yelled as he held out his hand.

"I never left," Caleb answered, keeping his hands at his side.

"Aren't you going to introduce me?" Monique asked Caleb.

"No, they were just leaving, and you don't want to know them, anyway."

"Aw, come on, Caleb. You know us. Let's go somewhere to talk over a drink or something. We can do each other a lot of good."

"I'm busy, and I have all the good I need," Caleb responded as he winked at Monique.

Caleb grabbed Monique by the shoulders and quickly began to walk her out.

"Don't be like that. We need your help!" the second man yelled after Caleb.

"What are they talking about? How do you know those guys?" Monique asked Caleb, trying to stop him from pushing her out the barn door.

"Just a couple of assholes."

"Somehow I get the feeling these guys aren't going away."

"Then we'll go away."

"To someplace with a shower, a cold drink, and hot food?"

"Of course."

"I know a place that has all of that."

"Let me guess—your place?"

"You have guessed right, and you have won tonight's prize."

"And what would that be?"

"Me."

47

Morality is relative to the circumstances. Nobody wants to admit that. Except when your circumstances are spiraling out of control and threatening your very existence. Then, if there's a way out that doesn't hurt anybody—at least anybody that matters—immorality becomes an option. You do what you have to do to survive.

Ben Guardian had a way out. He'd always known that there was a way; he just had to find it. The government had bailouts for other failures. A lot of those had been a direct result of fraud or at least gross mismanagement. Ben hadn't committed either of those sins. He'd worked hard, honestly, and always did the right thing, thinking it would pay off in the end. It hadn't. This was his bailout, and he was going to take it.

After meeting with Zane and hearing the complete plan, he told everybody he needed some time to think. He drove up to Taylors Falls. It was a beautiful drive on a beautiful day. The city is on the Saint Croix River, nestled among the bluffs. He'd gone out on the scenic overlook and was enjoying the view while contemplating sin and survival.

Ben reached for his phone and called his wife, Sue. She'd be home from the spa by now. Friday was beauty day. Lately, Ben had begun thinking of it more as spend-money-we-don't-have day.

She answered on the first ring. "What's up, Ben? Where

are you?"

"Just running some errands, but we need to talk. In fact, I want to talk to everybody. Family meeting in forty-five minutes. Can you get everybody there?" Ben asked.

"Tim is probably still at work, but I'll call Paula and Carol," Sue responded.

Ben knew everybody would be worried, but he wanted his daughters there too. This decision affected all of them.

"Yes, and please tell them it's very important."

"Geez, you're scaring me. What's going on, Ben?"

"Don't worry, everything is fine. At least it will be."

"That's not reassuring."

"Bye. Love you."

They met at the family estate for supper. It wasn't really an estate, but Ben liked to call it that. He'd always thought a jeweler should live on an estate. It was fifteen acres straight west of the Twin Cities off Highway 12. It bordered a small lake that was exclusive to their house. Long ago, fish had inhabited the lake, but several years of winterkill had dried up that recreational activity. Someone had named it Turtle Lake. Ben had never seen a turtle in or around the lake, so he was unsure how the name applied. It bore no resemblance to a turtle.

The Guardian house had five bedrooms, three levels, and three large porches bordering the lake. It had large overhangs and many windows. The house was an offbeat shade of green that seemed to complement the landscaping well. Upon entering, all their visitors were taken aback by the large, airy rooms. Both Ben and Sue were claustrophobic, and their house showed it. While it had been built in the 1970s, Ben and Sue had kept it up well, always undertaking some ambitious remodeling project on an annual basis. Lately, the remodeling projects had dried up along with the excess cash. Ben hadn't been quite honest with his wife about the reason, though.

He told her that he didn't have the energy to remodel anymore, which was a part of the truth.

Sue loved to have the kids come over. She also loved to entertain. Her weekly bridge parties were a highlight of her social circle. All of it cost money—money they didn't have. This family meeting was overdue. Ben knew that.

Tim arrived late and alone. Apparently, his kids had something going on, and his wife had to play taxicab. It was just as well. Only immediate family should hear this.

The girls were single, but both were in long-term relationships. Ben dreaded the day he'd be asked to escort them down the aisle. That would be an expensive walk.

Paula was a physical therapist, and Carol was an interior designer. He was financing Carol's fledging start-up furniture reconditioning business and loaning Paula's boyfriend money to get back into the finance world.

Everyone here tonight needed Ben and his money.

Sue had found enough time to bring in a catered dinner. It was absolutely delicious, yet Ben hated every bite. All he could think of was the cost and what Sue would think when he'd finally tell her that they couldn't afford these extravagances anymore.

The dinner dragged on. Nobody seemed to want to start this meeting, including Ben. Finally, he summoned up his courage and asked everybody to get a drink and retire to the great room. It wasn't going to be so great tonight.

"I know you're wondering why we're all here tonight. This is hard for me, and it won't be easy for you, either, but I have to go through with it and tell you," Ben said as he sat down on his favorite chair.

He took a quick drink of liquid courage, also known as scotch.

"Guardian Jewelry is going under. Under as in under, under. I can't compete with the Amazons and Walmarts of the world.

There's no way I can save the company." Ben paused for a split second, glancing at his rapt audience. Nobody said a word. Nobody even moved. Ben took a deep breath and sat back in his easy chair.

"Is this a joke? If so, this is one of your worst ever," Sue said.

"I would give anything, everything, to tell you this is one of my practical jokes. It isn't. Seeing all that your blood, sweat, and tears have earned you going down the drain will take the joke right out of you."

"How could this happen? Why didn't you say anything?" Sue asked.

"I should have told you, but I was too embarrassed. I didn't want to take away the life you were used to. You deserve better than this."

"I deserve to know the truth. I'm not just some wallflower wearing a negligee and waiting for you to come home every night and handing you a cocktail. We've worked through things before," Sue replied.

Paula just stood there gazing out the large window and sipping her wine. Carol, who was sitting on the love seat, leaned back and looked at Paula. Tim was looking at Ben, waiting for him to explain the solution.

This wasn't quite what Ben had expected. Other than Sue feeling left out, his family had shown more emotion when he told them the family car needed replacing. Denial apparently was a family trait.

"I don't know much about business, but I know if you're out of money, you're out of money. Liquidate and move on," Paula said as she turned to face the family and then walked over to the bar for a refill.

"I'm sure it's not quite that simple," Carol said, leaning forward and sipping her espresso, not looking at Paula.

"Tim may have found a way out that allows us to salvage

something," Ben said.

"Are you talking about Zane?" Tim asked.

"Yes, I am. Zane is a very interesting and creative man," Ben said.

Carol stood up, walked over, and sat down next to her father on the couch. "I'm here for you, Dad. Whatever you need, I'm willing to help."

"Oh, stop it," Paula said, leaning back against the bar. "If you really mean it, why don't you ask your lawyer boyfriend to pony up some investment cash? Except he won't even invest in your own crummy furniture start-up."

Silence greeted Paula's question as she took another swig. "Exactly."

"At least my boyfriend didn't declare bankruptcy trying to run an unlicensed check-cashing operation," Carol responded.

"Stop it, you two. I'm sure if we liquidate Guardian Jewelry, Ben will find another way to support us in the way we are accustomed to. Right, honey?" Sue said.

"I think that's what Dad is trying to tell you, if you would just stop your petty, hormonal bitching," Tim interjected as Paula stuck her tongue out at him.

"Liquidation isn't what I had in mind. And I'm too old to start a new business."

"You have an investor?" Tim asked, moving to the edge of his seat.

"Actually I do, sort of. It is not an investor in the traditional sense of the word. This investor would be buying the business in a very creative way. I'd be out—but out with money," Ben answered.

"Enough that we can keep living like this?" Sue asked.

"Yeah, spare us the details. 'As long as I can keep playing bridge and shopping at Saks, what difference does it make?'" Paula said, mimicking her mom.

"That's not my primary concern!" Sue almost shouted.

"Sure, I believe you. Just like I believe Dad that he can sell a business that has been run into the ground and come up with enough cash to support his greedy family," Paula stated.

"It's a unique solution, based on selling an asset that I didn't think had any value. And it's almost risk-free," Ben said.

"Who do we have to kill?" Tim asked while forcing a smile.

Ben drew a deep breath and looked at his family with an even gaze.

"Me."

48

Caleb came out of the shower feeling better. Monique had a cold beer waiting for him as they toasted his win. He took in her apartment while she returned to the kitchen to finish dinner.

She had pictures on the wall of herself and friends in various strenuous activities. They were all smiling in each picture and truly enjoying each other's company. While her apartment was small, it was comfortable. Stuffed with other mementos from her past, such as a wooden cowboy sculpture that added a southwestern motif and a quilt that appeared handmade from somebody in her past. All of the parts of her place were part of her. As he continued around the room, thoughts of domestic tranquility danced in his head. Could he be part of this someday? He needed to believe in something bigger than himself.

After they'd eaten a wonderful meal of beef fajitas, chips, and apricot salsa, exhaustion set in as they were sitting reasonably close on the couch. But Monique wouldn't leave it alone.

"Just tell me. We're enjoying a wonderful evening of postfight camaraderie. Regale me with your amazing training and fight stories. I won't tell anybody."

"Whatever. I think my second opponent found out fighting is more about doing than telling. But I already told you, I learned in the circus," Caleb stated as leaned back on the couch and took a huge drink of water. "Ice-cold water is the best drink on the planet."

"Uh-uh. What did you do in the circus?"

"Dirty, menial jobs like cleaning animal pens. I wasn't a performer of any kind. My mom and dad were, though. My mom was a trapeze artist, and my dad was the lion tamer. Seriously. It's the honest-to-God truth," Caleb said.

"I don't get it. How does that teach you to fight? Did you have to sleep with your dad's lions?"

"No, I slept in an Airstream travel trailer."

"With the pygmy act? And they would attack you all night?"

"Think about it."

"I'm thinking about it, but you're not telling me anything."

"My mom and dad were circus performers. We'd stay in each location for maybe one or two months, tops. New schools three times a year, no friends, and no siblings. Only child. My nickname was Monkey Boy. Now do you get it?"

"A lot of fights growing up, I guess."

"That's an incredible understatement. From the time I was old enough to swing my fists, I had a couple of fights every single week. First with kids, and then as I got older, with teens and adults who really wanted to hurt me. Bad. You learn what works and what doesn't the hard way. I had to fight to stay alive, literally. I did have help from some of the circus performers. Some of the trapeze artists were badasses, believe it or not. And the strongman also helped. Seriously."

"Wow. I guess that would make you good. Nothing teaches like experience. You sure don't look too beat up, so you must have won your share."

"I did, but I think I learned more from the ones I lost. I don't mean to brag, but when I left every one of those schools, they knew not to screw with me. The problem was, I had to teach the next school that same lesson all over again."

"Some lessons are learned hard," Monique said as she moved

closer to Caleb. "Maybe you could show me a few moves?"

Caleb could smell Monique as her arm touched his. It was a mixture of sun and something else—kind of earthy and very erotic.

He wanted to stay and see where the night led, but his body wouldn't let him. Monique said she understood. He really hoped she did, because he liked her. More than any woman he'd ever met.

Later, as Caleb lay in his own bed alone, willing the last bit of adrenaline to leave his body, he wanted to forget he even knew the men who'd approached him after the barn fight. It always ended violently whenever he listened to them.

But he needed money. Those two men knew the $1,200 he made from the fight wouldn't last long. He told himself he'd do just one more job. He knew where to draw the line. Except his skills always made them come back asking for more. And the line moved a little bit further.

Caleb first drew the line a long time ago, on a hot, humid night in Savannah, Georgia.

His mom had given him ten dollars, told him to take the night off to go see a movie or something. He relished those moments. Anything to get away from picking up elephant and tiger shit all night. He longed to do what other fourteen-year-olds did.

They'd been in Savannah about a month, and school had started two weeks ago. As usual, he hadn't made friends. The kids stayed away from him. He smelled different, which meant they couldn't miss that he was with the circus. He felt different, even abnormal, compared to his classmates. Sometimes he didn't even feel human.

So Caleb went to the movies alone. He didn't mind going alone; he did most things alone. Since they moved every couple of months, even if he did find friends, it was too hard to say good-bye. He was a loner and loved it.

The movie was a sappy love story, not really what he liked. But he imagined himself being the object of someone's love. He didn't know what that would be like, but it was fun to put himself in the leading man's shoes. Maybe someday a beautiful woman would love him.

He was still daydreaming when he left the theater. It was a two-mile walk to the tents of the circus. Caleb loved to walk. It gave him time to think. About a different life. About not being in the circus.

His thoughts were rudely interrupted. Someone was yelling at him.

"Hey, Monkey Boy! Come talk to us! We wanna hear about life under the big top!"

Caleb stopped and turned around to find the source of these words. Four boys, all older and bigger than he was, were standing on the sidewalk. It was a dark and desolate part of town. Caleb liked walking in those areas to avoid people. It hadn't worked tonight.

A kid named Raney was the leader of the foursome. He was always giving out shit, usually to kids smaller than he was. Everybody took it and gave little of it back. He was bigger than most, and that explained his victims' lack of response.

"Go home, leave me alone, and maybe someday I'll put on a show at school about the circus," Caleb responded.

"Show-and-tell? What the fuck. You think we're in kindergarten or something? Hey, Bill, he thinks we're in kindergarten."

Caleb knew the other kids. They were Raney's posse, Bill, Ted, and Smokey. Smokey got his nickname from trying to set the school on fire—more than once. Caleb guessed he was IQ challenged.

The four of them moved in closer. Caleb backed up slightly.

"He is in kindergarten. Or he'll wish he was after tonight," Bill responded.

"Good comeback, Bill," Caleb responded.

He didn't mean to taunt them, but it was too easy. Experience had taught him that no matter how hard he tried to avoid it, this scene would end the same as it had in many other towns like this one. Might as well get it over with.

"Don't be a smart-ass. Caleb? Is that your name? That sounds like a circus name," Raney said as took the lead and stared at Caleb.

"Actually, it is biblical, but you wouldn't know that since you can't read."

"Watch it, Monkey Boy. There are four of us and one of you," Smokey said, looking around for any witnesses. There were none.

"You have math skills too. I'm impressed," Caleb responded.

"Fucking A, you are a wiseass. This is going to be fun. Hey, Caleb, did your mom give you that name? It kind of sounds like something a bearded lady would do," Smokey said.

They needed more original material.

"My mom did give me my name. And I'm very proud that she's a trapeze artist, which takes more guts than any of you will ever have. She shits turds that have more character than the four of you."

Now it was on. He didn't care. He just wanted to do this and move on. He still had work to do at home. Life in the circus was busy, 24-7.

"You're a fucking turd. A little brown turd. Turds need to be flushed away and never seen again. Don't you agree, Smokey?" Raney asked, flexing his biceps and closing and opening his fists.

"You're damn right. Flush this fucker. For good. I don't even like the circus," Smokey responded.

They were making a circle around Caleb, getting closer, and he knew he had to respond quickly. The time for talking was over. If he waited for them to make the first move, it would be too late. He'd learned that the lesson the hard way.

Experience had taught him to take out the biggest, meanest

one first. And usually that was the one with the mouth. It was best to take him out violently, with a lot of blood. Sometimes that would scare off the rest of the group. Caleb wasn't sure with this crowd. They seemed intent on a beating.

Caleb faced Raney and rushed him at a full sprint. Raney stood there with a look of shock on his face and threw his hands up to protect his head. That's exactly what Caleb wanted. A virtual plethora of targets now opened up. Neck, chest, groin, knees, and feet. Which one was it going to be tonight?

Caleb chose chest. He wanted this to end quickly. He came in hard and threw a palm strike to the solar plexus, and Raney bent over gasping for air as his wind went along with his courage. Caleb brought up his right knee to the bent-over Raney, smashing it into his face, obliterating the little nub of a nose he had. As Raney fell to the ground, he rolled over, and Caleb had his bloody spectacle. The middle of his face resembled a bloody fountain. Caleb stepped behind Raney's prone body to use it as a barrier to more attacks.

It was obvious that it wasn't going to deter his other attackers. Bill came in hard with an overhand right, but he had to maneuver around Raney. This gave Caleb the time he needed to leap across Raney, block the right, and bring the same arm around, landing a vicious elbow to Bill's jaw. Caleb could hear the crack as it broke. The skin also opened up in a deep cut, and blood poured out profusely. Bill was in deep REM mode as he piled onto Raney. Caleb now had a two-body barrier.

That didn't stop Ted. He came in hot and furious. Caleb thought Ted was a brick short of a full load. He was coming in with head down and arms stretched out, leaping across the two prone bodies. Was it wrong if it was too easy? Oh well, they'd brought it on themselves.

Caleb simply moved to the side, letting Ted fly by, landing a vicious side kick to his groin as it flew by. Ted collapsed behind

Raney and Bill, adding to the mass of prone humanity. Caleb walked up to him, bent over, and hit him hard in the mouth a couple of times. Ted's head rolled to the side as he spit blood and a couple of teeth out.

That left Smokey. It was better to take a beating than to run. Running was for pussies, and Smokey never wanted to be called a pussy.

Smokey stood there looking at Caleb. Caleb stared back. He wasn't even breathing hard. He'd been in this situation many times. He couldn't let Smokey just leave. He had to hurt Smokey visibly. He had to send a message to the rest of the school to leave him alone. They wouldn't, but at least it was a warning.

"We could have a staring contest. Whoever blinks first has to hit themselves in the mouth. Does that sound like a winner?" Caleb asked.

Smokey didn't respond. He stood there with his fists clenched at his side. And then the unthinkable happened.

Smokey began to cry. Not in a desperate way, but nonetheless, huge wet drops were rolling down his cheeks. Caleb had never seen that before.

"Come on, dude. Not that. If you pick on people, you'd better be able to take it too. None of this crybaby shit."

Still no response from Smokey.

Oh well. Caleb needed to get home.

He stepped over the bodies and up to Smokey and swept his legs from under him. Smokey landed on his ass, hard. He wasn't hurt. Caleb landed with his knee on Smokey's sternum—not hard, as most of his weight was on his other foot. He grabbed Smokey's arm and began an arm bar. He was going to break the arm at the elbow. Walking around school with a cast would be a good deterrent.

Then he looked in Smokey's eyes. He had a look that Caleb

had not seen before. It wasn't fear, it wasn't pain; it was something else. It was a plea for mercy. His eyes were asking Caleb to spare him this misery. Caleb would never forget that look. It would change his life.

Something turned deep within Caleb. He had the power to show mercy and grace to somebody that had meant him harm. He was at a crossroads. One path would lead to a part of him dying. The other path would lead to survival and life. Self-defense was one thing, but purposely hurting another to send a message was something else entirely. Caleb's conscience was young and tender, and he strived to keep it that way.

Caleb stood up. He extended a hand to Smokey to help him up. Smokey took it warily and rose to his feet. He sniffled and wiped his nose with his arm.

"What does this mean? You're not going to hurt me? Is this some kind of trick?"

"No trick. There is a lesson to be learned here, and it's better to learn it now than later."

"Lesson? I don't understand," Smokey sniffled his response.

Caleb came up to him and threw his arm around his neck in a mock bear hug. He looked Smokey in the eye.

"Don't be a bully, don't be a smart-ass, and be nice. That will come back to you in many ways," Caleb said as he tightened his hug a bit. "And remember, what happened to your former buddies here tonight can still happen to you. I will be watching you."

There were times to show mercy, but never a time to be stupid. And, even as a kid, Caleb was anything but stupid.

49

To my dear family:

You've probably guessed this is my suicide note. This note and my dead body probably gave it away. I could say how much I've hurt people. I could say how depressed I was and that I couldn't go on. I could say I was tired, that I was just done with it all. While all of that's true, who really gives a shit? That's my final point. Everybody is better off without me. Don't feel sorry for me. That won't help me, and it's a waste of time.

Zanese and James, I love you. That might be hard for you to believe given my recent actions. But I can't be near you. That will only put you in danger. I killed your mother, and now I have to be wise and protect you. Betty is a good woman. Please listen to her. Your grandmother is a little crazy, but she knows a lot.

You'll hear bad things about me as you get older. I recently read a quote by Maya Angelou that said, "If I'd known better I'd have done better." That's the reason I did what I did. It isn't an excuse, but it is a reason.

I know this is a terrible day for you. It will fade from your memory. Time will help to heal this wound. I promise that.

Please take care of each other. You're all that's left of our small family. Always stay together.

I love you.

I never meant to hurt you, or to lie.

Good-bye.

Zane

He put the pen down and laid it on top of the note on the kitchen table. He threw away the several crumpled notes he'd started but couldn't finish.

It was strange to think about being neat when soon parts of his brain would be splattered around the room.

Zane was watching the raindrops hit and run down the window in the back door to his kitchen. His shitty window in his shitty little apartment. The day was bleak. His soul was vacant. He fingered the little key he had on a chain around his neck. It was the key to his tortured past. Always there but never forgotten.

He knew there was a better life out there somewhere. Just not for him. It would never be for him. His fate had always been this. He'd known that from the moment he was old enough to know things like this. People had been put in his life to tell him differently, but they were always taken away. Like Tina. He would stop the cycle today.

The driving force behind ending it all today had been an article in the paper that morning. It was about Billy Hot, the acquisition client who had preceded Ben Guardian. Billy Hot had owned a chain of boutique fitness centers called Hot and Fit. Too much debt, combined with Billy's propensity for late-night parties, had doomed them to a solution from SAS.

The article described how Billy Hot had died yesterday in a car accident on a remote stretch of Highway 169 north of the Twin Cities. Apparently, his airbag had deployed, inadvertently causing Billy to lose control of the car, go through a guardrail, and plunge one hundred feet to his death. Reading about his death didn't surprise Zane—that had been part of the plan. However, Billy had a passenger in the car, his cousin from out of town. He was dead too. Zane knew they could and would fake the principal's death as part of the plan, but not an innocent party. That could only mean one thing.

The deaths were real.

Zane was as guilty of murder as if he had been the one tampering with the airbag.

He'd bought a gun, a stolen .38-caliber revolver, from a guy he trained with at the dojo. It was old, but he was told it worked fine. It was unmarked and untraceable. As if Zane cared.

He had no options. Zanese and James had kept this choice off the table until now. But now he was sure they'd be raised better and happier without him. He had nobody, and nobody cared. Least of all him.

He picked up the gun from the kitchen table. He opened it and checked all cylinders. Six bullets. He needed one. Maybe he should do it the Russian way. Nah, that would take too long—and this was one thing he didn't want to leave to chance.

Suck on the barrel. Eat your gun. He'd heard those words somewhere in a movie.

He put the gun in his mouth. He tasted gun oil.

That couldn't be good for you.

Zane looked up to the ceiling. He thought about what a mess would be left of him. Blood and bits of brain all over. Maybe he should get a plastic sheet. God, what was wrong with him? He'd be dead! The mess would be someone else's problem. His finger tightened on the trigger. Hello, eternity.

Pink Floyd's song "Money" began playing somewhere in his mind. The pursuit of money was mocking him as he ended his life. Then he remembered—it was the ringtone on his phone.

Bad timing. He looked at the screen and saw it was Tec. He

knew he had to answer that call. He couldn't go into eternity with the phone ringing. Especially a call from Tec. He took his finger off the trigger and slammed the gun down on the table. He picked up the phone.

"What."

"We need to talk."

"Why?"

"Unfinished business. I'm in your parking lot and on my way up," Tec said as he clicked off.

Zane set his phone down and looked at the gun in his hand. This was going to have to be quick. *I guess Tec will get to find my bloody surprise.*

He put the gun back in his mouth, and his finger tightened on the trigger. Hello again, eternity. Zane closed his eyes.

Then his kitchen door burst open.

Zane opened his eyes and looked at Tec standing in the doorway.

He had enough bullets.

He took the gun out of his mouth and pointed it, center mass, at Tec.

"Fuck you, old friend," Zane said as he pulled the trigger.

Nothing but an empty click.

Tec stood there calmly with a look of exhausted sadness.

Zane pulled the trigger again and again and again.

Nothing but empty clicks.

Zane stood up and hurled the gun at Tec's face.

Tec caught it deftly by the barrel and set it down on the counter next to him.

"Now that we got that out of the way, let's talk."

50

Ann and Doug Torres had been customers of Guardian Jewelry for more than twenty years. They owned a chain of funeral homes in the Twin Cities and were doing well. People died on a regular basis. They were in a recession-resistant business. They came in every year before their wedding anniversary and bought an expensive piece of jewelry for Ann. They'd only shop at Guardian, and they'd only deal with Ben. They trusted him to give them the best quality and a great deal. Ben looked forward to their yearly visits. It was exciting to see the love between them and the way Doug Torres expressed it in jewelry. Ben would miss them.

Today, Ben was working at what had been his first retail location in Wayzata, an upper-class suburb of Minneapolis. His store matched the neighborhood. The display cases were marble and glass, the floors a black antique tile polished so well that you could see a reflection of the future in them. Lake Minnetonka twinkled through the front window like a large jewel that had been cut with meticulous care.

He wanted to do this last sale before getting out. No one better than the Torreses to give him one last piece of satisfaction for all his hard work over the years.

"What are you thinking, Doug? A ring? A necklace? Or maybe a bracelet? I have some new tennis bracelets—exquisite. I think you'll love them," Ben said.

"That sounds good, but I think this is the year for a new necklace. I've seen some designs in your window that looked so Ann. Can I look at those?"

At that moment, Tim came into the showroom from the back. He stared at Ben without moving.

"Hey, Dad, can you come back with me for a moment?"

"Sure. Doug, may I have Emily show them to you? I need to take care of something."

"Sure, as long as you come back. We need your judgment. I hope the day never comes when we lose that."

Ben smiled as he turned back toward Tim. This wasn't becoming any easier.

"Okay, Tim, what's going on?" Ben asked as they both walked into the back room.

"I need to talk to you about the family meeting," Tim said.

"Now? I'm kind of busy."

"Sorry, but this can't wait."

"Okay, what's on your mind?" Ben asked as he looked up at the ceiling and crossed his arms over his chest.

"What did you think of the meeting with the three witches, or should I say bitches?" Tim asked.

Ben smiled and leaned back against the jewelry repair counter. Tim never did get along with his sisters, and his relationship with his mom provided most of the ammunition for his weekly therapy showdowns with Ben and the family couch doctor. "They all have different agendas. That happens sometimes, especially with women. I'm still going forward with the plan."

"I was thinking—"

"Now, now, we talked about that. Let me do the thinking," Ben said, still smiling at Tim.

"Dad, really."

"Okay, what's your big new plan?" Ben asked while sighing

and beginning to rub his temples.

"What's going to happen to me? You sell the business, and I don't have a job anymore," Tim said while walking up to Ben and putting his empty hands out in a futile gesture. "What is your plan for me? You'll have enough money to keep supporting them, but what about me?"

Ben sighed again and crossed his arms over his chest. "The time has come, Tim, for you to figure out your own place in this world. You're an adult. You'll have to start acting like one."

"So you're going to continue to support Mom and the girls, but not me?"

"Of course, Mom. But I never said anything about the girls."

"Well, then, what good is this plan if we can't go on living like we are now?"

Ben pushed himself off the counter and walked around Tim to the door. He stopped and looked back at Tim. "Okay, I'll figure out how all of you can go on living exactly as you are now. Don't worry about me; death will be my reward." He turned and walked out of the back room without looking at Tim.

Tim was smiling, relieved.

Life was good.

51

Tec slowly walked over to the kitchen sink, grabbed a glass, and filled it with water, deliberately keeping his back to Zane. Slowly, he turned around and leaned back against the counter, crossed his legs, and looked at the brown water. "I didn't know you were a firearms type of guy."

"I didn't know you were a traitor."

"I hope you kept the receipt."

Tec threw the brown water into the sink and set the glass down, walked over to the table, and sat down across from Zane. "Suicide note?" he said, nodding at the note on the table.

"I'm sure one more death means nothing to you," Zane responded, keeping his hands on his lap and secretly wishing he had some other weapon.

"If I lived in a shithole like this, I might contemplate killing myself too. For someone who steals people's money, you sure don't have much to show for it."

"Some things are more important than money."

Tec laughed. "That sounds weird coming from you. Your whole life was about money. Any way you could get it."

"You know nothing about my life and nothing about me," Zane said while pushing his chair back slightly, thinking of Billy Hot and how much he'd loved his wife and kids.

"Then tell me."

"It's a little late for that. Your judgment has already passed. Especially for Tina."

At the mention of her name, Tec winced. Zane knew that was the chink in his armor.

"We don't judge, at least in this life. I've never judged you, and you shouldn't judge me. But you should listen."

"Come on, Tec, we both know you killed Tina. You didn't pull the trigger, but you might as well have. She'd be alive today if it wasn't for you taking her and the kids for those assholes," Zane said as he pounded home each word like a nail into Tec's cross.

Tec looked down for a second and then at the rain out the front window. "Yes, I need to own some of that. But we also know she wouldn't have been kidnapped if you hadn't been messing with people's lives. It's not all on me. Who knows where it all started?"

Zane stood quickly, knocking his chair to the floor in the process. He leaned over the table, resting his palms in the middle. "Yes, we're both to blame," Zane growled, watching for the slightest movement on Tec's part.

Tec stared up at Zane but made no move to defend himself as he kept both hands flat on the table. "There is a reason I did it. You may not care, but you should."

"You want me to care, don't you?" Zane asked as he backed up and leaned against the wall.

"Would make this whole thing a bit easier."

"I'll play. What's the fucking reason?"

Tec ran his fingers through his long hair and put his hands in his lap. "Several years ago, I did something bad—criminal, batshit-crazy bad—in a foreign country. Something I'll have to live with for the rest of my life. The people who made me take your family know about it and can use it against me. They can take something valuable away from me. And rather than deal with that, I decided that what I had to lose was more important than what you had to lose."

"So it's all about you. The rest of us are just mere tokens in your game."

"Sometimes it is bigger than us, Zane. Bystanders can get hurt when the stakes are high."

"They're never that high."

"Try telling that to the three thousand people killed on 9/11. They all had families too."

"So now I'm a terrorist?" Zane asked incredulously.

"I don't know what you are," Tec replied carefully. "You and I both know you haven't given me the complete story."

Zane looked down at his shoes and then at a point somewhere beyond Tec. "That choice is not up to me."

Tec stood up and moved around the table. "You have every right to hate me for my decision. But that doesn't do either of us any good."

"Maybe not, but it makes me feel better. If I'm going to go on, I need that hate. Without it, I don't have a reason to live."

"You have two reasons to live—Zanese and James. Can't find better reasons than that," Tec said, forcing a smile. "Trust me, I know."

"I need hate too. And you are the best bastard to hate," Zane spit out while moving up off the wall and taking two steps toward Tec with his hands forced into fists at his side. Zane began to rock slightly, trying to maintain his composure.

"No, I'm not," Tec answered, moving back a step. "You should be hating the people behind this. I know how hate enables."

Zane quickly turned around and walked to a small table in the corner. On it was a picture of Zanese and James, jumping off the dock at their Deephaven home. James wore a pair of black-and-white checkerboard shorts, and Zanese had a white one-piece bathing suit contrasting nicely against her summer tan. He picked up the picture and stared at it for a moment. He remembered them screaming with joy as they were about to hit the water. Tina had taken the picture. "So what do we do with all this hate?" Zane asked as he the picture back on the table, facedown.

Tec walked over as Zane turned around. Tec stood directly in front of him and put his hands on his shoulders.

"We fuck them up. You and me, together. We fuck them up."

For the first time since Tina had died, a small smile formed on Zane's lips.

52

Flameburger is always busy at 2:00 a.m. The bars are closed by then, and people need to refuel after a hard night of drinking. Caleb didn't occupy the bars late at night, but he loved the Flame. They had the best burgers and breakfasts in town, and their hash browns were legendary. The only drawback was its location in Columbia Heights, which was just above the Minneapolis neighborhood called Northeast. It wasn't the best part of town, but he didn't sweat it. Most people left him alone. And if they didn't, that was their problem.

The Flame was designed like an old-fashioned diner with a counter and chrome stools that spun. There were fountain drinks behind the counter, and all the employees wore little white hats that reminded Caleb of Gomer Pyle's marine hat. Booths lined the outside walls of the diner with large windows that gave the diners a panoramic view of the neighborhood.

In one of the booths, Caleb was waiting for the guys who had stopped him after the fight. He had thought that this part of his life was over, but apparently not. They'd told him they needed his help, and he was hooked. Caleb took the bait because he could use their money.

They were late. They always were. They thought that gave them control. Caleb thought it made them idiots.

He was finished with his meal and into his second cup of

coffee when they finally walked through the door. Their dark business suits were out of place, but at least they weren't wearing ties. One of them was short and bald, and one was tall with black hair slicked back with some type of emollient. The short one was skinny, and the tall one had never met a doughnut he didn't like.

"I was about to leave, but then I remembered you guys operate on congressional time, which means everything you do is late."

"We're busy. We have more of a life than just beating people," Baldy said as he slid into the booth across from him.

"Yeah, and what kind of place is this? There are nice restaurants in nice neighborhoods in this city," Slick piped in.

"I thought you could use the opportunity to meet some of your boss's constituents. You know, mingle with your subjects," Caleb said.

"You need to turn off the smart-ass persona for just a bit and listen to us," Baldy said.

"That's why I'm here. But I'm glad I'm done eating, because bullshit and food usually don't mix. But hey, you guys should go ahead and eat."

"Food poisoning isn't healthy," Baldy replied.

"The food is very good. They might even have clean plates."

The waitress arrived and asked if his friends wanted anything.

"They're not my friends, but sure, give them each a double burger with everything on it and hash browns. That will loosen them up a bit."

"They look like they need a little loosening up. Relax, boys; just sit back and enjoy. No more FiberCon for you," the waitress replied as she wrote down their order and sauntered away.

"My treat, guys. It is the least I can do for all the tough jobs you've given me."

"Tough jobs that you've been paid for very well," Slick said.

"That's true. Money motivates me, gets my adrenaline

pumping just like a good fight. So what mess did our congress-man get in? What do you have for me this time? Has to be some-thing nobody else would do. So whose fingers do you want broken? Whose head do you want busted?" Caleb said while taking a sip of coffee and putting one knee up on the booth and one elbow on the back of the booth, resigned to accept no matter what their answer was.

"Relax. We're not sure what this is. Right now, it's just an investigation. A constituent has asked the congressman to look into something. He was very impressed with your last investiga-tion," Baldy said.

"Let's be honest here; he was more impressed with how I elim-inated the evidence uncovered in my investigation. Why can't you get your other people to investigate this?"

"In the end, this situation may require someone with your special skills. We don't know yet. For now, we just want you to look into it."

"What is it?" Caleb asked while looking out the window, wondering if it would ever end. Or, to be more precise, if he even wanted it to end.

Slick slid a file across the table. "He received a phone call from a female constituent about a local business here in the Twin Cities that appears to be doing something not really kosher. She didn't say what exactly, but it sounded illegal enough for him to want to investigate."

"Businesses don't always follow the rules. You don't, either. Define what you mean by illegal," Caleb responded.

"It is a merger and acquisition firm called SAS, short for Stra-tegic Acquisition Services. The constituent who called said their methods of acquiring businesses appear to be illegal. When the congressman did some probing, he found out that Treasury is looking at them too. And possibly somebody else. He isn't clear on that," Baldy said.

"So just talk to Treasury and see what they know. Piggyback on their investigation," Caleb said as he leaned back and spread his arms on the back of his seat.

"He tried that, but Treasury told him to buzz off. They claimed they had it under control and would report back to him if and when they had something to report. They made it clear they didn't want any public scrutiny," Slick joined in.

"That makes sense. The public eye can be very perceptive. Of course, the Treasury guys don't want that," Caleb said.

"Yeah, except for one thing."

At that moment, their food arrived. The waitress slid two huge burgers and two huge plates of hash browns across the table.

"Here you go. Your life and bowels will never be the same."

"Thank you, ma'am. We may need a doggie bag for some of this," Baldy said.

"No doggie bags. There are kids starving all over the fucking place. The bathroom is in the back if you need to make room for more," the waitress said.

"Wow, this is a classy place, Caleb," Baldy said while using his fork to pick at the hash browns.

"Yeah, I bring all my asshole friends here."

"I'll leave you guys to it. If you need anything, just pretend you don't, because I'm going on break. And even if I wasn't, I don't really like your two friends," the waitress said to Caleb as she flipped her hair and walked right out the front door.

"I hope she didn't spit in our food," Slick said.

"Nah, she probably wouldn't do that. And even if she did, she's probably had all of her shots. Anyway, you were about to tell me the one big thing—why your boss thought he couldn't use Treasury's investigation?"

"Right. He didn't really trust what they were telling him,"

Baldy said.

"What, he didn't trust something the government was telling him? However could that be?" Caleb said.

"It wasn't something they told him. It was something they didn't tell him."

"And?"

"They didn't tell him they have a man on the inside, undercover."

"How come your boss knows that they do?"

"The lady who called told him."

"Does this lady have a name?" Caleb asked while leaning forward across the table.

"I believe he said her name was Betty."

53

Whenever Tec thought of her, he smiled. And then he would think of where she was now. And he'd stop smiling.

His mother was in a little nursing home in a northern Minnesota resort town called Fergus Falls.

He visited her as often as he could, but never enough to assuage his conscience.

Today's visit didn't serve that purpose, either.

He walked down the shiny, white-tiled corridor wondering how or if he would find her. Maybe this time her bed would be empty, and they'd be cleaning the room for another venerable soon-to-be resident. With all the death he'd seen and caused, hers was the one he feared the most. He held his breath as he turned the corner, but she was still with him.

Her mind was sharp, but her body was not. Ravaged by years of smoking and hard drinking, he hardly recognized her.

Her name, Willow, suited her well on this day.

One part of him wanted her to die so she'd be relieved of her tenuous hold on this world. The other part of him needed her. She was the only person who understood his conflict—not so much between right and wrong or good and bad but about what he should bring to the people around him. Should he bring them truth, in all its ferocity and stark certainty? Should he tell them who he was and what he was tasked to do? Truth: the whole is corrupt because it's made up of bent individual parts, but it must be protected. No matter who gets hurt.

Or should he take the other approach? Lie: even if we're treacherous at heart, we can harness a measure of our evil, protect each other, and by doing so bring honor to our world.

Some days, the struggle overwhelmed him.

That's when he needed her. She knew the demons within him. She knew that if he didn't let them out, they'd kill him—and possibly not spare those next to him, either.

He spoke to her quietly, fearing that if he raised his voice, she would simply shatter and the pieces would evaporate.

"I have a gift," he said softly, fearing he had caught her sleeping because her eyes were closed.

She briefly opened them, recognized him, and smiled with all the energy she possessed on this, her last stop in this world.

"The only gift I've ever needed is standing right in front of me," she replied in a raspy voice, betraying a past filled with too many Camel Lights and shots of Southern Comfort.

Tec flinched as he reached behind his back and set a bag of chocolate-covered pretzels on her nightstand. "Well, these will give you much more lasting satisfaction than one of my visits."

She looked at the bag and then at him with watery eyes. "Don't do that, Tec. I appreciate anything you bring me, but don't ever put yourself down. At least not in front of me. Remember, I know the truth."

Tec walked to her window, which looked out on the nursing home's front yard. Three elderly people were sitting in wheelchairs next to family members on a regular visit. Guilt washed over him for not being like one of those pious souls.

"How have you been?" Tec asked as he turned around and took a seat next to her bed.

"They tell me good, but I suppose you pay them to say that. I know I don't have long."

Tec did pay for her stay here, but not for them to tell her lies. "None of us know how long we have. You're the one who always told me that."

"That was to guide you to not place too much importance on this world but to prepare for the next."

"'Enjoy each day you have; when they're gone, they never return,'" he replied, quoting another of her sayings.

She smiled and reached for his hand. "I can tell you're troubled today. More than usual. Please tell me why."

Tec withdrew his hand, crossed his legs, and put both hands on top of the chair's armrests.

"I'm being asked to complete a task for different sides of the same coin. I'm in the middle, and I don't know which way to turn. Either way, people will get hurt, possibly innocent people."

"Is there one thing you do know?" she asked him, reaching for the bag of pretzels.

"I know that a close friend of mine has done something terribly wrong and he needs to be stopped."

"And?"

"I've been told that not stopping him and his plot could have wide-ranging implications." Tec sighed. "A lot of people could get hurt."

"How do you know this about this friend of yours?"

"He admitted part of it to me, and the rest I surmised on my own."

Willow raised her bed slightly and set the bag of pretzels down. "Can you please open my closet?" she asked Tec. "And close the hallway door?"

He did, knowing where this was going.

"Please reach into my snow boots in the corner and bring whatever you find over here."

Tec knew what it was, but he'd long ago given up trying to do anything about it. He took the bottle from her boot and brought it to his mom. She took it daintily and then opened it and took a long swig. He put it back and closed the closet door, half expecting her to be dancing around the room when he turned back toward her.

But she was still lying in bed, albeit with a growing smile on her face.

"And does this man trust you, the one who did wrong?"

"We had a falling out, but we've formed an uneasy alliance."

"Falling out?"

"I killed someone dear to him. Didn't actually pull the trigger, but might as well have."

"Alliance?"

"We have a mutual goal that will take our combined forces to accomplish. It's dangerous. We've put aside our differences for the time being."

"But you're still hedging your bets. Not sure which is the winning team?" she asked, resting her head back against the pillow.

"I'm positive he's doing the same thing."

"Winning or losing?"

"This is more about saving. What we all have," Tec responded, sitting down once more on the edge of her bed.

"Is this friend of yours selfish?"

"That's what I can't figure out. He's been doing some evil deeds, but maybe there's something I don't know. Who does he really work for? Is he just doing it so he can expose them later? Or does he just want to end up the top dog?"

"You're afraid. If you work to expose the truth, you might hurt him. If you believe in him, your friend, and help him, you might be complicit in the plot you're working to expose."

"That's about it, Mom. And on top of all of that, my friend has innocent people at stake, and I do too. It is not just our own lives we're fucking with."

"Please do not swear around me," she forcefully reprimanded him. "I'm your mom."

Tec nodded, mad at himself for forgetting that rule.

"Do you still have a minute?" she asked, knowing what his answer would be.

"Of course, but I wish this visit could be more about you."

"Any visit where you need my opinion is all about me. That means more to me than you'll ever know."

Tec smiled and waited. He knew he was about to hear a story. Like so many he'd heard before. But they'd always shown him the way.

The way to let his demons coexist.

At least for another day.

54

It was a little hole in the wall called the Trough, located in a former well-to-do strip mall a couple of blocks from his apartment. It was small and dark, not exactly the kind of place you recommended to your friends. It was for professional drinkers. For people who wanted to forget. Or maybe remember. Remember how good life used to be. The blues were playing and that, combined with scotch, had drowned many a sorrow. Zane stopped in, hoping it would work for him.

His drink was on the bar before him, untouched. He stared at the liquid as if just looking at it would help.

Zane didn't know what to think of Tec's offer of help. Working with Tec could provide the assistance he needed to follow the SAS money trail. On the other hand, he had understandable trouble trusting Tec.

He got up, paid his tab, and just stood there for a second as if suspended in time. He turned away, turned back, grabbed the scotch, and swallowed it in one gulp. He slammed the glass on the bar and walked away. He didn't look back. He drove home and went to bed immediately.

For the first time in over a year, he slept a deep, sound sleep. He didn't wake up once. He didn't dream. As he'd dozed off, though, he'd reveled in fond memories of the time spent with his children.

Zane got up at five the next morning. Refreshed and on fire, he clicked off ten miles, running like a gazelle. After his morning shower, he almost went out and ran another ten. But he had things to do.

He would accept Tec's offer to help. Tec was tough, smart, and resourceful. Who couldn't use help like that? Especially in Zane's circumstances. But Tec had a hidden agenda. Zane was sure of it. And until he knew what that was, Zane would keep a few cards up his sleeve.

Despite the likely mutual distrust, Zane and Tec had put together a plan. They needed one more person with expertise they didn't possess.

Monique.

It took Zane ten minutes to get to her place, not giving him much time to consider the best way to approach her.

He stood at the door for several minutes before he rang the bell. Zane had the courage, but involving other parties hadn't worked well for him in the past.

The door opened abruptly. No chain, no lock, no security. Monique just stood there wearing men's short boxer shorts and a wifebeater. Zane immediately felt guilty for gazing upon her lithe-some sexuality. He refocused on her face.

"Hello, Monique. I feel sorry for the bastard who dares to break into your house."

"Yeah, I'm secretly trying to draw them in by leaving the door unlocked. I need the experience."

"I'm not here to attack you, however much fun that may be. Can I come in?"

"Through me first."

"Don't tempt me."

"Okay, get your ass in here," Monique said, laughing.

"Thanks, I think. Do I need to keep you in my sight at all times, or is it safe to sit down?"

"Depends on your reason for coming here."

"Do you still have my laptop?"

"Safe and secure."

"I need some help."

"Kick-somebody's-ass help? Or the more mundane, sit-at-a-keyboard help?"

"For now, keyboard."

"Shit. I love kicking middle-aged white man ass."

"Why do you think that's the ass I would ask you to kick, if I were here asking you to kick ass?"

"I know the business world, and it's mostly populated by middle-aged white pussies."

"Not all of them are pussies."

"Case in point being you?"

"Of course."

She smiled at Zane and put her hand on his shoulder. "Obviously. Can I get you anything first? If I'm going to be bored, I'm going to need some caffeine."

"Me too. Black."

"Gotcha."

Zane watched her behind as she sashayed into the kitchen. Even though they'd always been friendly with each other, she was being extra saucy and nice to him today.

"Hey, Monique, why are you being so wonderful today?"

Monique quickly appeared with two steaming cups.

"I hope you like it strong. This shit will make your asshole pucker."

"If I ever need a puckered asshole, I'll know where to go."

"Just want to brighten your day," she said as she sat down on the couch with an inviting look.

He thought she might have an ulterior motive but quickly dismissed that as paranoia.

"Thanks, Monique. I need you to do some research."

"Anything. Whatever you need."

"Don't you want to hear the details first?"

"Nah, that takes all the fun out of it."

"Tom Moore, the guy who took my family and caused my wife's death. I need to know everything about him and his associates, especially his boss. And I mean everything, including his real name and personal history. And more importantly, his financial history. I need account numbers, balances, pretty much everything. And I need a forensic viewpoint—how he got his money, who he gives it to, and how somebody else can get it, if you know what I mean."

"I do. Except who is this guy? Other than the guy who took your family and lied about your wife getting killed in the house explosion?" she asked, taking a sip of coffee and leaning forward. Zane tried not to notice that she wasn't wearing a bra under her tank top and that the view was quite lovely.

"Apparently, he pulls the strings of the company I work for, SAS."

"You've told me SAS was involved in the abduction of your family, so then, by extension, this guy was too?"

"I'm not so sure SAS was involved anymore, but I'm sure Tom Moore was. I need some leverage that will allow me to determine how far up the ladder this really goes," Zane replied, averting his eyes to his coffee as he took a gulp.

"Why did you wait so long? A lot can change in a couple of months."

"I needed to get my head on straight. Tina's death really messed me up," Zane answered, looking down. "Death is not the final solution."

"If he messed with your family, then he deserves this. I love fucking with people and their ill-gotten booty."

209

"Monique, you are every guy's dream."
"I bet you say that to all the girls who do illegal shit for you."
"You're the first."
"You do make a girl feel special."

55

It took a lot to make Monique feel special. She'd worked her way through many guys. Most of them were typical. Meet the three basic needs on their chick menu and they were happy—food, sex, and sleep, usually in that order. The ones who weren't typical seemed to have emotional needs that hadn't been met, usually by their mothers. She didn't want to provide her men validation, whatever that was. She didn't need that shit. If you couldn't be a real man, she wanted nothing to do with you.

When she met Zane at the Warrior's Den, she quickly realized that he was pretty much everything she was looking for. Confident and tough. He didn't put up with any shit. He had a dark side, but she liked that. Except he was married. But then, all of a sudden, he wasn't. The circumstances weren't ideal, of course. His wife had died a violent death. Monique wasn't entirely sure how it had come to that, but she was sure Zane wasn't to blame. She could feel it. He was too heartbroken. It would take time, but if she was there for him, maybe he'd be there for her at some point.

And now he'd come to her for help. Normally, she wouldn't be comfortable messing with people's money, but somehow, she trusted him. Moore had taken Zane's family and killed his wife, which meant he was ruthless. That knowledge eliminated her reservations.

She knew she'd come on strong with Zane, but nothing

ventured, nothing gained. Yeah, good damn motto. Dream big and work hard. Or was it "Work it until it got big and hard"? Oh well; Zane was a dream, and in her dreams, it could work out.

At that moment, her doorbell rang. Could it be that Zane was coming back? Maybe he needed something more. Like a hug. That would be good. Yes, it could work out—except for one thing.

She ran to the door and flung it open. The one thing was standing there.

"Hey there, big boy. What do you need?" Damn, she'd been looking for the right guy her whole life, and now she had two of them. She felt like a traitorous whore.

"What makes you think I need something?" Caleb asked, trying not to look at her chest.

"The flowers you're carrying. Guys only bring flowers for two reasons. Either they fucked up, or they need something. Often both."

"That hurts. Are you going to invite me in?"

"Sure, come on in. I can't wait to see which one it is," Monique said, standing back and letting him pass.

Caleb laughed as he dumped himself onto her couch. "You're good, Monique. I'm sorry I left the other night. And I need your help with something."

"Actually, you don't know if I'm good yet, but depending upon what you want, you may find out," she answered, sitting on the arm of the couch and brushing her hair out of her eyes.

"I'm not sure what you thought when I left the other night. My mind wanted to stay, but my body wasn't cooperating."

"I was disappointed, but I understand. Too pooped to pop. You had a rough night. Most men wouldn't still be walking."

"Thanks for understanding, and I will take a rain check." Caleb said, looking at the creamy tan thigh perched on the couch's arm. She was wearing very short boxer shorts, and they were impeding his ability to think.

"Do you always dress like that around the house?" Caleb asked quietly, still staring.

"What do you mean by 'like that'?" Monique asked coyly.

"Those shorts look a size too small."

"I like wearing these, and I think you do too."

"I'm a bit fat to fit into those shorts."

"We'll see."

"Uh," Caleb muttered. "I need some help first, so you're going to have to keep it warm."

"I'm not sure what *it* is, but if it's what I think it is, then it's always warm. What do you need help with?" Monique asked, sitting down next to him on the couch and putting her hand on his.

"Do you have any objections to hacking into a government website?" Caleb asked her, staring at her face and breathing deeply while sliding his hand out from under hers.

"Which one and why?" Monique asked, putting her hand on his knee.

"The Department of the Treasury, but I can't tell you why. For your protection," Caleb explained, leaning back on the couch and putting both of his arms on the back and purposefully not looking at her.

"I guess I have no objections, as long as you can assure me that this will have no bounce back."

"If you're good, it won't."

"Come into the bedroom, and I'll show you," Monique said while she nodded her head in the direction of her back hallway.

"A little early in our relationship for that."

"Never know until you try," she said, smiling. "What are you looking for on their servers?"

"I need to know the details of one of their criminal investigations. I'd like to get a little background on someone working for them undercover. For starters, I need to know who the under-cover agent is," Caleb answered while putting his hand on Monique's knee.

"I could ask how you know about that undercover agent, but your hand is distracting me. And if you move it much higher, I won't even care," Monique said, leaning back on the couch and putting her hand on top of his.

"I'd move it higher, but I don't want you to misread my intentions, which are purely informational right now. But you never know what they may be later."

"All right. I'll do your hacking. But why wait for something that you can have now?" Monique said as she placed her hand behind Caleb's neck and drew him in for a long, passionate kiss. "By the way, what is Treasury investigating?" she mumbled darkly as she came up for air, holding her breasts against Caleb's arm. He could feel her arousal.

Caleb pulled her lips back to his, grabbed some tongue, and broke away. "Oh, a company called SAS."

56

Going back was difficult. This was where he'd lost Tina, the only love of his life, on the worst day of his life. He was going in with Tina's strength. It wasn't some spiritual, flaky kind of strength. It was real. Knowing what Tina had done gave him the power to do what was necessary.

It was better to go to Tom Moore's office early. Zane was most alert in the morning and more observant. He needed that advantage.

Involving Monique had been crucial. Regardless of the outcome, he couldn't have done this without her. Zane knew he was trading on her feelings for him, but be that as it may, he hadn't lied to her; he'd explained that he was trying to honor the memory of Tina. He liked Monique, but going beyond that wasn't even a remote possibility. Not now, anyway.

It only took her two days to come up with the information about Moore's organization. It was run simply, and Zane would use that against him.

He parked a block away, because he didn't want to be seen. He walked through the alleys on the outside chance they had observers on the street.

Zane's phone buzzed with a text. "Good to go, big daddy." He smiled. It felt good to have Monique on his side. There were cameras covering the exterior of the building, but working from her apartment, she'd hacked into their security cameras, which were now being frozen to their current view. He knew they'd catch on eventually, but he didn't need much time.

Monique had obtained the security code to the back door. He was a bit nervous, but it worked. "I'm in," he texted to Monique, but he didn't wait for her response.

The dark, narrow hallway was empty. He quickly went to the elevator. The same security code he'd used at the front door got him to the fateful floor where his beautiful wife and the mother of his children had been murdered. He put the terrible vision of his wife in a pool of her own blood out of his mind. He needed to be unemotional, cold, and efficient. A machine. He'd done it before, and he could do it again.

The elevator door opened.

The first obstacle was sitting behind the reception desk. The young man looked like he wouldn't take any shit. Too bad—he was going to get some. Zane walked quickly behind his desk and pulled out his gun. The same gun that wouldn't fire when he'd desperately wanted to kill his former friend was now pointed at the young man.

"Put your hands on the desk where I can see them."

The young man smiled and politely complied. "You just fucked up, dude."

Zane quickly flipped the gun around and hit the young man hard behind his right ear. He slumped to the floor. Zane reached under the top of the desk and found a button, pressed it, and heard the front door unlock.

He felt a vibration in his pants pocket. A text from Monique.

"Where are you? No alarms yet. I think I'm in control of them, but keep me posted."

"Will do," he responded. He didn't have much time.

He moved through the door quickly but took his time going down the hallway. He hoped he wouldn't run into Number One and Number Two. His main focus was Moore.

Suddenly, a door opened behind him. Zane spun around, wishing he had someplace to hide. Number One came out of the door and stared at him for a second. A second was all Zane needed. He sprinted the few feet between them and used a spear hand to Number One's trachea. He went down gasping for air as Zane hit him between the eyes with his gun. He was out, for now.

That scared the shit out of Zane. He said a quick prayer to Tina and then resumed his cautious trek. He was going down a tunnel with no clear way out. The walls were starting to move in on him. He passed door number seven and stopped at door number eight. He wanted to go in and see if he could still smell Tina, but that wasn't his mission today. He was soaking wet with anxious sweat, and his breaths were quick and shallow. There was a real possibility he was going to need a change of underwear when this was over.

He arrived at the fateful door. He stopped for a second and took several measured, deep breaths to slow down his heart. He needed to be calm. He took one last deep breath and tried the doorknob. It wasn't locked. Moore had misplaced his faith in his security.

He flung the door open and stepped into the room. Moore was sitting on his couch, alone. All of the blood and body matter had been cleaned up. Like it never happened.

But it had.

"Holy shit, Zane."

"Nobody told me you were actually killing them."

"Killing who?"

Zane walked up to Moore and put the gun up to his elbow on the armrest. He pulled the trigger. The blast was loud, and pieces of tissue and bone splattered across the couch and carpet. The gun was working fine today.

Moore screamed.

"Don't fuck with me. You made me a party to the murder of my former clients. Wasn't it bad enough we took their companies? Did we have to kill them too?" Zane retched out as his gun hand began to shake.

"God, you have to be the dumbest shit in the world," Moore uttered through clenched teeth. "Think about your children. Do you want them to die too?"

"I'm thinking about them. That's why I'm doing this."

"Doing what? What the fuck do you think you're doing?"

"We don't have much time. Who's your boss? Who pulls your leash?"

"No fucking way. Whatever you can do to me couldn't even come close to what they could do. People will be here soon. I suggest you get out of here, go find your kids, and run. Far, far away," Moore replied, gasping for air as he applied pressure to the hole in his elbow.

"That's what I thought you'd tell me."

Zane looked down at his feet, knowing it was best to leave. He and Tec would have to do it another way. Moore wouldn't give up his boss. Then he thought of Billy Hot, dying with his cousin in a hundred-foot ravine.

Zane looked up and pointed the gun at Moore's head, right between the eyes.

"Do you want to live?" Moore asked him, looking up at him indifferently and yet defiantly.

"Actually, I do want to live. Very much," Zane answered as he brought the gun down to his side.

Zane wasn't interested in revenge or justice. He needed information. He knew it didn't end with Moore and his organization. He knew that because Moore had told him that if he didn't go back to SAS, the money would kill him for what he knew. That meant two things. Moore wasn't the money, and whoever was would kill to protect their identity. But he needed more than just a name. Zane needed to expose the source of the money. He needed them to come to him. They would only do that if they were afraid of what he might do next.

Zane looked Moore straight in his beady little eyes, raised the gun again, and pulled the trigger.

There was no malfunction, and Moore's head exploded in several directions. Zane wiped bloody pieces from his arms and turned for the door. He wasn't happy, he wasn't sorry, and he wasn't satisfied. It was simply the only way to the truth.

As it had in his past, this killing served a purpose.

Zane wondered if Tec would agree.

As he neared the door, it was flung open, and Number Two was standing there with a gun in his hand. Zane chopped him hard on his wrist. The gun clattered to the floor, and Zane backed up a step and pointed the .38 at Number Two.

Two quickly took in the bloody scene.

"What the fuck is wrong with you?" Number Two yelled at him.

"People keep asking me that. Why is it when I shoot somebody, there's something wrong with me, and when you guys do it, you're geniuses?"

"You can't disappear well enough to run from this. When our bosses find out, I can't even imagine being in your shoes. You'd better kill me. That may be your only chance of them not finding out who did this."

"I'm not running. I'm not going to kill you. I need a witness," Zane responded as he grabbed a Sharpie out of his pocket and wrote his cell number on the wall.

"What a fucking idiot. Why would you want me to tell them?"

"Because I'm taking over."

57

"So this will be your office. I know it isn't much, but at least it has a door that will close."

"This will be fine. I don't care if it's a broom closet. The work is more important than the surroundings."

All the money SAS had absconded with sure didn't show in the offices. The lobby was plain, decorated in hews of dull brown and beige. The furniture was nice, glass and steel, but not luxurious. There were two well-tended plants in the lobby and several black steel chairs. SAS had the feel of a dentist's office rather than an acquisitions firm.

"That's a refreshing attitude. You don't see that often. If you need anything, just let me know. My name is Sally," she said as she led him back around some frosted-glass partitions to an office door along the outside of the building.

"Thank you, Sally. I always like to get to know the people I work with, so maybe we can talk more at lunch or something. You can just call me Caleb. Mr. Rider is way too formal," Caleb said as he opened the door and took in his office.

Sally dutifully retreated with a shy, subservient look on her face. Yeah, she might be a good source.

Caleb shut the door. His office had a leather executive chair, a large glass desk, and two cushy-looking office chairs on the other side of his desk. Lining the wall were two black lateral files. The office was clean, but he could tell that it had seen its last occupant some time ago. He wasn't sure how he knew, but he knew.

He was in, and it hadn't been that hard after the congressman's manipulation of his past. The congressman knew people who were good at manipulating data. Caleb thought he should be concerned about that but decided to push it to the back of his mind for the time being. He had thought of using the congressman for the Treasury information Monique was obtaining for him, but for now he wanted to keep those results to himself. He might need an edge later on.

He'd met Robert Holmes on a referral from a friend high up in financial circles who'd also spent a couple of days coaching him on finance and acquisitions. It helped to have friends in high places. Sometimes it helped having them in low places, as well.

Caleb's fake résumé had shown a wealth of merger and acquisition work for a large national company. When asked why he wasn't working for them anymore, Caleb replied that he'd been fired due to falsifying financial data to justify the acquisitions. He also told Holmes about a brief stint behind bars for his part in some of the devious transactions. When Holmes told him they didn't do background checks and weren't bothered by his past miscues, Caleb knew something was wrong.

Caleb also connected with Holmes on a different level. He lied to him about another illegal enterprise, one he was supposedly still involved in, but Holmes didn't respond to that. Caleb guessed that birds of a feather stayed fucked up together.

Holmes didn't get back to him for a couple of days, during which time Caleb was a bit concerned that the false background information wouldn't hold up to close scrutiny. Unnecessary worry, as it turned out, because Holmes finally called and took him out to dinner to welcome him to the company. He also told Caleb that he wanted special weekly reports directly to him. Caleb would be working with someone else he had yet to meet, but he'd be reporting to Holmes. It was obvious that there were trust issues within the company. That made his job easier.

Caleb was jarred from his thoughts by a knock on the door. *Here we go.*

"Come in!" Caleb yelled out.

"Welcome to SAS," Holmes said as he entered his office and stood with his hands in his pockets before Caleb's desk. "It's good to have you as part of the team."

"I'm thrilled to be at Strategic Acquisition Services. I appreciate you taking a chance on me," Caleb responded.

"I need someone like you. Someone I can trust. I think we speak the same language."

"We do. I'll justify your trust in me. I'm ready to get to work."

"Well, I have a list of prospects. However, before you start on that, I want you to review this case," Holmes said as he laid a file on Caleb's desk.

"Guardian Jewelry. Everybody's heard of them," Caleb responded.

"Yes, but few know they're in deep financial trouble. Someone else's loss can be our gain. I think we have a win-win plan."

"Win-win?" Caleb responded as he was looking at the file. Guardian Jewelry was clearly bankrupt. "For this to work, it must be more like win-lose. But I suppose the trick is making the client think they're winning."

"Our clients still get more than they would without us. In some cases a lot more," Holmes responded as he leaned against a lateral file. "I get up every day knowing my purpose is to get bankrupt business owners more money than they ever would with any other firm."

"I assume I'll discover how that works," Caleb responded, wondering if that was the real reason that got Holmes out of bed every day.

"You will, but keep in mind that our biggest job is convincing the client they have to be willing to do whatever it takes. Desperate circumstances call for desperate measures."

"I can be good at that. So what do you want me to do after I review this case?"

"I want you to talk to the man in charge of this case. He's the absolute best I've ever seen. Clients love him. They'll believe anything he tells them."

"Great. I love learning from a professional liar. Who is he?"

"Zane, Zane Donovan. You two will get along well."

"I hope we do."

58

Zane's ride home had been as uneventful as his exit from Moore's building. His heartbeat was returning to normal. It had been seven hours since he'd killed Moore, and it had taken most of that time to dump the adrenaline from his system and contemplate the events of the morning.

He had murdered Moore in cold blood. Never even given him a chance. That was the only way he could unravel the truth and protect his children. He needed to have something they wanted.

His phone began play Pink Floyd's "Money." He was surprised it had taken this long.

Zane wiped his sweaty palms on his jeans and swiped the Answer button. "Yes?"

"Do you realize what you're doing?" a gruff man answered.

"I'm at home watching *Good Morning America*. They're talking about the different types of car seats. What are you doing?"

"You don't lack for balls, that's for sure."

"Big, fucking nasty ones," Zane answered as he held the phone away from his ear, lest his caller could hear his heart pounding.

The man laughed. "This may be fun. We know where you live, and more importantly, we know where your kids live. In fact, we have someone watching them right now."

"I do too."

"I hope it's not the same person."

There was a pause, during which the death and mutilation of Zane's children played out like a horrible preview in his mind.

"Are you stupid or something? Maybe this will be a mercy killing."

"Whatever turns your crank. But give me just a second. They're getting to the part that explains which car seats are deadly," Zane responded, trying hard to get the vision of Tec as a traitor out of his mind.

"Just what do you think you know?"

"I know your name is Alan. Alan R. Thompson."

Silence. Long pause. Monique was good. Zane sincerely hoped Tec was too.

"What else do you think you know?"

"I now know that some car seats are actually worse than no car seats. Who would've figured?"

"You're starting to piss me off."

"Spending more doesn't always ensure you're getting the safest car seat. And I know you, Alan. You always like to spend more. And I also know you were Moore's boss. The key word is *were*. The last time I saw him, most of his head was missing. I also know that you bank primarily at the Bank of Scotland and Bank of America. Your account numbers are 01023423566 and 98700047211, respectively. Do you want the balances?"

The pauses were getting longer, and Zane's breaths were getting shorter.

"If you aren't going to answer my questions, then I don't want to talk. They're starting to talk about unsafe baby cribs. Can't miss this," Zane said as he hit the End button and let out a huge breath.

Five seconds later, "Money" played again.

"Geez, kind of busy here," Zane said as he answered the phone.

"You do understand you aren't going to live out the day, don't you?" Thompson said.

"The balance on your Bank of Scotland account is slightly over $40 million, and your Bank of America account has about half of that. I have both open on my computer right now. You may want to do the same, because if you're going to continue to talk like that to me, the plug will be pulled. Both accounts can go to zero within seconds. Trust me."

"You do that, we still kill you, and I hate to think what we're going to do with your snot-nosed kids."

"And you'll never see your money again. Did you know that certain cribs can contribute to crib death? Amazing," Zane said as he hit the End button, trying not to think about the fact that he was playing with his kids' lives.

Money, well, get back, I'm all right, Jack, keep your hands off of my stack. Zane hit the Answer button again.

"Come on, you're really ruining this crib story for me."

"Okay, asshole, we'll play. But here's the thing—did you kill Moore as part of your plan or somebody else's?"

"Trying to confuse me isn't going to protect you and your money," Zane answered as he wondered what Tec stood to gain from Moore's death.

"You'd better be sure that you know what you know."

"Nice riddle, but I do know your partners, and I know your ill-gotten financial interests and the interrelated entities. Do you want me to recite those?"

"You implicate us, and you go down. Not Dad anymore to your kids if you're put away for the rest of your life."

"As clichéd as this sounds, upon my death or imprisonment, a full report of all of this goes to the authorities and, more importantly, to the press." Zane paused. "And I have the laptop. All of it's on there."

"What goes around comes around. We may need you now, but that may not be true forever."

"Forever is for somebody else. I live for today."

"Live, eat, and be merry, for tomorrow we die."

"Tomorrow will take care of itself. As for today, I have your location, I know who you work for, and you need to listen, or I'll go over your head too. You know who I'm talking about, and you don't want that. And you know why?" Zane asked as he leaned back on his old couch. "Because I'm in charge. You guys take orders from me now, not the other way around. I'll be in touch," Zane said.

"Just watch your fucking back."

"Someone has my back."

"Remember, he works for us. Always has and always will."

"It's not who you think it is," Zane lied.

"They'd better be good."

"The best."

And untrustworthy.

59

Tec would miss Willow's stories, because they were more than just stories, and they were more than life lessons; they were his heritage and his blood. History that could show him the way.

"Forget about the names in this story," his mom began. "They aren't important. They were what you have become, and that is all that matters."

Tec nodded and leaned back in his chair, focusing on the events as if they were playing out in this little room full of sterile life-and-death needs.

"One of the men in the tribe was smart enough to realize that the end was near. Their lives as they knew it could never continue. The white man was too strong, but more importantly, they were backed by the conviction that their God was leading them on a righteous and moral path. The whites were bringing what they thought Native Americans couldn't get on their own—a better life, a just existence, and most importantly, salvation. Especially for the children. This man, whom we shall call Verity, knew what had to be done."

Tec sat up a bit straighter. "Many prophets are not understood by their people."

"*Prophet* might be too strong a word. Maybe he was just pragmatic, not unlike others who have saved lives and even nations."

Tec sat still and waited.

"Verity had to become what he did not want. He had to become white while still seeming red. He saw himself as a bridge from the past to the future. The only problem was, he knew something that all people know but are afraid to admit when facing great change."

"People," Tec muttered.

"People," Willow repeated, "are not perfect. If presented with an opportunity, some will use that change to their advantage. But truly, Verity didn't care. Regardless of what others believed, he proceeded based on what he knew was needed."

"He had to convince both sides that their interests lay within his heart," Tec interjected quietly.

"Verity had to prove to the whites that he was one of them while also bleeding for his people, which is where his heart truly lived."

"He had to be all things to all people," Tec said softly, fearing her response.

"He had to kill for the right to lie and save his people."

"Peace at any cost."

"Unity is not always right, but it is sometimes the only way."

"To what?"

"Progress. Fulfillment of the future. A future in which we can all become what God needs us to be."

Tec sighed and stood up. He moved to his mother's side. He squeezed her hand and kissed it. "I don't think I have that in me."

"Use what God has given you."

"Is it truth that he has given me, or the ability to use dishonesty so that I can get what I want?"

"They're both within you."

"Battling to come out. To see which one will win," Tec said as he stroked the hair on her head.

"That's where you're wrong, son," Willow said, grasping his hand tightly. "Telling a lie to get at the truth does beget a purpose. That is biblical. Rahab is a perfect example. Deception can be enlightening, although it may take a while to expose its purpose."

"Beguilement of two parties toward one end can be ugly."

"But we both know that is where you truly excel."

60

Caleb was waiting. He'd never heard of locked front doors for an M&A firm. The buzzer finally rang, and Caleb opened the door and trudged into the lobby.

"Good morning, Caleb. No suit today?" Sally asked him.

"I only own one. Ties make me feel like I'm choking. Too many bad memories," Caleb responded while sitting on Sally's desk with one cheek.

"Uh, okay. I'm sure being choked is very uncomfortable."

"I can tell you a lot of choking stories, maybe over beers at the company picnic."

"I don't like choking stories. And we don't have company picnics," Sally said as she stood up with a piece of paper she took over to the shredder.

"Why's that? Everybody just hates everybody else?" Caleb asked.

Sally quickly shredded the document and walked over to the coffee machine to pour herself and Caleb a cup. "Not sure. Don't care. As long as my check cashes, my coworkers can do whatever they want."

"That's the attitude. Give me mine and to hell with everybody else," Caleb said, grabbing the cup and taking a swig.

"That's harsh. I appreciate my time out of here and don't want to socialize with people I work with all day."

Caleb guessed Sally was in her midfifties. She was about as plain as a brown paper bag. She struck him as the classic underachiever. Her so-called career was just about a paycheck.

"I hear you, girl. You can pick your friends but not your nose. What do you do here, anyway, other than make very good black coffee?"

Sally sat back down at her desk looking up at Zane. "Typing, filing, answering the phone. Normal receptionist stuff."

"I never hear the phone ring, so it must be pretty easy."

"There isn't a lot of filing and typing, either."

"So what is it that you really do? Eye candy?"

"Very nice of you to say, Caleb, but my eye-candy days are behind me. I was hired mainly to sit here and look busy when people come in. Thank God for e-books."

"Do a lot of people come in?"

"No."

"I need a job like yours."

"It gets old. Except when the life insurance guys come in. I have to get the policies ready, and that's interesting. I'm not supposed to read the policy sheets, but I do. A lot of them are for very high amounts."

"What's high?" Caleb asked.

"Twenty, thirty, even fifty million sometimes."

"That gives a lot of incentive to knock off those policyholders."

"Not really."

"Why not?"

"All of them are dead."

61

"I understand, Zanese, but you have to listen to Grandma. When I'm not there, she has my authority. Whatever she tells you is the same as me telling you," Zane told his daughter.

Zanese was upset.

"She said I can't wear my favorite T-shirt. She said it's sexist. I don't even know what that means," Zanese pleaded with her dad.

"It means you can't wear it. What does it say?"

"Life's a bitch; deal with it."

"Sometimes that's true. And this is one of those times."

"No, that's what the T-shirt says."

Zane laughed; he had walked right into that one. "You can't wear a T-shirt to school that says *bitch*."

"You just said it was true, so why can't I wear it on my shirt? Mom always told us to tell the truth."

"The truth is a good thing, but we have to be careful how and when we tell it. You're saying it the wrong way and at the wrong time."

"So the truth is to do the right thing only at certain times. And you should never wear it on your T-shirt."

"The truth stands alone. But it's like telling somebody they're ugly. It may be the truth, but it doesn't do any good to tell them. In fact, it may do more harm than good. There isn't a lot they can do about it. If telling the truth hurts somebody, then you have to think really hard about it. Sometimes it is better for us and for others to not put the truth out there. You should be careful not to hurt people."

"Who does this hurt?"

"Well, for one, it hurts your grandma."

"I don't want to hurt her."

"Good; then put on a different shirt. And there is another reason you should change."

"What is that?"

"Grandma told you to."

"Okay. I miss you, Dad."

"I miss you too. Please put Grandma on."

"Hey, Zane. Thank you for having my back."

"Always; it's the least I can do. I need to take care of some business. I may not check in for a bit, but don't worry," Zane explained.

"I don't worry, Zane. God has always been there for me. But we need to talk."

Those words would strike fear into any man's heart, Zane thought as he sat down in his very used recliner. "I will tell you everything, but not now. I'm deep in the middle of this, and I need to protect you."

"I won't push you, but the day is coming. And you don't worry about me, either. I can take care of myself and the kids. I'm not just some little old grandma knitting shawls and shit."

"I don't even know what that means."

"Back in the day, the streets were my home. I did what I had to for survival. Then God used my ex-husband to bring me out of that. God can do the same for you."

Zane leaned back in the recliner and closed his eyes. "I'm sure He can, but will He?"

"God is able, and He will, if you let Him. But there is one requirement."

"Yes?"

"God requires an open receptacle. We have to allow Him to work through us. Don't forget that."

"I'll try not to."

"I'm praying for you. God has put His special seal on your life. You can do all things if you just believe."

"Thank you."

"And one more thing to remember."

"Okay," Zane replied with a large sigh.

"Many a man has tried to take advantage of me and come to wish they hadn't," she said as she paused. "Don't be another of them."

"Good to know," Zane said as he clicked off.

He wasn't ready to involve another person or even God at this point.

While the truth did stand alone, it wouldn't for him today. A lie would have to stand in its place. Zane hoped Zanese would forgive him.

Zane was almost at the office. It had been a few days. Contemplating suicide, almost killing Tec, and then conspiring with him while committing murder had kept him busy.

He stopped at Sally's desk for his messages, but there was only one: Call Ben Guardian. "He's called seven times for you over the last two days."

"Will do; it is the second thing on my agenda. I have to talk to Holmes first. Is he in?" Zane asked.

"Yes, he is. Zane?"

"Yes?"

"Something's different about you today. You seem more upbeat and in charge."

"I am in charge. And don't you forget it," Zane said as he smiled at Sally.

"It's about time someone sane took charge!" Sally yelled after him.

Zane walked to Holmes's office and flung open the door.

"Hey, Holmes. What the fuck are you doing?"

"Hello, Zane. Be careful," Holmes responded.

"My careful days are over, Holmes. And the days of you being my boss are over too. Get the fuck out of my office."

Holmes stared at Zane. He swallowed hard and wrung his hands.

"Zane, you have to give me more than that. I'm not going to just walk out of here and turn the company over to you."

Zane sat on the edge of Holmes's massive desk. Several expensive mementos from past illicit acquisitions sat on top, as did the latest version of any electronic gear anybody could want. Zane reached over and knocked it all to the floor with one sweep. The computer screen cracked, and the mementos weren't so expensive after they lay on the floor in a broken heap. Holmes got up and jumped back, knocking over his executive leather chair.

"Zane, what's gotten into you? Have you lost your mind?" Holmes yelled as he backed up against the wall.

"They're all dead, Holmes. All of our acquisition clients are dead. And don't even try to tell me you didn't know," Zane blurted out while staring daggers through Holmes.

"I have no earthly idea what you're talking about. I thought the deaths were fake."

Zane walked around the desk and shot out a straight palm strike to Holmes's stomach, watching as he retched and slumped to the floor. Zane picked him back up by the lapels of his tailored suit jacket and slammed him against the priceless work of art behind his desk, breaking the glass and frame.

"Come on, Holmes, work with me! Concentrate. I know who's pulling your strings. But not any longer. Moore is gone. I'm it.

Life's a bitch; deal with it," Zane said. The phrase may not have been appropriate for a little girl's shirt, but it worked just fine here.

"You have to believe me; I'm on my own here. I told you to follow the money, but I don't know who that is, and I don't know about any murders," Holmes pleaded as he struggled to catch his breath, with spit flying out of his mouth and sweat dripping off his face.

Zane believed him, which meant he held no value. "I'm following the money, and since it's not you, I don't need you," Zane said as he dragged Holmes by his lapels and dumped him on the couch. "I'm in charge now. You're out. If you fight it, you lose. Get your shit out of here. Now."

Holmes pulled himself off the couch rubbing the back of his head where it had hit the picture frame. He looked like he wanted all of this to end and run away. Zane almost felt sorry for him. Almost.

"Have it your way," Holmes responded. "I really don't care anymore. Whatever you started, you'll have to finish."

Holmes's easy surrender concerned Zane more than if he'd fought to try to stay at SAS. Holmes was scared. Not of Zane but of them.

Holmes stumbled out the door without turning back.

Zane knew that was the last time he'd see Robert Holmes.

62

Computers have no morals. They're machines that can be used for good or bad. They're simply a tool. Just like guns. Monique had used both, and she wasn't sure what gave her more satisfaction. Probably the computer. She'd rather see bad people fucked up than dead. Dead was final. Fucked up could go on and on.

She just wasn't sure she was fucking up the right people. After Caleb's admission that he was checking into a Treasury Department investigation of SAS, she realized she was working both sides of the same coin. For the two men in her life. Monique wasn't sure how she felt about that. Conflicted was an understatement.

Getting into the Treasury's servers wasn't difficult. She had hacked much securer systems. Like all government agencies, Treasury lacked creativity. She just had to think like a robot, and before long, she was in. Caleb had given her a code word for their investigation. Although she spent two days on it, she couldn't uncover anything about that investigation, let alone the person they had undercover. That particular investigation was locked down tightly. However, she'd found several e-mails from the Federal Reserve to an insurance company called AIS. All of them were about funding a life insurance company owned by AIS, which the Federal Reserve owned stock in. It seemed like the Federal Reserve was concerned about how much more money they needed.

She copied the e-mails and forwarded them to Caleb through

a secure web server.

Her work for Zane wasn't simple, either. He hadn't given her much to go on. All he gave her was an address. He'd told her his wife's death had occurred at that address, so she could assume they weren't good people. The address was enough, though. She established ownership through real-estate records. Even though Tom Moore's operation was a shell corporation owned by a shell corporation, she hacked into the secretary of state's records and tracked it backward. After two days of combing through corporate filings in multiple states and three phone calls to people who owed her favors, she had a name. Alan Thompson. He was the owner of all the shells, including the one that owned the building where Zane's wife perished. All real-estate purchases had been in cash, so Thompson didn't lack for funds. Tom Moore was listed as a corporate officer on all the various corporations, but he had no ownership. He likely worked for Thompson. However, all deposits into Thompson's account originated with the Federal Reserve via electronic deposits. She knew the Federal Reserve facilitated electronic funds transactions, but this was more than just facilitation. Zane thought the deposits looked strange, as well.

It was fun to hear the excitement in Zane's voice as they infiltrated Thompson's financial records. Their collaboration had felt right.

On the other hand, she wasn't stupid. As much as she was attracted to both Zane and Caleb, she needed to find out more about them to stay on top of this peculiar situation. Nothing came up when she searched for Caleb Rider. Obviously, his history had been sanitized. The question was, by whom? It was a thorough job. It was hard to believe anybody was better than she was, but it was possible.

Researching Zane would be easier. After all, she had his laptop. Monique was staring at it, wondering if it was betrayal to view its contents. Suddenly, her phone started playing "Kung Fu Fighting." She hit the Answer button.

"Hey, Caleb. Don't tell me you need more information," Monique said.

"My head is always working," Caleb replied.

"Yeah, just the wrong head."

"I think you've got head on the brain."

"My brain is actually in my head, but how is head a bad thing?"

"Right now, it is."

"There's always later."

"There is, but for now, I have a question."

"Go ahead, big shooter."

"Is everything a sexual innuendo to you?"

"Is that your question?"

"No."

"You need to learn to say yes more often."

"Never mind. I need some information. Background information. Nothing too illegal."

"I've already done illegal for you."

"I need more."

"Do you never get enough?"

"Sometimes I can be satisfied very easily. Other times if people play with me, they'll regret it."

"Is that a promise?"

"I'm not playing now."

"You're no fun."

"Don't you want the name or something?"

"Okay, back to work. What a buzzkill."

"Are you ready, like with a pen and paper?"

"Aye, aye, sir."

"It's my boss, and I need this pretty quick. His name is—" he started.

"Am I just supposed to guess? I ain't that good."

"I'll tell you later; he just walked into my office," Caleb said as he quickly hung up the phone.

63

They were all dead? That was messed up. Caleb wasn't a mathematical genius, but he knew the chances that all your clients with life insurance would die were about equal to the chance of the Minnesota Vikings winning the Super Bowl. He wasn't a Minnesota native, but he understood the Vikings were cursed. Apparently, so were the clients of SAS. Caleb had to get a look at those policies. Sally could help with that.

The Guardian Jewelry file didn't shed any light on the situation. They were in deep financial trouble; that much was clear. They needed cash to upgrade their marketing and Internet presence. Cash they didn't have, but SAS did. It seemed pretty straightforward. SAS would take over the ailing company and make a shitload of money, some of it through life insurance proceeds, while the Guardians would be debt-free. But one comment in the file by Zane Donovan seemed out of place, even downright weird. *Prospect is excited about potential outcome.* Caleb had been around finance enough to know that excitement and distressed acquisitions didn't go together. The former owners usually ended up with very little to show for their life's efforts. That's the definition of being in trouble. They might feel good about walking away from their debt, but never excited.

He also saw the word *viatical* in the file. He'd never heard that term, but he'd learned from a quick Internet search that it had to do with life insurance and getting the money early.

There was a knock on his door. Then it flung open. The man standing there looked calm and focused, as if on a mission.

"Caleb? Caleb Rider?"

"Yes?"

"Zane Donovan," Zane said as he extended his hand.

"Nice to meet you, Zane. I've heard a lot about you. Why don't you have a seat?"

"You can't believe everything you hear," Zane said as he remained standing and crossed his arms.

"Modest too; that's a good trait. Okay, what's up?" Caleb replied as he pushed his chair back while looking up at Zane.

"There's been a change of management at SAS. Holmes is out."

Caleb tried to hide his surprise. The sudden ouster of Holmes confirmed his earlier suspicions that something was wrong.

"My second day, and the guy who hired me is no longer here. Never a good sign," Caleb said, leaning back and putting his feet on the desk.

"Don't worry; you still have a job," Zane replied, sitting on the edge of the desk. "For now."

"I don't worry. Who's taking his place?" Caleb asked, now putting both hands behind his head.

"Me."

Zane didn't lack for boldness. That could mean he was hiding something.

"How did that happen? It may not be any of my business, but when the guy who tells you about a change of management *is* the new management, it probably means it was hostile."

"It was."

"And?"

"That's all you need to know. Holmes is out, and I'm in. If you still want to work here, you report to me, and I sign your check. If not, there's the door."

Zane was going to be difficult.

"Relax. I'm still here. It's just nice to know what's going on with the company providing your livelihood. I'm kind of funny that way."

"It's your second day."

"Chill out. Let's move on."

Caleb knew something more was going on than what was being said, but he knew better than to push it. It would come out. It always did.

"What did Holmes have you working on?"

"You."

"Me? What the hell does that mean?"

"Checking up on your ass."

"Now you know why Holmes is gone."

"If some guy is checking up on you, just fire him. Very Donald Trump. I like it."

"You're either with me or against me. You'd better decide which," Zane replied, standing up again and pointing at Caleb. "And if I ever catch you checking up on me again, you're out," said Zane as he leaned over and swiped Caleb's feet off of the desk. Caleb abruptly came to a standing position while bringing both hands up in a defensive position.

Zane seemed surprised by his reaction.

"I'm in, Zane. How many times will I have to tell you?"

"As many times as I ask you," Zane replied as he grabbed the Guardian file and walked out the door.

64

Caleb was a potential problem. He was asking too many questions and didn't seem to possess much financial knowledge. Was he a plant? By Thompson, perhaps? He'd have Monique do a little digging on him. But first things first. Zane left the building. He assumed Thompson was bugging his office, perhaps even the whole place. He went downstairs and out into the alley. It had recently been redone with landscaping on the edges and bright red pavers. Looked like a park now.

He dialed his Treasury contact.

"Finally. We haven't heard from you in a while. You need to stay in closer contact with us, Zane."

"I've been busy. I have a new development that will interest you."

"Do we need to meet?"

"Don't have time. Listen," Zane answered as he nervously looked up and down the alley.

"You're being recorded," the agent told him.

"There's another party. They're behind the kidnapping of my family and seem to be supplying the money behind SAS," Zane said as he began pacing up and down.

"Who are they? How much do you know about them?"

"Not sure who they are, but I'm in control now, and whatever they want doesn't matter anymore."

"In control? Of what? What does that mean?" the agent raised his voice.

"It means that even though I don't know who they are, I have control over some of their money."

"Do you think that's a good idea? Combined with what you know?"

"You need to take care of me. You said you would."

"It's hard to do that when you're running your own operation."

"Because you guys aren't doing a damn thing."

"Tell us more about this other operation. Tell me everything you know about them and how you found it out."

"I know it's a lot bigger that just SAS."

"Sounds like you're peeling back the onion. We need to know who they are. We need facts. Otherwise, we can't take any action, and we can't protect you."

"I'm going to draw them out for you. Shine the light on all of them."

"Draw them out? Sounds like a cloak-and-dagger operation. Don't go rogue on us. Facts. We need hard facts. And we need to meet."

Zane feared a meeting with them would end up with him incarcerated. He'd gone rogue because the Feds weren't getting the job done. But he still needed them. He would dump the case in their laps, and they'd have no choice but to prosecute. And if not, then something else was going on.

"You'll have the facts. Later. In the meantime, I need you to do something," Zane said.

"What about your wife's death? The last time we talked, you were convinced your boss was behind that," the agent said.

"A guy by the name of Tom Moore was pulling the strings behind SAS. He took my family and is responsible for my wife's death. But someone was pulling his strings. And that's who I'm after," Zane said.

"*We* need to be after him. Vigilante action isn't going to do the trick, Zane. But we can't do anything until you provide more information. We need to meet. Now. Today."

"Help me do some research on the SAS account. Since you're the Fed, that should be easy," Zane said, trying to keep his voice down.

"What kind of research?"

"Deposits. I need to know the source of all deposits into all SAS's accounts. I'll text you the account numbers."

"What's this for?"

"Part of the package I'm going to dump in your lap. A package that's going to include other murders, as well."

"We're going to need a lot more than deposit slips to prove a fucking murder."

"I'm also going to get you a video, which will be conclusive evidence of how SAS completes acquisitions," Zane said more quietly as a lady from the opposite building entered the alley and lit up a cigarette. She nodded at Zane. He walked away from her briskly.

"We can get you the source of the deposit, but I don't want to send it to you," the agent cautioned. "Give us a place and a time, and we'll meet to hand it to you, in person, today."

"We'll meet soon, at a place and time of my choosing."

Zane wasn't stupid. He would give them everything, but he would control the timing and the place of its delivery. He needed to show, not tell.

"Why should we listen to you?"

"Because you need me. Don't forget that."

No response.

"Yeah, that's what I thought."

Zane clicked off, leaned against the building, and breathed a sigh of relief while nodding in acknowledgment to the lady who was desperately working on getting her nicotine fix before her break ended.

65

He had nothing substantial. Viaticals? What the hell were they, exactly? Caleb spent most of his day researching them. One thing was certain: viaticals were controversial and borderline illegal. Criminal prosecution seemed to go hand in hand with most research on viaticals.

Caleb learned that a viatical is the sale of a policy owner's life insurance policy to a third party, called the investor. The original policy owner is typically terminally or chronically ill and desperately needs money. So the investor steps in, buys the life insurance policy for a fraction of its worth, and pays the premiums, and when the policyholder dies, the investor receives the full death benefit. The investor profits by paying less for the policy than the amount of the death benefit. Apparently, viaticals were really popular in the early 1980s when the AIDS epidemic peaked.

He got up from his chair to stretch. Manual labor was more suited to him, but this was hard mental labor that would hopefully lead to a clue, although he wasn't sure what a clue would look like in this case.

Caleb didn't get life insurance. If you were dead, you couldn't use the money. For those who cared for you, money didn't replace your presence. Maybe money could buy happiness or at least financial security. Apparently, a lot of people thought so; life insurance was big business. And viaticals were too. As the principal gets older or sick, it becomes more certain that the beneficiaries will collect. This is also the time when the principal could really use the money to wrap up final business or personal debt, to give it to those they really want to give it to, or maybe just to blow through it. Caleb thought that if you're paying the premiums and you're the one dying, you should get the proceeds.

Investors thought so too. Investors were willing to pay good money to purchase policies from people who would likely die relatively soon. The only potential challenge for the investor was if the principal lived too long, the investment could turn out to be a bust, because the investor had to continue to pay the premiums. In other words, the investor had a strong interest in the principal's quick death. At SAS, those deaths came exceptionally quickly.

That much made sense. But there was more. Caleb knew enough about life insurance to know that insurance companies would only issue a policy for the amount the principal was worth. In the Guardian case, for example, that seemed to be almost nothing. Ben was broke. So how did he convince a company to give him such a high death benefit? And even if a company was stupid enough to issue a life insurance policy worth more than Ben's net worth, who would be stupid enough to step in and purchase the policy from Ben? He was healthy as a horse! And if by some miracle somebody did buy the policy from Ben, how did SAS profit from this transaction? It didn't make sense.

Unless Ben suddenly passed away. But even so, no life insurance company would just pay out a huge premium on a sudden death involving a new policy without extensive investigation. And that investigation would focus on whoever would benefit. And that pointed the finger at the investor, who had bought the policy from Ben. Caleb decided the investor was the best place to start. Except he had no idea who the investor was.

Caleb decided to make a call. It was the end of the day, and what better way to enjoy a ride home than to spend time on the phone? Caleb hated talking on the phone unless he combined it with another activity like driving.

The congressman's office answered on the first ring. Caleb loved when they answered on the first ring. His tax dollars at work.

"Hey, let me talk to the big kahuna."

"Caleb, dear Caleb. You're the only one that can get away with calling him that," a young woman answered.

"Yes, ma'am. Now get his treacherous ass on the phone. I didn't give him all those damn contributions to be sitting here shooting the shit with some peon like you. Besides, how can I tell him how to vote unless you get him on the phone?"

"I'll do that right away, sir. I don't understand most of what you're saying, since I'm such a loser and since the only job I really do around here starts with *blow*. But I do understand contributions. Let me get him on the phone right away, and please have your credit card handy," she said as she started giggling.

"Caleb," the congressman answered. "About time you checked in. Don't forget who you work for. And stop giving the help a hard time. I don't pay them much as it is. Some people in Washington work for a living."

"Really. I think you need to come out to Minnesota, constituent land, and see what real work is. Not kissing-ass work, but sweaty, I-wish-it-was-break-time work."

"Someday. But kissing ass can be hard work too. Especially the big, stinky ones."

"I guess you're the expert on that. But I'm calling about something else. There's something going on with SAS, but I can't figure out what it is. It has to do with acquiring businesses."

"Duh. I didn't need you to tell me that. They're in the acquisition business."

"Let me finish. It's tied into life insurance, specifically viaticals, with the principals all dying immediately after buying life insurance and selling their businesses."

"I don't know much about viaticals except that most of them are fraudulent. Particularly if the principals are all dying. Which life insurance company?"

"Subsidiary of AIS."

"American Insurance Solutions?"

"One and the same."

"They're owned by us. The government. Bailed out in 2008 by the Federal Reserve."

"Interesting. In addition, there has been an abrupt change of management at SAS. The new guy, Zane Donovan, seems to have a hidden agenda. I'll have someone look into him. I could have your office do that, but it might be better to keep you out of it for now. No use stepping on Treasury's toes."

"Make sure they don't find out you're the one looking."

"I understand the definition of undercover."

"It's more than that," the congressman replied and then paused. "I need deniability, and I need you loyal to only me. Regardless of what you uncover. And that's a lot easier to do if nobody uncovers you."

"Or you."

"That goes without saying."

"We don't have a contract."

"What we have is better than a contract. I know what you've done, and you know what I've done. That keeps our mouths shut and us in bed together 'til death do us part."

"Or until I get tired of your shit and your money and just disappear."

"You're not that stupid. By the way, we did find something that might be useful."

"Are you going to tell me?"

"I showed his picture around to a few people at Treasury, and one of them remembered seeing him at their Minneapolis office not long ago."

"So you think he might be the guy on the inside?"

"Maybe. Would fit with something else I found out."

"Yes?"

"The lady who first called me about this, Betty, is his former mother-in-law."

66

The fund-raising dinner had gone well for the chairman of the Federal Reserve. Everybody in attendance was addicted. As long as the drugs kept coming, the addicts didn't care about anything else. In this case, the drug of choice was money, the addicts were the politicians, and he was the dealer. Eat, drink, and party, for tomorrow we may all die. Or go broke—which, for many, was the same as death.

The only problem with the fund-raiser was that the people the chairman really needed weren't in attendance. Typically, the conservative, right-wing Tea Party crowd didn't attend functions where a drink was a necessary lubricant to promote the easy flow of money and favors.

There was one person, though, who held great sway over the far right. The Tea Party leader from Minnesota. He could deliver them, but there would be a condition. There always was.

The chairman pushed his computer keyboard away and picked up the phone. He leaned back in his chair and swiveled around to face the window overlooking the expansive green yard. On the fourth ring, somebody finally answered.

"Don't start with the pleasantries. Skip that shit and get to the point. But please use lubrication this time."

"My, my, are we having a bad day?" the chairman asked, smiling into the receiver.

"I was having a perfect day until you called."

"You're making assumptions. Maybe this call is about giving

you something."

"Is it?"

"Yes and no."

"The no is what I'm worried about."

"So I'll start with the no."

"Good."

"Well, Congressman, I need your support. Quantitative easing. Bond purchases. Our economy is on life support, and I can't keep it going without buying more bonds. Eighty-five billion per month, minimum. Your colleagues on the right have a problem with this, and that's causing a problem for me. If they don't back off and I lose support on the right, I may lose the president's support. And we both know that's not good."

"I'm not so sure anymore. Quantitative easing is putting tons of greenbacks into the money supply without anything behind them. In the short term, it looks good, but in the long term, our children will pay the price in the form of inflation, credit bubbles, and unsupported run-ups in asset values due to low interest rates. So how is ending QE not good?" the congressman answered.

"Wow, you paid attention in Economics 101. I'm impressed," the chairman said while putting his feet up on the credenza behind his desk. "We've had this conversation before. While all those risks you talked about do exist with QE, the risk is much greater without it."

"Risk of what?"

"Interest rates going up, housing values going down, business investments falling, unemployment rates rising, consumer confidence faltering—and ultimately recession. You don't want that."

"Why not? Maybe we have to tighten our belt a bit to get through this. Reduce the deficit."

"We can't. We need easy money and low rates. As we found in 2008, recession is only a part of it. Easy money keeps us from finding out how deep the hole really is. The world depends on our economy. It depends on our money. And it depends on our good faith. Without it, we may be unleashing the four horsemen. Apocalypse. Is that what you want?"

"Someday, we'll have to find out how deep the hole is, won't we?" the congressman asked. "Faith is only good if it is based upon something that is real."

"We will need to go down the hole. But it has to be done the right way. The way that prevents this from happening again," the chairman answered, putting his feet down and reaching for a cigar in the humidor on his desk.

"I assume you're going to tell me the right way?"

"Deniability has its privileges."

"Give me something."

"The best way to control the economy is to *be* the economy."

"The government that governs best is the government that owns the most."

"You're getting it."

"I'm not sure I can deliver the far-right caucus."

"Oh, you greatly underrate your persuasive powers," the chairman said while snipping the end of his cigar and putting it into his mouth, unlit.

"And this is where you tell me what I get."

"Keep the far right quiet and you'll have power to shape the new economic order. Trust me."

"I need more than some pie-in-the-sky platitudes," the congressman answered while admiring the rear view of one of his assistants as she walked from his office.

"You know, 2008 was just a dry run. The next financial meltdown will be a lot worse. It's not a matter of if; it's a matter of when. And when it happens, I have the answer. And QE is the vehicle that drives my plan," the chairman said while taking the cigar from his mouth and rubbing a smudge from his real mahogany desk.

"Yes, but it could be quite a while before another crash."

"QE is not the underlying cause of our decrepit financial house. Deficit spending is. So all I have to do is turn off the spigot, and presto, we have a crash. I control the timing. But in the meantime, I need QE."

"What is your plan?"

"This is where the aforementioned deniability becomes valuable for you."

"What about your deniability?'

"I have mine."

"You might as well tell me; I'll find out, anyway."

"Knowledge can be dangerous."

"Keeping me in the dark can be dangerous too."

"You aren't the only one with a loyal operative."

"So QE is the money. The money behind your real scheme?" the congressman asked, ignoring the chairman's last statement.

"I wouldn't say *scheme*. More like *plan*. But yes, pretend money is needed until it isn't. Then real money will be the savior, and you will be too."

"Political savior or real savior?" the congressman asked.

"They're the same thing. We both know that the current president and his party aren't willing or able to address the real financial issues. They can't cut spending, and they can't cut easy money. When our plan goes public and you're the one who cleans up the mess, we'll be the only ones the people trust. And that will translate into power. Presidential power."

"As in Germany pre-Hitler? Democrats and Republicans won't matter. For all intents and purposes, a coup."

"Now you're getting the socialist picture. Please keep me posted," the chairman answered while hanging up the phone. He grabbed the silver lighter on his desk and held the flame to the end of the cigar, breathing in the distinct Cuban aroma.

67

The middle can be a good thing. People like to lick the middle before eating the Oreo cookie. The middle child is usually well adjusted. The middle of the T-bone is always the tenderest. But Monique wasn't sure this middle was quite the same. She was being asked to check on and facilitate two illicit and probably illegal operations—operations that were directed against each other by two men she found attractive. If that wasn't the definition of a double agent, then what was? Except she didn't do it for money or country or politics. She did it for love.

She'd just gotten off the phone with Caleb. Now he wanted her to hack into a life insurance company, a subsidiary of AIS, one of the largest insurance companies in the world, and find out what she could about a few specific life insurance policies. Monique wished she had more information. She hated doing this and not knowing what her client was after.

But she had agreed. Caleb had that effect on her. She didn't know anything about him, but she trusted him, and she wasn't sure why.

She knew she'd have to pick sides—and thus a man—eventually. This couldn't go on much longer. She hoped that something, anything, would make the decision for her.

A knock interrupted her reverie. Whoever was knocking was impatient.

"Chill out! You're going to break the door."

She peered through the peephole. Son of a bitch. The other half. She slowly opened the door.

"What the hell do you want?" she said, smiling as she opened the door all the way.

"You know what I want."

"What?"

"Never mind."

He had been through a lot. God, what a stud.

"Come on in, Zane; you know I'm here for you. Always will be."

Zane came in, dutifully took off his shoes, and plumped down on the recliner. He did look beat. *Damn, why didn't he sit on the sofa?*

Monique did sit on the sofa, toward the end with her feet curled up under her. She hoped it was her inviting look.

"Why the sad, tired vibe?"

"Thanks for caring. Just a lot going on. I've taken over as the head of SAS, and I hope it was the right thing to do. Doubts are invading," Zane said.

"That's a bold move. Sometimes the decisions we make seem right at the time. Then later on, we wonder what the hell we were thinking."

"That happens to me all the time."

"Don't worry. It'll work out. I promise."

"You haven't been peeking at my laptop, have you?"

"No," she answered truthfully.

"Good. I knew I could trust you. So how are you sure this will all be good in the end?"

"Because that's what you deserve. By the way, have you heard from Tec lately, or are you guys on the outs or something?" Monique asked.

"Something like that."

"Like what? I mean, you guys seemed inseparable during our drink excursions after training. And you started this together. What changed?"

"Sometimes you have to take a step backward to make two steps forward."

"I hope Tec agrees. Now what is it you want again?"

"Is that the only reason I stop over?"

"It has been. And that's fine. I like being needed. Especially by you," Monique replied, thinking she could be using that line on Caleb too.

"I'll have to change that. I do need something. I need you to appropriate some funds from one of Thompson's accounts. Fifteen million," Zane said while closing his eyes and then rapidly reopening them. She was still here. "And I need you to make sure he doesn't know I'm the one who took it."

Holy shitballs.

"Steal his money? Um, that's more than a tad illegal. Are you going to visit me if I'm caught?"

"If you do this right, you won't get caught. I know I'm putting a lot on you, but I have nowhere else to turn. And I need some information on a man called Caleb Rider."

Monique stood up and went over to the window. Staring at her back gave nothing away.

"Do you also have a small video camera that I can hide easily?" Zane asked, still speaking to her behind, and although it was quite nice, he'd rather talk to her face.

"I do," she answered quietly.

"Last, I'm also going to get you originating accounts on deposits into the SAS account. I want you to verify the ownership of the originating accounts," Zane said, trying to will her to turn around. "Those electronic funds transfers by the Federal Reserve to

Thompson have me thinking. Were they just transactions cleared by the Fed, or was the money from the Fed? I need to trace the money backward."

"I take it that's all the information I'm going to get," she said as she continued staring at the sky.

"I don't want to give you any more. The less you know, the less you can be held accountable for," Zane replied.

Monique turned around and sat on the arm of Zane's chair. "That didn't give me a warm, fuzzy feeling,"

"I get the strong feeling that you've done this type of work before."

"In case you don't remember, I'm in it for you," Monique replied, quietly wishing she didn't have two men she was telling that to. Somehow it seemed traitorous.

"Can you promise me Thompson won't know I took the money? I don't want him to think I'm reneging on our truce."

"Yes, I can hide that, but he'll assume that you stole it, since you have control over the accounts. Are you sure that's what you want?"

"Can't you make it look like somebody else took it? In fact, I'll give you Holmes's account number. Run it through his," Zane said, looking up at her. "Also, I need the camera to be online, streamed, and saved to my laptop, which you still have."

"I can do that, but I wish I knew more."

"You don't trust me?"

Monique turned and looked at Zane. "I do trust you. Just don't abuse it."

Monique felt guilt wash over her as the words left her mouth. She was abusing his trust.

"I feel like I'm taking advantage of you," Zane said, his eyes probing for her physical response.

"Then why don't you?" Monique replied, putting her hand on his knee.

"What?"

"I'm just a girl. I need big men like you to protect me since I have a pussy and everything."

Zane raised his eyebrows. "I know you can handle yourself. But I will protect you."

"It is nice to meet a chivalrous male. Not many of you left. The last guy I was with would hear a bump in the night and ask me to check it out."

"That's because he was a pussy."

Monique laughed. "His penis was kind of small."

"But then again, pussies are good, on the right sex."

"They are. They're very good."

She stood up, leaned over Zane, and moved his arms out of the way so she could sit on his lap, facing him.

"Is this pussy being too forward?"

"I don't know. I really don't know. I'm attracted to your pussy. Er, you know what I mean."

She laughed again. "I'm attracted to your lack of pussy. If you know what I mean."

"Absolutely. Except I don't think I'm ready. You don't know what you're getting into."

"No, you don't know what you could be getting into. I could show you, though."

Now Zane laughed. "That's what I'm concerned about. Once I see that, it could be all over but the moaning and sighing. I need to be careful. You do too. I'm not who you think I am."

She must like guys who weren't who she thought they were.

"Apparently, I like that."

"Huh?"

Monique leaned in and kissed Zane. Long and slow and with tongue. He didn't resist. Finally, he gently pushed her away and stood up.

"Surprises aren't all they are cracked up to be, Monique."

68

He'd been through this before, but it was different this time. He would make it different. Now he was trying to do what was right. He was trying to turn around the damage, if that were even possible. Zane knocked on the large front door of the Guardian home. He silently wished nobody was there.

Zane's wish went unfulfilled when Ben opened the door. "Good evening, Zane. Thank you so much for stopping by. Come on in. We're all in the great room," Ben said as he ushered Zane into the house.

Zane grabbed his arm to stop him before they left the entryway. "Hey, before I go in that room and talk to the whole Guardian clan, you have to tell me what's going on. Don't just put me out there blind."

Ben stopped, looked at the floor, and slowly turned to Zane. "I've discovered that my family has competing interests. They all want me to save Guardian Jewelry, but for different, selfish reasons. If I'm going to pay the price and do this, they need to know what this is going to cost them."

"You tell them. Why do I have to?" Zane replied, still holding on to Ben's arm.

"Because it's your idea. If you're going to eat the sausage, you need to see how it's made," Ben replied, twisting his arm out of Zane's grasp.

Zane stepped back. He needed to be careful. While he had to give them something, he couldn't give them too much, or he risked exposing his plan before he was ready.

"Okay, just remember you asked for this," Zane said as he followed Ben into the great room.

Ben made the appropriate introductions and explained to Zane that he had laid the plan out to his family but that they had questions for Zane—questions he wanted Zane to answer, bluntly.

"Okay, but remember, anything said here stays here. Violation of this rule can have severe consequences," Zane explained.

Tim, Sue, and Carol all nodded in agreement. Paula stared at Zane with a slight grin on her face. "Scary stuff."

"First of all," Sue started while glaring angrily at Paula, "why does it have to be life insurance? Why can't it be a loan, an investment, or any other financial vehicle that could introduce cash into the company?"

That actually was a very good question.

Zane turned to face Sue. "There are multiple reasons, but all of them have to do with the critical state of Guardian Jewelry's financial health. There is no collateral for a loan; nobody will invest in an old-school jewelry store. Buying and selling a life insurance policy on Ben is the only way we can get the money and get it quickly."

"How soon do we get the money?" Carol asked while sitting on the edge of the ottoman.

"Not soon enough for this family," Paula said while flipping the La-Z-Boy to full recline and taking a sip of her drink.

"As soon as the investor makes sure the policy is bona fide," Zane answered, ignoring Paula. "Usually, that takes about a week."

"So then some of the money goes to Ben, and the rest goes to your company, SAS?" Sue asked.

"Yes, we use some of the money to purchase the company, and the rest we keep as our profit," Zane answered.

"So other than—well, *the event*, we're out of the picture?" Carol asked nervously.

"Until the investor gets his money back from the death benefit of the policy. You'll have to sign a few forms then," Zane answered.

"We'll be on easy street soon enough," Tim said while smiling at Zane.

"It seems pretty simple," Sue stated while staring straight ahead, looking at no one.

Paula laughed. "Let's cut through the bullshit. The 'event' you so eloquently referred to is the death of our father. That's the fucking elephant in the room nobody wants to address. So I will. Dad seems healthy to me. How does he die? And when?"

"We know Dad's death will be faked and that we may never get to see him again, but how will it be faked? Details will help us feel better," Carol said quietly.

Zane sighed. This was his first acquisition since he'd found out the truth, but he couldn't tell them the truth. Disclosing that the principals actually died would jeopardize everything. "We'll take care of that. The family doesn't need to be concerned about that," Zane lied.

"Will you now? Well, then, I guess that's it," Paula said, pouring down the last of her drink and flipping the La-Z-Boy back to upright. "I've got shit to do." She stood up and walked past everybody and out the front door.

"My death will be faked," Ben said quietly, watching Paula walk out the door. "It won't be real."

As Zane silently nodded assent to this latest comment, a vision ran through his mind of Ben lying dead in a car at the bottom of a ravine with Tim dead beside him.

69

Running around Lake Harriet early in the morning was comparable to rush hour in downtown Minneapolis. People of all shapes and sizes, colors, and ethnicities loved to run there. It was trendy. It seemed to be more about being seen than it was about fitness. And the jealous looks Caleb received confirmed his suspicion that it was also about who you were seen with.

"Are you getting what you want?" Monique asked as she effortlessly glided down the well-worn path wearing very short black silk running shorts, black Pumas, and a black running bra that was more for exhibiting the goods than support.

"Yeah, I'm starting to sweat," Caleb answered, struggling to hide the fact he was struggling to keep up.

"I mean from this, you and me."

"Depends."

"On what?"

"If you slow down and let me catch up," Caleb responded, dropping behind her a bit, enjoying the one benefit to running behind Monique—her behind.

"Kind of like our relationship," Monique responded with no loss of breath.

It was obvious this run wasn't much of a workout for her.

"Kind of like that. Our pieces are there, and they're falling into place, just not on your timetable," Caleb said as he pulled up to a grassy spot.

"My timetable says don't postpone to tomorrow what can be done today, especially when the fish may be looking at other hooks."

"Oh, now I get it. There's somebody else, and you need to know where we stand."

"Maybe. Maybe I need to know your true intentions. Like do you intend on sampling the goods, or are you just content to look? I saw you back there."

"That answer will have to wait. Did you notice the guy over by the band shell?"

"Running with his jeans and button-down shirt? I'm not just another pretty face."

"He's been on us for the last couple of miles. Before I let you know my intentions, I intend to find out his intentions. Wait here."

"Don't you want backup? Or is feminine backup not cool?"

"You can have my back anytime. Watch for his cohorts. I'll approach him one-on-one."

"Gotcha. I'll just stand here and wait for your return, oh big, strong, quiet one."

Caleb stared back at her and walked away shaking his head. He liked her a lot, but he sensed it was getting complicated. He didn't do complicated.

When he was about fifty feet away, the tail made him. He turned abruptly and headed for the parking lot. Caleb began to run. His quarry did, as well. It was going to be a footrace. Caleb had not lost one of those, for, well, he guessed his whole life. What he lacked in endurance, he made up for in speed.

The man he was hunting realized that and disappeared behind a row of cars. Caleb immediately sensed where this was going to end up. He took the shortcut. He came around the other end of the row and, sure enough, there he was. A big guy with a gun. It was a small Beretta, hidden in his palm.

"Just to get your attention," Big Man said.

"You got it."

"Don't make the mistake of not taking this seriously. Other people have done that, and that became one of their life regrets."

"I'm beginning to regret this conversation," Caleb said as he moved a bit closer.

"Stay back. Any closer and you'll regret more than this conversation."

Caleb stopped. Something about Big made Caleb realize he had done this before. He was no stranger to violence.

"Okay, what's the point? Get to it."

"You need to stay away from SAS and Zane Donovan. A long fucking way away. In fact, I'd suggest taking your little lady friend and going on a trip. Today is as good a time as any."

"Why would I want to do that?"

"You're getting involved in something that's not going to end well. There is nothing for you in this but pain."

"Sometimes pain serves a purpose."

"This kind will hurt those around you. Just leave. Or else."

"That just makes me want to stay. You have no idea who you're talking to here. The last guy who pulled a gun on me never lived to regret it."

"I'm not the last guy. I'm the guy you need to listen to. Now and always."

Caleb was about five feet from him, and his options were limited. And then they weren't.

"Hey, big boy, don't you remember there were two of us?" Monique said as Big turned around.

That gave Caleb his opening. He covered the five feet in less than a second and applied the sleeper hold before Big could respond. Big was unconscious within another five seconds, and Caleb took his Beretta and tucked it into his shorts. Monique drifted back into the scenery. There had to be another one.

There was. A short, skinny guy. He stepped out from behind the tree, pointing another gun at Caleb. Monique stayed still because she knew he'd seen her.

"Drop him and the gun and step back," Skinny said. "Way back. Farther yet."

Caleb complied. He sensed that Skinny was more dangerous than Big.

Skinny walked up to Big and kicked him in the ribs. Big moaned softly, came to, and stood up unsteadily. A small crowd was beginning to form.

Big glared at Caleb. "It's sunny today, but the rain always comes."

Skinny helped Big to his feet as he glared at Caleb. "You had better make sure you have a big fucking umbrella."

The crowd was getting larger.

"Come on, Rocker," Skinny said as they disappeared into the sea of people.

70

Zane was ready. He was sitting in the SAS conference room, waiting for Ben and Sue Guardian and the life insurance representative from AIS. This would be his last closing, and that gave him a small sense of satisfaction. Until he thought about Ben—dead.

The conference table had a glass top and chrome legs, with twelve black, modern-looking chairs surrounding it. A wet bar occupied one corner, and a large-screen, closed-circuit TV was hanging on the front wall. It wouldn't be needed today.

The only video equipment needed for this meeting was Monique's camera, well hidden on top of the TV screen.

Zane looked up as Caleb walked into the room with his cell phone and a large yellow legal tablet. Caleb grabbed a bottle of water from the fridge and sat down next to Zane.

"Your presence is not needed," Zane said as he looked at Caleb and pointed at the door.

"Sally told me you're handling the Guardian closing today," Caleb responded, and he took a long swig of water. "Man, I love ice-cold water."

"The Guardian closing is in a few minutes, and you need to leave."

"Relax. How am I supposed to learn from the best if I can't observe?"

"I don't care. I can't explain your presence here, so vamoose."

"Just tell everybody I'm new and just watching."

"You are new, but you aren't watching."

The intercom beeped, and Sally began to speak. "The agent is here. Should I escort him to the conference room?"

"Yes, and please do the same for the Guardians when they arrive," Zane replied while pointing at Caleb and pointing to the door again.

"I'm staying," Caleb said, standing up to shake the hands of the insurance agent as he walked in.

"Hello, Zane. And who is this?" the agent asked.

"My associate, Caleb Rider, but he was just leaving," Zane said as handshakes were exchanged.

"And what is your name?" Caleb asked as he shook the agent's hand.

"Ryan Anderson, AIS."

"I thought the life insurance company was a subsidiary of AIS?" Caleb asked.

"They are, but for acquisition closings, we send an actual AIS employee," Ryan answered.

"And why is that?"

At that moment, Ben and Sue Guardian walked in, and another round of handshakes and introductions was exchanged.

As all parties were seated, Caleb asked his question again. "Why would an employee of AIS be here for the closing and not an employee of the subsidiary insurance company?"

Ben shot Zane a quizzical look while Ryan responded, "I'm afraid I'm not prepared to answer that question, and we won't be able to proceed with this closing until Mr. Rider leaves."

"As I said earlier, he was just leaving. Right, Caleb?" Zane said.

"Okay, I get it. Party is over, at least for me." Caleb stood up with his tablet and half empty bottle of water. "I guess I'll just have to learn some other way," Caleb mumbled as he shut the door behind him.

"Thank you, Zane," Ryan said as he opened his briefcase and brought out a large manila file with the words Guardian Jewelry stamped across it. "The fewer people, the quicker this will be."

"Before we do any signing today, for the benefit of my wife and me too, can you explain exactly what is transpiring here? I mean everything. I want to know how the sale of my company affects my former employees, what happens to my customers, and how the money flows from the life insurance, to the viatical, and then to me," Ben said while letting out loud sigh. "And most importantly, I need to know—"

"Wait a second, Ben," Zane replied as he walked over to the place Caleb had been sitting. "It looks like Caleb left his phone, and it's in the middle of a call. Hello, hello?" Zane asked into the phone as the call promptly ended.

"Now, what again was the most important thing, Ben?" he asked as he calmly took the battery out of Caleb's phone and dropped both on the table, hoping that it would render it defunct as a recording device.

Ben stared at the now battery-less phone and then looked at Sue and then at Zane, who winked at him and smiled. "The most important piece of this agreement that Sue and I want to discuss is the—well, the death. How will my death be faked, and how do I disappear? As you might guess, this is a big deal, and we both need to know more."

"Who was that man who just left?" Sue asked with more than a little trepidation in her voice.

"An associate of mine," Zane answered calmly and confidently. "He's in the learning phase. But he must learn to walk before he runs. Isn't that right, Ben?"

Ben nodded as he put his hand reassuringly on top of Sue's.

Ryan was also staring at the phone and battery on the table

and then looked up to Ben. "Well, now that the phone is off, I can answer all of your questions. And since the death is the most important part, I'll start there. First though, Zane, can you get me something to drink? This is going to take a while."

71

New Ulm, Minnesota, twenty-one years earlier.

Ray's childhood had been a game. Hide-and-seek. He hated his home life, so he tried to spend as much time away as he could. His parents would often question him about where he'd been, and he'd lie. It didn't matter where he went, as long as he was away from them. He'd rather live in a cardboard box under a bridge with the homeless than in his crazy household. The day he could leave couldn't come soon enough.

As he grew older, his father's beatings were harder to take. His friends from school didn't have to live like this. They didn't have to be scared to go home. When Ray would visit friends, he'd witness the peace and love in their homes. He wanted that too. He wanted to be happy.

But Ray knew he deserved his punishment. He was a bad person, and that's why his parents were angry with him. He just couldn't figure out how to be good.

He couldn't hide the abuse forever. He would change for gym class in the bathroom instead of the locker room. Otherwise, someone might see his bruises and scars. It was better to be thought sexually weird than to suffer the embarrassment of being a bad child who was beaten. If teachers approached his dad and asked what was going on at home, the punishment would be doubly bad.

Telling on Dad wasn't an option.

Then one day, a teacher did find out. Ray had to go to the front of the class to point out Siberia on a world map. As he stretched his hand above his head, his shirt rode up, exposing the lower edge of his rib cage. Mrs. Danielson caught her breath and quickly asked about those marks and scars on his side. He was able to convince her that it was due to an ATV accident. She seemed to buy the story after he told it over and over.

Ray knew that the deception wouldn't last.

The time had come for him to act. He had to do something. Ray didn't care what happened. It was better to be dead than to live in constant pain and suffering.

His opportunity came on a rainy Saturday afternoon two weeks after he turned fourteen. His dad always worked until late afternoon on Saturdays, but that day, he came home early due to the rain. His crew couldn't work in the rain. He arrived with a full case of beer and drank half of it before supper. He sat at the table in a drunken, surly mood, complaining about the food in front of him. His mother yelled at him, telling him to go straight to hell. That was Ray's cue. He got up from his place at the supper table, walked to his dad's seat, picked up his plate, and smashed it on the floor. He looked at the food and pieces of plate strewn about the floor and then looked up at his dad with an emotionless stare.

His mom screamed, "Ray!" Then she ran to the bathroom to hide.

He could hear the bathroom door lock as his dad took a slow drink from his beer bottle.

Ray turned to his dad. "If you don't like this shit, then don't eat it. We all have choices to make in life."

His dad put the beer bottle down. "Get in the fucking basement. Now." His drunken slur was crystal clear in Ray's ears. "You fucked up big time. You won't be sitting tomorrow. I'll teach you to ever fuck with anything of mine."

He stood up and stumbled to the cupboard and grabbed a shot of courage, Canadian Club Whisky.

Ray had a club of his own. He stared at his dad, burning this moment into his memory, and went down the basement.

At the bottom of the stairs, he retrieved the Louisville Slugger he'd placed under the shelf where his dad kept his horseshoe-pitching trophies. No trophy for Dad tonight.

He stood to the right of the stairs, where his dad wouldn't be able to see him as he came down.

He heard his dad put the shot glass down, come closer to the stairs, and take them one by one.

Ray was only fourteen, but he was tall and strong for his age. And his plan relied on leverage more than strength.

Ray shivered, but he was happy the end was near.

As his dad stepped off the bottom step and headed straight for the "beating room," Ray stepped up behind him. The first swing caught him flush on the back of the neck, and his dad went down like the sack of drunken, old shit he was. Ray stood over him and hit him again and again. Ray, soaked in the blood of his revenge, had two thoughts.

It ends tonight.

I hope this bat doesn't break before he's dead.

72

"Hey, Zanese, what's going on?"

"Just wondering if we could spend tonight with you. We miss you."

Zanese could evoke feelings in him nobody else could. How could he say no?

"Sure. We'll make spaghetti for supper and play cards or something. Make sure to bring all your money. I feel a lucky streak coming on," Zane said with great enthusiasm.

"Dad, you never win when we play cards for money. But that's fine; we need some money, anyway. Grandma is pretty stingy with the candy around here."

"Well, I feel sure my luck is changing. Bring it on, girl."

"Same crap, different day."

That sarcastic crack wasn't like Zanese. She knew her mom wouldn't have tolerated that.

"Watch it. You know Grandma doesn't like that talk. Tell her I'll be over in a half hour. I know she'll like not having to cook tonight."

"See you soon," Zanese said as she hung up.

Tec was right about one thing. Zanese and James were two reasons for him to go on.

Zane checked the fridge and cupboards to make sure he had

the makings for spaghetti. He was only missing sauce. Thirty minutes should give him enough time to stop for sauce. He also needed to pick up some pop and maybe even some candy. If Betty was making them go cold turkey on candy, he could surprise them with a little treat. Maybe they'd play for candy tonight instead of money. That would be fun.

He grabbed his keys, his cell phone, and a jacket and headed out the door. He couldn't wait to see them. Zane needed to forget about SAS for one night.

His car was parked in a small lot next to his apartment, front end in up against a wall. As he approached the driver's side door, he stopped next to the rear door, trying to find the remote button to pop the locks.

Suddenly, the rear door sprang open, slamming into Zane and knocking him against the neighboring car. Momentarily stunned, he rolled to his right to get out of hitting range of the large man who exited the backseat. As he rolled against the car, another man approached from behind. He had a gun in his hand. He pressed it against Zane's neck and pulled the trigger. Zane immediately went numb. He fell to the ground and began to spasm uncontrollably. Just before he lost consciousness, he stared at the familiar face that was now inches from his.

"Sorry, Zane, but this is for your own good," Tec said as he removed the stun gun and stood up, carefully making sure no witnesses would spoil this abduction.

73

MINNEAPOLIS, NINETEEN YEARS EARLIER.

All the kids there had problems or had caused problems. Maybe nobody had ever loved them. It didn't matter now; he hated every one of them. He wished they would all go away. He wanted a bathroom he felt safe in that smelled nice and had decorative little soaps on the counter. He wanted a room of his own where he could read adventure stories or watch TV or just daydream, like other boys did. Yet that wasn't his reality. His reality was living out his punishment in hellholes like this one with demon-possessed, ravaged boys who constantly wanted to do him harm.

Since the hearing, Ray had been in two other correctional facilities for boys. This was his third. From the outside, it looked like a large, older, yet well-maintained home. On the inside, it also looked like a home, except for the barred hallway and bedroom doors and the smell. It wasn't a bad smell, but it wasn't good, either. It smelled institutional. The bedrooms were large enough for two boys. Ray had no privacy. They had tried him as a minor and found him guilty of second-degree assault and attempted murder with extenuating circumstances. The circumstances being that his dad beat the shit out of him. His dad had survived, which hadn't been Ray's intention at all. In fact, his father's death had been all he cared about.

Ray was remanded to the state for the rest of his years as a minor and would be released upon his eighteenth birthday, if he was found mentally competent. He knew he was mentally competent. He knew that because he'd almost killed a man who deserved to die. Ray didn't have one bit of remorse or regret. The counselors asked him about that constantly, and when he explained why he tried to kill him, they didn't seem the least bit concerned about his lack of remorse.

They didn't let him out for any day trips. The counselor said it could upset his mom. It might. It should. She'd let the abuse happen day after day. In Ray's book, she was as guilty as he was. Who cared if it upset her?

His mom never visited him, even though the facility was less than a two-hour drive from their home in New Ulm. Ray wasn't sure if it was because she felt partially guilty or if she just hated him. He didn't care either way.

His sister, Joan, came to visit once a month. She brought him books and magazines, and didn't talk about the attack or their father. She was his lifeline to the outside world. Ray wished he could be more like her. Then one day, she changed his world.

Sundays were visiting days, and she'd driven up after church, dressed like the unblemished saint she was. Her white dress contrasted sharply with the dirty past of his life. He wished he could someday have a wife like her. Never once did she accuse him of being wrong for what he did. Her grace and love seemed limitless and unconditional.

This day, he was allowed to go outside with her. They walked to a bench in the front of the building. It wasn't much better than sitting inside, but at least the sun was out. The bench faced the street with a small wrought iron fence separating the two.

Ray sat down first, leaning his head back to soak up some of the rays, trying to burn the smell of that place out of his skin. Joan sat down next to him and grabbed his hand.

"Mom asked me to tell her how you are. Is that okay?"

"Yeah, that's fine, as long as you tell her I'm great."

She dropped his hand and grabbed Ray behind his neck, forcing him to look at her.

"Even if you're not?"

"Especially if I'm not."

Joan smiled, dropped her hands, and began to wring them in her lap.

"You need to cut her a little slack. She suffered through some of the same stuff you did."

"I know, but she's the one who could have done something about it. She chose not to," Ray said, now looking at her intently and spitting out the words. He stood up, walked over to the fence, and leaned his arms against it, keeping his back to her.

"Maybe she didn't have a choice."

"We all have a choice. And we live with the choices we make. She has to, just like I do."

"None of us are perfect."

"Let's talk about something else. What's in the bag?" Ray said, turning around and sitting down again.

"A gift. A very special gift for you."

"I don't deserve a gift, especially not a special one."

"It isn't about merit."

"Sure it is. If we don't deserve it, we don't get it. Anything other than that's a lie."

She put her hand to his face and stroked his cheek. "I have never lied to you, and I hope never will."

"We'll see."

His sister looked extremely excited about whatever it was. She told him to close his eyes. Ray had to admit that his excitement was growing too. Before he closed his eyes, he checked to see if anybody was looking. They were alone. Good. He closed his eyes tight.

"Okay, open them. I really hope you like it."

He opened his eyes and saw a black scrapbook laid out before him. Across its cover was written "Celebrating 16 Years of Ray!"

"I know your birthday isn't until next week, but this was my closest visit. Come on, open it," she said, anxiously tapping her feet.

"I'm scared. What if I don't like it?" Ray said, keeping his hands from even touching the book.

"You have to like it. It's you!"

Ray tentatively took the book and opened the first page. On it were various pictures of Ray as a baby. Opposite was a written letter about Ray from his grandma and grandpa on his mom's side. It was short and to the point.

Ray was the baby boy this family needed. We had only daughters, and Ray's birth fulfilled our greatest dream. He was a beautiful baby and a joy to take care of. He didn't cry much, and when he was old enough, he always listened to what we told him. I'll never forget the day he first walked. He was so proud of himself, and at nine months! We knew it was the beginning of very big things in his life. We still believe that. It is up to you, Ray. Only you have the power. We love you and miss you.

The book went on and on. Each page had pictures of different stages of his life, with the facing page being a letter from someone who had an impact on him during that time. It was surprising to him that there were so many. He'd always felt that he had no friends, no one who cared for him.

There were letters from his junior high football coach who said Ray was a leader. One from his best friend in third grade who said Ray was the best and craziest friend he'd ever had in his life.

Another was from his fifth-grade teacher, who'd recommended Ray skip a grade because he was so smart. And one from his eighth-grade sweetheart. She'd never forget him and how nice he was to everybody, no matter how they treated him.

Ray was stunned. He never knew he had such an impact on people. He saw himself as a loser who deserved his crappy life. He began to get a small glimpse of the idea that maybe he deserved more.

The second-to-last page was about him and his sister. It had pictures of the fun times they had enjoyed. There were quite a few of them. And the letter.

> My wonderful and dearest brother,
>
> Life without you is boring, stupid, and sad. I miss you all the time. I miss you stealing my underwear off the line and hiding it around the house. I miss you and your friends playing baseball in the field next to our house and trying to act all macho so my friends and I would notice. Remember that time we followed you to the swimming pool and stole your bike and you had to walk home? You were so mad.
>
> We'll always be together, no matter how far apart we are. You're the best brother any sister could hope for. Don't let this ruin you. You are too good for that. If you don't believe me, then believe all the other people in this book. They believe in you. We all do. It is all the truth. I know everything that's happened to you has sucked. I figure you can either let it make you bitter or make you better. Weaker or stronger. Please allow it to make you better and stronger. I can't wait until you get out and we can share good times again. It won't be long.
>
> Sayonara, little bro.

She grabbed his knee and squeezed it. "Exciting, isn't it! Come on, one more page."

There was one page left. He was afraid to turn it. All of this has been so good, why ruin it now?

"Go ahead. You can do it."

He turned the page. It was from his mother. His eyes began to fuzz up with tears. Why did she have to be in this?

Ray,

Don't hate me. I haven't been perfect. Far from it. I've done you physical and emotional harm. I'm sorry. I know it's changed you, and that thought keeps me awake at night. Some days I hate myself and wish I could stop this tortured life. I have no excuses and don't want you to feel sorry for me. Just know, though, that there were reasons for what I did and didn't do. They don't sound like good reasons now, but at the time they did. I was the best mom I knew how to be. Please forgive me. I love you. You are part of me.

Mom

Ray couldn't take his eyes from that page. He was glued to it like a gawker at an accident scene. Tears were streaming down his face. Could they be a family again? Somehow, someway, could they all be repaired? Please, God, make it so. For the first time in his short life, he had hope. Life could be good again.

He closed the book softly and looked up at his sister. She was crying now too, but smiling at the same time. They hugged so hard he thought his back would break. They finally unclenched.

"This is the best gift anyone has ever given me. I'm too stunned to say anything. You're an amazing sister."

"You're the amazing one. I love you, Ray, and always will. But I have to go now. Time is up. I'll be back soon. Try to remember that life will be good again. I promise."

They both stood up and wiped the tears from their faces. Ray walked her back into the building and to the front lobby. She opened the door into the bright, sunny day and turned to wave at him. She looked like a heavenly vision framed in the golden rays.

She didn't keep her promise.

74

The fighters called this place "the House of Pain." It had certainly brought Zane his share of pain. He'd also administered his share of pain. Tonight, he'd be on the receiving end of a different kind of pain. A pain with a purpose.

They were at the Warrior's Den. It was deserted, since there were no classes on Sunday nights. He was stripped to his underwear and sitting in a chair with his hands tied behind his back and his socks stuffed into his mouth, covered by a gag. The only light in the room was the one over his head. Tec was standing in a dark corner. Spaz and Rocker stood off to the side in front of Zane. And there was a woman. A beautiful woman. She was tall and slender with long auburn hair. She had prominent cheekbones and full lips. She was the most beautiful woman Zane had ever seen. She was dressed casually in jeans and a T-shirt, with black Puma running shoes. She was smiling at Zane. The smile contrasted sharply with the wicked-looking instrument in her hand. It was a probe of some sort with a switch at the end. Zane had two alligator clips attached to his nipples with a cable running to a car battery. They were serious.

"Mr. Zane Donovan. I'm pleased to make your acquaintance. My name is Chastity. I work for Mr. Thompson. Don't worry; my name isn't indicative of my intentions here. You won't be a virgin when I'm done."

286

"Let's just get this over with," Rocker said as he began pacing around the room.

"Yeah, let's be quick about it," Tec said without moving from the corner. "Someone else has a set of keys."

"Relax. It will take as long as it takes. You don't want to rush me."

"Let her work," Spaz said as he stood with crossed arms. "You said the lady never shows up this late."

Chastity turned back toward Zane. "We had a truce. You promised you wouldn't fuck with Mr. Thompson's money and we wouldn't hurt your kids. But then you took $15 million, anyway. We need that money back. And the video of the Guardian closing."

Monique. She must have told them.

Chastity was standing behind Spaz, and she was reaching around him to rub his crotch. "You're trying to get information about money going into SAS. Mr. Thompson doesn't want you making inquiries into that."

"If you take his socks out of his mouth, maybe he'd tell you where the money and the video are," Tec said, moving up a couple of steps.

"You could tell me where they are now. But you won't. And even if you did, you wouldn't have learned your lesson," Chastity said as she grabbed Zane's shoulders and leaned down with her face close to Zane's. "You fuck with us, we will fuck with you. Anytime, anyplace. I call it fun," she said as she yanked the key off his neck. "I need to find out what this key unlocks."

Her breath was sweet. Like candy. Candy made Zane think of the kids. What did they think when he didn't show up?

"Is this the key to your future, Zane, or your past?" Chastity asked as she threw the key to Tec.

Zane knew they would never find out what that key unlocked, and that gave him some small sense of relief.

"Just do this damn thing," Tec said as he moved up a couple of steps.

Zane glanced at Tec. He was showing no emotion. Zane hoped very much that all of this was going according to plan as he steeled himself for whatever was about to happen. He had to separate his mind from his body. Remove himself from the pain and look for an opening. He'd sat in this chair before.

"Okay, pay attention here. This is an electric cattle prod. And *prod* is the operative word. I'm going to put this on or into a part of your body. Then we'll flip the switch on the nipple clips, and you'll decide which hurts most. You won't die, but you may wish you would. Then, after you think you can't stand it any longer, I'll shut it down. You'll have approximately sixty seconds to tell us the location of the money. If you don't, I pick a different orifice, and we start all over again. I have all night. Let's begin."

She took the gag off his mouth and removed his socks. Zane worked his jaw around a bit. Spaz came up behind him and tied his forehead back against the chair. Chastity nodded at Spaz, and he stood by the battery, ready to flip on the power.

Chastity opened Zane's mouth and rammed the cattle prod in until Zane began to gag. She then turned the switch, and Spaz did the same.

The pain and convulsions were immediate. Not only was he gagging on the prod, it felt like his throat and esophagus were on fire. He couldn't remain calm as the electricity racked his body. He was trying to breathe through his nose, but the convulsions prevented him from concentrating. His whole chest was on fire. It felt as if his skin was being burned off. The restraints did their job as Zane thrashed violently.

Tec came out of the shadows but didn't say anything. Why wasn't he putting a stop to this?

Zane's vision began to gray around the edges. The tunnel was closing in. It was similar to being choked out in training, but much more painful. Were they actually going to kill him? At this point, that would be a welcome option.

His vision was just a pinprick of light rapidly closing to nothing. Complete darkness engulfed him as he saw Tina holding out her arms to him.

75

Ray's fellow juvenile delinquents had privileges not afforded to those who were incarcerated for second-degree assault. Some were in for running away from home. Others had been nabbed for auto theft and other lesser crimes. Good behavior earned them overnight passes. Not Ray, though. He wouldn't be eligible until six months before his eighteenth birthday.

Howard was in for multiple counts of various crimes, the most recent being auto theft. His English teacher had flunked him, causing Howard to be held back a grade. He got even by stealing a brand-new Buick and crashing it into the teacher's suburban home. Howard had been in here for two years and was five months from being released.

Ray hated Howard. Howard was always picking on Ray, teasing him because he didn't get any passes and only had one visitor. One day in the cafeteria, Howard gave him his slice of apple pie with the comment that he was having supper with his family at his favorite restaurant tomorrow, and their pie was much better than this shit.

That was all Ray could take. He turned from his chair and landed a right uppercut, slamming Howard's lower jaw upward. His tray of food went flying as he landed on his back with his head hitting the tile floor with a dull thud. Blood and pieces of teeth began to bubble out from his mouth as his eyes rolled back into his head.

The guards were on Ray immediately. They wrestled him to the floor and handcuffed him. He was put in solitary detention for two days. Well worth it. They went by very quickly.

Howard had a broken jaw and a concussion. Several teeth had to be replaced with bridges. Howard was in the hospital for four days. On the first day Howard returned, Ray found a note on his bed.

Hey, Ray,

I have to suck my food through a straw for six weeks because you hit me. They say my jaw will never be the same. I still have six visits of dental work to sit through. You know I didn't deserve this. Something is wrong with you. I don't think you should ever be let out. But there is probably nothing I can do to keep you locked up. I will do something, though. I'm going to fuck your life up just like you did mine. Someday when you least expect it. Count on it.

Howard

Ray threw the note in the garbage. Howie was garbage. He couldn't give a shit what he wrote. Howie couldn't hurt him. His life was so far down now, Howie couldn't send it any deeper.

He was wrong.

Howard had watched Ray and his sister together many times. He studied them the day of the birthday gift. He knew they were having a special moment. How touching.

Howard had a one-hour pass to go shopping or whatever else he could legally do in sixty minutes. He used it while Ray and his sister were out on the bench. He went outside and waited.

When she didn't come home after four hours, Ray's mom called the police. They started their investigation at the detention center. Someone had seen Howard getting into her car with her. That was the last time anybody ever saw Ray's sister. Or Howard. They conducted an official search but didn't turn up anything. Not one clue.

Ray was told the next day.

He didn't cry.

He showed no emotion.

He stared at the *Book of Ray* his sister had given him.

All of it is a lie. Every single word.

76

Monique had given her set of keys for the Warrior's Den to Caleb. He liked to go there after hours to work out. Sometimes on the heavy bag, sometimes the speed bag, and sometimes just to shadowbox. It made him feel good.

Something was wrong tonight. The front door was locked, but there were two cars in the parking lot. And a light was on. His radar went on full alert. Usually, things were what they seemed to be. This seemed to be an abnormal situation.

Caleb quietly unlocked the front door and moved through the lobby. If something illicit was going on, they were stupid not to watch the front. Being stupid didn't make them less dangerous.

There was light under the door to the training room. He could hear muffled screams and thrashing. It didn't sound like sparring.

Caleb stood by the door. It was obvious somebody was being hurt. He had two options. Go in low and hard or go in high and easy. He chose the latter. He needed to observe and react. To act and then observe could cause innocent people to get hurt.

Caleb flung the door open and stepped through. He scanned the room. He should've gone in low and hard.

Zane was tied to a chair, shaking uncontrollably, while a beautiful woman was pulling a long slender cylinder from his mouth that was hooked up to an extension cord. Caleb recognized the big guy named Rocker from the warning in the park. Rocker

293

was silently observing while his little friend reached down to flip a switch next to a car battery.

"You all having a special class?"

"Special training session. For special members," Tec said as he stepped from the shadows, silently willing Caleb to leave.

"Let me guess; it's on how to survive torture." Caleb said, surprised to see Tec.

Caleb knew that if Zane was being tortured, he must have something this torturess wanted. Caleb needed to get whatever it was from Zane before this gorgeous witch did.

"Yeah, something like that," Tec responded as he faced Caleb about five feet away. "I have it under control."

"Since I wasn't invited, I guess I'd better leave," Caleb said as he turned to go. The very act of him leaving created a moment of indecision. Would they let him go? Would they try to stop him? What was Tec going to do? This moment of indecision gave Caleb his opportunity.

As he turned, he bent down and scooped up a focus mitt lying by the door. As he stood back up, he flung it at Tec, causing Tec to swat it away. Rocker came at him hard from the other direction. Caleb swung open the metal door, catching Rocker full on in the face and dropping him down in a daze. Caleb grabbed the pistol stuck in Rocker's pants and whirled to face his little friend, who had let go of the battery switch and was reaching for his gun.

Caleb fired once, hitting the little guy in the shoulder and causing him to fall back. Caleb then turned the gun on Tec and the beautiful bitch with the long dildo.

"Foreplay's over."

"Not quite yet," Rocker said behind him as he stood up shakily.

Caleb moved back against the wall as Rocker reached back and flipped the light switch off.

Caleb was on the wrong side of the inward swinging door, and it bumped against him hard as Rocker and Tec sprinted by him out the door. He heard the back door open and assumed that meant Chastity and the little injured friend's exit.

As he flipped on the lights, his assumption was proved correct. He was alone in the room with Zane. Caleb considered following the abductors but was unsure which party was better to chase. He also was unsure of Zane's condition.

Caleb untied the restraint from Zane's head, which flopped down on his chest. Caleb removed the restraints tying Zane to the chair, and Zane collapsed on the floor.

Caleb knelt down and rolled Zane on his back.

"What the hell were they after?" Caleb asked while going to get him some water.

"Money. Money I supposedly stole. But I was after information," Zane gasped out.

"Boss, there has to be an easier way of getting information," Caleb said while helping him sit up and giving him sips of water.

"Maybe," Zane whispered with a raspy roar as he tried to sip the water without coughing.

"Maybe? You have a warped sense of research. I can take care of these guys if you want me to."

"Leave them alone. I think this was part of Tec's and my plan. Which is why Tec chose this place," Zane said as he crawled to a corner of the mat and picked up the key that had been around his neck. Apparently, Tec had dropped it.

Caleb wondered how Tec fit into the plan, but knew he would discover that later as he befriended Zane. And maybe Tec.

"So he could control events?"

"Pain can be gain," Zane answered as he fastened the key and chain around his neck again.

"How does that apply here?"

"I'll know more after I have a little spiel with a lady friend of mine."

77

Monique was having a hard time falling asleep. Maybe because she was lying to the two men in her life. That's not what she wanted. She wanted love and security, not this mess. That brought back memories of her childhood in Santa Fe.

"You need to squeeze the trigger, not pull it," Monique's dad commanded her.

"I don't understand the difference. You have to pull the trigger to fire the gun," Monique said, obviously frustrated.

"If you pull the trigger, then the barrel will move, and your accuracy will suffer. Just lightly caress it, like you do the cat's ears at home."

"Dad, I'm not one of your men. A natural-born killer. Lighten up."

"You're fourteen today. Your birthday present won't do you any good unless you know how to use it—and are willing to do so. This lesson is my other gift to you, and it's worth far more than the gun."

"I don't think Mom agrees."

"Mom lives in a different world. A world where everybody loves everybody and nobody ever means harm. That world doesn't exist."

"For Mom, it does."

"Just shoot. Someday you may look back at this and realize it saved your life."

"I want to learn. But it doesn't have to be perfect today. I don't expect to kill my first person, until, oh, maybe when I'm . . . sixteen? Yeah, that would be a good age to bag my first person. What do you think?"

"Just keep firing. Smart-ass remarks have no place on the range."

"Yes, sir, Big Daddy."

Monique continued to fire. And fire. And fire. She learned to love the gun and the firing range. It was therapeutic. Three days a week after school, she trained in a secluded valley outside of Santa Fe. She became good. Very good. She began to experiment with action shots as she dived, as she ran, and from different positions. By the time she was sixteen, she was proficient with a handgun and a rifle at good distances. Monique began to enter tournaments. Her parents set up a room in the house just for her trophies. Monique would put them in the room, but she never looked at them again. You're only as good as your last shot, her father kept saying. If you missed your last shot and your adversary made his, you were dead.

New Mexico had been a wonderful place to grow up. The weather was good year-round and the scenery idyllic. Monique had always told herself she would live there for the rest of her life. It fit her and her mom just fine. The shooting didn't. Her mom was the polar opposite of her dad.

Monique and her mom loved to suntan topless wearing nothing but a thong in the backyard of their small adobe desert home a couple of miles from the city limit. Dad had put a pool in a few years back, and it helped keep the heat at bay.

"I wonder when Dad will be home. I'm so excited to show him my new self-defense moves. With the gun, I'm becoming almost as badass as he is."

"Being a badass and a sixteen-year-old girl don't go hand in hand," her mom responded while rubbing more lotion on her arms.

"Mom, I'm not your little girl anymore. I don't have to be like you."

"That's true. But you don't have to be like your dad, either."

"I don't think anybody could be like him."

"True again. I love your dad very much, and I know what he does serves a purpose. We need men like him," her mom said as she took a hit off a joint and held in the smoke while she held out the joint to Monique.

"But?" Monique said, taking the joint and inhaling.

"It's a lot for me," her mom said, blowing the marijuana smoke out. "I never know when he'll be gone. I never know when he'll be back. I never know *if* he'll be back. And when he does come back, it always takes more and more time for all of him to come back. It's as if he leaves a part of him over there. He's forbidden from talking about it, even with me. I can't share any of it with him. I know he goes through hell, but I do too. I don't want to see you live that life. Not your dad's and not mine."

"I don't think I want to. I see what it does to both of you. I think somewhere in between both of you would be just fine. Right smack in the middle," Monique said, putting the joint on the table between them and lying back on the lounger while closing her eyes and exhaling.

"Maybe a little more toward my end. Toward the love end."

"Mom, I agree love is a powerful thing. I just don't know if I need it spray-painted on my car. You and your flower-power friends lay it on a bit thick at times. Free love, smoking pot, and wearing little to no clothing seem to be your main purposes. Just like Dad is a bit much, sometimes you aren't enough. I love you, but I can't be you."

"Hard for me to believe that, watching you enjoy that joint while lying there half-naked."

"I try out Dad's way, and I try out your way. But in the end, I have to decide who I am," Monique said, rolling over onto her stomach.

"I know. I really do know. You must be your own person. I hope that when you meet that special other person, neither one of you lies awake at night, wondering where they are, who they're with, and who they're having to lie to and possibly kill. I can't take much more of it," her mom said, reaching for the rapidly disintegrating joint.

As it turned out, she didn't have to.

Monique's dad came home from his mission two weeks later. In a flag-covered box. Monique never had a chance to show him her new moves. She never again heard his stern admonishments for discipline, and never again felt his loving embrace before bed at night. They were told he died honorably. Gave his life for his country. So they might live free.

Two weeks after the funeral, her mom remarried a long-haired, bearded younger man whose sole source of income was the pot he grew in a commune up in the mountains.

Two months after that, her mom and her new man moved to a seaside villa in Mexico, where the pot-growing laws weren't so harsh.

Monique stayed in Santa Fe. Sixteen and self-sufficient.

She talked to her mom once a month.

Her mom was happy. Happier than she had ever been. She told Monique, "Every night when I go to bed, he's holding me in his arms."

Someday, Monique would have that too.

78

Zane was on his way to Monique's. His body still ached from the torture, but he needed to talk to her. She was the only other person who knew he'd taken the $15 million. She must have ratted him out. And she had the laptop. She might simply know too much by now.

His watch read 12:10 a.m. as he trudged up the stairs to her apartment. He hoped she was alone but really didn't care if she wasn't. She deserved what she got. Tucked into the back of his jeans, the gun felt safe and secure.

Zane stood outside her door and called her. He didn't need any neighbors waking up.

She answered on the fifth ring. "Booty call?"

"Can I come in?"

"Where are you?"

"Right outside your door."

"Be right there, honey. I have to put something on. Or is this the kind of visit where clothing would just get in the way?"

"Put something on."

"Oh, I like a man in control."

God, why did she have to be a lying bitch? In another life, she could have been the one.

The door opened suddenly, and Monique was standing there in a very short, flimsy nightgown, her hair all tousled. Double shit.

Zane moved inside as Monique slammed the door shut and immediately gave him a big hug. And a kiss. A long, slow hug and kiss. He could feel her sensuality through her negligee as she rubbed against him. She was grabbing his ass and kneading it while she kissed. Then her hands moved up to the small of his back.

"Do you always bring your gun to your booty calls?"

"Only when I've been fucked already."

Monique dropped her hands and moved back. She looked up at him while she crossed her arms across her chest.

"Geez, who beat the shit out of you?" Monique asked as she noticed his still-swelling face. "And why is your voice so raspy?"

Zane moved toward her, not fast but steady as he backed her up against the wall. His body was up against hers as he moved his hands to her throat and grasped it firmly.

"I don't mind rough foreplay, but let's get rid of the gun first. We don't need any premature shooting off," Monique said as she reached around him with one hand for the gun.

Zane beat her to it and pulled the gun with one hand and left it dangling by his side. Monique now had one hand on the gun barrel and one over Zane's hand on her throat.

"We can do this here, but I think the bedroom would be better. I like my men horizontal. It's easier to play with their gun."

Zane leaned his head in close and whispered into her ear, "You have no idea who I am and what I'm involved in. I have killed and will again if I have to."

Monique looked up into Zane's eyes. He expected to see the fear. But there was something else. Defiance.

Monique leaned into him and spoke into his ear. "You're right; I don't know what you're involved in. You asked me to help you, and I did. If you think I did something else, then let's do this. Don't play games."

Zane twisted the gun from her grasp, removed his hand from

her throat, and stepped back. They both looked into each other's eyes. The pivotal moment. Violence or love. Faith or fear. Trust or doubt.

Zane dropped the gun to the floor. He brought his right forearm across her throat and his other hand to her waist. He brought his head in hard.

And kissed her.

Then he picked her up. And carried her.

To the bedroom.

79

"That didn't go as you had planned, I'm guessing," Rocker said to Tec.

"Too early to tell," Tec answered.

Rocker looked at Tec quizzically. "So this was a Chastity operation?"

"Chastity isn't all it's cracked up to be."

"She isn't, either," Rocker replied while checking his gun.

"I don't know what the hell they see in her," Tec agreed.

"I think I know."

"T & A?" Tec asked, knowing the answer.

"She's sick. That's what they see in her. You have to be demented to do what she does. I don't even like being in the same room."

"Then why were you?"

"Same reason you were," Rocker replied.

"I doubt that."

"Why are we torturing this guy? What do they want from him?"

Tec looked hard at Rocker. The fact that he asked those two questions said something about him. He doubted Spaz would have cared.

Rocker and Tec were driving on Interstate 494 heading back to the shed. This debrief wasn't going to be fun.

"Zane is messed up, but he may know something that we

need to know. They must think so too, if they're willing to bring in Chastity," Tec explained.

"A wife's death would affect any husband."

Tec looked at Rocker with a raised eyebrow.

"Just because I kill people doesn't mean I don't care. Sometimes I kill people because I care," Rocker explained.

Tec drove on in silence.

"Maybe that's what Zane did. He killed the Man because he cared," Rocker suggested.

"He needed information."

"What kind of information?"

"The kind that exposes the truth," Tec answered, hoping that it wouldn't be quite all the truth.

Now it was Rocker's turn to stare straight ahead. The silence stretched out. The only sound was the tires slapping the joints in the concrete.

"I think torture is only acceptable if we're trying to gain information that will help us stop an attack or a crime. Chastity wasn't even concerned with that. She was only worried about money. Shit, that type of backward thinking is what contributed to 9/11," Rocker said.

"Maybe there is something we don't know. Or something Zane doesn't even know."

"Maybe."

"There is one way to find out."

"Damn straight there is."

80

Ben Guardian and his daughter Paula were sitting in a nail salon in Wayzata called Roxy Nails. No matter how busy their schedule, every two weeks, they made time for manicures and pedicures. This would be their last time.

Ben and Paula had always had a special connection since she was a little girl. It was a feminine connection, but Ben didn't care. Paula was different, and anything they could do together was better than nothing.

They could talk about anything here because the nail technicians spoke no English.

"How many times does this make?" Ben asked Paula as he leaned back in his recliner, letting his feet soak in the bubbly warm water of the footbath.

"Too many times to count," Paula replied as she cracked open a can of Miller Lite. "I think you enjoy it more than I do."

The nail technicians didn't like that Ben and Paula brought beer in while getting worked on, but one hard look from Paula stopped any protest.

"I don't know about *more*, but I sure hope they have nail salons wherever I end up," Ben said while grabbing a beer from the small open cooler between them and popping it open.

"You're a pussy, Dad. Not many guys will admit they like to have their nails done."

"Not many guys will willingly die to provide for their family, either."

"Fake die," Paula said while taking a good long gulp of frosty beer.

"Fake or not, I have to leave my life forever. You won't see me much, if at all," Ben replied, wincing a bit as the technician began pushing on the cuticle of his big toe.

"Don't do it, then," Paula said, setting her beer down and closing her eyes as a Roxy lady began to massage her feet.

"How did you get so tough? You show less emotion than Tim, and you don't seem to care much what happens to Guardian Jewelry."

"I care, but it is what it is. If you think this deal with Zane isn't for you, then just stop it. Do something else. I'm sure it'll work out; it always does," Paula said, keeping her eyes closed and wiggling her toes in the warm water. "And to answer your question about how I got so tough, I just looked at Carol and Tim growing up and how pampered and wimpy they were, and it disgusted me. I wanted to be self-reliant."

"What about your boyfriend and his finance career? Aren't you concerned he'll lose his opportunity for another chance if I don't fund it?"

"He can find something else to do."

"You are really something, Paula," Ben replied, now holding both hands in a green liquid. "What do you care about?"

"You, Dad. I care about you. But I don't have to show it by hoping you'll save Guardian Jewelry. That damn jewelry store is not you. I've seen it just about kill you with long hours and sleepless nights. You look fifteen years older than you really are. And if my boyfriend needs you to become a success, then he ain't going to be my boyfriend much longer."

"It's already done. The wheels are in motion."

"You could stop it if you wanted to."

"Tim and Carol will never survive. Your mom won't, either."

"Let all them bitches figure it out on their own."

At the word *bitches*, the two Roxy technicians began to giggle. Apparently, *bitch* was international.

"The decision you make about Guardian Jewelry should be based on what's right for you. Nobody else. Mom and Carol and Tim have about milked you dry. They've had their good life; now have yours," Paula replied, draining her beer, crushing the can, and throwing it ten feet into the garbage.

Ben began to laugh. "Are you sure I'm really your father? You have more balls than I do."

Paula smiled at her dad. "You'll have to talk to Mom about that, but just because you have good nails doesn't mean you can't kick some ass. You should start with your own family."

Ben drained his beer, crushed the can, and sailed his over the garbage can by three feet. "Maybe you're right. I need to toughen up."

"Being tough is good, but don't be stupid. Once you're fake dead, SAS could easily make you real dead, and nobody would care."

81

Usually, Caleb could sleep on command. Just say *sleep*, and his eyes began to close. Not tonight. When his mind worked on something, sleep was the furthest thing from it. A lot of people could sleep on a problem and the solution became clear. For Caleb, the reverse was true. He couldn't sleep until he had the solution.

Right now, the solution called for coffee. And lots of it. That meant a Flameburger run. Coffee is always better with eggs and hash browns.

Particularly at 1:00 a.m.

His fourth cup of coffee and a huge plate of browns and eggs later, the solution still evaded him.

He knew something screwy was going on. That much was obvious. People don't just torture other people, even if it is for money. And who was the chick with the electric stimulator? She was seriously hot, but Caleb wasn't into rough foreplay.

Who was the man on the inside at SAS working for the Treasury? Had he met him yet?

He needed more information. And that only meant one person. Zane.

But he would start with Monique. She would have a way of getting to the bottom of Zane.

82

Monique was still up. Zane wasn't. In any sense of the word. Why did the two men in her life always have to be exhausted when it came time for the big show? She'd had more action when she was a virgin.

Zane had carried her into the bedroom and thrown her on the bed. She loved that. He stripped down to his sexy Under Armour briefs and followed her in. She had asked him about the key around his neck, but he wouldn't answer. They kissed and messed around a bit, and then he leaned back for a second. That was all it took. Out like a light. She didn't have the heart to wake him. His face looked like an old rug, and she could tell by the way he talked that he was hurting. He needed his rest more than she needed to get laid.

She covered him up and then crawled into bed beside him. At least she could pretend he knew she was there. Then suddenly, a loud knock on the door.

What the hell? She slept alone night after night and all of a sudden, the whole world was at her doorstep.

"I'm coming." She wished.

She looked through the peephole before opening it. Shitballs. Caleb. *Man, it never rains until it pours.* And she had Zane in his underwear, sleeping in her bed.

She guessed that wouldn't fall into the category of an aphrodisiac for Caleb.

She opened the door but kept her foot wedged behind it.

"I don't know, Caleb. Should I trust letting you into my tiny home at almost two in the morning?"

"I need to ask you another favor. Open the damn door."

"I don't think cussing is the way into my home, let alone my pants."

"Okay, let me ask my favor, and then we can talk about your pants."

"I'm not wearing any."

"Where are your pants?"

"Don't change the subject."

"Okay, we'll talk about you and me."

"Talk?"

"Yeah, I know, a little less talk and a little more action. Elvis's words, not mine. But I need to come in first."

"You ain't goin' to get into nothing with that attitude, if you know what I mean."

"You look real sexy tonight."

What is it with these guys? First none of them wanted to make a move, and now she had to find separate rooms to store them.

"I don't think those are the magical words to the enchanted forest, but come on in. I can't have my neighbors hearing me say no to a booty call. What will they think of me?"

She let him in, and he quietly shut the door behind him.

"The neighbors and all," Caleb whispered.

Monique stood in front of him in the hallway.

"Okay, what do you need?"

"Judging by that nightgown, I won't need any Viagra. Can we at least sit down?"

"Yeah, where are my manners? I guess it's hard to concentrate at two in the morning," Monique replied as she led him into the living room.

310

The longer he stayed and the farther he went into her apartment, the more nervous she became. *Get to the damn point.*

"I kind of took you to be a night owl. Aren't most techies?" Caleb asked as he sat next to her on the couch.

"I guess. Um, you're sitting a bit close, aren't you?"

"How else do we get to know each other better?"

When she wanted them to make their move, they acted like twelve-year-old boys—but when she didn't, they were damn Casanovas.

"Well, I guess this is one way. Maybe I should go brush my teeth first," Monique replied.

"I don't give a shit about that." Caleb wrapped his arm around her waist and drew her into him and kissed her hard. At first, she mildly resisted and then gave in. It was long and passionate and seemed to be leading elsewhere.

They both came up for air.

Caleb grabbed her head with both hands and looked her in the eye. "My favor can wait. I don't think this can."

What a slut. Two men and they both wanted to get busy. Except one had petered out on her, and this one looked like he was about to take his peter out.

"I think you should ask your favor first, 'cause otherwise, I'll be bound to do anything for you," Monique replied in a deep, husky voice.

"It'll wait. I guarantee you," Caleb said as he stood and picked Monique up in his arms.

He was ready, and she was ready. It was going to be a big downer when he threw her on the bed right on top of Zane. *Think, woman.*

She would have to use the oldest trick in the book.

"If you had been a night earlier, you would have missed Aunt Flo, but tonight you arrived just in time to see her in all her glory.

So you'd better put me down before we need a mop."

"You know the sight of blood turns me on."

Why didn't she remember that?

"Yeah, but this is different; it isn't blood from violence. Kind of gross, huh?"

"No. Blood from violence or blood from love—it's all the source of life."

It could be the source of death tonight if she didn't get one of these men out of here.

"I have to tell you something first. Very important."

Caleb looked into her face as he slowly let her down on the couch. "Sometimes I can't figure you out. I thought this is what you wanted. I know I do."

"Timing. It's all in the timing."

"So what do you have to tell me?"

"Women just like talk sometimes. I need to fill you in on a few things first. From my past," Monique replied. She didn't even know what she was talking about. She desperately wanted Caleb and now. But she also wanted Zane and now. Maybe a ménage à trois? No, that wasn't her. Two on one in hockey maybe, but not sex.

"Just kiss me again."

"I need to find your on-and-off switch. It might be shorting out or something."

"I'm a woman. Besides, it might be better if we just started slow. You know, with my aunt here and everything."

Caleb kissed her again. Slowly and passionately. He leaned back this time, and she stretched out on top of him.

"Did you bring a gun, or are you just happy to see me?"

"No gun."

This was getting beyond her control. She kissed him again and reached for his pants zipper.

Then just as she unzipped it, she heard something. A brief

swish of cloth somewhere else in the room. She turned her head and looked up.

It was Zane standing there in his Under Armour briefs, looking down at Monique.

"When I ask you to check somebody out, you sure do a thorough job."

83

The shed wasn't a shed. It was a warehouse located north of the Twin Cities in the suburb of Fridley. It was small and tucked up against a railroad track. An office out front faked a shipping business. The large rear section of the building was used to store vehicles, guns, and other equipment. Tec and Rocker pulled in the back right after Chastity and Spaz arrived.

Alan R. Thompson was in the front office talking to Chastity.

"How's Spaz?" Rocker asked as they joined them.

"What a fuckup. How could you let this happen? Who's the guy that saved the day for Zane?" Thompson asked.

"I asked, how is Spaz? Take care of your men first, and then we can debrief."

Chastity was sitting in an easy chair with her legs crossed. She didn't look happy, and she didn't look sad; she looked bored. "Spaz will live. It was a clean shot, through and through. He's lying in the break room. The doctor will be here soon."

Rocker and Tec each split up a bit and stood to the side of Thompson, who was seated behind the desk.

"Who was the guy? Just straight answers, no bullshit," Thompson asked again.

"Just some guy who trains at the Den. He had a key and came to practice. Unforeseen," Tec replied.

"If you prepare properly, unforeseen doesn't happen. You

know that. So what do we do now? We can't let Zane keep the $15 million. It's evidence. And now some guy has seen all of you, and he's still running around out there. Not good."

"We need to know what you know about Zane," Tec replied, walking up to Thompson and standing directly in front of the desk.

Thompson began to laugh. He was a large man, not necessarily fat but everything about him was big. He had a long beard and long black hair. When he laughed, it seemed jovial enough, but everybody in the room knew better.

"What does it matter to you, Tec? Your spot in the car is insured," the man answered while Rocker looked quizzically at Tec.

Tec did not look at Rocker while he replied. "We're risking our necks too."

"What a joke. You guys fuck up an operation and you need answers? What gives you the right, if I may ask ever so politely?"

"Why did we torture Zane?" Rocker asked.

"Against my better judgment, I will answer. And then you need to find Zane and his knight in shining armor and reel this whole thing in. I also want to grab Zane's kids. I don't care how. We need to make sure he's under our control. Enough is enough," Thompson said, slamming both hands on the desk.

Tec interrupted, "We'll do that if you tell us what's going on. The time for withholding is over."

Thompson shot Tec a cold look. "I said I would answer your questions, but you know better than to give me ultimatums. Remember, you have a lot to lose and a lot to gain."

Tec looked down at the ground.

"I'm getting tired of your shit too," Rocker piped up.

"Zane went back to work just as we asked. But then he went rogue. He killed one of our people, a key person, and he stole $15 million. We don't know his goals, but we need to make sure they align with ours. We can't have him exposing SAS before we're ready."

"Wouldn't exposing SAS get the bad all out in the open and stop all this torture and chasing around?" Rocker asked.

"It's all in the timing. If you remember correctly, we initially took Zane's family to get Zane to cooperate. We told all of you that what we were doing was in everybody's best interests, including his. Exposing SAS and their illegal acquisitions of large businesses could weaken the confidence in our national economy, which is weak enough as it is. We have to control it and keep it out of the headlines for now. Unfortunately, Zane is the definition of *out of control*, and you know best, Tec, that sometimes extreme measures are needed to bring a participant or situation back in control. It's that simple."

That wasn't what Tec wanted to hear. *Could it be that Zane was part of the problem rather than part of the solution?* Tec wished he knew more about Zane's past. On the other hand, he knew he didn't have the full story from Thompson. Thompson had always colored the truth to accomplish his goals. Tec had the battle scars as proof.

"So are we all still in the game?" Thompson said as he looked at Tec and Rocker.

"Who is the *we* you keep referring to?" Tec asked.

"For your purposes, the *we* is me. It's not in your best interests to know more," Mr. Thompson said with a note of finality. "Again, are you still able to do this?"

Both men nodded reluctantly.

Chastity stood up and smiled. "You know how to reach me. Next time, don't call me until you're good and ready for my special skills."

"Good. Now let's get Zane and his cohorts. Bring them all in. We could really use them."

"Use them for what?" Rocker asked.

"A successful conclusion. One that best serves the majority," Thompson answered.

"Don't you need to sort out the good from the bad first?" Tec asked.

"That's why I want all of them. Use the good and do away with the bad."

"Even the kids?" Tec asked.

"They're our leverage," Thompson replied. "We can't end this without them."

84

It was beginning to make sense. Caleb and Monique. They must have been working together all along. The whole act at the dojo last night had been put on. Caleb came to the rescue so Zane would trust him. And when he initially came to Monique for help, it had been with Tec's guidance. Zane was confused—and angry. Were they all in on this?

His full bladder had led him to wake up to find the bathroom. Instead, he'd found this dilemma. He approached the couch and made his presence known.

He'd put his gun in the waistband of his underwear before he walked out of the bedroom. He wasn't sure why at the time, but now he was glad he had it.

Caleb immediately lifted Monique off him and stood up with his hands held loosely by his sides. Monique moved to the adjoining easy chair. Zane thought the easy chair was an appropriately named seat for her.

"Zane, stay calm. I had no idea you were here. We were just hanging out."

"By the looks of your zipper right now, something's about to hang out," Zane said, and he smiled while walking around the couch and approaching Caleb, flexing his fists.

"I told you why I was here, but what about you? Why were you in her bedroom? Combined with the earlier scene at the Warrior's

Den, I think I deserve some answers, as well," Caleb said while holding his ground and zipping up his pants.

Zane stood face-to-face with Caleb. "I'm not sure what the fuck is going on here, and I don't give a shit about you and Monique. I only want to know about you. Who are you really, and why did you show up tonight? Truth and consequence."

"Back it down, boys," Monique said, springing to her feet and attempting to get in between them. "You need to listen to me before you two go at it. I'm the guilty one here."

Both men turned toward Monique while keeping a wary eye on each other.

"Monique, I trusted you to keep our dealings private. But it seems like you ratted me out to some very bad people. That's why my face looks like this," Zane said while pulling the gun from his back and holding it at his side. "Caleb caught them in the act and saved me, but now I'm not sure if he really saved me or if it was just an act to make me trust him. Are both of you conspiring with my enemies to bring me down?"

Caleb backed up a couple of steps to bring both Monique and Zane in his line of vision. "I helped you at the dojo because you needed help, Zane. Nothing more. But I think we really need to listen to Monique." Turning to her, he said, "You said you're the guilty party. What exactly are you guilty of?"

"I'm guilty of wanting both of you and not telling either of you about the other!" Monique exclaimed loudly while sitting back down and putting her arms around herself in an attempt to cover up her nakedness. "I'm also helping both of you without telling the other. Caleb has me checking out SAS—and Zane didn't trust you, Caleb, so he had me check you out. You guys put me in the middle. I didn't; you both did. There's a lot of blame to pass around."

Zane exhaled loudly and pointed the gun at Caleb. "So you haven't been honest with me. Why are you at SAS? I know it's more than just a job for you."

"I'm working for somebody else, someone who wants to know what's going on at SAS. He is on the right side, and I think he can help us get to the bottom of this," Caleb answered while taking a step toward Zane.

Zane took a step back against the wall and now turned the gun toward Monique. "What about the money, the camera, and the videotaping? Who did you tell?"

"Nobody. I did what you asked, and I didn't mention it to anybody. Swear to God," Monique said, drawing her knees up to her chest.

Zane wasn't sure. Who else knew he took the money?

"Put the gun away," Caleb said, looking Zane in the eye. "Nobody has to get shot tonight. There is a way we can figure all of this out."

Zane stared back at Caleb as waves of exhaustion washed over him.

"I'm not sure who to fucking believe, but I'm headed home," Zane said emphatically. "I don't have a clear head. I think the best thing for me is to be on my own. I don't know who to trust except myself. Always has been that way and always will be. And I'm taking my laptop."

Monique and Caleb exchanged a look of desperation and something else, but Zane wasn't sure what. He just needed to get out of there, and he slowly put the gun back. He turned toward Monique as his phone buzzed.

It was a text from Tec. Three words. "It is on."

"Zane, don't leave like that. We want to help. Let us."

"I don't know if I can trust you. I really like you, Monique, but I'm not sure where your interests lie, as evidenced by this," Zane said, motioning between her and Caleb. He turned to leave and stumbled, falling against the wall and landing on one knee.

Caleb rushed to him and helped him up while Zane pushed him away.

"You need us, Zane. You're in no shape to be on your own. Whatever you have to do, three are better than one. Let us prove we're not the enemy," Caleb said, holding out both his hands as a gesture of peace.

"I need to protect my children," Zane said, grabbing Caleb's hand and standing up. "Tec just texted me, and our plan to do just that is happening now."

"So you and Tec are working together?" Monique asked.

"It sure didn't look like that at the dojo," Caleb interjected. "Are you sure you can count on him to protect your kids?"

"I think so," Zane answered while sitting down on the arm of the couch and running his hands through his hair and becoming more worried by the second about Zanese and James. Did he fuck up a second time by trusting Tec?

"Well, let's go. Children shouldn't have to pay for any of what's happened," Caleb said while Zane winced.

Monique stood up and ran into the bedroom. "I'll throw on some clothes. Be just a minute."

Zane looked at Caleb and quickly looked away.

As Monique came back fully dressed, she brought Zane's pants and shirt. "And you shouldn't leave without these, either."

In their mad rush out the door, the laptop was forgotten.

85

It was a job, and he'd done others like it. This one was the same as all the others. Except it wasn't.

Tec was abducting his former best friend's children yet again. At least that's what Thompson thought. Tec had a different plan. The children needed to be removed from the equation.

Tec had tried to convince Thompson it was best if Rocker and he grab them alone while Spaz recuperated, but he demanded they take Spaz along. Tec didn't want to, but he would be good as a look-out. Rocker and Tec would make the grab.

Tec knew the kids would be with Betty, because Zane had told him.

They would hit the home at about 3:00 a.m. Attacks at dawn meant hitting the enemy at its weakest. Betty lived in a northwestern suburb of the Twin Cities called Maple Grove. They drove by twice before parking a half block away. It was a large one-story rambler with a spacious yard and long driveway. That meant it was fairly secluded and offered some privacy for their job. Tec wasn't worried about an alarm system, because even if there was an alarm, they wouldn't be there long enough for it to matter.

They were wearing lapel mikes and radios. Spaz's job was to warn them of any nosy neighbors or other unwanted arrivals.

They would pick the lock on the front door, enter quickly, and go straight for the bedrooms. Rocker would find Betty's bedroom and subdue her with a Taser, while Tec would grab the kids. They'd meet at the car. It was simple, but often the simplest plans proved anything but. Battle plans rarely survived first contact. Adapt and improvise. That was Tec's battlefield motto.

Tec and Rocker rushed across the front lawn. There was a dim light glowing in the front window.

"What do you make of the light?" Rocker asked Tec as they crouched behind a hedge surrounding the front walk.

"Probably just a night-light for the kids or something. But have your Taser ready just in case."

"Roger that. Let's rock and roll."

"Rock and roll? A little clichéd, don't you think?"

"How do you think I got my name?" Rocker replied.

"Never mind. Okay. Here we go. Anything out front, Spaz?" Tec asked.

"Some car just drove by but didn't stop, so we're all good."

Tec sincerely hoped so.

They leaped over the hedge and made it to the front door, crouching low. Tec took out his lock pick and inserted it when the knob turned, and the door opened. There stood Grandma in her pink flannel pajamas with feet, holding a twelve-gauge double-barrel shotgun pointed right at their heads.

"Come on in, boys. I just started morning devotions. Do you have Jesus in your hearts?"

86

There were benefits and drawbacks to having to travel fast early in the morning. The good part was no traffic; the bad part was no traffic. That made it hard to hide from the police. So they traveled fast, but not too fast. Ten to fifteen miles over the speed limit, no more. Since Monique's apartment was in Uptown and Maple Grove wasn't far away, they arrived at Tina's parents' house within fifteen minutes. Caleb was at the wheel, because Zane was still a bit shaky. Caleb wasn't sure if it was from the beating or from seeing Monique lying on top of him. Probably both.

"After we secure your kids, what's next?" Caleb asked as they passed by the house slowly.

"Smoke 'em out," Zane answered.

"And how are you and Tec proposing that will work without somebody getting killed?" Caleb asked while driving around the block.

"One step at a time," Zane said in his best I-don't-trust-you-yet voice. In truth, he was unsure of the answer.

"Did you see the car parked down the street?" Monique asked.

"I did. It appears empty, but you can never tell. Why don't you and Zane go in, and I'll stay out front to monitor? I can intercept any intruders and honk a warning. If you get into trouble inside, text me," Caleb replied, shrugging his shoulders. "Not perfect but the best we can do."

"In and out, fast," Zane said.

"The story of my life," Monique said as Zane shot her a penetrating glare.

They slowed in front of the house, and Caleb pulled in the driveway.

"The light's on in the front room. Is that normal?" Monique asked.

"Morning devotions. Betty's very disciplined."

"Nothing wrong with that," Caleb replied.

Monique and Zane got out and walked up the sidewalk. Caleb got out and leaned against the car holding his phone.

Ready for anything.

$ $ $

Tec and Rocker followed Grandma to the sitting room. She sat in the chair facing them while they sat down on the couch. She knew enough not to get close. Don't let them grab the weapon.

"I assume you boys were up to no good. Why would you come here at three in the morning trying to bust in my house? I'd call the police, but I want to give you the benefit of the doubt. Jesus would do the same."

Tec was ready to reply as his earpiece buzzed.

"Car in driveway. Three peeps. Driver is dude who spoiled party last night. Zane and some hot chick are headed to the door. What do you want?"

"Copy. Hold for now."

"No, no. Take those earpieces out and turn the mikes off. I was born at night, but not last night," Betty said, waving the gun barrel at their faces.

Tec and Rocker looked at each other sheepishly and complied. They'd never been covered by a pink-flannelled grandma and her shotgun. How did this happen?

"Better. Now one more time, why are you here? Fine with me if you don't want to say; I'm sure the police will have better ways of finding out," Grandma said while she picked up the cordless phone on the side table.

"Put the phone down. You've involved yourself in something that's way over your head. Put the shotgun down before you do something you'll regret," Rocker replied.

"You need to tell me what I'm involved in. Help me understand. Or not. Up to you."

"Your son-in-law's company, SAS, is involved in an illegal insurance scam. The implications reach far and wide. We need you to cooperate so we can uncover the potential damage to the country," Tec said as he began to rise from the couch.

"To the country? Come on. Actually, no. Stay there, big boy. Don't tempt me. I have used this thing many times. Nobody would ever prosecute me for defending my home against two big, tough guys like you. So explain: how would busting into my home help Zane?"

At that moment, the front door burst open.

$ $ $

Zane and Monique stopped at the front door. They thought they could hear voices or a low rumbling inside.

"What is that? Are we too late?" Monique asked.

"I'm not sure. Could be Betty praying in tongues. She can be pretty loud sometimes."

"Can't wait to meet this woman."

"She's a trip, but I love her. She gave me Tina."

"What's the plan?" Monique said as she put her hand on Zane's shoulder and squeezed.

"Go in and deal with whatever," Zane replied while shaking

her hand off his shoulder.

"I suggest an alternate plan."

"Like what?"

"I open the door, you go in low, and I follow. We don't have any weapons, but we can take cover as we enter and then react to whatever we see. Or you could call her first."

"I don't like the calling option. Knowing her, if it's a bad situation, she's probably in control. A phone call could cause her to lose control. Let's just go."

"Okay," Monique replied as she flung open the door.

Zane dived in, rolled, and took cover behind a low entryway wall. Monique followed. As they peered around the corner, the scene before them gave Zane another reason to appreciate his mother-in-law.

$ $ $

For a split second, Betty looked toward the door and saw Zane and Monique rolling on the floor. That was all Tec and Rocker needed. Tec dived low for Grandma, and Rocker went for Zane at the bottom of the wall.

Tec grabbed Grandma's ankles with one hand and pulled her off the chair while grabbing for the shotgun barrel with the other. As he did, the gun went off into the ceiling. The blast was shockingly loud in the small room and gave everybody pause—enough pause for Tec to wrench the gun from her hand.

Rocker arrived at the wall just as Zane reacted to the shotgun blast by rearing his head back. Not enough, though, because Rocker caught his chin with his right boot, snapping Zane's chin hard enough to stun him. Monique dived hard at Rocker, driving a hammer fist to his groin. Rocker deflected it with his thigh and had his gun out to thump Monique on the back of her head.

Zane and Monique were barely conscious as Rocker held his gun on them. Tec held the shotgun covering Betty. She'd only fired one barrel, so he had one shell left.

"You had better know how to use that thing, son. Because if you think I'm going to stand here and do nothing, you are mistaken."

$ $ $

Spaz couldn't reach Tec and Rocker on the radio, so something had to be wrong. He didn't want to give his position away, and Tec had told him to stay in the car no matter what. Also, he really didn't want to tangle with the dude in the driveway. At the dojo the night before, he'd shown that he could handle himself.

Then came the gun blast. It was more than Spaz could handle. Hence the nickname. He ignored the pain from the bullet wound he'd suffered earlier, bolted from the car, and ran toward Caleb. Maybe he could confuse him with a full-speed frontal attack.

Caleb heard the gun blast too and turned toward the house to investigate when he heard the car door slam. Spaz was sprinting right toward him. He couldn't be that stupid, could he?

He wasn't. A couple of feet from Caleb, Spaz stopped. Usually, the sprint disoriented the foe enough to have them react rashly and leave an opening. Caleb wasn't a normal foe. He assumed a ready stance but left all his options open.

Caleb knew his best option was to act rather than react. As Spaz tried to stop, Caleb knew this was the moment to grab the initiative. With a spear hand to Spaz's throat. The combination of his leftover momentum and the hard strike collapsed Spaz's trachea like a can of cheap Schlitz beer. Spaz fell to the ground, unable to breathe. Caleb ended his misery by several boot stomps to the head.

"I should have shot you in the head earlier. Now my boots are all messed up." Caleb said as he turned toward the house.

Spaz deserved grace and forgiveness, but he didn't deserve to live.

$ $ $

Tec was shocked by Betty's behavior. It didn't go with the image of a distinguished old lady performing her daily devotions. That observation was interrupted by Betty's one-handed lunging toward the gun. Her other hand went for his eyes. *Grandma was good.*

Tec had no choice. He brought his knee up to her forehead, and she dropped to the floor. Out for the count. He quickly spun to cover Zane and Monique.

"Grandma, are you all right? Dad, do something!"

Zanese was standing in the hallway holding James's hand.

$ $ $

As Caleb neared the front door, he came face-to-face with another man who appeared from around back. He had a gun and looked like he wanted to use it.

Caleb took two steps toward him.

Another voice came from behind him.

"I wouldn't do that if I were you. I don't think he'll let you get his gun, and I know for damn sure I won't," spoke the voice from behind.

Caleb turned sideways to face both men. Two on one weren't bad odds for him, except they had guns. It was going to take some trickery to pull this off, and these guys didn't look easy to fool.

$ $ $

"Zanese! James!" Zane yelled. "I have everything under control!"

Monique gave Zane a bewildered look.

Tec walked quickly across the room while covering them both with the shotgun. Rocker maintained his distance and kept his gun trained.

Tec knew better than to talk to Zanese and James. After all that had happened, it was quite likely they'd only listen to their dad. So as he neared them, he stopped, smiled, and winked at them. They both turned and looked at Zane, who did the same, although it was one of the most difficult things he'd ever done. Tec grabbed them with minimum resistance and headed for the door.

"You motherfucker!" Zane screamed as he went for Tec. Rocker had seen that coming and drove his boot into Zane's nuts as he leaped by. Zane fell to the floor clutching his crotch. Monique went for Rocker's back, but he sensed her and drove his other boot back in a hook kick that caught her in her solar plexus. She collapsed next to Zane.

"Take the boy. I'll take the girl," Tec told Rocker as they both grabbed a kid and started for the front door. As they neared the door, Tec heard an all clear from the front. Thompson must have sent backup. Tec hadn't planned on that.

"Just remember this—take good care of my kids! You're responsible!" Zane yelled after them as they stopped at the front door.

Monique sat up spitting and coughing. "I'm with him on that. You're looking at the queen of finding people. And I love to fuck with them before I find them. You're going to seriously regret this."

Rocker opened the front door and prepared to leave.

Tec came over to Zane and grabbed him by the front of his

shirt as he was kneeling on the floor. "I know you can't see this now. You think I'm bad and you are good. But I'm not bad. I'm doing what has to be done. You do the same, and it'll all work out. I promise." Tec dumped Zane back to the floor and stared at him for a moment and then followed Rocker out the door.

Zane was left wondering what Tec was talking about.

That speech hadn't been part of their plan.

87

"They chose the wrong person to visit with evil. This is the last time they'll pull this shit on me. They mess with my kids, they mess with me. I will find every last one of those sons of bitches. I will hunt them down like the dogs they are. I will get my kids back. If they've been hurt, I'll kill those two ugly dudes in a very slow, painful way. They're going to regret this day."

"Okay, Grandma, we get the picture," Caleb said, trying to calm her down.

"I'm not sure that you do. I'll get dressed, and let's go. Now."

"Um, Betty? I think Zane said that's your name. Let's let cooler heads prevail. Maybe they want us to go after them hard. It could be a trap," Monique said as they were all sitting on the living room floor, regrouping and trying to figure out what to do next.

"Hopefully it is a trap. Then we'll have them all in one place and turn the tables. Do unto them what they did to us. Fuck 'em," Betty replied as she pulled herself back up to the couch.

"Monique is right. Let's just chill for a minute. We don't even know who all those people were. We need information before we run off half-cocked," Caleb said, standing up.

"I'm going to make sure those nasty men have half a cock if they even so much as touch one of those kids," Betty replied.

Monique smiled and shot a glance at Caleb, who couldn't help but grin back.

"I understand where the emotion is coming from. I would go into battle with you any day, Betty. You have more desire and mental fortitude than a lot of people I have trusted in dangerous situations. However, we need to figure out what's going on. Information equals power," Caleb said.

"Yes, the Bible teaches that a man of understanding is more powerful than a mighty warrior. I get it. I just can't believe they got the drop on me."

"It happens. They got the drop on all of us. Why don't you go take a shower, tend to that nasty bruise on your forehead, and rest for a bit while we figure this out?" Monique suggested.

"I suppose. Just don't leave me out of any action. I may be older, but my heart is young, and I can shoot with the best of them."

"I believe every word. We won't leave you out of anything. You earned that right today," Caleb replied.

Betty stood up and wobbled a bit. Monique stood too and steadied her with a hand on her shoulder. Betty shrugged it off violently.

"Don't try that with me. I've seen worse than this. I can take care of myself," Betty replied as she stalked defiantly to the back bedroom.

"I hope I'm like that at her age. She has balls, so to speak," Monique said.

"Just like her daughter," Zane chimed in from the corner.

"Good. I thought you were comatose."

"Just thinking," Zane replied while also trying to stand up. "Monique is right; we need to slow down a bit and understand this."

"Has Grandma always been like that?" Caleb asked as he walked over to Zane with his hand out to help him up. "She doesn't fit my definition of any grandma."

Zane refused Caleb's hand and stood up on his own, gingerly making his way to the kitchen, which was next to the living room in the open floor plan. "Tina told me her mom had experienced some violence in her past and had vowed never to be a victim again—although, right now, we all look like victims. And I feel like one too."

"I can't imagine why. You've been tortured, you think your friends have deceived you, and then your kids are kidnapped," Monique said. "A second time, no less."

"Speaking of your kids," Caleb piped in, "are they all right, or do we need to go find them?"

"I think they're fine," Zane replied while grabbing a bottle of water from the fridge and a bag of frozen peas from the freezer. He held the peas to his groin while sipping the water.

"I love you, Zane, but you are seriously wrong. I'm ready, so let's go!" Betty yelled as she reentered the living room, completely dressed and with a bandage on her head.

"Based on Tec's last words, I think we'd better make sure," Caleb also said urgently while heading toward Zane.

"I sincerely appreciate your sense of urgency, but I know where he has them. This is all part of a plan. For now, I have no choice except to trust it," Zane said while dropping the bag of peas down the front of his jeans. "Oh my God, that feels so good."

"What plan? This is part of a plan?" Monique asked.

"Tec's plan. Well, I helped make it too. That's why I had to come here, to make sure the kids knew I was in on it and would go somewhat willingly. If I don't follow the plan, my kids could be in worse trouble. So far, it seems to be working, even though my nuts disagree."

88

"I think we may have our leverage back," Thompson stated as he put his feet up on the desk in the plain office back at the barn, holding his cell phone up to his ear.

"How can you be so sure? Zane seems to be a pretty resourceful guy. I can't imagine he doesn't have a contingency plan," Thompson's boss replied on the other end of the line.

"Doesn't matter. No contingency plan could survive the reality of what we have."

"I heard you lost a man."

"Yes, a casualty. Sometimes that can't be helped. If we had to lose anybody, he was the one."

"So you have the kids?"

"We do," Thompson replied, taking a sip of Perrier. Sparkling water was his favorite beverage. It was so refreshing.

"One of your strategies was mutual destruction. He doesn't take your money and you don't take the kids. Now with the kids gone, what stops them from taking all your money? Not that I really care, but I don't want you to lose your incentive," his boss asked.

"He already took $15 million, but I don't think he'll risk the kids' lives and take more. And besides, he can't get to my money anymore. He has the goods on us, and he could still expose us, but I'm sure the kids' safety will prevent him from using it."

"What about the video?"

335

"We'll get it."

"What does that mean?" his boss asked in a worried tone.

"Chastity."

"I'm still very uncomfortable. I thought you were going to finish them all."

"Tried, but they were a bit much. Some old lady got in the way. Tough old lady. At least that's what I'm told," Thompson said while draining the last of the Perrier and sitting up in his chair. He looked out the window at a train slowly passing by. He wondered where it was going and how hard it would be to run alongside and jump on.

"Spare me the details. Without Zane, you're not in complete control."

"True. We'll get Zane and his cohorts. Ultimately, he knows he can't expose all of our operation. He has too much at stake."

Silence.

"Hey, you still there?"

"Yes, I just don't know how much I can believe," his boss answered faintly.

"All of it. Within a couple of days, we'll wrap this up."

"What about you? Are you willing to give up something here?"

"I'm willing to give up all of it. The money, the people, everything. I'm committed. All the way."

"What about my group? Nobody can find out. They must be protected at all costs. No matter what."

"No one will ever know. We'll conduct an operation today that will clean all files and get the policies. It will also protect you and yours. Place the blame where it needs to be placed. On all of *them*."

"And Tec?"

"He's upholding his end of the bargain."

"End it today."

"Today."

"Well, just remember, this isn't about you, Alan Ray Thompson, and it isn't about me."

"What's it about?"

"The continued financial dominance of the United States of America."

89

"What do I get to do? You can't just leave me here. Come on, Zane," Betty pleaded as she was tying her boots. "You're going to need me."

"We need you here," Zane replied.

"Not an option. I know you think the kids are fine, but I need to know that. Don't leave me here."

"I can't tell you everything. Look, we need a home base, and somebody has to stay in case we need something. Trust us on this."

"Bullshit. Sitting here makes no sense. What can I do here that I couldn't do if I were with you? I have a laptop and a mobile Internet connection, and we all have that beautiful invention called a cell phone. I'm going," Betty said, standing up to confront Zane.

"Can you guys try? She isn't listening to me." Zane looked at Monique and Caleb as he backed up to a chair and sat down.

"She's your mother-in-law; you deal with her," Monique mumbled through a mouthful of the energy bar she'd found in one of the cupboards.

"Yeah, she said she can shoot. Bring her with," Caleb said while reaching for one of the energy bars. "But if the kids are all right, where are we going?"

While hoping Zanese and James were safe with Tec for now, Zane needed to get and control as much of the evidence against SAS as possible. There were client names, life insurance policy numbers, and investor records on the computers at SAS. He needed all of it. That meant going to the office.

Zane also needed his laptop, because it already held some proof of SAS's illegal acquisitions, along with the video of the Guardian closing. In the video, the insurance agent proudly had gone on and on about the scheme but hadn't disclosed the true source of the funds. Zane kept wondering where Thompson's money really came from. Monique had unearthed a clue, but it wasn't definitive. Somehow the Federal Reserve was involved.

"We're going to SAS. We need to get something," Zane explained.

"We need more than that," Caleb stated while unwrapping an energy bar. "You can't expect us to just go along and risk it all without telling us why."

"I need evidence of SAS's wrongdoing,"

"What is their wrongdoing?" Caleb asked.

"Wait until I get everything, including the laptop, and then I'll show you," Zane said as he stretched his triceps.

"The laptop is safe," Monique said, licking the last of the energy bar from her fingers. "We can get it later."

"They're not just going to let us take the evidence," Caleb stated flatly.

"That's why we need to hurry. I need it before anybody else. Then I need to see what they'll do to try to get it back."

"So you're expecting them to go after it too?" Monique asked.

"That's what I want."

"Does *they* include Tec?" Caleb asked.

"I think so; at least that was our plan. But I'm sure he won't be alone."

"We'll need all the help we can get, then," Monique said.

"Listen to your friends. I can be an asset; trust me," Betty pleaded.

"Fine, come along. What a fucking circus."

"I like the circus," Monique said as she winked at Caleb.

"What the hell was that?" Betty said as she noticed the wink.

"Yeah, what was that, Caleb?" Zane asked.

"My story is pretty simple, but I don't think Caleb's is. I know a part of it, but there has to be more," Monique said.

"I'm working for somebody," Caleb replied. He finished his energy bar, took a sip of coffee, and leaned against the counter.

"Duh," Monique said.

"Who?" Zane asked.

"Even as corrupt as this guy is, he's the one who can wrap this up for us."

"Elected?" Monique asked, having figured it out on her own through some of her research.

"Bingo. The pretty lady in the front row wins the prize. I'll fill you all in as we get ready," Caleb responded as he stretched his triceps. "Now, who do we see about getting some guns?"

"Let me take you to the basement. Every gun you could ever want is in my doomsday shelter," Betty said.

"I think we just found our name for this little operation." Caleb said.

Operation Doomsday.

90

I t was one of those famous sunny Minnesota September days—dry and cool with just a hint of fall in the air. Tec always felt it was the calm before the storm of the equally famous Minnesota winter days. Kind of like his life. Just when he could sit back and enjoy beautiful fall weather, a season-changing storm would erupt. Then he'd spend the whole winter shoveling.

They were headed to SAS to retrieve the evidence and destroy it, according to Thompson's instructions. But Tec didn't know whose best interests would be served by the destruction of key evidence. Maybe nobody, and maybe everybody.

Rocker broke his thoughts. "Do you think we'll find Zane and his companions there?"

"I'm not sure. If we do, we have to be careful not to hurt them. We have to figure out who's good and who's bad."

"We aren't the only ones who've been violent. That dude from your dojo is one cold mofo. There was no love lost on Spaz, but I still wouldn't mind getting a little crazy on that dude's ass."

"This is not a revenge mission; remember that. We're there to retrieve the goods and close it down. Don't do anything out of anger."

"I'm just saying. If that guy is there, why not?"

Tec looked at Rocker and smiled. "I hear you, but restraint will pay dividends. Trust me."

"Speaking of trust, what did Thompson mean when he said your spot was insured?"

"He thinks I'm one of them."

"What makes him think that?"

"The kidnapping, I suppose. But something else bothers me," Tec answered, trying to change the subject.

"What?"

"Something Zane told me at the beginning."

"Did he know you'd taken his wife?"

"No, but that's not the point."

"It may be the point. Things always change when the truth comes out."

"Astute observation. Still, Zane told me he was working undercover for the government. Treasury Department."

"So?"

"Well, if he was working for Treasury and he was going rogue, why wouldn't Treasury reel him in? So Treasury must have approved of Zane's actions. But Thompson doesn't. Or Zane lied about working for Treasury," Tec said while rolling down the window.

Rocker brought his palms up to his temples. "So that means either Thompson and Treasury are working against each other, or Zane is working against all of them."

"Exactly. Who do we trust?"

"I may not be the brightest bulb on the tree, but I can answer that," Rocker said while checking his pistol and pointing at himself.

"It seems like Thompson tells us enough to get us going, like he always has. And Zane is doing the same," Tec replied.

"I just don't want to end up in a small, windowless room talking to myself for the rest of my life," Rocker said.

"Well, then I think we need to take care of ourselves. Nobody else will."

"How do we do that?"

"Thompson told us to destroy the files and computers and to get everybody and bring them in. But he didn't say we couldn't look at the information first," Tec said, smiling at Rocker. "However, I don't think all of it will be at SAS."

"How do we get the rest?"

"We need to bring the cockroaches out of the woodwork," Tec explained. "Put them all in one room, start stomping, and see who survives."

"We need bait for this roach trap," Rocker replied, smiling back.

"Couldn't agree more."

91

Grandma wasn't lying when she said she had guns. She had shotguns, rifles, pistols, machine guns, and even grenade launchers. She was ready to defend hers and her own should the end of the world draw nigh. She expected it any day and was ready. She target fired at the range on a weekly basis and took Krav Maga for self-defense. She was not a grandma's grandma.

They ended up taking two cars. It wasn't the best operational security, but the women rode in Betty's Yukon, and Zane and Caleb rode in Caleb's Wrangler. Grandma said she needed some time alone with Monique to ascertain her true intentions with her former son-in-law. Zane was sure that Monique didn't know her intentions.

"Do you trust the congressman? If we lay it in his lap, will he do the right thing?" Zane asked Caleb as they pulled onto I-494 South. Traffic was light since it was still early, even for a weekday morning.

"I don't trust any politician. I think he'll do the right thing, but if not, we need another plan. I'm working on that."

"Are you going to fill me in?"

"When I figure it out. It may involve the press; I'm not sure. I know a guy at the *Wall Street Journal* who may want to get involved, but we're going to need a lot more evidence of all the transactions, especially the purchase of the insurance policies. Hopefully we'll get it today."

"If I decide that's the way I want this to go," Zane replied forcefully. "This is my operation and my investigation. Don't forget that."

"Well, it appears this may go way beyond you. I work for a congressman who is elected by the people, so I would guess the results and solution must be for the people," Caleb said as he checked the rearview mirror. "I think something else is going on, Zane. And it has to do with AIS."

"I know AIS is owned by the Federal Reserve."

"Right. The Fed bailed out AIS in 2008. And AIS is writing the life insurance policies you're selling as viaticals, although they are fronting it through a wholly owned subsidiary."

"How do you know that?" Zane asked suspiciously.

"I'm not just another pretty face," Caleb responded, grinning at Zane. "Monique found out through some e-mails from the Fed to AIS that they were asking how much more money they needed for this subsidiary. So if AIS is writing the life insurance policies for the companies you're acquiring and AIS is owned by the Fed, then maybe the Fed is more like club Fed, with the money flowing just like the drinks at Club Med."

Zane remained silent for what seemed like an eternity. E-mails. The Fed funding AIS. Worried about AIS needing more money. *Wow.* "And the Federal Reserve may be behind the money for Thompson. Which may not mean anything since the Fed sends money to a lot of parties, but I do know the transactions to Thompson do not look like the normal wire-clearing process."

"Maybe the Federal Reserve is a player in all of this. Maybe they have a motive beyond just funding AIS."

"It has to be about control." As soon as the words were said, Zane broke out in a cold sweat. He knew something Caleb didn't. AIS owned SAS. The Fed owned AIS. The Federal Reserve was funding AIS. It was a direct line from SAS to the Federal Reserve and back again. Suddenly, Zane felt his phone buzzing in his jacket pocket. He debated letting it go to voice mail, but he looked at the screen. *Shit.* "Yeah, what is it?" he answered tersely.

Caleb looked at him with a quizzical look.

"I understand."

Caleb mouthed the words, "Understand what?"

"It'll work out. Just remember what I told you."

Caleb mouthed, "Put it on speaker."

Not a chance.

"I'll get it. It won't be long."

"Get what? What won't be long?" Caleb whispered.

"Enough. I won't do that, and you know that. Good-bye." Zane clicked off.

"Who was that?" Caleb asked.

"Personal."

"At this point, I'm not sure anything is personal."

"Nothing to do with this."

"What does it have to do with, then?"

"Full disclosure isn't in the cards for either of us," Zane said, looking straight ahead.

Caleb thought about that for a minute. "At least tell me you were just talking to one of the good guys."

"Of course I was," Zane lied to Caleb as he turned off on the downtown exit toward SAS.

92

"Why such a big truck? It's just you, right?" Monique asked as they pulled out of Betty's garage in her GMC Yukon, following Zane and Caleb to SAS.

"It is. But I like a lot of car around me. Besides, I need four-wheel drive," Betty explained.

Monique leaned her head against the headrest and reclined the seat. "I know. Until I moved here, I never knew how bad winter could get."

"That too."

"What else?"

"Depending upon how it's going to go down, I like to be able to maneuver. You never know when the end will come and how it will affect the roads. Be prepared at all times."

"Apocalypse?"

"Exactly."

"Are you ready for this today?" Monique asked as she closed her eyes. "I'll have to admit I'm a bit nervous. Zane expects confrontation."

"I'm anxious, but I have my faith in God," Betty said as she floored the big truck toward the on-ramp.

"You really believe that shit, don't you?" Monique asked, opening her eyes and turning her head toward Betty.

"Don't you?" Betty asked, pointing her finger at Monique.

"If you ask me if I believe the Bible, the answer is yes. However, I don't think it all applies to today."

"You either have to believe all of it or none of it," Betty said while again stabbing her finger in Monique's direction. "You can't pick and choose."

Monique laid her head back down, "Of course you can. It is like any book; some of it's true, and some of it ain't."

"No, no, no. It's the inspired Word of God, given to man by God's inspiration. It's either all true or none of it. A made-to-your-liking God is a God that doesn't exist," Betty replied stoutly, closing her mouth as if the debate was over.

"I've never looked at it that way."

"You'd better start."

"Even though I do believe, I've never gone to church much. It just seems like a bunch of rules. Do this, don't do that. That's all preachers tell you. None of us can ever be perfect. I get frustrated just trying," Monique explained.

"Anybody would. God is not a set of rules. That's religion. Religion kills, and God gives us life, through His Son, and He came to give us life more abundantly. It's called Grace. Once a person really understands Grace, then the rest of the Bible makes total sense, and life becomes so much more fun and exciting," Betty said and slapped Monique on her knee.

Monique sat up quickly. "Ouch!" She brought the seat up and looked at Betty. "I never thought of it like that. That's amazing."

"Thus the song 'Amazing Grace.'"

"I love to talk more sometime. Right now, my mind is a bit preoccupied."

"With thoughts of Zane, or is it Caleb? Or both?"

Monique laughed. "Ah, there's your real motive for having me ride with you."

Betty smiled. "No, it's much more important to know your

relationship to our Savior, especially with what may be in store for us today. But, since we stumbled on that subject, let's linger awhile. What are your intentions with my son-in-law?"

"Former son-in-law," Monique corrected her.

"Former nothing. As the father of my grandchildren, he'll always be my son-in-law."

"Even though he played a part in your daughter's death?"

"Grace. God showed it to me, so I need to show it to Zane. I'm not sure what he's involved in, but I'm sure he had his reasons. His best days are ahead of him. God has brought him to this for a reason. You'll see."

"I've got a lot to learn," Monique said, now looking out the window at the billboards and commercial buildings they were passing.

"All of life is learning. God has something for us to learn in everything that happens, including the bad things," Betty said, trying to keep Caleb's Wrangler in view.

"What do you think the lesson was today?"

"Yet to be determined, but you changed the subject."

Monique grinned. "Not on purpose, but okay, you want to know my intentions with Zane and Caleb."

"What do you think?"

"Right now, I want to help them through this. They both need my help, and I hate to see the bad guys win."

"How about after right now? What happens then?"

"Pray that God shows me the wisdom to know what to do then, because I haven't the slightest idea."

"I pray wisdom will be shown you. I will also pray that you'll treat Zane with that same wisdom. Because if you don't, and you hurt Zane, then I'll have to hurt you. With God as my witness, I promise you that."

93

It became Ray's mission to find Howie. Ray was released on his eighteenth birthday, but the rest of his life would have to wait. Eventually, everybody died, and this life was over. But that inevitable outcome couldn't come soon enough for Howie—and Ray didn't care how soon it would be for himself.

Week after week, Ray faithfully attended to his court-ordered counseling. He developed a close relationship with his counselor. An inappropriately close relationship. They would conduct their counseling session, Ray would leave, and then they would meet later at a less than four-star hotel. Much less. Minneapolis had a lot of those. They would use a different one almost every time. She told him she could lose her job, her career, and her whole life's work for this. She had court-ordered authority over him and was exercising that authority for her gratification. Ray didn't care.

She would do almost anything for him. She was in love, or so she said. It didn't take long for her to find Howie's residence, even though it was private and not in his file. He was living in Winnipeg, Canada. She asked Ray how he was going to use this knowledge. Ray told her he wanted to visit Howie to see what he knew about his sister. He'd been with her just before she'd disappeared, so he must know something. If Howie was guilty of something,

350

he'd forgive him and turn it over to the authorities. She said she believed him.

Everybody uses somebody.

94

Zane knew Tec would be at SAS, and he wouldn't be alone. Thompson wouldn't trust him that far.

Caleb was able to park in a parking garage that had a clear sight line to the front door. Monique and Betty had parked next to him. Monique, Betty, and Zane would go into the office building. Monique would monitor the back door from the inside, and Caleb would stay in the parking garage and monitor the front. Everybody was tense but ready. Including Betty. She loved this. At her age, any adrenaline rush was welcome.

They all wore bulletproof vests, courtesy of Betty's doomsday shelter. Zane had two pistols—a .45 in a shoulder holster and a .38 in an ankle holster. He had four spare magazines, which should be enough if they ran into trouble. Guns weren't foreign to him. Monique carried the shotgun. She needed to discourage anybody from the rear entry, and a shotgun was a master of persuasion. She was also an excellent shot, so she had a .45 tucked in her waistband. Betty carried a .45 in a waist holster and held a rifle under her jacket. Her sharpshooting skills could prove necessary from the high vantage point of the office windows. As they crossed the street, Monique and Betty argued about who was the better shot.

"Let's hope we don't have to find out," Zane told them as he brought up the rear.

"At least not today," Monique responded.

Caleb stood in front of the car facing the front door of the building armed with a rifle and pistol. He'd won several shooting contests over the years. He'd been firing guns since he was old enough to hold one. During an act in his parents' circus, an old-fashioned duel was staged with each participant shooting off various parts of his opponent's apparel. The trick shooters had taught Caleb well.

Betty's grenade launcher was on the front seat. Caleb wanted to keep this whole operation on the down-low, but if firepower was needed, he wasn't opposed to using it.

He'd thought about informing the congressman of today's operation but decided against it. With something like this, informing him after the fact was better. After all, he was an elected politician. He needed deniability.

As they entered the building, Monique assumed the position by the back door, and Zane and Betty took the elevator up to SAS.

Caleb keyed his radio, telling the others, "All quiet out front."

Monique replied, "Ditto that."

"So far, so good," Zane agreed.

"But ready for anything," Betty chirped in.

Caleb smiled. He'd follow that woman to hell and back.

$ $ $

The elevator opened to proof that Tec wasn't alone. A guy in a suit was seated at the front desk. No receptionist in sight. Zane brought his pistol up and shot him in the forehead before his hand could touch the shotgun on the desk.

"One at desk, eliminated," Betty said into the mike.

Zane stared at Betty. "Holy shit. Where did that come from? You just saw me kill a man, and you're no more bothered by it than if I'd swatted a fly."

"I have a past too. I'll cover the elevator. You go get your stuff. How long?"

Zane was still staring at her incredulously. "Ten minutes. Fifteen, tops."

"Nothing takes ten minutes. The longer we're here, the more bad stuff can happen."

Zane grinned at her.

The more he was around Betty, the more he loved her. He regretted that he'd never been able to show the same love to his own mom.

Caleb and Monique had caught Betty's terse statement. They both knew what that meant. Tec had backup, and their intentions were violent, or they would've never killed someone.

Caleb keyed his mike. "Do you want me up there? We could put Monique on the front and leave the back for now."

"No. We've got it. You guys need to stop anyone from entering. Stick with the plan," Zane answered while checking out the waiting room area for more unfriendlies.

"And gals. There are gals here too."

"Sorry, I'm a bit too preoccupied to be politically correct," Zane replied, motioning Betty to crouch down behind the receptionist desk.

"Whatever you say, boss. Are you all right, Betty? Can you still cover Zane?" Caleb asked.

Betty was behind the desk with her rifle aimed at the elevator door. "Why couldn't I? I've seen people shot before. Blood doesn't bother me. You do your jobs, and I'll do mine."

"10-4. But if you need help, remember I'm just an elevator ride away."

"We should be fine. Give me ten minutes, and I'll have what I need," Zane promised.

"Ten might be a bit long. We've got company," Caleb replied, trying to stay hidden behind the concrete pillar of the ramp.

"Who?"

"Two cops, and they're going in the building."

"I got it," Monique told them as she set the shotgun in the corner by the back door. "I'm going to the front to get rid of them. Getting rid of guys is my specialty."

"Well, you have at least one to get rid of now," Betty said into her mike.

"No, three's company."

"Watch it, girl; remember who you're talking to," Betty responded.

"Right. I meant three as in husband, wife, and baby."

"I don't want a baby," Caleb said.

"I don't think you're the husband," Zane chimed in.

"We don't know who the husband is," Betty said.

"Who said anything about a husband?" Monique responded. "Or a baby."

"You did!" Betty, Caleb, and Zane all responded, happy to indulge in a little comic relief in this life-threatening situation.

"Well, I guess you guys had better get to courting when this is all over," Monique said. "And may the best man win. But for now, I got to get rid of the po-po, so you all better just shut the hell up."

Monique was at the glass front door, where two cops were looking in. One was a young lady who didn't seem too far removed from the academy, and the other was an older cop who could be her father. The lady was pleasantly plump with ample bosom and short brown hair. She looked like a real ballbuster. The older guy was bald on top, with short gray hair on the sides and a gray handlebar moustache. He looked like a no-nonsense kind of guy. Monique knew she had to keep it real.

She opened the door and let them both in. They both seemed tense and wary. Not a good sign.

"How can I help you, officers?"

"We had an anonymous complaint about possible prowlers on the first floor of this building. Do you know anything about that? Or are you the prowler?" the lady cop asked.

"I just got here for work and saw you guys pull up. Don't know anything about any prowlers."

"Isn't five a bit early for work?" the old cop replied.

"Not for me. I've got to get everything set up, and this is my most productive time. You know, before the phone starts ringing and everything. You can call my boss. He's usually here by now too."

"That can be faked easy enough. Who do you think called it in?" the lady asked.

"Probably just a passerby. There's this old guy who does his power walking around here every morning. I think he owns a downtown condo. I hear he's always calling in when he sees somebody in an office building this early."

"Could be. Just to be safe, do you mind if we look around on this floor?" Old asked.

"Nah, be my guest. Nobody here 'cept me."

And the shotgun. *How stupid*, Monique thought, kicking herself mentally. They find that, and the whole gig is up. *Think. Think, woman, think.*

The cops were checking the lobby and looking in the doors and the bathrooms. Did she have time to get to the back door without them seeing her? Each cop was in a bathroom as she hurried by them toward the back door. She just made it and picked up the shotgun.

"Do you take a shotgun to work every day?" The lady cop's voice came from behind Monique. "Now slowly set that back on the floor and turn around with your hands laced behind your head. No sudden moves, or you'll wake up talking to dead relatives."

Monique did as she was told, turning around to find that the lady had her pistol drawn and was covering her. *Fuck, fuck, fuck, fuck.* Now she'd really messed up. Maybe she could minimize the damage.

"Yeah, you got me. Shit. A fucking ride downtown," Monique said.

"Shut up. Lie facedown on the floor with your hands behind your back."

Again, Monique did as she was told. "I need an attorney."

The lady leaned down and tore the radio out of her ear and put the cuffs on. That's what Monique wanted. The best that could happen was for them to get out of here and take her with them. With her attorney and no evidence, she could probably be free by noon. She only hoped Zane could get his proof.

The lady cop picked Monique up by her hair and set her in the corner, propped against the wall. She brought out a radio; at least it looked like a radio. She spoke quietly and clearly, "Back entrance neutralized. She's bagged and harmless. You're free to come in and go upstairs. Repeat, you now have clear entry."

The lady cop then swung her boot hard in a vicious side kick at Monique's head. She didn't have enough time to get out of the way and took most of the blow right above her ear. The tunnel began closing in on Monique as she wondered if Zane or Caleb could really love someone as stupid as she was.

$ $ $

Zane assumed Monique had the downstairs covered. If anybody could get rid of the police, she could. She was a very resourceful girl and had proven that many times.

First he had to go to his office and hope his computer was still there. Then the network server, which housed the digital backups, and then two drawers of files. Along with his laptop, he'd have all the evidence. He had to hurry before Thompson's minions got it before him or Tec.

Zane arrived at his office, flung open the door, and stepped to the side. Better to be safe.

"Come in, Zane. We've been waiting for you," Tec said in his usual taciturn and cool sort of way.

$ $ $

Caleb called Monique. No answer. Not a good sign. Caleb couldn't stay here any longer. He had to go help her. It could be a trap, but he'd survived a lot of traps.

"I'm going to check out the lobby. Monique isn't answering."

"Gotcha. I would, but I have Zane's back," Betty answered.

"I agree."

Caleb put the rifle and grenade launcher in the trunk of the car. A pistol was best for close combat. He walked across the street slowly, trying to discern any unusual activity. Everything looked normal for five in the morning.

"I'm at the front door. I don't see a soul, including Monique. I'm going in."

$ $ $

The police officers had opened the back door and were awaiting their compatriots. It was taking them a bit longer than expected. Early morning and quickness weren't compatible for these two. They were dressed in matching gray suits and appeared to be going to a business meeting. However, upon close inspection, one could discern the slight bulge under their jackets.

The look in each man's eyes revealed that they'd seen a lot, fought a lot, and were satisfied to be alive. Not happy, but satisfied.

They both glanced at Monique, now gagged and handcuffed to a water fountain. She was conscious and looked at them with careful, watery eyes.

"She's a looker. Hey, babe, maybe we can have some fun later. I've got the gun; you provide the fun. Whatcha say?" the short suit said.

"Shut the fuck up. Let's get this over with," his taller companion replied.

They pushed the Up button.

$ $ $

Tec was sitting behind Zane's desk, which used to be Holmes's desk. Rocker was sitting on the sofa facing the desk. The server and a computer were stacked on the floor.

Zane breathed a sigh of relief until Tec opened his mouth.

"A little bit late, Zane," Tec said as Zane came in and stood between the desk and the couch.

Rocker stood up and approached Zane.

"Not too late. Are we good to go?" Zane asked, keeping a wary eye on Rocker.

"Is this our bait?" Rocker asked.

Tec smiled at Zane. "Of course."

Zane took two steps toward Tec. "What the fuck is he talking about? Let's get this shit and roll."

"We will. But remember, we have to peel back all the layers of the onion, get all of them and the full story," Tec answered as he stood up and picked up the server.

Zane stopped and stared at Tec. "Some of it should be here," he said, motioning at the server and computer.

"Some of it," Tec replied. "But you always knew that getting the complete story behind SAS wasn't going to be this easy."

"And how do we get the rest?" Zane asked in a low voice.

"We use you," Tec replied.

"We already did that."

"We need much more," Tec replied flatly.

"I thought it was you and me against them?" Zane said as he stepped between Rocker and Tec and held out both arms toward them.

"It's me for me and you for you. Always has been," Tec replied, slapping Zane's arm out of his way.

$ $ $

Caleb slowly opened the front door and looked around. His pistol was drawn. It was way too quiet.

"Monique?" he yelled through the lobby.

No response.

Caleb went in. He had read that for some reason, defenders always expected intruders to enter and go right. He needed every advantage, so he went left.

Sure enough, three shots rang out to the right of the door, where they expected him to be. They were coming from opposite corners by the elevator.

Caleb dived behind the front entrance security counter. Now he wished he had his rifle.

Obviously, these guys weren't cops. At least not good cops. He had to smoke them out. Shooting at them wasn't going to do anything, and a frontal assault was sure death.

Caleb needed an edge. Any edge, no matter how small. A distraction would be best.

But he couldn't think of one. And time was wasting.

"You may be getting visitors," he radioed to Betty.

"I sincerely hope so. I'm bored."

No fear. That was his edge.

When all else fails, do the thing your enemy least expects.

Run to the battle. Just like David ran to Goliath—with no fear.

Caleb quickly stood up and sprinted for the elevators. He counted to two before he heard the first shots. They fired several shots, but they all blended as one. The adrenaline propelled him on. The shots were behind him, and by the time he counted to three, he was at the corner.

The old cop stood up and pointed his gun straight at Caleb's head. At this distance, he couldn't miss. Except Caleb already had his gun aimed and pulled the trigger a split second before the cop, catching him between the eyes and blowing his brains out through the back of his head.

The lady cop was behind him, momentarily distracted by the explosion of her partner's head. Caleb dived to his left and pivoted as he aimed at her. He didn't have the time to bring the gun up to a vital organ, so he shot her in the knee. She went down, hard, howling in pain. Her pistol slid across the lobby on the hard marble floor.

Caleb stood up quickly and walked slowly over to her. He stood over her with his gun casually at his side.

"Where's the pretty lady? It is your only chance of living through this day."

"By the back door," the lady cop spat through clenched teeth. She was starting to go into shock.

Caleb went toward the back of the lobby and looked around the corner. Monique was handcuffed to the water fountain. She was trying to scream through the gag.

Caleb slowly walked back to the lady and pointed the gun at her head.

"You said you were going to let me live!" the lady cop screamed up at him.

"I said it was your only chance. I never told you how good of a chance," Caleb replied as he shot her twice between the eyes.

He walked back to Monique and took the gag out of her mouth.

"That was kind of harsh, don't you think?" Monique said as she worked her jaw around to loosen it up.

"Sometimes it's necessary to send a message."

"And what would that be?"

"Fuck with us and you wind up dead."

$ $ $

Betty heard the elevator before it arrived at the SAS offices.

She crouched behind the reception desk so just the top of her head was showing. She aimed the rifle straight at the elevator doors only fifteen feet away.

The doors opened. She fired two shots straight into the elevator. Luckily for them, the two occupants had anticipated a welcoming party and were hidden in the front corners.

"Hey, we just want to talk. We'll throw our weapons out and come out to talk. No shooting."

The short suit held his pistol upside down by the trigger guard in the elevator opening.

Betty shot him in the hand.

He dropped the pistol and screamed. "What the fuck? Haven't you heard of a truce?"

"Truces are for pussies. I suggest you hit the Lobby button and get out of here before I come in there and kill both of you," Betty calmly stated as she continued to aim into the elevator.

"Fuck it," the tall suit said. "We'll do this another way." He hit the button to the floor below him.

Betty knew that meant one would try the stairs and one the

elevator. She couldn't cover both entrances.

"Zane, you'd better finish up. I need help out here," Betty said into the mike.

"I'm right behind you," Zane said as he walked up. He was carrying a computer. Tec followed behind him carrying the server, and Rocker juggled two boxes of files.

"What the hell is this?" Betty said as she took in the surprising entourage.

Suddenly, they heard the stairwell door open behind them. They all turned as Caleb came out dragging the tall suit behind him with two bullet holes in his forehead.

"I knew taking the stairs was good for your health," Caleb said as he dumped the dead man on the carpet.

"Where's Monique?" Betty asked.

"Covering the lobby, like we asked her to."

"Well, we'd better get out of here. I think that elevator is about to open, and the guy coming out of it is going to want to shoot people," Betty said.

"Are these guys going with us?" Caleb asked as he gestured toward Tec and Rocker.

"They are," Zane replied.

"And why is that?" Caleb asked, pointing his pistol at Rocker.

"We're going to see what we have and go from there," Zane said as he held up the server.

Rocker set down the files and smoothly brought up his pistol and pointed it at Zane. "You'd better tell your boy to back down."

"I knew Tec was in on this, but what about him?" Betty asked, pointing her gun at Rocker, as well.

"I'll let you explain, Tec, as it seems you have a clearer picture," Zane said while moving closer to Tec.

Tec took a deep breath, set down the server, looked at them all, and smiled. "I fear the SAS fraud and its implications go way beyond what we can conceive at this moment," Tec said while moving up to Rocker and pushing his pistol down toward the floor. "We need to look at what we have here and then dig deeper."

"What do you base that theory on?" Betty asked as she put her gun under her jacket.

"Thompson's boldness and lack of discretion. He blew up Zane's house with bodies inside. He takes the kids, and then we came here in broad daylight. And I've never seen him employ Chastity's special skills here on US soil. I know he's trying to protect himself and hide something bigger than we can imagine. We need to find out what that is," Tec answered.

"How do we dig deeper?" Caleb asked while putting his gun away and leaning against a desk.

"Continue with what Zane and I were doing," Tec said while picking up the server again.

"What about you, Tec?" Caleb asked while Zane stared at Tec. "One moment you're taking Zane's family, torturing Zane, and then taking his kids again. Now you show up here grabbing the evidence. Prove to us that you're on the right side."

"Tec is a free agent," Zane said quietly. "Free to do what suits him best."

Tec sighed and placed the hand not carrying the server behind his neck and began to rub. "Let me show you something, and let's look at this evidence together. In the meantime, they'll expose themselves. I promise."

"And how do you know they'll do that?" Rocker asked.

"I've worked for them a long time, but we need to get out of here first," Tec said, moving toward the elevator. "Then watch Zane. Now that we have this evidence, they'll go after him. Whatever happens to him will lead us to it, and we all need to see it for ourselves."

"What is *it*?" Caleb asked, following the others onto the

arriving elevator.

"Why Zane's family was really taken, why they think our actions will benefit everybody else, and why they think torture is acceptable," Tec answered, pushing the Lobby button. "The capital-R reason."

The door opened to an empty elevator, proof that the short suit had decided his life was more important than what he thought was just computers and files.

They were all quiet as they descended to the lobby, lost in their own thoughts. Nobody paid attention to Tec as he looked at his phone and pushed Send on a prepared text.

Four words.

We're on our way.

95

WINNIPEG, FIFTEEN YEARS EARLIER.

Patience was a powerful ally. Ray had learned that when he was young. He'd endured the wrath of his father and waited until the right time to do something about it. If you waited long enough, the tables would turn.

Ray rented a small apartment in Winnipeg about three blocks from Howie's house. Ray had saved his money while in the juvenile homes and had also worked and saved since his release nine months ago. He could afford to wait. And watch. He had to do this right.

Howie worked in an office of a financial company on the outskirts of Winnipeg. He appeared to be well paid. He lived in a newer split-level home and drove a new BMW. He was always dressed well and hosted parties on a regular basis. His life seemed comfortable, happy, and full.

Ray's wasn't.

Ray had to figure out the best place and time to approach Howie. Alone. There were two options. One was in his car. The other was in his home. Either way, he'd break in late at night while Howie worked late or was out to supper, and he'd confront him.

He chose Howie's home. More room. He might need the room. And it would be easier to clean up.

First, though, he needed to fuck with Howie. It wasn't for fun; it was for retribution.

He began to call Howie late at night or early in the morning. He would disguise his voice and tell him that he knew what he'd done and where she was buried and that soon everybody would know. Howie never responded. Ray could hear him breathe, but never a response.

Then Ray began to call Howie's coworkers. He would ask them if they knew about Howie, about what and who he was and what he'd done in his past. And then he'd hang up. He didn't want to be specific. Just spark their imaginations. That could do more damage and was harder to refute than the truth.

Then Ray began to break into Howie's house. Just to mess with shit. And to leave pictures of his sister. Reminders of the young life he'd snuffed out. Howie had to have some type of conscience.

Then Ray began to plan the final confrontation. He'd break into Howie's house the next day while he was out to supper and wait. In his bedroom. Ray had been thinking about his dad a lot lately and how good that had felt. He didn't know if he could restrain himself much longer. This was for his sister. Had to be.

He woke up the next morning, ready. It was a Saturday, and he knew that most Saturday evenings Howie went out. This was the day.

Ray got ready and went out for breakfast. He never kept groceries at his place. Cooking wasn't his strong suit. He put on his jacket, grabbed his keys, and went out to his pickup. He felt good. Soon it would be over.

Just as he stuck his keys in the lock of his car, his world erupted. The back of his head was the epicenter of the eruption as he slumped down against the side of his truck.

Daylight soon faded to black.

$ $ $

Gradually, it lightened to gray. And orange. And purple. Ray didn't know his head had the capacity to contain this much pain. Ray wondered if his dad's had hurt like this. He hoped so.

Slowly, his eyes began to focus. The place seemed familiar. He'd been here before. Not too long ago. Ray tried to yell, but his mouth wasn't working properly. His tongue felt swollen, as if it wasn't a part of his body. Suddenly, he realized he had something in his mouth. God, it tasted horrendous. It tasted like rotten, bloody meat.

He was in a small barren room. He was tied to a chair. He was naked. A single bulb in the ceiling gave some light. It was a bit melodramatic. Suddenly, the door burst open, and two men walked in. The second one was Howie. He was smiling from ear to ear.

"God, that was easy. You are so fucking predictable, Ray. Like a cow being led to slaughter," Howie said as he giggled like a schoolgirl. "Don't worry; you haven't been shot or anything. Just a bat to the back of your head. Now you know a little of what good old Dad went through."

Ray couldn't believe he'd let this happen.

"You're so gullible. Thought she'd do just about anything for you. That your counselor loved your dick and you controlled her with it. But it was all a lie. Money, not your dick, is what controlled her, old boy. I had the money, and so she gave up her virtue to get some of it. She gave you my location to get more of it. I had to promise her she'd never see you again. She wasn't scared of you but couldn't bear the thought of letting you down after she was trying to counsel you up. Pathetic, wouldn't you say?"

Howie was right. He was pathetic. How could he have trusted her?

"Then you came here. Just as I knew you would. You couldn't pass up the chance to confront me. You just had to come and get revenge. Like that was going to do any good. I *made* you come up here. I've always been better than you and always will be. Do you see any marks left on me by your stupid attack on me? No, I'm fine. But you aren't."

Howie was right. He was a long fucking way from fine.

"Your sister had to pay for your pride. So sad. And now you miss her and have to find out what happened. You think that will settle it. It won't. You're here, and now you have to deal with it. You have to live with this the rest of your miserable fucking life. Nothing will ever change that."

Nothing would ever change that.

"Now, you get to learn my lesson."

He was afraid to ask what that lesson was.

"If I pulled that cow tongue out of your mouth, you would probably ask, 'Well, gee, Howie, what lesson is that?'"

Cow tongue. Ray began to gag and cough. Breathing was difficult.

"Actually, I'm not going to teach you the lesson. That friend of mine in the corner is. You aren't going to get along with him very well."

Howie's friend was just standing in the corner, grinning. He had a short piece of chain in one hand and a vise grip in the other.

"And now the lesson begins. But first, just so there is no confusion, what is the lesson for today?" Howie asked his friend as he began to swing the chain.

"Never—no matter what—never, ever fuck with Howie. Because if you do, you'll live to regret it."

96

They rode together in separate cars. Not as friends, more like associates. It was a two-car caravan. Tec and Zane were riding with Caleb in the lead car. Rocker was riding with Monique and Betty in the trailing car.

The retrieval of the laptop would have to wait until after the inspection of the contents of what they'd just taken from the SAS offices.

Tec was navigating them to his house. He lived in the western suburbs of the Twin Cities, out past Wayzata on Highway 12. He had a little acreage set back in the rolling hills on the shore of a small lake. It was his retreat. They needed privacy to view the contents of the computer and the files. And Tec had something else to show them.

"It appears Zane is our bait," Betty said as she leaned back in her seat. The foray had been exciting so far, but it was also tiring for someone her age. "Why do you think he agreed to this? It seems weird that he's trusting Tec, after what he did."

"I don't know. Hopefully they have a plan," Monique replied. "And hopefully Tec shows us something that will help us all trust him."

"I think God has given him His wisdom and put him in this place for a specific reason and that it'll work out. But that doesn't mean I'm not concerned. Zane has been through a lot."

"Well, let's hope it works out, because I don't think I can

handle any more screwups today."

"Yeah, let's hope that never happens again," Betty said as she winked at Monique.

"Remind me never to play poker with you."

$ $ $

Silence permeated Caleb's car. They all had questions but were afraid of the answers. Caleb took the plunge.

"I know you used to be friends. That isn't all water under the bridge. I also know a lot of bad shit has happened, some of it caused by both of you. Let's figure it out."

"I don't really care about that," Zane said.

"You have to care about it. If not, why did we take this ride?" Caleb asked.

"Whether you care about me or not, we still need to peel back this onion," Tec responded.

"Are you sure that's what you want?" Zane asked.

"It is," Tec answered haltingly.

"Did you set me up to kill Moore?" Zane asked very quietly. "It seems as if you may have had a personal motive to see him dead."

The only response to Zane's question was the sound of bugs hitting the windshield.

"Hello? Tec?"

"Why would you ask me that?"

"You aren't the only one who has talked to Thompson."

Tec sighed and put both of his palms on his forehead. "We're all better off with Moore out of the picture."

"Answer the question," Caleb demanded.

"I only want the truth," Tec lied.

"Whose side are you on?" Zane asked. "You never answered that back at SAS."

"I work for Thompson, but only so I can get some answers and influence the outcome."

"We all want something," Caleb interjected.

"We did what we did for different reasons, and we're doing this for different reasons," Tec replied.

"That's very deep," Caleb said mockingly while looking at Tec in the backseat. "What are those reasons?"

Tec laid back and pushed his hands up against the roof of Caleb's Wrangler. "I can't answer for Zane."

They'd been traveling west on Interstate 394, which had turned into Highway 12. The scenery had progressed from suburban office low-rises and the typical restaurant chains to rolling hills with trees, grass, and the occasional farm-implement dealer.

"How about it, Zane?" Caleb turned to look at Zane sitting next to him in the front seat. "Tell us your reasons."

Zane was looking out his window. "Every time I drive here, I want to live here. Life seems slower and more meaningful."

"What do you mean by *meaningful*?" Tec asked, putting his hands on the back of the front seat.

"Here, everything seems real. All the shit I've done in my life pales in comparison. I've always had to pretend to be somebody else. How can anything you accomplish mean anything if it isn't even *you* actually doing it?" Zane asked, looking straight ahead and pounding his fist into the dash.

"Who were you pretending to be?" Caleb asked quietly.

"Doesn't matter," Zane answered just as quietly. "We need to expose SAS."

"Exposing you may help us expose SAS," Tec said.

"Is that what we really want?" Zane asked, looking around Caleb's jeep. "We all have a past, and we all have secrets. We did things we aren't proud of. We need to work together and forget the past. There's a reason for what we did and a reason we're all here together now."

"Yeah, except you are SAS," Caleb said while staring at Zane. "Just saying."

"I show you my shit, but you don't show me yours," Zane said as he looked out the window at more of the slow life. "That was never part of our plan."

Caleb looked back at Tec and shrugged his shoulders.

"I think your secrets are more closely intertwined with SAS's," Tec said. "And you'll find out some of mine in just a bit."

"How close is your place, Tec?" Caleb asked, trying to deflect any questions about his past.

"We aren't going there," Tec responded.

"What? I thought we were going to look at these computers, and you had something else to show us," Caleb said as he turned around and shot a hard glance at Tec.

"That's going to have to wait," Tec responded.

"For what?" Caleb asked quietly, almost as if he knew the answer.

"For some revelation straight from the source."

"What the hell are you talking about?" Caleb asked.

"Be prepared for anything," Tec said as they approached an intersection. "Turn right here, on County Road 4."

Before the words left Tec's mouth, Zane reached in his pocket and pushed Send on a prepared text message of his own.

The meeting is on. At the shed.

Caleb slowed and completed the turn.

Suddenly, they were sideswiped by a car swerving into their lane.

Caleb's Wrangler was pushed violently off the edge of the road down a steep embankment. It rolled once before it came to rest back on its wheels.

Caleb's question remained unanswered.

97

Howie stood with his back to the door. He didn't look happy. He looked anxious. This would begin a journey. The journey of Ray.

Ray feared the pain. He feared the injury. But most of all, he feared losing and Howie winning. Ray couldn't live with that. He couldn't die here today. His only goal was to stay alive. Stay alive, confront Howie later, find out what happened to his sister, and make him pay. Ray had to stay breathing, at all costs. No matter what.

That fear was soon relieved.

"Don't worry; you aren't going to die today. You're going to wish you could. But you won't," Howie's friend said as he began to twirl the chain faster. "Have you ever seen the movie *Pulp Fiction*? I'm sure you have. I think it's Tarantino's best work. It was raw and didn't have a social message like his more recent movies, but it had a message. Sometimes when your situation looks the bleakest, it turns around, after all. And vice versa. Just when you think two rednecks are going to fuck you up the ass, you're the one fucking them. You thought you were coming to Winnipeg to fuck Howie up the ass, and instead, I'm going to get medieval on *your* ass. And there is nothing you can do to stop it. It will take a while too. Try not to tense up. The less tense you are, the less it will hurt. I know that's difficult, but try. Just fucking try."

Howie's friend began to laugh. He seemed to be enjoying himself.

Ray had seen *Pulp Fiction* several times. It was a good movie. He agreed that any situation could easily turn around. This situation could too. He just needed an opportunity. Ray had to stay within himself to look for that opportunity.

Howie's friend was short, thick, and strong. He had a crew cut and a large nose. If he had a neck, Ray sure couldn't see it. He wore a blue medical smock hanging out over blue jeans with rubber boots up to his knees. The medical smock and boots bothered Ray. He was prepared to get dirty. Dirty with Ray's blood.

He moved toward Ray slowly, swinging the chain low in a circle. As he got close to Ray, he stopped swinging it and snapped it like a towel at Ray's shin. The pain was immense as the chain snapped against the bone. Ray screamed; he was sure the leg was broken.

"I'm going to leave you two alone. Three's a crowd for this party. Let me know when you're done. The money is upstairs," Howie told his friend.

"Aw, you always pay me. I told you I'd do this one for free. Keeps me in shape and sharp."

Now Ray remembered where he was. In Howie's basement. He'd reconned this room.

"Yeah, that's right, Ray. I do this shit all the time. For Howie. He's not the man you think he is."

"Have fun, boys." Howie waved as he left and shut the door.

"What next? Arms or legs? I say we switch it up."

He moved in again behind Ray. He flicked the chain, this time at Ray's forearms, which were bound behind the chair. The chain flicked short and hit the restraints instead. It split a palm wide open, but also cut the restraints. Ray's hands were free.

Opportunity.

"Woohoo! Now you think you can turn this around? Your hands are free, but your leg is broken. What are you going to do with that?"

With his good leg, Ray pushed the chair up and back. With his hands free, he was able to reach up behind the friend's neck on the way down, and he brought his face crashing down on Ray's forehead with a kind of reverse head butt to the chin as they both landed on the cement floor. The friend dropped to the side, momentarily stunned.

That gave Ray all the time he needed to free his legs and roll over onto his torturer. He brought his knee down hard on his sternum and felt the bone crack. The friend cried out in pain as Ray grabbed the chain, which had fallen to the floor, and wrapped it around the friend's neck. He wound it tight, like a noose, and brought his lips close to his ear.

"This won't take long. You can tense up if you want. This isn't about pain, it's about death," Ray whispered as he pulled both ends of the chain around his neck until the thrashing and moaning stopped.

Ray stood up and put on his pants. He grabbed his shirt and wound it around his hand. It was quickly soaked with his blood. He limped to the door, cringing at the pain in his broken leg. The door was unlocked. He opened it and limped to the stairs.

It was time for a face-to-face.

He screamed, "Asshole!" at the top of his lungs as he dragged his broken leg up the stairs.

98

They'd stopped for gas and fallen far behind Caleb's Wrangler. Tec had texted Monique directions, and they were almost there.

Betty stepped on the gas to catch them and then made the turn onto County 4, which was the last paved road before Tec's driveway.

Suddenly, Betty hit the brakes and pulled onto the shoulder.

"Holy Jesus, woman, what the heck are you doing? I've been through enough today, I don't need whiplash too," Monique complained.

"Something is wrong. I know it," Betty responded as she put the vehicle in park and stopped the car.

"Did God tell you?" Monique asked while shooting her a sly grin.

"His Spirit did. My Spirit is troubled, and that comes from His Spirit."

Betty and Monique got out of the car just as Rocker jumped out of the backseat.

"Look at the skid marks. They go off in the direction of the ditch," Rocker interjected, pointing at the asphalt.

"I don't think we have to look very far," Monique responded from the edge of the ditch while peering over the embankment. "That's them at the bottom. That's Caleb's Wrangler!"

Betty ran to the edge and carefully began her descent.

"Here, let me go first. They may need more help than you can give," Rocker replied while scrambling down, trying to reach the damaged car first.

Rocker ran down so fast he almost fell over himself and still arrived at the same time as Betty. Monique was only seconds behind. They looked in the car, expecting the worse.

They found nothing but blood. A lot of it.

But no Caleb, no Tec, and no Zane.

The computers and files were gone too.

99

"I guess Tec's plan worked," Caleb said as he looked over at Zane, who was tied in the chair next to him.

"I'm not sure that makes me happy," Zane replied.

"If the next person walking into this room is the dildo chick, you'll have your answer."

Caleb tried to work his arms around, but they were tied tightly to the chair; movement only brought pain. Zane's face was bloody from several deep cuts incurred during the accident, and he had no energy left to move any part of his body. The only things holding him up were the zip ties tying him to the chair. He was relieved he could still feel the key around his neck.

They were in what looked like a garage. It had a cement floor and workbenches along one side. A van was parked next to one of the workbenches, and a small car with front-end damage from a collision was parked next to it. The floor was shiny and clean, and it was obvious that this place was rarely used for vehicle repair. The walls were cement block, painted a high-gloss white with illumination provided by banks of fluorescent bulbs. A large overhead garage door was on one end of the garage. On the other end was a small door with a window next to it that looked into a lighted office area.

There was a floor drain between Caleb and Zane. It was shiny, as if it had just been cleaned.

Three people walked through the small door—a small, thin, muscular man, Tec, and Chastity.

"We were just talking about you. I sure hope you got a better torture device than that dildo you used last time. The thought of that kind of turns me on," Caleb said while staring at her and smiling.

Chastity chuckled. "I guarantee you, nothing I do will turn you on."

"Aw, come on. You never know until you try," Caleb said while continuing to stare at her and smile.

"I also guarantee you that the smart-ass remarks will stop as soon as I start," Chastity said while standing in front of Zane.

Zane appeared to be asleep. His head hung down on his chest, blood dripping from his face onto his shirt.

"And you, Mr. Zane, look worse than the last time I saw you," Chastity said while picking up Zane's chin and turning his head. "That will make my job easier."

Zane abruptly opened his eyes and violently shook his head from side to side, spraying blood over Chastity, who immediately jumped back.

"You bastard! You got blood on me!" Chastity screamed while jumping in again and grabbing Zane on both sides of his head. She squeezed as hard as possible in hopes of somehow making it burst. "Defiance is the breeding ground for pain!"

The small man moved in quickly and pulled her back. Tec watched silently.

"Leave me alone, dickhead!" Chastity yelled, trying to free herself. "This doesn't involve you."

"No, but it involves me," another voice interjected. They all turned to see a large, long- haired, bearded man walk in the room. "Back off, Chastity. Not now."

Dickhead carried her to the corner and dumped her on the

floor. She got up and charged at Zane, but Dickhead held her at bay while she frantically tried to brush Zane's blood off herself.

"You need to keep your pet monster on a leash, or I'll do it for you," Caleb said, looking at the large man.

"Yes, she is a bit unruly at times, but none of us are perfect. By the way, my name is Alan Thompson. I'm the guy Zane thinks is the mastermind behind this operation. In the flesh. Are you happy to finally meet me, Zane?"

The silence was deafening.

"I know you've had a rough couple of days. It'll soon be over."

"It'll be over for you too," Zane said hoarsely through swollen lips. "In the meantime, you'd better take good care of my kids."

"We will. And you had better take good care of my $15 million."

"So what happens now? Where do we go from here? Exchange money for kids?" Tec asked.

"Isn't it nice to see your friend's concern for you and your children's well-being?" Thompson said as he positioned himself between Caleb and Zane. "Tec has served us well. He even endured the little rollover you guys experienced. Of course, he's the one that set it up."

"Get to the bottom line. Why are we here? What do you want?" Zane asked while moving his head in circles, trying to get his neck muscles to stop hurting. Nothing about Tec surprised him anymore.

Thompson took out a knife and held it in front of Zane's face. "It isn't what you think." He brought the knife down quickly and cut through Zane's zip tie restraints.

"I need you. I need Caleb. I need Tec. I need all of you. I have great plans for you, and it really doesn't matter if you like me or not. And, sad to say, it doesn't matter if we use Chastity or not," Thompson looked sideways at Chastity. "Sorry, honey."

Caleb shot a glance at Tec that Thompson didn't catch because he was still staring at Chastity. Caleb's was a look of surprise mixed with resignation, at which Tec simply shrugged his shoulders.

"What does matter?" Zane asked while standing unsteadily to his feet. "And where are the computers and the files?"

"I'm going to show you what matters. I'm also going to show you what this is all about, but we won't need the computers or the files. They're safely tucked away," Thompson answered while leaning over and cutting Caleb's restraints.

Caleb stood up suddenly, tipping his chair over and coming face-to-face with Thompson. "I wouldn't be too sure of yourself just yet. We won't settle for being your bitches."

Thompson flipped the knife closed and put it in his pocket. "Mr. Rider, the day will come very soon when you will give anything to be my bitch."

100

"So what now?" Monique asked as they climbed out of the ditch. Betty started walking to the Yukon. "Ask Rocker! He should know!" she yelled over her shoulder as she hopped into the car, slamming the door.

Monique and Rocker were standing on the side of the road. Cars whizzed by without stopping. They didn't need or want some Good Samaritan to stop.

"Let's get out of here first. Then we can figure this out," Rocker replied, amazed that it was going to be this easy as he got into the car. Monique followed.

Betty made a U-turn and turned back on Highway 12 toward the Twin Cities. "So, Rocker, what gives?"

"We all need to figure out the truth," Rocker replied, putting both hands on the backseat next to him and looking out a side window. "I know no more than you guys do."

"You know who is behind this," Betty said, stepping on the gas. "Take us to him."

"To the shed, then." Rocker smiled as he looked out the window. "I just hope it's not a trap."

101

Zane and Caleb were seated next to each other in hard metal folding chairs around a cheap eight-foot metal folding table in the office area of the building known as the shed. Thompson was seated at one end of the table with Tec at the other. Dickhead and Chastity occupied spots on a leather couch in the corner. The floor was unfinished concrete, and the walls were concrete block. One door opened to the outside, and another opened to the garage they had just occupied. In addition to the window opening to the garage, one window looked out over the parking lot.

Zane was staring out the window noticing the train track and wondering when the next train would go by. Then he noticed a vehicle crossing over the railroad tracks and pulling into the gravel parking lot. He knew the SUV. It was Betty's. This wasn't part of *his* plan.

Zane watched as Betty, Monique, and Rocker exited the black Yukon. They started walking toward the front door and then stopped and turned around. A black Chrysler 300 sedan was pulling into the parking lot behind them. Two men got out of the front seat and stretched, slowly looking around.

The two Treasury agents.

"Well, it looks as if now we're going to have a real party," Thompson said, looking at the five people walking in the door.

Relief washed over Betty and Monique as soon as they saw Zane, but they were reluctant to express their emotion. The time and place didn't seem sufficient for a joyful reunion.

"Have a seat, ladies and gentleman. There are more chairs in the corner," Thompson said while each new participant grabbed a metal folding chair and sat down.

Amid the commotion, Tec leaned over and dropped his phone in Caleb's lap. Zane nodded at Caleb as he looked up at him.

"Why don't you make the introductions, Zane?" Thompson said, referring to the two men from the Chrysler now sitting on either side of him. "After all, it was your text that brought them here."

Zane drew a big breath and let it out slowly. "These are the Treasury agents I've been working with, Ralph and Rick." Zane then smiled at them. "I never gave you the address."

"Oops," Thompson said while chuckling slightly.

Caleb nodded. "That answers that."

"And the older lady is Betty, your former mother-in-law; and of course, there's Monique, your friend with the computer skills; we all know Rocker. He's one of ours," Thompson explained finishing the introductions.

Zane was surprised that Thompson knew the identities of Monique and Betty.

"I don't get it," Monique spoke up. "If Thompson is associated with SAS, he must be associated with the crimes SAS has committed. Why don't you two arrest him?" she asked, nodding to the two Treasury agents. "After all, the guys in the white hats are the government, right?" Monique asked.

Zane suddenly realized how Moore had obtained the tape of Zane's confession to the Treasury that Tina had watched. From the two Treasury agents.

"Things have changed," Ralph said.

"What has changed?" Caleb asked.

"You'll see. But first of all, take a look at this," Ralph said as he threw a newspaper on the table.

The paper was opened to the obituaries, and one of them in particular was underlined.

Caleb snatched the newspaper and read the name aloud. "Ben Guardian, owner of Guardian Jewelry, died today at his home of a coronary embolism."

Zane stared at Caleb without moving.

"What do you know about that?" Caleb said, looking at Zane as he was rising up out of his chair. "I know Ben Guardian had an insurance policy. And I also know he was in perfect health. You told me about SAS illegally acquiring businesses, but that explanation didn't include the premature death of the former owners."

All eyes were now on Zane. He was sitting calmly like a rock with both hands flat on the table.

"Ben needed a way out."

"What do you mean, *a way out*?" Tec asked.

"He was in desperate financial straits—losing his business, his personal wealth, heck, even his pension plan. I offered a way out. The SAS way."

"Bottom line. He died," the second Treasury agent, Rick, threw in. "That made the whole plan come to life, pardon the pun." Rick chuckled. "It also made our investment pay off nicely. Right, Zane?"

"What in God's name is he talking about?" Betty asked Zane.

"Yes, Zane. Do tell," Thompson invited.

"Life insurance. Ben was worth $25 million—dead." Zane said.

"So because he died, his family gets the money and is taken care of?" Monique asked.

"If only that were true. No, his policy was sold as a viatical," Zane replied.

"Viatical? What the hell? Sounds like sabbatical. Are they similar?" Monique asked.

"Not even close. A viatical is a life insurance policy that has been bought by an investor. The investor waits for the principal to die to collect on the policy, hoping to get back the investment and then some."

"So what's so bad about that?" Betty asked.

"That depends upon who owns the viatical," Zane responded.

"Who owned Ben's viatical?"

Everybody was looking at Zane.

"SAS," he stated flatly while looking at all of the occupants.

"But I thought SAS sold him the policy. Is that legal?" Monique asked.

"Why don't you answer that question, Ralph?" Zane asked.

Thompson was smiling as he looked to Ralph for the answer.

"It is," Ralph replied as he folded his hands on the table.

"SAS bought the policy for less than the death benefit, and therefore, SAS will profit," Caleb said as he looked from Ralph to Rick several times.

"Yes, it's a financing vehicle for SAS to purchase business interests from distressed owners. The proceeds from the purchase of the life insurance policy go to the owner of the business, and he signs the business over to us, and SAS profits from the death of the business owner, who is the principal insured," Zane answered.

"So let me understand this. Let's take the late Mr. Guardian as an example," Caleb said. "His business was in trouble. SAS offered to purchase his business. A life insurance company issued a policy on Ben, who was healthy as a horse. SAS bought the policy from Ben and waits for Ben to die so they can make back their investment and reap a huge profit."

"Yes."

"What does Ben get?" Betty asked.

387

"The money from the purchase of the life insurance policy, so he can live out his life debt-free and with a bit of change," Zane explained.

"Live out his life?" Caleb mocked. "He died."

"Yes, he had to. Only then can SAS make back its investment and profit," Thompson spoke up.

Nobody wanted to ask a follow-up question.

"This puts things in a rather different light," Monique said, staring at Zane.

"I didn't kill them."

"They agreed to be killed?" Betty asked. "Why would anybody agree to that just to get some money?"

"They didn't agree. In Zane's defense, he thought they were going to fake their deaths and disappear never to be seen again," Thompson explained.

"Sometimes the principal's families knew, and they'd stay in touch, sometimes even visit periodically. Sometimes they didn't know, and the principal just disappeared. The principal's choice. Or so I thought," Zane's voice trailed off.

"We weren't comfortable with that. Having the principals live out their lives on some remote island in the eternal sunshine was a loose end. Too dangerous for us."

"So the family members thought they were going to fake die, and then they really died?" Caleb asked. "Didn't that piss them off or make them wonder?"

"They thought their loved ones' death were fake and that they were just choosing to stay out of touch. If the family members asked too many questions, we would threaten them too. Since they were complicit in getting the money, they wouldn't want any of this exposed. It's worked so far."

"I read about a car crash with two people dead. Billy Hot and his cousin. Both way too fucking young to die. Thing is, this was my case, and I knew that only the principal should have died and disappeared. I realized that the deaths aren't fake at all. That the principals were killed. Murdered. And I was a party to that," Zane explained.

"This doesn't make any sense to me," Caleb said. "How could a broke business owner get a large enough policy to make it worth everybody's while? And if this insurance company kept doing this over and over again, they would go broke. What was their incentive?"

"The insurance company owns SAS. Robert Holmes and I worked for them at a huge profit. They made huge fees on each transaction, but I never figured out their real incentive until now," Zane replied.

"But the insurance company couldn't keep paying out on these policies. It would ruin them," Caleb said.

"At first, I thought they made their money from owning the businesses they bought. It would take a while, but they would make enough to justify paying out on the policies," Zane responded.

"Why would SAS want to own a bunch of broke businesses?" Caleb asked.

"They were dirt cheap. But there's more," Zane said.

"Spill it already," Caleb demanded.

"SAS and the insurance company are financially backed by the Federal Reserve," Zane said looking at Rick.

"Very astute," Rick said.

"What?" Betty said. "The government goes around killing people?"

"Let's not put it so bluntly," Ralph replied. "After Zane came to us with his evidence on fraudulent insurance policies, we thought we'd have an open-and-shut case. But we were told to back off. We had no idea really what was going on at first, but hey, we did our jobs. We kept you on a leash, asking you to collect more and more evidence of the insurance fraud. But then when one client found out and we weren't attempting prosecution, our boss was afraid you'd go public. So Thompson and his subordinates took your family to ensure your cooperation. And by subordinates, I also mean Tecumseh here," Ralph replied.

"We considered having Zane killed too, but a higher power wouldn't have that," Thompson explained. "This person felt he was better alive and in our control."

"Higher power?" Tec asked.

"Believe it or not, there are those higher than me," Mr. Thompson replied. "Higher than even the president of this great country. They're the ones who are really behind this."

"Federal Reserve," Zane restated.

"Some things still don't figure," Monique said.

"How did this insurance company get away with this? I mean everybody dying right after buying life insurance," Caleb asked.

"It's very simple. The Fed owns the insurance company and therefore SAS," Ralph said. "And we didn't always have the business owner die. Sometimes it was somebody else, a family member or a key employee."

"I guess it didn't really matter, since the thieves were guarding the henhouse," Caleb blurted out.

"I didn't know the Federal Reserve was in the insurance business," Betty said.

"We are. Courtesy of the 2008 financial crisis," Thompson answered. "Our version of TARP, the Troubled Asset Repurchase Program."

"So if you didn't own these businesses to make money, what was your goal?" Rocker asked.

"Control." Zane sighed and pointed to Ralph.

"The next time a financial crisis hits this country, we'll own enough businesses to control the economy. Therefore, any effect from a financial fallout will be contained. We won't have to lay off people; we won't have to worry about missing debt payments. We rescued these dying businesses. We'll pump money into them to keep them afloat, so that, if need be, they can keep the country afloat. In 2008, we funneled money through this same insurance company to give to other broke businesses, but this time, we want to own them so we can control them—to avoid a repeat of 2008."

"I knew it!" Betty exclaimed. "End-time prophecy being fulfilled right before our very eyes. If the government can control our money, they can control us."

"The government is broke too. How do you come up with the money to pump into these broke businesses or the money to pump into SAS to buy the policies or the money to pump into the insurance company to pay out on the insurance policies?" Rocker asked.

"We are broke. But that's not the same as being out of money," Rick said.

"Does that mean what I think it means?" Betty asked.

"The Federal Reserve can do whatever it wants, and their pockets are infinite," Zane said.

"The Fed has the power to do whatever, including making money. And I don't mean making it the old-fashioned way by earning it. I mean, making it by manufacturing it. Quantitative easing. Printing money," Ralph said.

"Thompson's group works for the Fed," Zane added. "They're part of the Federal Reserve."

The room became very quiet as everybody processed what they'd just learned.

"I have a question," Rocker said, looking at Thompson. "Why didn't you just print the money and use it to purchase the businesses outright? That way, you don't need the viatical program, and you don't need to kill people."

"That would be too easy to track straight to the Fed. By

running it through the insurance company and SAS, the Fed's role is not as apparent."

"So people have to die so the Fed's role in all this wouldn't become public? Why are you telling us all of this?" Monique swallowed hard. "Aren't you afraid that we'll go public?"

"Only if you're allowed to leave," Thompson said, staring at Zane. "And that option is not on the table."

Zane looked at Thompson with a slight grin. "You may not be in the position to make that decision."

Thompson looked at Tec and Rocker, who were smiling back at him. "What kind of shit has he told you?"

Caleb cleared his throat. "Here's the thing, guys," Caleb said, looking at Ralph and Rick. "I work for somebody who might have a little problem with what you just said. He is more US of A than either of you. He is of the people, by the people, and for the people. Everything that was just said, he heard through my cell phone, because I called him just before we started in on this little explanation. Isn't that right, Congressman?" Caleb said into his phone as he took it from his lap and hit the Speaker button.

"Oh yes, I heard it all. And so did this gentleman from the *Wall Street Journal* who just happened to be in my office. I don't know what kind of shoes Ralph and Rick are wearing, but I hope they brought their running shoes."

102

Interstate Park is one of the most picturesque parks in the United States. It straddles the Saint Croix River north of Saint Paul, with parts of the park in Minnesota and parts in Wisconsin. The Wisconsin section is bigger and easier to get lost in. It also has better trails leading up the rocky bluffs overlooking the river. Zane was now hiking on one of those trails at five minutes past midnight.

It had been two days since the confrontation with Treasury and Thompson, and things were still being sorted out. Seconds after the phone call ended with the congressman, the FBI had entered the place and detained them all. Only Thompson was being held for questioning, because the rest of them were cooperating with the investigation.

Zane didn't know what their cooperation entailed, but he needed to take care of some unfinished business, because his days of freedom were likely numbered.

The trail was steep, almost straight up, and full of rocks. It was a treacherous hike in full daylight and almost impossible to navigate safely at night, especially with the moon afraid to show its face. Zane didn't dare use a flashlight, lest he be discovered. After everything he'd been through recently, it would be a shame to fall from this trail and die on the rocks below. He slowed his pace and carefully picked his way through the boulders and tree roots.

He reached the top slightly winded. He laced his hands behind his head and took several deep breaths while slowly walking in circles. Then he proceeded to the end of the trail and looked out over a bluff to the Saint Croix River below. He was several hundred feet up and wondered how deep the water was below. This was known as Suicide Cliff, and he could easily imagine how it earned its name.

"I thought about it," a voice spoke out. "Since I'm already dead, maybe it won't hurt as much."

Zane turned around and saw a familiar figure emerge from behind a large pine tree and approach him.

"Hello, Zane."

"I need to touch you," Zane said as he shook Ben Guardian's hand. "Just to make sure you aren't actually dead."

Ben laughed. "Not yet, anyway. Although I'm not sure how much longer I'll remain not dead. You need to fill me in."

They both crossed several feet to a bench that overlooked the bluffs and the river.

"I'm going to miss this place. This was my thinking spot," Ben said, putting both arms on the back of the bench and stretching his feet out.

"I understand. Change is hard, but this is what you wanted. Right?" Zane asked him.

"After running jewelry stores almost all of my adult life, anything other than that would be difficult. But, yeah, this is what I want, and more importantly, it's what I need," Ben answered, putting one hand on Zane's arm.

Zane stared straight ahead at the bluffs on the Minnesota side of the river. "When I first saw the obituary, I thought you were dead. Just like my other clients."

"In spite of our plan?"

"Plans don't always work."

"I was home alone, so it was easy. Also, having a longtime

customer and friend who owns a funeral home sealed the deal. He showed up with the hearse and took care of the newspaper notice. He knows the coroner—and cremation avoided any questions at the funeral," Ben explained as he crossed his arms over his chest.

"Good planning. How did you split the $15 million?"

"Three million for each of us. It was the only fair way." Ben explained. "I don't know where you got the money or how, but quite honestly, at this point, I don't care."

"Just know that you have to disappear. If the people whose money I stole find out you're still alive, you won't be much longer."

"I know how to disappear, courtesy of some friends of mine in the international jewelry business."

"I'm not sure anybody can truly disappear," Zane said, kicking at the rocks by his feet. "How are your wife and kids taking it?"

"I hear they're sad. But if the way they're spending the money is any indication, they're getting over it. I don't feel bad about leaving them behind, thinking I'm dead. This will force them to live for themselves and within themselves. They need that."

"Money makes things easier, but its comforts aren't eternal," Zane said, looking at Ben.

"Maybe they'll learn that lesson the hard way," Ben answered. He got up and walked toward the cliff.

"I've learned a lot of lessons about money lately the hard way," Zane said as he got up too and approached Ben. "The problem with that way is that it usually means other people get hurt."

"Like your wife."

"Like your family, mourning your death."

"Death does seem to solve some problems." Ben stood on the very edge of the cliff, looking out.

Zane silently stood behind him. Ben didn't move a muscle for fear of what would happen next.

"Am I a loose end you need to tie up now that my family is

taken care of?" Ben asked.

Zane reached up and put his hands on the back of Ben's shoulders.

"You're a good man," Zane said, gripping Ben's shoulders tightly. "But you are evidence."

"Evidence that's about to disappear," Ben said softly. His muscles tensed.

"You're the only living survivor of the SAS viatical scheme." Zane held on to Ben tightly.

Both men stood stock still, afraid that any movement would set off irrevocable events.

Zane would have to face the music for his crimes. Leaving Ben as a witness could come back to haunt him. If he pushed him off the cliff now, he'd have to find and dispose of the body, because as far as the world knew, Ben Guardian was already dead. But nobody would miss him. Zane wasn't opposed to killing. In fact, he had no trouble killing those who deserved it.

Ben didn't qualify.

Zane removed his hands and looked up at the stars on the clear night. Why was there so much more darkness than light?

Zane slowly turned around and headed back down the trail.

103

COLOMBIA, FOUR YEARS EARLIER.

Tec couldn't process what his eyes were telling him. He sat down on the front step and put his hands on either side of his head and squeezed. Maybe it was the heat and humidity. Everything was shimmering and moving. Maybe it was dehydration and low blood sugar. Maybe it was the taste of failure.

The two missing team members were slapping each other on the back, laughing. Nito stayed in the background, confusion on his face.

"The tip came from an American," the tortured Colombian had said. Why would an American give a Colombian drug gang a tip that would lead to the general and his family? The general was helping the Americans. It didn't make sense.

"Did you think we were dead?"

"Maybe you should be," Tec responded as he drew his combat pistol and pointed it at his head. "What the fuck happened?" he shouted.

"Spill your fucking guts. Or we'll spill your fucking guts," Nito claimed.

"Just settle down. Everybody stay cool. This place is not worth it, and the people in it sure as hell aren't, either. Obviously, we weren't abducted, and we have more good news."

"I wouldn't count your blessings just yet," Tec flatly stated.

"Things aren't always as they seem."

"You're going to regret you came back unless you seriously clarify what the fuck just happened." Nito pulled his pistol and pointed it at the other reunited team member.

"It's very simple, numbnuts. We're fighting an undeclared war. If we don't show some results, Washington will pull us back, and we'll lose funding. So we needed a surefire way to smoke out the drug gang. Going into the jungle day after day wasn't working," the first missing team member explained. He looked quickly from Tec to Nito, hoping to rapidly defuse the situation.

"We had the satellite phone number for the drug leader, but couldn't pinpoint it on GPS. So we called him and told him where the general and his family lived. We told him the general was a leading proponent of the war on the drug gangs. We provided classified information so they'd buy our story. And they did. It didn't matter that we were Americans; they couldn't pass up the offer of getting to the general. We suspected it would be a bloody massacre, but having the drug gang kill the general's worthless family served our purposes well," the second missing team member explained while walking up to Nito and putting his arm around him.

Nito shrugged the arm off and turned away from everybody.

Tec tried to slow down his breathing. He took a deep breath through his nose and expelled it through clenched teeth as visions of the children's heads played in his mind.

"They were just casualties of war, but their deaths will actually help our case. We can publicize this incident back home. When the public finds out what these savages did, they'll scream for results. The political hacks that fund our program will only be too eager to throw more money our way. This is a win-win for everybody. You get credit for nabbing the Colombian drug gang, and our program gets much-needed publicity," the second missing member explained to Nito's back.

Nito had seen it coming. He turned and stepped in front of Tec and grabbed his pistol, forcing the barrel down. Tec wanted to struggle, but knew he would lose and didn't want to hurt Nito. The general and his family had died for nothing. Or worse, they died for military funding. His bloodlust rose. All he could see was red. He felt responsible. It was his fault. He couldn't live with that. He needed his knife.

He spun back into the house with Nito close on his heels. He ran up to the chair where he had left the gang leader. Blood was pumping out of the two holes where his ears had been. Only the restraints kept him upright.

He only remembered pulling his knife out of the chair—and then suddenly the gang leader's head was staring up at him from the floor with blank, empty eyes. But his body was still restrained to the chair. There was blood everywhere. Everywhere. But it still wasn't enough.

Tec spun out of Nito's grasp. The family was in the basement. His last memory was going down those steps. Going down fast.

He had lost all control.

104

"What happened to the two team members who set you up?" Caleb asked.

Before Tec could answer, everybody looked at Rocker, who was quietly staring out the window and looking at people in the cars around them. Could they possibly have problems on this scale?

"Well, one of them is in this truck," Tec replied as he steered Betty's Yukon through traffic on the western edge of the Twin Cities. Now they were heading out to Tec's.

"Spaz and I. We did what they told us to do. We were doing what we thought was right," Rocker said, continuing to look out the window.

"I've forgiven them. I've had a harder time forgiving myself," Tec said.

"Colombia was a bad place. A thorn in the side of America. You did what you were sent there to do," Zane said as he stifled a yawn, still tired from his late night rendezvous with Ben. "But I'm not sure how that relates to me and this situation. This is not Columbia."

"Regrettably, there are some similarities," Tec explained.

"It's hard to know the innocents in a war zone," Monique said, and she looked at Zane, hoping he'd understand her veiled reminder.

"I had orders, but I went too far," Tec said.

"Looking back and figuring out what we did wrong serves a purpose, but only to avoid doing it again. Not to feel the guilt," Betty said as she reclined the seat back in her Yukon.

"I need to learn that lesson and apply it to this situation," Tec said as he slowed down to turn. "But it's difficult to disobey my superiors. In this situation, one Alan Thompson."

"Disobedience is our duty at times," Zane muttered as he looked over from the passenger seat.

"I wouldn't be too hard on him," Monique said from the back row. "Without Tec, all of us wouldn't have been there to witness and tape Thompson's confession."

"Caleb was in on that too," Betty offered up as a way of leveling the playing field in Caleb's favor. "Without his phone call to his boss, we wouldn't have an influential witness."

Monique looked at Betty out of the corner of her eye.

"Tec knew about my phone call idea, and Zane saw it happen. And don't forget Rocker," Caleb said quietly.

"What was Rocker's role?" Monique asked.

"Get you and Betty to the shed," Rocker answered, trying not to look at Betty or Monique.

"So you thought Monique and I were a guilty party?" Betty asked incredulously.

"No, not really. But I didn't know about Zane, and I knew your allegiances were with him, so I didn't know if we could trust you," Tec answered.

"Wow," Monique said quietly.

"It was always Zane's and my plan to get everybody to the shed, including the two goons from Treasury. But I didn't know what was going on and who was who, so I talked Rocker into getting you two there," Tec explained to Monique. "Don't blame him."

"We just wanted to nail the bastards responsible," Rocker said, pounding his fist into his hand.

"I hope that's what we did," Tec said.

"It is," Monique said forcefully and loudly. "Zane knew who they were going in. He really brought this all together."

"There is enough guilt to go around," Zane said, crossing his arms. "Some of us more than others. It remains to be seen how that will all play out. And condemning the guilty does serve a purpose."

Betty sat up abruptly and cuffed Zane in the back of the head. "It isn't our job to condemn anybody."

"Holy geezers, is this your place, Tec? This is incredible," Monique said, trying to change the subject.

"I hope I can keep it," Tec answered.

They were driving up a long, winding gravel driveway that stretched like a lazy snake between old cottonwoods and maples and over a slowly meandering stream. They couldn't see the house yet, but just the driveway was a scene from *Little House in the Big Woods*. A covered bridge crossed over the stream. Tec stopped the van in the middle and stepped out, reached around a post, and flipped a switch.

"Security?" Caleb asked.

"Not anymore."

The house came into view as they left the bridge and took a turn over a hill. Laura Ingalls Wilder would have written four chapters on the house alone. It was a log cabin with a green metal roof and a wraparound front porch. Trees dotted the front yard in an effort to camouflage its true size, but as they pulled around, it became apparent that this was no ordinary log cabin. There were three split-level stories and multiple entrances. The width of the porch would have provided enough living space for at least two families. It was a log cabin mansion.

"Let me guess—you're the builder?" Monique asked.

"It's amazing what you can do with money," Tec responded.

"And God's help," Betty chimed in.

"That too."

They got out of the van, turning around slowly, marveling at the expansiveness of the dwelling and the surrounding lot. The landscaping was rustic and yet had a sophisticated touch. Someone had put a lot of toil and love into this place.

"Let's go into the house. I need to show you something," Tec stated as he led them up the porch and into the side entryway. "It'll explain everything."

"Will it explain why you stabbed me in the back and took my family?" Zane asked with more venom in his voice than anybody expected.

"Family, yes," Tec said. "Once we do something, it can't be undone. Ever. The past haunts us." Tec's posture slumped. "There was the family. In Colombia. Two kids and the mother. Still in the house. In the basement."

"Two kids and a mom?" Zane said. "What the fuck?"

"I went into the basement, needing to kill them. I don't know if any of you can understand that, but I wasn't in control of my own thoughts or body," Tec said.

"Yes, I can understand that," Zane responded.

Everybody looked at Zane and then quickly looked away. Except for Caleb.

They were all sitting or standing around the center island in Tec's kitchen. Many a Twin Cities restaurant would have given a month's worth of patrons for a food preparation center like that. But they didn't notice the magnificent surroundings anymore. They all waited for Tec to continue.

"I don't remember much even now, except how out of control I was. I had to have my revenge for the brutal killing of the general's family with those sweet, innocent children."

"How does that compare to my situation? How does any of this explain why you betrayed my friendship the way you did? I then trusted you with my kids a second time. And you still didn't believe me and had to trick my family and friends into going to the shed. Where are your loyalties, Tec?"

"Yes, I put your wife and kids in danger. Zane, you always told me that I shouldn't be too hard on myself, that war is war, that what happens in a war zone should stay in a war zone," Tec pleaded.

"We're not at war," Zane spat.

"I went to Colombia to do what had to be done." Tec struggled to remain in control. "That's what I thought I was doing in your situation too." He looked up at Zane, his eyes old and sad. "I know that your wife died because of what I did. I'll have to live with that."

"We all have reasons for what we do. The bad and the good. The reasons make sense at the time or we wouldn't have done it. We did the best we knew at the time," Betty said. "God's Grace is big enough for all of us."

Zane's voice wavered. "So is this when you tell me where my kids are buried?"

Tec gave Zane a grim smile. "When I arrived in the basement, my whole body became extremely warm, even though the basement was cool. I started to shake, and my heart seemed to stop beating. The whole room seemed foggy. It was like I couldn't see. I knew they were down there, but I couldn't find them."

"Will I be able to find mine?" Zane asked carefully. "This time, you were supposed to take them and take care of them."

Tec walked to the back of the kitchen, opened a sliding door, and whistled. All of them followed Tec onto the back deck. They were staring at a metal door set in the ground about thirty feet from the house. Slowly, it opened.

Out stepped James, Zanese, and a Hispanic lady with two teenage children.

Zane ran off the deck, sprinting to get to his children and

bear-hug them until it hurt.

The rest stood around watching as the lady and the two teen-agers walked up the stairway to the deck, stopping at the top.

Tec approached them and put his arm around the lady while the two children hugged him from behind.

"I would like you all to meet my wife, Margarite, and my two children, Diego and Isabella. They're from Colombia."

105

Caleb and Tec were the whole crowd for the fight extravaganza. And they only watched because they were next to fight in this four-person tournament. Monique was the only nonparticipant in the room; she was the referee. She was to stop only egregious acts and to ensure the participants maintained some order. This was a tournament without many rules, including no fight stoppages, except by the participants.

They were at the Warrior's Den on a Sunday afternoon. No classes were scheduled that day, and nobody had the keys but them. They wouldn't be interrupted. They'd fight on open mats. They didn't want the cage; it could slow them down.

Each fighter wore shorts, MMA gloves, a protective cup over his manhood, and a mouthpiece. They had discussed protective headgear but decided getting a concussion was a risk that should be on the table. Besides, maybe the loser would want to forget this fight.

"The only way to Tec is through me," Rocker said while shaking out his hands and smiling at Zane.

"Whatever it takes," Zane said while jumping up and down to get his blood pumping.

"Well, come and get it, then," Rocker said and motioned for Zane to move in.

Zane knew better than to be the aggressor in this fight; let the fight come to him. Rocker was only too willing to oblige.

Rocker moved in and quickly spun, giving up his back. Zane went for it. Rocker tried to catch him with a backward side kick, but Zane moved out of the way, caught the side kick, and swept his other leg, driving Rocker to the mat. He had Rocker's leg and attempted a knee bar. Rocker had seen that coming and was able to drive Zane off with a lying side kick. Both fighters somersaulted backward to a standing position.

"You ain't the only one who can fake," Zane said.

"Your ruse didn't work, either," Rocker responded.

"Maybe this one will."

Zane dropped to his knees while Rocker came in. The second he got in range, Zane used a palm strike to his groin, slapping Rocker's cup against his precious jewels. Rocker grabbed them, allowing Zane to stand up and use another palm strike to his chin. Rocker pinwheeled back but didn't go down. Zane followed him in driving a front kick to his stomach as Rocker fell against the wall. Zane moved back, smiling.

"Come on, Rocker! Go after him! He's too confident!" Tec yelled.

"He's confident, because he's going to kick ass," Caleb responded.

"Is that all you got? You ain't much!" Rocker yelled at Zane as he picked himself off the wall.

Zane moved in again quickly and dropped his hands as if going for a clinch or takedown. Rocker hit him with a jab, driving his head back and opening up his chin for a straight left. And another right cross. Zane backed up, momentarily stunned.

"Oh yeah! Keep going!" Tec yelled.

Rocker followed him around the mat. Zane stopped abruptly, and Rocker couldn't get out of his range. Zane threw his own jab, catching Rocker lightly in the forehead—but it opened up his midsection as his hands flew up. Zane threw a quick side kick directly into his solar plexus, taking his wind. Rocker dropped to his knees and gasped for breath.

Zane backed up into a corner. "Do you want more?"

Rocker was barely able to breathe as he gasped out, "It ain't over."

He struggled to stand but couldn't straighten up.

"It's over if I want it to be," Zane responded.

"Were the hands dropping just a ploy?" Rocker asked, still gasping.

"Deception is only known by the truth."

Rocker coughed twice and brought his hands up and moved in. "And your face needs to know my fist. I've got more."

"Not much," Zane responded as he threw the jab again and spun away while Rocker chased after him, catching a backward spinning side kick in the solar plexus yet again. Rocker dropped, this time almost out of all his wind, gasping and spitting up something that looked a lot like lunch.

"Always wait one hour after lunch before undertaking strenuous activity," Zane mocked.

Rocker dropped to all fours and rolled over on his back.

"Fight over. Sorry, Rocker," Monique said as she moved between them.

"Don't be too disappointed," Zane said as he helped Rocker to his feet. "I needed you to get to Tec."

106

There were things worse than death. Being locked up for the rest of your life with no human interaction and only one hour a day outside of your eight-by-eight living area was one of those things. The prosecutors couldn't use this threat against Thompson. Knowledge was power, and since he had the knowledge, they didn't have the power. He was at the center of a financial scandal that threatened the US economy—possibly the global financial system. He knew the players and the source of the money.

The story hadn't gotten out yet. The government regulators and law enforcement had used their combined influence to force the *Wall Street Journal* to keep a lid on it. For now. The damage had to be contained. Thompson was their vehicle for that containment. However, he wasn't cooperating.

This was the eighth interrogation session in the last three days. It appeared Thompson enjoyed them. He was drawing strength from the interrogators' frustration.

They couldn't keep Thompson at any type of detention facility; that would raise too many questions. So he was being held at a small, run-down motor lodge north of the Twin Cities. They had rented the complete eighteen-room facility. The hotel had cinder block walls, and each room was equipped with those small air conditioner–heater combo units that didn't cool the room below seventy-eight degrees. The carpet was stained in too many spots to even care, and the drapes didn't match. The smell of the room was a cross between a dirty ashtray and the perfume strippers wear to hide their body odor.

Security was extremely high; ten federal agents were posted around the building at all hours, and another three agents were in the room, watching Thompson even as he slept.

It was the middle of a warm afternoon, and Thompson was alone with his interrogator one more time.

"Let's start over," the interrogator going by the name of Steve said as he sat across from Thompson at a little round table by the window. Thompson was staring at some artwork carved into the window's wood sill containing the initials, "WIFMI." Below that: "Will I fucking make it?"

Thompson was dressed in jeans, black dress socks, and a large short-sleeve gray camp shirt. The armpits were stained with perspiration down to his waist. He stroked his beard while leaning back in the chair to put his feet on the bed.

"Same questions, same answers," Thompson replied and smiled at Steve.

"We need different answers. The right ones this time. The truth."

"At the risk of sounding clichéd, you can't handle the truth."

"So you won't say anything?" Steve asked calmly.

"Sometimes the best thing said is what isn't said."

"Maybe it will hurt, but the healing can't start until we know the depth of the illness. It's our only way out," Steve said, closing his file and taking a sip of tepid water from the bottle on the windowsill.

"There is no way out. If I expose the rottenness at the core, you think you can just cut it out? If you do that, it will bring down the whole structure."

"Let us decide that. It can't get much worse than it is."

Thompson laughed. "You have no idea."

"Tell us. Show us. Help us," Steve said carefully, afraid to admit how much they needed him.

Thompson leaned forward and looked intently at his interrogator. "Do you remember when the insurance company AIS got into trouble a while back? I don't mean going-out-of-business, shut-the-doors trouble. I mean trouble that made the regulators shit blood. It made the politicians stop having sex with each other."

"Yes, it just about brought down the whole economy."

"How was the bleeding stopped?" Thompson asked, taking his feet off the bed and sitting up straighter.

"Bailout. Financial rescue. The government took an ownership stake," Steve answered, backing his chair up slightly.

"Yes, they did. Why?"

"Because that insurance company had creatively guaranteed a lot of bad debt using credit default swaps and derivatives. Debt that, if it wasn't made good, could bring down the financial structure of Europe, China, Russia, and us. They had to rescue them."

"But why couldn't they just have given them money?"

"Because they didn't have congressional approval for that type of funding," Steve answered.

"Right. They took ownership for another reason. It gave them control over that insurance company and control over the debt they guaranteed," Thompson said. He stood up, moved to the bed, and sat down on the edge close to Steve. "And that, by extension, gave them control over the banks and the countries holding that debt. Our government had the world's financial structure in their grubby, greedy mitts."

"We know that the same insurance company is involved with this scheme. But I thought the government sold their stock." Steve turned to face Thompson, holding the lukewarm water bottle up against his forehead.

"That's what they said, but they didn't. Even if they had, it didn't matter. You're talking about the government here—the all-knowing, all-seeing, federal, democratic government. They still own, and more importantly, control that insurance company."

"And therefore, they control other banks and countries holding debt they guaranteed. We get that. But isn't that enough control? Why do they need to also control or own businesses?" Steve asked quietly.

"During the 2008 financial crisis, they needed AIS as a vehicle. The Federal Reserve funneled money through that insurance company to give other insolvent companies. It was called a back-door bailout. AIS is the only company the Fed took an ownership interest in so they could do this type of rescue without congressional approval. Well, now they're trying to preemptively avoid another crisis by doing a different version of the same thing, utilizing SAS, the same insurance company and the viatical scheme."

"So they're trying to avoid another meltdown?"

"Assets and debt are parts of the balance sheet. The other part is equity. Ownership. They need to own and control not just the assets and debt but the equity, as well. By controlling the equity, they control the party that owes the debt and the party the debt is owed to. The debtors don't default on the debt since the government owns them and makes the payments. They control the businesses, and that protects their investment and the economy."

"Were the businesses you acquired about to default?" Steve asked, now standing up and clumsily moving away from Thompson. He leaned against the cheap dresser, crossing his arms.

"Some of them," Thompson answered, moving down to the end of the bed to again get closer to Steve. "But we called the debt due even with those that weren't. It made the business look worse than it really was and ripe for the picking."

"So they concocted this scheme. We get that. But who? We

know the rot is deep, but give us somebody so we can start the carving. We need to bring the whole house of cards down. Let the chips fall wherever they may."

"You still don't get it, do you? The who is *us*," Thompson answered, falling back on the bed and staring up at the ceiling.

"What?"

"Let's not play Abbott and Costello here. Our government is of the people, by the people, and for the people," Thompson said, sitting up again. "We want easy credit, a growing economy, and the government to be our fail-safe. There isn't enough money for all of that. But we can't say no. So we say yes and keep writing the checks. Except there's no money in the account until the Federal Reserve puts money in."

Steve sat next to Thompson on the bed.

"You guys were buying businesses that were supposedly bad. You did that through the viatical scheme of the life insurance company, which was owned by the Federal Reserve. We know that now. Who else knows?"

Thompson winked at him. "My revelation knows its limits."

The interrogator put his arm around Thompson's neck. "We need names. We need to know who knew."

"I can't give you names, because you can't expose this. If you do, SAS will fail, a lot of businesses we bought will fail, but most importantly, the insurance company will fail. And if the insurance company fails, banks and governments around the world will fail too, because they need the insurance and derivatives to prevent default on their debt. Not to mention quantitative easing. That printed money is debt owed by the US government to the Federal Reserve. If people start to realize that this debt represents funds used to purchase businesses to prop up the economy, the Federal Reserve will fail. My, my, what a tangled web we wove when we first set out to deceive, or print money," Thompson said, putting his arm around Steve's neck.

"So let me get this straight. Those bonds the Federal Reserve bought from the US government also represent a whole bunch of other programs and funding. Quantitative easing was more than just money given to that insurance company and SAS," Steve responded, beginning to look ill.

"Exactly. It's now inherent in the financial fabric of this country. The Federal Reserve is the government, yet it's buying the government debt. Making money the easy way. It's addictive. They can't stop. Even if they say they're tapering, they aren't. They know they can't. Exposing this SAS scam will make people wonder how easy it is for the government to have enough money to do whatever the government wants. So if eventually you're able to overcome all of the other bad shit, you'll also destroy the confidence in our entire economy. At the end of the day, confidence is really all that keeps this economy going. You know that."

"So what are we to do? What about the people who know about this?" Steve asked, staring straight ahead. "Can they be trusted?"

"Well, I don't know. I'd say that if you don't want to pay for a week's worth of groceries with a pickup load of cash, I suggest you'd better find them."

"Are you talking about Zane and his cohorts?"

"Yes, but there are more. You'll need to deal with all of them."

"How do you suggest?"

Thompson removed his arm from Steve's neck and grabbed his chin, forcing Steve to look into his eyes. "I have a plan, but let's save that for another day. I guarantee you'll need higher approval," he said as he removed his arm, stood up, and stared out the dirty window. "Much higher."

107

Caleb was the better striker, and Tec was better on the ground. The classic matchup.

The anticipation weighed upon all in attendance like the fog in an early morning New England harbor. Neither Caleb nor Tec had lost a match in a long time.

They bowed to each other ceremoniously and touched gloves, and it was on. It was time for a fight.

Caleb knew he had to stuff any takedown attempts as Tec circled to his left, stopped, and threw a jab-hook combo to the head. Caleb slipped the punches but only barely, while backing up and circling to his right. Tec gauged Caleb's response carefully and threw the same combo again with the same results. The third time was his charm. As Caleb backed up and circled, Tec dived for his knees, keeping his head up while slamming Caleb on his back on the mat. Caleb couldn't defend the takedown since he had been backing up at the time.

"Nice takedown, Tec!" Rocker yelled out. "Two points!"

"Points don't matter. Blood does!" Zane yelled in reply.

Tec was in between Caleb's legs on the mat, in his guard. He began to throw punches and elbows at Caleb's head. Caleb minimized their effect by coming up quickly, clinching with Tec, and bringing him down to the mat. Tec drove a knee sharply into Caleb's groin as Caleb went for a choke. Tec turned his head to

415

avoid the choke while Caleb turned his hips to avoid the nut shot. Caleb then got his leg under Tec's hip, sat up, and flipped Tec on his back. He wound up in top mount on Tec and then threw two elbows in quick succession, opening up a cut.

Blood flowed out freely, masking the calm and unconcerned look on Tec's face.

"Work it! He only has so much!" Zane cried out.

"Don't worry, Tec, blood don't hurt," Rocker responded.

"Geez, maybe we should have recorded this; that way, you guys could hear the idiotic comments you're making," Monique said.

Tec and Caleb barely heard them. It was all about the contest. Who was better, at least on this day.

Tec was able to bump Caleb off him, because Caleb had slid up a bit far. Both rolled to a standing position. Immediately, Tec threw a roundhouse right. Caleb easily stepped inside and threw a palm strike to Tec's chin. His chin was tucked, minimizing any damage and giving Tec the chance to grab Caleb in a tight clinch while head butting him on the bridge of his nose, opening up a cut that also gushed blood. He then tripped Caleb to the mat, ending up in side control. Caleb spun, putting Tec in his guard again.

"All that fighting just to end up in the same position! That's tiring, huh, guys?" Monique yelled.

Not yet. Tec passed guard, gaining side control but allowing Caleb to balance him and flip him over his prone body. Again, both rolled out to a standing position.

"I guess Caleb has some ground skills, after all," Zane said.

"Must be the blood in Tec's eyes. He is a jujitsu black belt; no way would he lose to Caleb on the ground," Rocker said.

The ground fighting had tired Tec out, and he had a hard time seeing through the blood from the cut. Caleb's nose cut wasn't bleeding as badly and therefore wasn't hindering his vision.

Caleb kept up the pressure, throwing jab cross combinations

and mixing them up with some body shots. Tec was backpedaling furiously to stay out of the way. Suddenly, he stopped and was able to catch one of Caleb's right crosses. He spun Caleb around and drove a knee into his thigh, numbing Caleb's right leg. Caleb responded with a backward spinning elbow, catching Tec just above his ear and stunning him as he stumbled into the wall. Caleb limped after him. It wasn't going to last long now. Both fighters were hurt. Their blood had covered most of their upper bodies, and the mat was getting slippery.

"Let's just call it a draw! You're both badasses! Leave it at that!" Monique yelled as she stood up.

Caleb and Tec both stopped for a second, breathing hard and dripping blood.

"You know what?" Caleb said, wiping blood off his face. "I agree with the lady."

"You forfeiting?" Tec asked. "You quit, and I win."

"That's fine," Caleb responded while grinning at Tec. "I was just softening you up for Zane. He's the one who really wants your ass."

"Bring it on," Tec said, wiping the blood out of his eyes with a towel. "One question, though—where did you learn to fight like that?"

Monique groaned. "Don't ask."

108

At the same time as the round-robin fight tournament was happening at the Warrior's Den, the Minneapolis police SWAT team was meeting to refine their tactical plan for a Sunday afternoon assault.

The pictures were on the large screen at the front of the room. They looked like normal people: Rocker, Tec, Zane, Caleb, Monique, and Betty. Next to them were pictures of the front and back of the Warrior's Den.

The police briefing room was crowded and hot. Anticipation was high, and the adrenaline was flowing. They lived for this.

"Any hostages?" a SWAT member asked.

"Not to our knowledge. Should be clean," a federal agent answered.

"What is this place?"

"Dojo. Mixed martial arts. All of these guys—even the ladies—know some. Be careful when you cuff them. They're most dangerous up close."

"Armed?"

"They have a large arsenal and have killed before," the federal agent answered.

"Dead or alive?" another SWAT member asked.

"We want them alive, but that's up to them. Do not give them a chance. Repeat, take them down with extreme force if threatened.

You won't be second-guessed."

"What the fuck does that mean?"

"It means that they decide their fate. They're wanted for murder, kidnapping, fraud, and probably about ten other felonies."

"No due process? We just shoot them, no questions asked?"

"Bag 'em or tag 'em," the federal agent answered, looking around the room for the response.

"Hey, we're a SWAT team, not some hired assassins. I've heard about shooting first and no questions asked. That's how we end up sitting in a six-by-eight until our gray hair has gray hair. We need to know the deal," another SWAT member said while moving to block the exit door.

"They're threatening national security. They're considered the most dangerous people in the country right now. If you want to be part of the team that takes them down, then let's do this. If not, stay here. The only questions you have to ask yourself are, do you want to be on the side of history that prevents another 9/11, or do you want to be on the side that stayed home while glory passed you by?"

"What's the source of our intel? How do we know they will be at this training hall, dojo place?"

"Inside information."

"Reliable?"

"We think so."

"Why not use military or paramilitary, like the FBI Hostage Rescue Team?"

"Can't use military on domestic; you know that. This is not a hostage rescue, so HRT isn't the best choice. Do your job, everybody goes home happy, and your country will owe you. You'll be heroes."

"Well, I guess we'd better mount up and drag the Feds out of another mucking fess. At least this time, we're doing it before three thousand people burn to death."

"Watch it."

The twenty-eight SWAT members looked around at each other, made their last equipment adjustments, and then filed out.

They all said the same thing as they passed the watch commander and bumped fists. "Just do it."

109

This was the main attraction. The one everybody would pay to see. The spectators were antsy. It was time to fight.

There were only three spectators. And no ref. Let them go at it, do what they have to do, and whoever is left standing is the winner.

"How long is this fight? Till one of us is dead?" Tec asked.

"Works for me," Zane replied.

"Be careful. Revenge rarely gets you where you want to go," Tec said, still wiping the blood out of his eyes with a towel.

Zane was sitting on the mat stretching his hamstrings. "I need this."

"Should we do the Rocky and Apollo Creed thing and touch gloves to ding the bell? Ding, ding," Tec asked as he watched Zane jump to his feet.

"No, let's just fight."

Both fighters moved to the center of the mat and touched gloves; the fight was on.

Zane circled warily in a tight circle, reluctant to move in quickly. He stepped in a couple of times, feinting his right jab and front kick.

Tec didn't bite on the feints and stayed out of range. Zane felt he was stronger with his striking and weaker on the ground. He didn't want to roll with Tec.

"Are you sure you want this?" Tec asked Zane.

"I do. You made some bad decisions, and now you'll pay," Zane responded.

"I don't have the market cornered on bad decisions," Tec said as he feinted and moved away.

"Come on, guys, play nice!" Monique yelled out.

"None of that matters. All that matters is kicking your ass," Zane said.

"Win or lose, the truth will set you free," Tec responded.

"Winning is the truth," Zane said as he feinted a jab and dived for a double-leg takedown. The feint caught Tec off guard; he knew he was better on the ground and was shocked at Zane's takedown attempt.

Zane got both legs, picked them up, and slammed Tec hard on his back.

Caleb and Rocker hooted and howled, and that drove Zane on.

Zane was in Tec's guard and caught Tec with an elbow to the forehead before Tec could establish any control. The elbow opened up the previous cut, and blood flowed. Zane reveled in his success a second too long. Tec attempted a triangle choke, which Zane successfully defended, but it left him open to a sweep that Tec pulled off nicely. The tables were turned with Tec in mount position on top of Zane's chest. Zane attempted to bump him off, but Tec's balance was too solid. Tec began to move to side control, grabbed Zane's left arm in the process, and went for an arm bar. They were both too sweaty to make it stick, though, allowing both of them to disengage. The flurry ended with both back in standing position.

"Good job, Zane. I don't think ground and pound is your best way to win, though," Tec blurted out, with blood starting to fill his eyes again.

"Doesn't matter. I don't care how I pound your ass," Zane responded as he moved in fast, backed off, and caught Tec on the counter with a side kick to the thigh.

"You've gotten better. Who've you been training with?" Tec asked.

Zane shot a look at Caleb.

"Don't pay any attention to him. He's just building you up to tear you down. The best defense is a good offense," Caleb coached.

"Come on, Tec! Stop talking and show him what we know! Our experience outweighs any training!" Rocker shouted.

"You two aren't the only ones with experience! Right, Zane?" Caleb yelled.

Zane sidestepped to his right, faked a jab, and caught Tec with a spinning back fist.

"Many paths lead to the same destination," Zane replied.

"Just remember that later," Tec said as he bobbed down and came up with a palm strike to Zane's groin.

They were wearing cups, but still.

"Love tap to the balls! *Brokeback Dojo!*" Rocker yelled.

Both fighters were wary, but not tired. Zane's revenge made Tec careful, and Tec's hard edge made Zane careful. Zane knew he needed an edge.

He dipped down low and faked the takedown. Tec responded with a half sprawl in defense, and Zane came up hard with his right knee. Tec was able to get his forearm in the way, but the force was enough to drive his forearm back into his chin, stunning him.

"Finish him!" Caleb yelled.

"Go, Zane!" Monique yelled as Caleb shot her an inquisitive look.

The knee opened Tec up, driving him backward. Zane took advantage of that, driving a backward spinning side kick into Tec's midsection. Tec let out a loud sound of air from his mouth and fell on his ass. Zane followed that with a roundhouse right that caught Tec flush on the temple. Tec fell back flat on the mat.

"Be careful! Tec is best on the mat!" Caleb yelled.

"You've got him where you want him!" Rocker responded.

Zane came down on top of Tec with one knee hard on his chest, driving the air from his lungs. Tec was in serious trouble. The mats were slippery with his blood, and he was having a hard time seeing. Zane smelled blood, literally. It was time to end it.

Zane felt his resolve harden as he began to rain down blows on Tec's bloodied face. The thought crossed his mind that Tec was letting him win, but he didn't care. If Tec was that stupid, he deserved a beating.

This fight had started as a friendly competition, but now visions of Tina lying dead in his arms ran through Zane's head. His fury knew no bounds.

"Come on, Tec, do something! Don't let this office boy whip your ass!" Rocker cried out.

That drove Zane into a new frenzy of punches as Tec was only offering a feeble defense briefly getting his forearms in the way.

Zane suddenly stood up.

"Don't stop! Keep on pounding him! Don't let him stand!" Caleb yelled as he stood up and moved closer to the action.

Rocker stood up next to Caleb. "Tec, get up. Now's your chance."

Monique shot a glance over to the onlookers. "You two stay out of this. We don't need a tag-team match."

Tec was having a hard time catching his breath through his bloody nose. Blood was also streaming from at least two cuts above his eyes. It didn't look like he'd be standing up anytime soon.

"Just do it, Zane. Finish him. Now!"

"Fuck it. This one's for Tina," Zane spat as he brought up his bare foot for a stomp to Tec's sternum. Normally in MMA, a kick to a downed opponent was prohibited, but they had no such rules today. The reason for the rule was that a downed opponent didn't have much of a defense to a kick from a standing opponent whose kicks were very powerful in their downward arc and could do a lot of damage. It was obvious Zane didn't care.

Tec suddenly turned his body slightly to his right and brought his hips up off the mat and snaked his right leg up through Zane's right leg. He also grabbed the ankle of Zane's left leg and pulled hard while using the leverage in his right leg to lever down Zane's hip. Zane fell hard on his back while Tec raised his upper torso off the mat, secured an Achilles lock on his right leg, leaned back, and applied it hard.

Zane knew he was facing a snapped Achilles tendon, immediate surgery, and six months of painful recovery if he didn't submit. But submission wasn't on the menu of revenge. Tina didn't tap, and he wouldn't, either.

Rocker howled in delight. "Tec da man. Wow, close but no cigar, Zane."

"He hasn't tapped yet!" Caleb shouted out.

Tec applied it even harder to the point where the tendon was about to snap, and still, Zane hung on. Zane worked his other leg around to try to kick, but Tec was able to slide out of the way.

"Come on, Zane," Tec said between gritted teeth. "Don't make me hurt you."

No response as Zane, salted with his vengeance, continued to work frantically for his freedom.

Finally, at the point of no return, Tec released and rolled backward to a standing position.

Zane kipped up to his feet and came in on Tec immediately, snapping off a right jab, left cross combination that stunned Tec as he fell against the wall. Zane pinned him there with his left hand and began teeing up with his right, throwing punch after punch. Tec dropped his hands, and his shoulders sagged as his eyes began to dim.

Rocker moved between them and forced Zane back. Zane gave

up his ground grudgingly, trying to get back at Tec until Caleb stepped in, as well. "It's over, Zane. You won. Revenge is complete."

Zane stood with his hands by his side, breathing hard and glaring menacingly at Tec, knowing he'd won only as a result of Tec's mercy.

Monique kneeled down to make sure Tec was all right, using a towel to wipe the blood off his face. She helped him feebly to his feet.

"Things aren't always what they seem," Tec said as he held his head back to try to get the blood out of his eyes. "Sometimes we learn more from a loss than ten victories."

"That's a lesson we all need to learn," Zane responded, still staring at Tec.

"There was no other way."

"There was, but not for you."

"Yes, not for me."

"Well, this is over for now," Zane said as he bent down to pick up a bottle of water.

"For now," Caleb interjected. "But probably not forever."

No sooner had Caleb stopped talking than they heard the words that strike fear into any heart.

"We have you surrounded! Come out with your hands raised in the air!"

110

Tec snapped to attention and reacted immediately. He grabbed a towel and began wiping blood from his face while throwing one to Zane. Tec sprinted toward the back door that opened to a small hallway in the back of the building.

"Come on, move!" Tec yelled as he ran.

They followed as if shot out of a cannon. No one had to tell them twice.

"Damn! Sure wish we'd brought guns to this fistfight!" Caleb yelled, furiously trying to put his pants on. The others were also dressing quickly in the back hallway.

"Not a problem," Tec responded as he led them to a stairway down to the basement.

"Holy big balls, I never even knew this place had a basement," Monique said.

They were obviously concerned but calm. Getting upset wouldn't help.

While they were still in the stairway, they heard the bullhorn again.

"Five minutes. You have five minutes to come out on your own. Then we will come in to take you out. That way is the dead way."

"I guess that rules out talking our way out," Monique said as they continued their rush down the stairs.

"We all should've known this day was coming. The Feds

weren't going to just forget us with what we know," Caleb said.

"Of course not," Zane said.

"Can anybody say cover-up?" Caleb responded.

"Well, if you knew this day was coming, why aren't we prepared?" Rocker asked.

"I am," Tec said as he flipped on the lights and opened a large metal locker. He began throwing bulletproof vests to everybody. And assault rifles.

"That's what I'm talking about!" Rocker yelled as he caught a vest in one hand and a rifle in the other. "At least we have a chance."

"What are you talking about, a chance?" Zane asked, not showing any fear at their abrupt change of fortune. "There are probably a hundred of them and five of us."

"Maybe we should just surrender and talk our way out of this," Monique said as the first shadows of fear began to cloud her face.

"No, no, no. That wouldn't work. The time for talking is past. They're here to kill us or put us away forever. I'd rather die fighting than be locked in solitary twenty-three hours a day," Caleb said as he grabbed Monique by the shoulders. "We can put up a lot of fight. Don't give up. If we are able to shoot our way out and escape, at least we live to fight another day. There has to be a safe place for us somewhere."

"Yeah, but chances are the SWAT team outside doesn't even know who we are. They're innocently thinking we are bad guys. How can we take it out on them?" Monique asked.

"Anytime you take up a weapon against somebody, you'd better be damn sure who they are. This is on them. If they don't know who we are and they're prepared to kill us, anyway, then they're in the wrong. They're standing in the way of us getting the truth out and maybe saving whatever is left of our collapsing economy," Caleb said.

"I agree. Fuck 'em if they can't take a joke," Tec said calmly as he now handed out full Kevlar helmets with night-vision goggles strapped to the top.

"WTF. Why do you have this shit?" Monique asked.

"He used to be a Boy Scout," Zane said as Tec looked at him quizzically.

"I guess you took their motto seriously," Monique said as she fastened her helmet in place.

"Hey, what about Betty?" Rocker asked.

"They'll go after her too, if they haven't already. Another reason to survive and get to her quickly," Tec responded.

"I'm not sure what dreamland you're living in, but in about ninety seconds, they're going to blast their way in here to take us out in a body bag," Zane said.

"Quick, in here," Tec said as he opened a large thick door into what looked like a vault. "This is a vault, safe room, whatever you want to call it. Nothing will touch us in here."

"Unless you have a lot of everything in there, they'll just wait us out. They have all the time in the world. We don't," Rocker replied as they all moved hurriedly inside.

"We don't need time. I have this instead," Tec said as he produced a small switch in his hand while spinning a large wheel on the door, closing it with a loud *whooshing* sound.

"What is that?" they asked in unison.

"My contingency plan. Always have an escape route. Plug your ears," Tec said as he flipped the switch and five hundred pounds of TNT exploded instantly, obliterating the building formerly known as the Warrior's Den.

"Up and out! Now! Caleb, Zane, go to the front! Rocker and Monique, cover the rear!" Tec yelled at them as he flung open the door of the vault.

The stairway was intact. Nothing else was. The building had been evaporated. Nothing but a memory of blood, sweat, and a lot of pain.

Pain was evident in the parking lot surrounding the former Warrior's Den, as well. The SWAT team had been only twenty yards away when the building blew. Several of the team members were lying on the ground, not moving. Several were rolling around on the ground and holding their heads, arms, legs, and stomachs, writhing in pain.

Some of the team members were still in position behind vehicles and barricades. They were still in the game but in a state of shock. It appeared as if a ghostly apparition was coming at them out of the smoke and fire.

"Fire into their chests if necessary! They have vests on!" Tec yelled into his helmet mike. Tec had thought of everything, including goggles.

They had to use the temporary shock as an edge. It was important to get out of there and now. They had to find Betty.

Their cars had been parked next to the building and were damaged beyond use. However, Rocker and Tec were trained in

430

securing emergency transportation.

They came at the barricades in a dead sprint, leaped the temporary fences, and dodged the vans and trucks. The SWAT team was beginning to come out of the fog.

Two SWAT members swiveled their rifles and aimed at Tec and Zane. They fired into the SWAT members' vests, putting them down. Caleb and Monique had a similar encounter.

It actually looked like they might make it.

That's when they heard the scream.

$ $ $

The SWAT team leader and the federal agent were in the main battlewagon, named that because it carried all the necessary ingredients to wage full-scale war. It also had a small cage for prisoners. It wasn't soundproof.

That's where they held Betty.

"You need to shut your sandwich hole, lady. Got it?"

Betty screamed again and began pounding her feet on the bottom of the truck. "Kill me! Or haven't you got the guts?"

"Don't tempt me, lady. I knew we should have gagged you. I think your asthma story was a crock of shit."

"Slap her; that'll shut her up. I'm going outside to see if we anybody is still alive."

The team leader opened the wagon's back door as Betty let out an even louder scream, calling Zane's name. The federal agent slapped her so hard her head bounced.

At that moment, Zane's and Tec's figures filled the back door entry and brought their guns to bear on the team leader. He fell back into the truck as Zane followed him in, driving the butt of his rifle into his face, rendering him unconscious.

"Zane! Get me out of here!" Betty yelled as she shook her

head, attempting to clear the cobwebs.

"I don't think so! You guys back up and out, or I shoot her right fucking now!" the federal agent yelled as he put his pistol up to Betty's temple.

Betty drove her head so hard into the pistol that it slapped hard into his head, opening up a deep cut and stunning him. Tec then double tapped him between the eyes. The federal agent was no more.

Zane shot the lock off the cage and helped Betty out of it. "I'm so sorry, Betty."

She looked at him with understanding, and then the three of them were off and running.

Then they suddenly stopped.

Monique and Rocker were backed up against a van with their hands up, guarded by two SWAT members. It was the last van on the edge of the parking lot. All they had to do was get past it and they'd be in the clear. But that task appeared to be quite formidable.

Tec looked back toward where they had come, but that escape route was quickly closed off by two other SWAT members. It wouldn't be long before more SWAT officers would arrive.

"Drop your weapons, right now, or we'll shoot your comrades. And don't think we won't. Just following orders," the leader of the four barked out.

Tec and Zane dropped their weapons and put their hands up, just like Betty.

"I'm not sure your plan is working, Tec," Monique observed.

"Yeah, it's a little harder to shoot law enforcement than I thought it would be," added Rocker.

"Don't look at them as law enforcement," Zane replied. "They're obstacles."

"What do we do with them?" one of the SWAT guys asked his team leader, keeping his rifle trained on the fugitives.

"Find that Fed and let him decide. I've got the feeling it wasn't the plan to bring 'em back alive."

Tec agreed with Zane but was having a hard time formulating a solution. He kept staring at the team leader. Something seemed wrong with his head. Suddenly, it wasn't there anymore as it burst like a melon into gray matter and blood. His body slumped to the asphalt.

The solution was lining up his second shot through the scope of his tactical rifle while trying to conceal his position behind the corner of an upturned car. The head of the SWAT member next to Tec opened up the same way, allowing Tec to grab the guy's knife off the back of his belt. He sunk it deep into the neck and carotid artery of the remaining SWAT member closest to him, while Rocker brought his knife into the groin of another. Rocker pulled the knife out and coolly slit his throat. The line had been crossed.

"This changes things," Monique quietly stated as she looked at the ever-widening pool of blood around each former SWAT member.

"The only thing it changes is our freedom. They stood in the way of that and the truth." Tec stated calmly.

"Okay," Monique muttered as Betty put her arm around her.

Caleb strode up to them while slinging his assault rifle over his back.

"Good shooting, Caleb. You still haven't told me where you got your skills," Rocker said.

"You wouldn't believe him if he told you," Monique flatly stated as they began to run away.

"Life can be a circus," Caleb said as he ran after them.

Finding wheels was easy. They were all over the place. The trick was to find one that wouldn't be missed. They needed to vacate the area quickly and covertly.

Two blocks down was a used-car lot, which was perfect. Tec and Rocker were into a gray minivan within seconds and had it running a couple of minutes after that.

Tec was in the driver's seat, and as he accelerated away from the carnage, he turned and looked into the back of the van.

"You need to make a call, Caleb. I think we need some help."

112

Paul Manson had been a reporter for the *Wall Street Journal* for seven years. Seven very good years. His career was on a constant upward trajectory. He wasn't a great writer, but he had the right contacts. He always knew where to find a good story. But he hadn't encountered anything like this.

When Paul had listened in on the phone call with the congressman, it was hard to fully comprehend the depth of what was happening. It was like hearing the pope was actually Satan in disguise. There was no way it could be true. The government was probably corrupt, spent money like it was water, and couldn't manage very well, but they didn't kill innocent people and buy businesses just to control the economy. And they sure didn't fund all their nonsense with worthless printed money.

Except it appeared they did.

Paul wasn't given full access to all the coconspirators, but he was allowed to look at the files and to interview a couple of the federal agents. He knew he wasn't being given all the facts, but he also knew this story could affect the immediate stability of America and maybe the world. Paul knew that because he'd received a visit from the lead investigator with a letter from the attorney general threatening him should he decide to go public with the story at this time. His superiors at the *Journal* had all received the same threat. For the time being, they would sit on it, but Paul didn't know for how long. At some point, he'd have to go public. Paul wanted to be on the right side of history. The side that made money.

He lived in New York but had spent almost all of his time in the Twin Cites after the meeting with the congressman. He needed to be close to his source.

He was set up in a Residence Inn in Edina, a western suburb. Paul hated hotel living, but maybe this would end it. Expose this story, write his book, and tour the world living off royalties.

It was a one-bedroom unit with a kitchen and living room area. In some respects, it was better than his apartment back home. Not for long. The future looked bright.

Right at that moment, he was hungry. After 11:00 p.m., his options were limited. But there was always pizza. He found a Little Caesar's two blocks away that delivered. Ten minutes after his call, the doorbell rang. Pizza, pizza.

As soon as he opened the door, he knew something was wrong.

The guy at the door didn't have a pizza.

And he was wearing a suit.

113

"You don't have them? How can you not have them?" Alan Thompson asked as he sat up on the hotel bed. "SWAT could fuck up a wet dream."

"Shut up and listen. They had the building rigged, and it blew sky high just as the SWAT team was making their entrance. It threw them off, and they used the confusion and debris to make their escape. They've even got the old lady. She's with them," Thompson's boss explained to him as he stood by the bed.

"This is bad, very bad. You have to find them."

"You don't have to remind me how bad it is. I know we need them. They fucked up, though. They killed some SWAT members."

"That doesn't seem like their MO. Accident?" Thompson asked as he slowly stood up from the bed. He was only wearing boxers. No shirt. His large hairy belly paired well with his full black beard.

"Possible, but who cares? They killed the good guys. The public will brand them cop killers. We can file murder charges and use the full strength and power of the law enforcement community to track them down. Then once we have them, we pull a fucking Guantanamo on them. Make 'em disappear," his boss said as he moved quickly back toward the wall to allow Thompson to pass.

"We'll make them out to be terrorists attacking the financial system. We can pin SAS on them but spin the story to our benefit—like leaving out the insurance company and Federal Reserve,"

Thompson said while rummaging around in a plastic Walmart bag.

"Killing those innocents was the best thing that could have happened to us. People wouldn't believe that shit before. But if someone would kill innocent SWAT members, they must be bad and trying to cover up something. Like a plot to bring down the United States," his boss answered, turning away as Thompson brought out a new pair of boxer shorts.

"There is a problem, though. What about the congressman and that journalist, Paul Manson?"

"Mr. Manson is no more. And the congressman will play ball. He has a lot at stake."

Thompson took off his old boxers and threw them on the bed. "Yes, but he is kind of a wild animal. He could just say fuck it and expose us and let the chips fall where they may."

"He wouldn't," his boss answered while closing his eyes, not wanting his gaze to fall on the smelly undergarments that had just hit the bed.

"Dirt?"

"Yes, he has a problem keeping his pants up," his boss answered, trying to keep his focus on Thompson's face lest his eyes wander to the hairy protuberance dangling from the middle of his body. "But he also has a role to play. After the meltdown, he'll emerge as a political savior and leader of our new financial future. Or at least that's what I told him."

"He must be thinking with his small head," Thompson answered as he grabbed the new boxers, smelled them, and put them on. "Otherwise, he'd know that you have more power over our financial future than any elected official of this great country."

"Chairman of the Federal Reserve is a title that comes with privileges."

"Don't I know it."

"So we'll use the congressman to reel this whole damn thing

in. And everybody who knows about it. You haven't given the names to the investigators yet, have you?"

"Of course not, Mr. Chairman; you and I are the only ones with that knowledge," Thompson answered as he sat back down on the bed with his hairy belly roll covering the top of his boxers like a mudslide after a heavy rain.

"Good. Zane and his team won't even see this coming."

"Yes, while we use them, we destroy them."

"Am I part of this new financial order?" Thompson asked as he stroked his long beard.

"That depends on whether or not I still need you. Right now, I do."

"How will I know when you don't?"

"You'll be dead."

114

Walking was good exercise. Walking to a meeting that would begin to bring resolution to a life-threatening situation was even better exercise. The fact that it was another one of those incredible fall Minnesota days only enhanced the pace. It was two in the afternoon, the temperature was sixty-five degrees, and there wasn't a cloud in the sky. The smell of colorful leaves warming in the sun drifted up from the ground. Zane was sure nothing could ruin this day. Absolutely nothing.

Zane and his friends were meeting in an abandoned schoolhouse in the small town of Elk River, a far-flung northern suburb of Minneapolis. Nobody was around, but they were still nervous. Being spotted by police would abruptly end their wonderful walk.

They had parked three blocks away and walked to the schoolhouse in concentric circles to determine if any unwanted guests were present. Trust was a virtue they couldn't afford.

"Do you think the congressman is here?" Monique asked.

"I don't know. Usually, you can smell shit a long ways away, but he knows how to disguise it well," Caleb responded.

"I don't get it. Why are we talking to him if we don't trust him?" Betty joined in the questioning.

"This is the best of a lot of bad choices."

"Maybe," Tec responded.

"He's always been on the side of right for me, and I think at the end of the day, he'll be for us too. Don't look at the speck in your brother's eye when you have a timber in your own," Caleb answered.

"My, my. Quoting scripture. No atheists in foxholes?" Monique queried.

"No atheists in Caleb."

"I will have to file that away for future perusal."

They were sitting on a large concrete step leading into the school, soaking up the late fall sun's warm rays. Global warming was far down their list of concerns.

Just as Zane stood up and began pacing, a Lincoln Town Car with dark-tinted windows drove up. The back door opened, and a middle-aged man stepped out. The wind caught at his thick white hair, but not a single hair moved out of position. He was tall, dressed in a casual ensemble of a blue button-down oxford, a navy cashmere blazer, light-gray wool slacks, and tasseled black loafers. He was carrying a Starbucks Frappuccino. He was the perfect male specimen, oozing confidence.

"So this is the merry band of marauders," the congressman asked as he walked up to the group.

"Yep, the people who are going to save the country's ass," Caleb responded as he stood up.

"That's a lot of ass," Zane said seriously as he also stood up.

"He likes a lot of ass," Caleb said.

"Now, now. I think there are more important things to discuss than my sexual preferences. And doing it on the front step probably isn't the best idea," the congressman responded as he fiddled with the lockbox on the front door. Introductions were made as they were led in to the building.

Soon they were walking through a cobweb-filled corridor of what once was an institution of middle-school education. The walls were lined with rusty old lockers, and announcements were pinned to the walls telling of forthcoming wrestling meets, basketball games, and pep rallies that happened over fifteen years ago.

"I can close my eyes and vividly remember these days. My only worries were why some pimple-faced dude was too scared to ask me out and why my period always happened on days I had gym class," Monique stated.

"Not much has changed, then. Except now you have two dudes too scared to ask you out, and your period seems to always happen when some bad men are trying to kill you," Betty said.

"Trying to stop a worldwide depression is a tad bit more important than wondering who has a date on Saturday night," Caleb responded.

"I hear you, but I'm just trying to get our minds off our present problems for a moment. What does this place remind you of, Caleb? Maybe we can find a few more pieces of the puzzle," Monique said.

"Lots of fights, lots of blood, and lots of trips to the principal's office."

"Kind of like the past few months, then. Betty is right; not much has changed," Zane added.

"Maybe not, but we have the power to change it," Betty said.

"Maybe we can have a party right here in the school library after this is all over," Caleb said.

"We could invite all our friends from Treasury and SWAT here. I'm sure they'd like to party with us," Rocker said.

"Those who are still alive," Tec said.

Those words had the intended effect; everybody finally shut up. Being wanted for multiple murders and conspiring to commit terrorist acts never made for entertaining chitchat.

"Just to make you feel right at home, Caleb, we'll be meeting in the principal's office. This is more serious than your previous visits here, but I also agree with Betty. There is a way out. A way fraught with danger," the congressman said while holding the door open.

"People can sleep well tonight knowing that tough and dangerous men are willing to do things that they couldn't," Rocker replied.

"Never changes," Caleb said.

Next to the principal's office was a conference room of sorts with a long table ringed by several hard plastic chairs. Middle-school chairs.

"Hemorrhoid chairs. I guess they didn't want their students to be too comfortable while they were chewing them a new one," Monique said.

"No, and I don't want you guys and gals too comfortable, either," the congressman replied. "Ever again."

They all assumed their positions around the table, wishing they were middle schoolers, even if only for a day.

The congressman passed out a binder to each one of them. It was bound in black, inexpensive plastic, not that different from what you would find at the local OfficeMax.

"Don't open your binders yet. In fact, don't open them until I tell you. I can't answer any questions about them, anyway," the congressman uttered.

"Just get to the point. We know if caught, our lives are over. We want to know how you are going to get us out," Zane said.

"If I know the congressman at all, he isn't going to get us out. We will have to get ourselves out," Caleb stated. "Isn't that true, shitbag?"

"Shitbag? A bit offensive for an elected official, don't you think?" Betty asked.

"Not most of them, including this one," Caleb replied.

"What's the use of having power if you're unwilling to use it?" Rocker asked.

"Let me guess. You can do us more good being on the inside,"

Caleb said. "Which really means they have his ass over a barrel, and he can't turn them in without getting his short hairs burned."

The congressman smiled at all of them, crossed his arms, and sat back. "My life is complicated."

"Complicated by whores, other men's wives, and young women aspiring to political careers. Very young women," Caleb said.

"I don't check IDs at the door. But don't throw the message out with the messenger. I can help you. Nobody can know about it, though."

"So it's the short-hair thing?" Betty asked.

"I don't have any hair in that particular location, but yeah, I'm compromised."

"I don't want to know anything about that region," Monique said.

"That's what they all say until they try it."

"Enough. Why are you doing this? Who are you loyal to?" Zane asked.

"His true loyalty is he, him, and himself. He also knows he has to risk his position at times to protect himself. He'll only do that if it involves something big. So big that if nothing is done, a lot of us will suffer, including him," Caleb interjected. "He'll do the right thing if pushed, hard, into a corner."

"Yeah. But I don't give a shit if you don't trust me or my motives. You don't have a choice. I'm the only game in town. You're in some deep shit," the congressman replied.

"We know that."

"How deep?" Betty asked.

"First, I have a question for Zane," the congressman said. "What was your plan? You must have had one."

"This is it. I knew that taking over SAS and killing Moore would bring out the true puppet master. Thompson. And I hoped it would expose the plot. Which it did. As you know, everything was recorded on Caleb's cell phone."

"Well, your plan worked. Except what about Ben? Ben Guardian. Is he just a casualty of war?" Monique asked.

"He's not dead."

"What?" they all chimed in unison.

"He faked his own death. He wanted a new life, unencumbered by his greedy family and his failing business. He lives somewhere by himself with part of the $15 million we stole from Thompson. His family got the rest," Zane answered.

"The money Thompson was so worried about?"

"Exactly. Monique stole it, and Ben got it."

"Good job," Tec said.

"I'm very happy for Ben and his family, but what about us?" Betty asked.

"First, I have a question for you, Betty," Caleb asked while pointing at her. "Why did you make a congressional inquiry to the congressman about SAS?"

Zane looked at Betty disbelievingly. "I wasn't aware of that."

Betty took a deep breath. "After Tina's death, I knew Zane needed some help. I also knew he was working with Treasury, and I know they're playing an evil role in end-times prophecy. I prayed about it, and God led me to the story about the faithful two, who said that the giants didn't scare them and that the land would be flowing with milk and honey. So I knew Zane had to concentrate on the future and not be afraid. But he needed help."

"How did you know Zane was undercover with Treasury?" Caleb asked.

"I followed him to one of his meetings with them," Betty answered while smiling at Zane. "Don't get mad at me, but I knew something was wrong by the way you were acting, and I needed to find out to protect my daughter."

"Who were the faithful two?" Tec asked.

"Joshua and Caleb. And if I remember correctly, the congressman's first name is Joshua, and of course that led us to Caleb."

Nobody said a word as the weight of Betty's words hit home.

"I'm not sure I'm worthy of being compared to a Bible figure," the congressman noted, raising his eyebrows.

"None of us are, but we'll get to that later," Betty responded. "But now, please tell us more. How deep are we?" She was unable to hide her concern.

"Remember the 9/11 hijackers? That deep and maybe deeper. Risking the financial solvency of this country, and maybe the world, has more impact than taking down two skyscrapers and damaging the Pentagon. Killing SWAT members hasn't helped, either," the congressman replied. "If they find you guys, you wouldn't see the light of day. Ever. That's if they let you live through your capture and you survive the torture."

"Sometimes killing is necessary, even if they're good people," Caleb said quietly. "If it prevents greater harm."

"I'm not judging you," the congressman replied. "But there are those who will."

"So again, why are you helping us?" Zane asked.

"I'm not helping you, if you listen to what Caleb told you. I'm doing this because it's the only option left to keep our country from tearing itself apart in financial turmoil," the congressman said. "And my motives are a bit more altruistic than Caleb would have you believe. I do believe in this country, and it's our best hope to turn the world around."

"And?" Caleb asked.

"And I love what I do and don't want to lose that."

"He loves *who* he does more than *what* he does," Caleb said.

"We get that. Let's say we don't trust you, but we also know we have very limited ways of getting out of this situation. What's your plan? Show us, and then let us make up our minds," Tec said.

"I will, but acceptance of the plan won't require trust or belief on your part. It's the only plan available," the congressman said. "And I never said you guys would get out of this. That ship has sailed. This plan is beneficial for everybody else, not you."

"Where have I heard that shit before?" Rocker asked rhetorically.

"Just fucking tell us. Endless debate drives me insane," Monique said.

"Insane may help, actually," the congressman responded. "The information in those binders is necessary for your assignments. You may now open them, but only look at the first page. Under no circumstances may you show your folder to your companions around this table. The consequences would be dire."

Each person carefully opened the folder directly in front of him or her. The folders weren't the same.

The first page was a summary.

He waited until each one of them was finished reading and looked up at him.

"You'll be working on your own. In a vacuum. No one will ever admit to giving you this assignment. This meeting never happened, and I don't exist. I can be contacted, but only under extreme circumstances," the congressman said. "Don't look at them now, but the rest of the pages in your binders contain information about several important people. There's information about who they are, what they know, their associates, and their roles. Some of your folders include only one person, and some of your folders include more, but all the people in your individual folders are tied together by a common thread in the fabric of the overall conspiracy."

"Who are these people?" Zane asked.

"An inside source high up in the administration gave them to me. He's involved in the cover-up of the SAS debacle and knows everybody involved. There are seventeen people in all," the congressman responded. "All of these seventeen people know about SAS, the role AIS played, and, more importantly, the fact that the Federal Reserve's quantitative easing program funded the scheme."

"And they each told other people?" Monique asked.

"That's a safe assumption," the congressman answered.

"Why can't we tell anybody else, not even each other, what's in our folders?" Betty asked.

"It's very simple," the congressman answered. "The plan's success hinges on exclusivity and each of you performing your individual duty. It will only work if your assignment is only known by you. Otherwise, it is certain to fail—and the country with it."

"Why do we have to do this now?" Monique asked.

"Too many nonconspirators who aren't in your folders know about this. They won't keep quiet forever. So after your assignments are complete, we need to go public with this. But it will be our version of events—a version where we control the variables, the flow of information, and the outcome."

"In other words, you'll spin your own warped edition of the truth," Rocker said.

"There is no truth, only a version of it," the congressman said. "Through these events, you have discovered a little-known fact that must be protected at all costs."

"Which is?" Zane asked.

"Faith," the congressman answered, looking around the table. "Our dollar, our banks, our whole financial structure—it only exists because we believe in it. Without our faith, it dies a very ugly, immediate death."

"That is true for all that we cannot see," Betty interjected. "In every area of this life and the next one too."

Zane looked at her and closed his eyes. "Now I know."

They all looked at him quizzically until the reality of the here and now came crashing back toward them in the form of another very good question.

"And you can't tell us who this mystery guy is that gave up these seventeen?" Rocker asked.

"I can't."

"Can you trust him?"

"Don't know. He put sixteen profiles in the folder, and I added his," the congressman replied. "So now there are seventeen."

"Why did he give this to you?" Zane asked.

"The government needs to cover this up. If any of it ever became public, the national and world economy would crash and burn. He thinks that with each of your backgrounds and special skills, you can rein all of them in and contain the damage, and then he can run the program for the benefit of the country."

"Or the benefit of himself," Zane added.

"Precisely. And because we can't take that risk, his profile makes the total seventeen," the congressman answered.

"Maybe you just want to remove the competition?" Monique asked.

"Not so, but even if it were, it wouldn't matter. This scheme can never go public." The congressman smiled at Monique.

"It matters to us," Rocker said. "And it should matter to you, if you don't want us to remove you too."

"You won't," the congressman answered. "I'm your lifeline."

"Now what?" Tec asked.

"Caleb knows."

"What does he mean, you know?" Betty asked.

Caleb stood up and stretched. He picked up his black folder and pushed his chair in. He zipped up his jacket after carefully placing the folder inside.

"He means all the evidence of this conspiracy needs to disappear by our hands, and then we disappear," Caleb said as he began to leave the room. "End of story."

115

They were riding in an older Suburban Tec had borrowed from a friend of a friend of one of his students, lest the license plate lead to them. Tec was driving as silence held sway.

"I can't do what they're asking," Monique flatly stated while staring blindly straight ahead.

Nobody spoke for a minute as each considered his or her individual assignments in light of Monique's flat refusal.

"Before making any rash decisions, we need to consider the consequences," Rocker said softly, trying not to minimize Monique's concern.

"Such as?" Betty asked.

"These seventeen people are corrupting our financial system and hence our future. Our assignments may be the only hope," Caleb, who sat next to Monique, commented.

"Everybody dies someday," Zane commented dryly.

"I hope your assignment isn't about murder," Betty responded.

"Killing them would be easier," Caleb responded.

"It doesn't make any difference. Do you really think everybody who knows about this is in these folders? Take the congressman. He knows about it and isn't on the list," Zane said.

"We can always pencil him in," Caleb said while putting his hands flat on his thighs and staring at each car as it passed them.

"I know I can't tell any of you what my assignment is, but

it has an element of danger," Betty said, purposefully ignoring Caleb's comment. "It would just help knowing who gave us these."

"Danger doesn't scare me. After all, the country's future is at stake," Monique said while staring at Zane. "It's just that what he is asking me to do requires blind faith, and like Betty said, we don't even know who he is. I will sacrifice a part of me that I'll never get back."

"I'm not sure we have time to find all the answers to our questions," Tec replied as he pulled the Suburban into a secluded grove of trees, shutting down the engine and rolling down his window. "My whole life has been based on the premise that the only way through it is to just do it."

"What do you say, Rocker?" Betty asked.

"I have signed up for a lot of shit in my special forces career, and rarely have I asked any questions," Rocker answered while turning around in the front seat to face Betty. "But this time is different. I have to know more. I can't just do this. For all we know, we're being set up."

"We can talk about this all day long, but I'm out," Monique stated emphatically, leaving no room for discussion about where she stood. "I'm not the person they think I am."

"That won't end it for you, Monique," Tec said slowly, emphasizing each word. "You're either in or out. And if you're out, then you're just another person who knows about this, which puts you on the list."

"Why not just kill me now? Is that what the fuck you're saying, Tec? Right back to your same old double-faced ways, huh?" Monique asked loudly, pointing her finger at Tec.

"When it comes right down to it, we all only watch out for ourselves, right, Tec?" Zane asked.

"I'm just saying, if we each make our own decision based on what's best for us as an individual without considering the bigger picture, then we must live with that," Tec explained, staring a hole through Zane.

"Obviously, it's worked for you," Monique answered bitterly.

"We need to stick together, make our decision as a group," Betty said, putting both hands out in a gesture of peace. "Like the congressman said, all of us have to be in for this to work."

"Well, then, Monique seems to already have made our decision," Rocker said.

"There are other factors other than just what's best for us and even other than what's best for the country," Zane said haltingly.

"Yeah, our families," Tec said, again drawing distrustful looks from Monique.

"I thought you said they'd be protected," Zane and Betty said in unison while looking at Tec. "Out of the country, watched by a close and trusted friend," Zane continued quietly as Betty nodded.

"They will be, but probably not forever. Nobody can protect anybody forever," Tec answered, letting out a big sigh. "Someday, they'll become bargaining chips again. We need to be sure we have the upper hand that day."

Everybody was quiet as they listened to a bluebird singing in the tree next to them.

"We could have Monique research the seventeen. Find out what they know," Zane said, seeming to grudgingly admit that they may not be able to carry out their assignments, given Monique's and Rocker's reluctance to carry out their assignments.

His comment was greeted by more silence as all parties pondered their situation and alternatives.

"We don't have to decide this minute," Caleb said finally. "More information may be needed."

"Rest assured, the solutions will require blood," Tec said.

"Let's not jump to that conclusion," Zane interjected. "Although you're probably correct."

"There will be some pain," Betty said. "Getting America's financial house in order won't be pain-free. The Bible even predicts that for the end times."

"Let's not write ourselves into Bible prophecy just yet," Caleb responded. "Maybe this will delay the end and allow this country to heal its many wounds, financial and otherwise."

"Dream on," Zane said with a sarcastic tone. "We can't even pass a budget without tearing each other apart."

"The book of Revelation," Betty said loudly. "But there is a happy ending."

Caleb looked at Betty and shook his head, looked away, and then looked back at her again, this time with a smile. Then he spoke to all of them. "I like the research suggestion. Monique is good at that. Get some information on these seventeen targets and see what we can do with it."

"Doing that will require us looking at each other's folders," Monique said. "That was expressly forbidden by the congressman."

"If we do this right, he won't know," Caleb answered. "He may not want us working together, because if we do, we're stronger. In fact, I firmly believe that working together is the only way to protect ourselves."

"He'll know," Rocker asked. "I'm sure he has his ways."

"Unless he's gone too," Caleb stated quietly.

"As in dead?" Tec asked.

"Gone is not dead," Caleb said, stretching his neck in circles. "Just ask Ben Guardian."

"Ben couldn't trust his family, either," Monique added dryly.

"Caleb is right; we have to trust each other. All for one and one for all, lest we fall," Betty said.

"That's what we may have to do," Zane responded with a note of regret. "Until the time comes that we can't."

116

Weather permitting, the Wayzata High School band practiced their parade march and songs every Tuesday and Thursday morning. This Thursday morning, the weather was granting its permission. Their practice area was a road that carried them past the local cemetery.

The march music reminded him of better days. Days without murder, theft, and grave financial consequences. Zane stared at the band members. Only to be one of them.

He was taking a chance being here. Zane hoped his new hair, clean-shaven face, and shabby clothes would keep any surveillance at bay.

Kneeling at Tina's grave provided him encouragement for the days that lay ahead. No matter how dark the nights became, the sun always rose the next day. Listening to the band playing its rowdiest, loudest victory song along the road provided a celebratory setting, and it seemed fitting for Tina. Celebrating instead of grieving. Life was a party.

He was beginning to understand that God had answered his prayer to protect Tina. What better place for protection than with Him in heaven instead of down here fighting through all this and the mess his life had become.

He didn't know how to pray. Betty had told him it was just talking to God. Like you talked to anybody. Not too difficult.

Zane prayed out loud. "I need Your help. I can't do this on my own. Nobody could. If there's another way, please show me. Killing can't be the answer, but it seems to be here. I pray for the souls we are about to send to eternity. Give them a chance to spend it with You. Help my children to understand. They must know I did this for them. For us. For everybody. I have always had a reason for what I did, even though it may not always have been a good one. My reason now is to save our country, our way of life." Zane paused as he bowed his head. "Give us Your strength, Your wisdom, and Your power. Have Your righteousness go before us. Also, I pray for him. He has to see Your power in this. He has to know he is forgiven but must now do the right thing. Have him see it Your way."

Zane felt a hand on his shoulder. He knew it was him.

"Praying for me? How nice. Except it's a bit late, Zane. Or whatever you're calling yourself these days."

Zane slowly stood up but didn't turn around. "It's never too late. I'm a perfect example of that, Chairman."

"It was too late for the one lying in the grave you're kneeling on. Neither God nor you could protect her."

"It's all about perspective."

"Yes, the eternal perspective. Someday, we all die. The question is, where will we go? Eternity?"

Zane turned around and purposefully kept his hands at his sides. "Exactly. Death loses its sting." Just like it had for Tina.

"Why do you kill people, then, if death has no power?"

"It doesn't for eternity, but in this world, it still does. Power to stop this country from becoming a third-world cesspool." Zane smiled, seriously doubting Monique and Caleb would find another way.

"Ah, so true. That's why I need to talk to you. Can you walk with me to my car?" the chairman of the Federal Reserve asked him.

"Only because I have to," Zane responded.

They strolled, looking like two friends in quiet mourning. The cemetery lent gravity to their walk.

But they weren't friends. Far from it.

They slipped into the backseat of his black Town Car. The driver was standing one block away, smoking a cigarette.

"You don't even trust the soundproof partition?" Zane asked.

"Not for what we're going to talk about. Besides, he needed a cancer stick."

"If you lose any more weight, you're going to start looking like a cancer stick."

"I'm the picture of health. Lean, mean, a double-agent machine," the chairman said while leaning back in the seat.

"You're on the list."

"I'd better worry about eternity, after all."

"Alan Thompson is on the list too."

"Just because I'm his boss doesn't mean he gets my protection."

"Do the people on the list think you're their collaborator?"

"Of course. They pulled off the scheme with my knowledge."

"And they profited?"

"Immensely. That's why they have great incentive to keep the conspiracy going."

Zane sighed and shook his head slowly.

"I still have the recording of our little visit at the shed."

"Its value has depreciated."

"Are you sure?"

"I don't have to be."

"I have the laptop."

"You mean this one?" he answered as he reached under the seat and produced Zane's laptop, giving it to him.

"How did you end up with this?" Zane asked incredulously as he took it.

"From the person you gave it to."

Zane stared at the laptop. He set it on the seat and leaned back, staring up through the sunroof.

"Why did she give it to you?"

"You'll need to find that out yourself. Sometimes asking the question is enough of an answer," the chairman replied. "And you should also ask yourself how Thompson knew you took the $15 million. That's still a mystery."

"As you taught me, only trust myself."

"That's the way."

"I won't lose any sleep over killing you, you know that."

"Do what you have to do. I think you'll find that killing me presents you with a dilemma."

"Not so much."

He laughed. "You think you're tougher than you really are. Killing the chairman of the Federal Reserve will cost you more than you think."

"We'll see. Why are you doing this?"

"Our country is the world's last great hope. It must be saved at all costs."

"And after, you remain. With the spoils."

"Why not me?"

"Through the Federal Reserve and quantitative easing, you'll own a good share of the country's debt and businesses, so you'll have control, and any solution must come through you."

"Control that this country needs."

"The Federal Reserve. Don't leave home without it."

"Priceless."

"You're the money, the power—and I'm your bad boy."

"That's why I recruited you."

"To keep the scheme under your control?"

"So it can be used for good."

"Your good."

"Everybody's good."

"We'll see."

"You shouldn't have gone to Treasury."

"So you *were* behind the abduction of my family."

"I couldn't stop it. You were too close to your family."

"But you stopped Thompson and his gang from killing me."

"Remember that."

"If I had a choice, I would do this differently."

"Just remember you're my eyes, ears, and hands. You can do things for me that I can't do."

"The dirty work."

"You owe me."

"I think that debt has been paid. Over and over."

"It has worked well for you too."

"It has, although I'm not sure for how much longer. It's taken a toll."

"Just be careful," the chairman reminded him as he took a cigar out of the humidor under the seat.

"I have been," Zane replied while looking out the window at a young family standing over a small tombstone. He wondered who had died. "Although at times the thought has crossed my mind that maybe I just need to expose myself. Let everybody know who and what I really am."

"Did Tina or the rest of your family have any clue?"

"That I've been working with you for years? That I have a double identity? No, even in death she trusted me."

"Perfect. How about your new friends? Do they know you gave up their location at the Warrior's Den for the SWAT team?"

"They needed the proper motivation to help me," Zane replied while watching the family kneel at the tombstone. The father and mother were crying and holding hands. Their two young children were staring at the ground, possibly wondering why death came for some and not others. "But no, they don't know I gave them up. They trust me."

"Don't trust them. I don't think any of them are survivors."

"Maybe."

"The lady knows more about you than you think," the chairman said while producing a knife and cutting off the end of his cigar.

"She doesn't really know." Zane smirked. "The truth."

"How long can you pretend to be something before you become it?"

"I learned from the best."

"You did. Even after what I did to you, you still believed me," the chairman said, licking the sides of the cigar.

"You caught me at a vulnerable time," Zane replied.

"By design. Now go out and do what you do. Kill, steal, and do my bidding."

"Aren't you scared that your solution will allow more bad men to thrive, even if your solution is good?"

"Sometimes bad men are needed to keep other bad men away," the chairman answered while holding a lighter to his cigar and inhaling the acrid smoke.

"How do I live with that?"

"I can't have you dying with it."

"Maybe you will do the dying."

He laughed again and unlocked the door.

"Maybe, but not by you. You could never do that to her. As hard as it is for you to comprehend, she loves me."

"One question."

"Yes?"

"Why did you choose me?"

"I didn't. You chose me."

117

Ray was scared, more than he'd ever been in his life. But he knew he had to go in. He knew that not going in would require him to forget this day, and he never wanted to forget this day.

She was sitting in the bedroom, in a chair looking as peaceful and heavenly as the last time he'd seen her. She didn't look hurt; she was even smiling, telling him without words that she loved him and would love and support him no matter what. He would never forget that look. It would make him do anything for her.

"I thought I'd never see you again," he said, limping into the bedroom. As he stood by the bed, he held his blood-soaked hand behind him so she wouldn't see it.

"I knew I would see you again," his sister replied. "That makes me so happy, even though you don't look too good."

She stood up, walked over, and hugged him. He hugged her back with one arm, trying not to get any blood on her, not quite believing what was happening. Life never turned out for him this way. Why would it now?

And then the asshole came in. He stood just inside the door and spoke softly. "I didn't hurt your sister. I saved her."

"Is that true?" he asked her.

"It is," his sister answered, holding Ray's face in her hands.

460

"That day at the detention center, a man was lying in the backseat of my car, waiting for me." Pointing to the asshole, she said, "He dragged the man out of my car, hit him hard enough to knock him out, threw me in the car, and drove away with me."

"So you saved her and then took her?" Ray asked, turning to face the asshole. "That doesn't make you good."

The asshole took two steps toward Ray. "I never said it did. I needed bait. I still needed you to pay. Which you did," he said, pointing at Ray's broken leg.

"Are you all right?" his sister asked, grabbing his shoulder and trying to get Ray's attention.

"I'm fine," Ray answered, shaking off her hand and looking at the asshole. "So now what? I get that knife sticking in the floor and cut your fucking heart out?"

"No!" his sister screamed, grabbing Ray and turning him around. "In a strange way, I think that's what he wants. There's another way."

"So you've been locked in the bedroom since then?" Ray asked her. "Two years?"

"Yes, and I knew he was sucking you in, but I couldn't warn you."

"Forget about that," the asshole said, walking in a circle to face them both. "Your sister is right; there is another way. A way that works for all of us."

"I know there is—me and my sister walk out of here and let you live your rotten, stinking life while we try to forget any of this shit happened."

"You know you can't do that. You either have to kill me or do it my way," the asshole said as he sat down on the bed.

Ray knew he was right. He didn't know how he knew, but he knew. It was like knowing that smoking was bad for you. You didn't need the surgeon general to tell you, but they put those warnings on the package for a reason.

"Why do I have to do it your way?" Ray asked, standing next to the bed and towering over the asshole.

"We weren't put in that detention center together by accident. I need you, and you need me."

"I need you?" Ray mocked. "Hardly."

"Look at yourself. You're nothing. You beat your dad so bad he's a vegetable. You can't even look at your mom because she allowed him to beat you. You have no job, no money, and no prospects. You have anger issues, you have no self-respect, and you'll probably never be able to love again," the asshole said, glancing between Ray and his sister. "I can give you those things. I can give you a life. And I think you want that. But there's a more practical reason too. There's a body in my basement, and I have a video of you killing him. Hardly self-defense."

"You set him up for that," Ray's sister said grimly, looking at the asshole. "You knew if you pushed, that's what he would do."

The asshole smiled and nodded.

Ray turned and went to the window, looking out over the asshole's large lawn. "As much as I hate to ask, what is your way?"

The asshole stood up, approached Ray, and spoke quietly to his back. "I come from a rich and powerful family. I have many contacts, and my family wields a lot of influence in American and international finance. They have the power to eliminate my past. I won't always be a financial analyst. Someday, I'll be much more. In the meantime, I need an assistant. I need somebody to be my ears, eyes, hands, and feet. That somebody is you."

"Why?" Ray asked, still looking out the window.

"I'm going up, and you're going down. Tie yourself to me, and reverse your descent. But my way will come at the expense of other less ambitious, deceitful people. I'll need these roadblocks to progress removed. That's where you come in. I have to keep my hands clean. My way is brutal, but it's the only way. I have some great fiscal ideas, but I need the power to implement them. I also have some other, less altruistic motives," the asshole said, putting one hand on Ray's right shoulder. "The beautiful thing is that both of our juvie records are sealed. Forever."

Ray turned around and shoved the asshole out of his way. He walked up to his sister, grabbed her hands, and looked her in the face. "What do you think of this? I value your opinion more than anyone's in this world. Just say the word, and I'll kill the asshole."

"It's your choice, but to me, that answer is obvious," his sister replied, looking into his eyes with tears in her own. "Everything that's happened to you—to us—has happened for a reason. I hate to admit it, but I think this," she said, nodding toward the asshole, "is the only way you can discover what that reason is."

118

"Alan."

"You don't get it, do you?"

"Answer my question," he said.

"What was the question again?" Thompson answered his question with a question while lying on the dirty little bed in the dirty little hotel room. His visitor was sitting on one of the flimsy little chairs next to the table. It was dark outside and dark in the room; the only light came from the bathroom. The darkness had kept Thompson's visitor's identity secret while security allowed him into the hotel room.

"Do not fuck with me. What the hell did you tell them?"

"Well, I'm still here, ain't I?" Thompson said while crossing his bare feet on the bed. He was wearing boxer shorts and a large white T-shirt. The smell in the room wasn't kind.

"That doesn't mean a damn thing. You could give them the world and they aren't going to let you go. You're too valuable," he stated while raising his voice. "And please, start bathing. This smell is not how I want to remember you."

"I'll get out of here a lot sooner than you think."

"If you had something to bet with, I might take you up on that. Now, tell me what you said. You're not safe, no matter where you are."

"Is that a threat?" Thompson asked while casually glancing at him.

"Of course it is. You have no power over me anymore."

"Remember what happens to you if something happens to me."

"It's gone way beyond that."

"How do I know I can trust you? Do your loyalties lie with them or with me?"

"If I kill you, then you'll know. The Man found that out."

"Even after he promised you a bigger slice."

"He couldn't deliver. He didn't have the power."

"And now you think I can deliver?"

"I know you can't. I'm just using you the way you used me. You're the means to an end."

"Which is?"

"You are fucked up, our country is fucked up, and this whole mess is fucked up. I may have to be the one to unfuck it."

"And enjoy the spoils. The chairman may have a problem with that."

"You're rapidly losing value to me."

"I was just fucking with you."

"I'm going to count to five, and then I'm leaving. I guaran-fucking-tee you that will be bad. You don't want me to leave with-out filling me in," he said as he stood up.

"It doesn't matter."

"One . . . two . . . three—"

"Okay, okay. Relax."

"And?"

"I told them everything. All of it. They know it all."

"Why? Is there a plan?"

"No plan, just the facts."

"Which are?"

"Think about it."

"Killing you would be a beautiful pleasure."

"Go for it. It would be the biggest mistake you ever made," Thompson said while sitting up on the edge of the bed directly across from him.

"We've all got to pay for our mistakes, just like I do for ever deciding to work with you. Okay, I'll play along. Why did you tell them everything?"

"Because it doesn't matter. Doesn't make a difference. Doesn't matter in the least," Thompson answered, standing up and walking to the bathroom. He left the door open and began to urinate in the toilet.

"Of course it matters!" he yelled after him. "And close the damn door. I don't need to hear that."

"Who cares what they know? The beauty is, they can't do a fucking thing about it. Nothing. Criminals have been looking for the perfect crime for years, and we found it." Thompson came back out of the bathroom pulling up his boxers. There was a little wet spot on the front.

"Perfect? How is that? And how about washing your hands and putting some pants on?"

"Yeah. The perfect crime isn't about not getting caught; it's about getting away even though you've been caught. Allowing it to be exposed would reveal a far greater crime committed by the infallible leaders of this great country. It would cause too much fundamental damage to our economy and society for decades to come. We have endless funds to continue our criminal enterprise, because our source is the engine that keeps our economy going. Quantitative easing. Printing money. The politicians, the Federal Reserve, and the Treasury are stealing in exactly the same way I am. And we're all doing it to keep our damn papier-mâché economy going. It's just that we're profiting along the way. All of us—including you."

"So because they need you, your plan is just to keep this conspiracy going until you have so much money it doesn't matter?"

"It'll blow up long before then. And when it does, they'll need me."

"That doesn't mean they have to let you go. You could be a long-term resident in these fine accommodations," he said, standing up.

"Could be, but I don't think so. Even though I've given them the people who know about this, they still need me. I'm the link between the Federal Reserve and AIS. I'm the only one that can do what has to be done out there," Thompson said, pointing to the window while plopping down on the bed again.

His visitor looked out the window, thinking about what he had just been told. The link. Thompson was right; the link was needed, but it didn't have to be Thompson. There was another far more suited and far more attractive.

His visitor moved over to the bed and stood over Thompson. He bought his knee up quickly and drove it hard into his sternum, driving all the wind momentarily from his lungs. While Thompson flopped back on the bed gasping for air, his visitor cut off the possibility of any resupply using one of the dirty little pillows greased with stains from the long, stringy mess Thompson called hair.

Contrary to popular belief, suffocating someone with a pillow wasn't easy. The ability to fight back had to be removed first. Thus the knee to the sternum.

Tec had learned that move a long time ago.

At the same time, he had been learning that murder wasn't the reprehensible task that righteous people would make you believe.

One down and sixteen to go.

119

Zane took the long way home. He risked stopping at a local burger joint. He had a beer and a Juicy Lucy—a Twin Cities favorite, a burger stuffed with cheese. Then he had another beer. No one seemed to notice him. Zane and his group were perfecting life on the lam, with considerable help.

He paid for his meal and drinks and continued the journey to his hotel. Betty and the kids were gone. Out of the country. Protected, along with Tec's Colombian family. That had been a surprise. Tec maybe was good after all. Maybe.

Time would tell.

Zane had tried to do what he thought was good. His inner compass was corrupted, though. He knew that and was trying to fix it. Or let God fix it.

He needed to go to his bank. Not for a withdrawal or a deposit. It was more like checking his balance. He walked in and signed the little safe-deposit card. The attendant left him alone. He removed the key from around his neck, opened the box, and removed a book.

He opened the book, trying to really look at it. Even though it was his touchstone to the past, sometimes he wished his mom hadn't given it to him before she died.

Zane closed the book and placed it back in the large safe-deposit box. Someday, he'd read it again. Maybe after all this was over; maybe after killing the man he'd met with just an hour earlier.

Could he kill him?

Could he kill his brother-in-law?

Zane didn't like him. Despite all he'd put her through—maybe because of it—his sister had fallen in love with him. Or so she said. He wondered if that was a lie too, fueled by Howie's possessiveness or her desire to keep tabs on him. Regardless, Zane knew he owed him. Howie had helped him through and out of his past.

He'd given him a new life. In that bedroom in Canada many, many years ago. To become what he was today.

A dad, a brother, a son, and a killer.

The reason he was here at this place and at this time.

The reason our economy existed and the reason he would save it.

Faith.

Believing what could not be seen.

Zane looked at his book one last time.

Celebrating the Life of Ray.

Let the party begin.

For a more in-depth look at the author and the characters and entities involved in the fictional world of *The Reason* visit:

QuentinBrent.com

ACKNOWLEDGEMENTS

Many people have made this book possible. If I miss anyone, please forgive me as you know who you are, but apparently I don't. I may have forgotten you, but I still appreciate what you have done.

Someone that I do remember is Helga Schier, my first editor who saw this manuscript before it was ready for anybody to see. She showed me how to believe in myself and how to put on paper what was inside of me. I learned so much from her and am eager to use that knowledge for years to come.

Wendy Weckwerth, another editor, massaged this story and inspired me to develop the characters and expose the plot in a way that was suspenseful even to me until we truly reached the end.

Hanna Kjeldbjerg, our managing editor at Beaver's Pond Press, is such a bright star. She always brightened my day with her sincere, heartfelt enthusiasm that made me feel like I was the next great thing. Actually, everybody at Beaver's Pond Press made me feel that way. I guess maybe I can fool some people, some of the time.

James Monroe of James Monroe Design, was the incredible talent that made you want to buy this book just by looking at it. His cover design left me speechless and wondering what the reason for this book really was, even though I knew. James also went way above and beyond developing our website. If you don't believe me, please check out our website. It will deepen your understanding of this book and the characters in it. It will also prepare you for the next one. It can be found at quentinbrent.com.

My sister, Gwen, was also a huge help and inspiration to this story. She has always believed in me through the darkest days of my life, when nobody else cared.

My brother-in-law, Justin, and his wife, Betsy, were such a gracious supportive team. He is a professional photographer who had the unenviable job of making my face look mysterious and like I wrote a book that makes you want to read it. I don't know how he does it, but after he was done, even I was wondering what secrets lie within me.

And, last but not least, my exquisitely beautiful wife; I would have never started this book without her love and support. I certainly wouldn't have worked for three years on it and finished it without her extreme sacrifice. Her criticism, motivated by a genuine desire to make me a better writer, and helpful ideas always seemed to arrive at the exact moment I needed them. Whenever I would thank her for all she has done, she would say that's what spouses do and she loved doing it for me. Most of us know that is not all spouses. I am amazed on a daily, if not hourly, basis on how much God has blessed me with this incredible, ethereal human being.

I hope you have enjoyed this story. The characters and events are fictional, and not based upon any real person, dead or alive. Regrettably, the dire financial condition of our country is all too real, and if you're not concerned about our financial future after reading this novel, you should be.

That is why my last thanks goes out to our wonderful Federal Reserve. They have a very tough and impossible job, but if they keep on performing it the way they have, they will supply me with substantial writing material for years to come.